Blue Moon

Blue Moon

The Bad Moon Rising Series

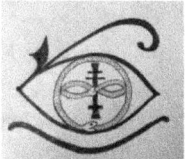

Johnny Bryan Ward

Beyond Thought Productions

Blue Moon

©Copyright 2013 by Johnny Bryan Ward

Acknowledgments

First and foremost, I would like to thank my husband Clay for standing beside me in life and throughout the writing of this book. He has been my inspiration and motivation for continuing to improve my knowledge and move my writing career forward. He believed in me when I didn't believe in myself. This book would not be what it is today without his guidance, editing, promotional push and website design. He is my rock, the love of my life, and I dedicate this book to him.

I realized during this process that it takes a team to make this come to life and I feel fortunate and extremely supported by my team. My daughters Lupe and Nataya, thank you for the promotional support and your tireless social media work.

To the beta readers, Margaret Bedard, Eli Jeremiah, Shar F. Grant, Rebecca Howard and Keith McNeal. I cannot tell you enough how much you helped to guide me and challenge me at the same time. Thank you for agreeing to do this project.

A special thank you and shout out to the brave and creative artist, Nate L. Spangler and Jennifer Renne' Spangler of Blanc Kanvas Art Productions. You took on the vision I had for my characters in this book and turned them into works of art which you will see displayed on JohnnyBryanWard.com

Thank you Brandy Walker of Sister Sparrow Graphic Design for creating a beautifully, haunting book cover. You were able to use a picture we took of downtown Tulsa and create the perfect book cover.

Thank you Brenda Donelan, author and friend, for your encouragement through this process.

This book was a labor of love and I hope you enjoy it as much as I enjoyed writing it.

Prologue

Screaming as she was ripped back from her vision, tears filled the wretched looking woman's eyes. Torture for over three hours had given way to information, which held the attention of all in the room.

"You will fail demon. You who claim to be all powerful will find your demise by the hand that is closest to you. So much death, so much death, all because of power and greed and in the end it will be for naught. You walk this earth when it is not right to do so. You don't belong here. Darkness fills the land as it fills my dreams, but the darkness has an end. You will die demon, maybe not in the true sense of the word, but you will leave this world and be banished back into your own. You will rot there as it should be, and the world will rebuild itself, it will see the light again," the old woman moaned as she spoke through her pain. "But just as you will meet your death in this world, you will have the opportunity to come back; a small window of time in which you will meet the biggest threat you will ever face. Three thousand years this world will have to build itself up again, three thousand years you will have to wait in your hellish confines before you can attempt to be born again. When the moon shines blue, you will be able to cross over if you have the powers to do so. Three sacrifices are required for your journey, but beware demon; the powers that kill you in this world are not dead in

1

the new one. Now kill me, for I will tell you no more." She screeched as she spat bloody spit at his feet.

The man whom the demon embodied reached over and snapped the old woman's neck knowing she had told him all she would. She fell to the ground dead.

The demon turned to the two men in the room, two of his most trusted confidants. "I have no reason to believe this oracle is not telling the truth, so listen to me as if your life depended on it. If and when I meet my death here in this world, you will prepare for me the way back. You will keep this from the world, from prying eyes who would deny me what is mine. You will silently build an army, an army to infiltrate every aspect of this life, to know everything that might work against me. You will be brave; you will be strong, you will be deadly, and you will be called Balashon."

Chapter One

Demetri ran down the unlit street, sweat dripping from his face, his breathing labored, and his heart racing. How uncanny he found himself running, running for his life, running scared, when it had been so many years since he feared anything. But this fear inside him, this head splitting fear would not subside. His powers failed him here. All around him darkness and *them*. Those who held to the shadows, those who dare not reveal themselves sank deeper into the dark. He could hear their whispers, their thoughts, and they all were saying the same thing in unison "*He* is coming, and we will all die, *He* is coming and we will all die."

These creatures of the night, creatures of the shadows steered clear of Demetri. They feared his abilities, but tonight they feared something much worse. For the supernatural world to run in fear and to share that fear with Demetri was new. They needed Demetri to protect them, but from what. "*He* is coming and we will all die."

Demetri's head was aching and adding to his discomfort the sweat dripped down his face making everything sticky. Summers in Tulsa are known for their muggy, heat filled nights. This night was no exception. The temperature topped ninety degrees, and the humidity made it difficult to breathe. Demetri continued to run, but could feel fatigue overcoming his body. He wasn't sure if the physical drain was from fear, from running or if the *He* the supernatural world referred to was trying to make contact.

As Demetri ran down Riverside Drive, he couldn't help but think *where are all the lights? There were no cars anywhere.* The Arkansas River, which was typically bone dry, flowed heavily tonight. *Could this really be happening? Could the vampires, lykens, witches, and who knows what, be turning to him for protection? What the fuck was going on?*

Demetri saw an image in his head. Faint at first, but Demetri knew it was *He*. Standing next to the noise reduction wall, a five-foot ten inch man with black hair, wearing an even darker black linen robe, which hung to the ground. The ebony robe split down one side from shoulder to the chest, down to the navel, revealing a chest full of intricate tattoos. A big, full orange colored moon filled the sky and cast a beautiful glow onto the folds of the robe creating an even paler complexion to his skin. *He* was looking down at the ground; his head cocked to the right. He was beautiful; he was dark and mysterious, but why would someone with such beauty have the entire underworld of Tulsa shaking in the shadows?

Another image flashed through Demetri's mind and this time he found himself standing near the water's edge, no longer running. This time the same man, stood next to the same wall, with his hands covering his face revealing more intricate tattoos on every inch of both arms and hands. *Was he crying? Was he praying? If he was praying, it wasn't to any god Demetri could make out.* He was chanting, but the language failed Demetri.

Then with a swift, sudden flourish, the mysterious man shed himself of his robe letting it fall to the ground at his feet, leaving him totally nude. *He* looked up at Demetri revealing his face for the first time, and it was pure beauty. His eyes, which were black as night, piercing and longing, looking out to the world. His lips were plump and luscious still chanting a language Demetri had never before heard. Then *He* looked Demetri directly in the eyes and said "I have been searching for you for over three thousand years and I have found you."

Searching for me? Three thousand years? Was this guy high? Demetri didn't need to answer the question because he already

4

knew. The man with no name the underworld is calling *He* was not of this world, but something more, yet still something familiar. As if reading Demetri's mind, the man with the black eyes began speaking to him, but his lips were not moving.

"Calm yourself, this is but a dream. I am not of your world, but I am in everything. I am your savior, your redeemer. I am your enemy, your death. I am your breath, the blood that flows through your veins. What is to come has been three thousand years in the making and nothing you do can stop it. Don't fight the inevitable. For when we meet, when your moon is blue, you will know the true power, you will see the world fall before me, before us. You will be by my side, my warrior. They will beg for mercy, beg for their lives," the man said staring at Demetri.

"Why me, why would you pick me?" Demetri questioned, once again wondering why he was so afraid. *If I am dreaming, this can't hurt me*, Demetri thought to himself.

"How do you think you came about these special gifts of yours," the man asked smiling so beautifully at him. "Do you think these gifts you call psychic, these miracles you do, happen to you by circumstance? You come from a long line of magical beings. Do you not question why these vile ancient creatures, these modern-day, earthly demons you call vampires and werewolves fear you," he said laughing softly, almost condescendingly. "You are a god among men; once you know the full meaning of your gifts you will be able to squash armies, crush cities."

The man stepped away from the wall and advanced towards Demetri. He was still nude, and as he came closer, Demetri could see his body was covered from head to toe with the most exquisite tattoos he had ever seen. Skeleton heads graced his hips, with bats and serpents on his arms. A zombie looking creature covered his leg. An extremely large face, attached to a body, wrapped around from his back across his torso onto his stomach. It could be described as a giant, maybe a troll, with large yellow eyes and yellow sharp teeth. The man was only five feet from Demetri when he stopped and looked amusingly at Demetri. It may have been the shock he saw on Demetri's face, or the way Demetri was looking him up and down as if he were a walking art exhibit. He was art, a beautiful walking art exhibit with stunning dark eyes, dark hair and a face that drew you in closer than you ever thought you wanted to be.

As Demetri stood staring at the man's body, he began to notice something. It was subtle at first, but as he looked closer he began to see movement on the man's body. The tattooed serpents seemed to move up and down the man's arms; the face on the man's abdomen winked at him. Startled, Demetri stumbled backwards tripping and falling onto his ass. He attempted to get away from the man by moving crablike, in a backwards crawl.

The man laughing at Demetri begins to lift his arms out to his side. "You have yet to see my powers, but you will," he said staring Demetri directly in the eyes. As if trying to scare him even more, the man, with his arms still raised to his side, began to chant in a non-familiar language so foreign yet so evil. The tattoos, which were once winking and moving up and down his arms, began to take on other forms. The ink started moving through the flesh of the man's body forming new creations. A vampire started to form on his chest, as a werewolf grew on his leg and hip, and a witch looking as if she were throwing a fireball formed on his arm.

"You think these creatures that fill children's nightmares, those hiding in the dark can save you," the man questioned. This time he wasn't smiling but looking at Demetri with impatience. "These creatures of your underworld cannot help you. They are a disgrace; a wasted speck of demon blood not worthy to be let past the doors of hell," the man shouted with a disgusted, angry voice, his lips pursed in a snarl.

"I can wipe these creatures out with just a whisper if I cared," sneered the man as if taunting the creatures still hiding in the dark.

Right on cue with the man's insults, Demetri began seeing glowing eyes lighting up in the darkness. The taunting worked because Demetri heard rustling in the bushes.

6

The man stepped closer to Demetri with an arm outstretched in front of him. At first this appeared to be a helpful gesture but then the man's fist slammed closed and with it Demetri's air was cut off. As his arm began to rise, so did Demetri's body. He was floating in mid-air, breath lost to him with the man looking intently into his eyes.

He tried with all his might to summon up enough power to knock the man backwards, but no matter how hard he focused his powers of telepathy and telekinesis seemed to be lost in this dream world. Demetri tried to focus on what the man had said earlier, this was only a dream, and he started telling himself over and over in his mind, *this is a dream, wake the fuck up!*

"You can't fight me," the man said. "Whether in a dream or when I pass through to this earthly realm, you will be mine."

Demetri called out in his mind for help to all the creatures stirring, irritated in the dark. But with each second that passed, he felt his life force being drained from him.

Then out of the darkness, the creatures began an advance towards the man. Werewolves were running at him; vampires hurled themselves at him. Witches stepped out of the darkness chanting their spells at him.

What happened next was something made from dreams. The tattoos from the man's body began to crawl outward from his flesh, stretching, pulling themselves free from his body, taking on their intended forms. No longer were the tattoos of werewolves, vampires, and witches, but of bats, serpents, walking skeletons, and the giant troll like creature. With a flick of the man's other arm, these tattoos had taken on a form of their own, flew free of his body attacking with supernatural speed and strength. The vampires who were trying to help Demetri attacked the massive troll, hitting it with supernatural strength, ripping at the troll with razor sharp fingernails and teeth. But their effort was to no avail. The troll was not fazed by this attack. One by one the vampires were grabbed up by the giant creature, their heads bitten off with its fang-like teeth, and their bodies tossed to the ground as he grabbed up another morsel.

The werewolves advanced on the skeletons, taking for granted they were just bones. As they bit down viciously onto the bones of the skeleton expecting to hear a satisfying crunch, the wolves howled in pain as their teeth broke on the mystically hardened calcium. As the groups collided, one of the skeletons grabbed a werewolf in mid-air by the mouth as it jumped towards the skeleton in an attempt at beheading. Demetri could hear the yelps of pain as the skeleton ripped the wolf's mouth apart until the bottom jaw was torn completely from its head. Tossing the limp body onto the ground, the skeleton set itself for defense against the advancing pack of werewolves.

The witches had no time to take cover before the bats and serpents attacked. The bats were attacking their faces and arms, biting them while the serpents made their way up the bodies of the witches. The serpents wrapped themselves tightly around their victim's necks. Squeezing with supernatural force and speed until the heads of the witches popped off like dandelion heads, flying high into the air before falling to the ground. It was a complete bloodbath, and it seemed like it was over within a matter of seconds.

As the carnage lay on the ground before them, the killing machines from the man's body, made their way back, where they were absorbed into his body, taking on their original tattoo form.

Demetri still suspended in the air, was in shock by what had just happened. What he couldn't see by moving his eyes back and forth, he made up for by hearing the events. It was a massacre. All the while, the man continued to look at Demetri with a smile on his face, pleased by what he had just accomplished.

"Join me or watch the world suffer the same fate as these underworld beings," commanded the man, only inches from where Demetri was suspended in the air. As the man pulled his arm a little closer to his body, Demetri in return was pulled closer. The man's lips pursed as he pulled Demetri in and gave him a kiss. *What was this man's game?*

Reading Demetri's mind the man said, "All in good time. Now wake the fuck up," shouted the man as he hurled Demetri backwards in the air.

Demetri opened his eyes just before his body hit the wall in his bedroom. Crashing into the wall, he felt the pain ripple through his body while he fell onto his bed, bouncing off the mattress and hitting the floor. Gasping for air and feeling blood dripping down the back of his head onto his neck, Demetri struggled to get up onto his feet, righting himself. He had dreams before, but none like this. Was he actually levitating when he woke up from the dream? His mind was reeling; his head and body aching. What the fuck had just happened?

Stumbling into the bathroom, Demetri flipped the switch on the wall turning on the lights. He made his way to the bathroom sink and turned on the cold water. Leaning forward, Demetri's hands joined beneath the stream of water as he splashed his face, letting the cool wetness shock his body into waking up. As he did, a steady stream of red water made its way down the drain. Reaching for the hand towel to dry his face, he froze as he saw himself in the mirror.

Wrapped around his neck was a red and inflamed handprint as if the man's grip of power burned his neck. Alarmed, he touched the handprint on his neck and winced at the pain that shot through him. His mind was racing and just when he was almost ready to make sense of what could have happened Demetri heard a voice in the room with him, the man's voice.

"When your moon is blue, you will know true power, my power!"

Demetri turned around looking for the man in the room but found himself alone.

Chapter Two

Alex Rogers woke up at his usual time, rubbing his eyes; he got up out of bed and made his way into the bathroom. As he stood there pissing he tried to remember the night's events, but not having much luck. Alex knew he should not have taken the ecstasy Brandon offered him. Brandon always had the best shit in town. If you ever wanted to try the newest, latest party drug, Brandon was your man.

Shaking his cock of the excess piss, he walked into the kitchen where he started making his morning cup of coffee. Caffeine would be needed, tons of it. Feeling shaky and not quite himself, he knew he needed steady hands today.

Alex loved his job; the artistic freedom, which so many customers gave him, to come up with their dream tattoo, the vibrating of the electric pin. Most don't even know the electric pin used to create the tattoos is made from the same mechanics as a doorbell. The energy of the shop, his workers and the customers made Alex extremely proud he chose to open his tattoo studio. Alex knew some people carried with them stereotypes about tattoos and tattoo artists, but he truly couldn't have chosen a better career path for himself than this, it completed his love of art and creativity.

Alex remembered today was Saturday, August 10th, and he had agreed to come in early to accommodate clients who were getting matching tattoos as a birthday gift for their daughter. They were a gay, married couple who thought it would be a cool idea to have them, their son and their daughter's fiancé all do matching tattoos. Their daughter had been in earlier in the month and gotten "beautiful" tattooed on the inside of her wrist, and his clients were going to do the same. The thought around it has such a beautiful sentiment; a reminder for all, when they were feeling down about themselves, they could always remember they were beautiful, inside and out.

Alex's three roommates, John, Carrie, and Seth, were never around, so he didn't even give a thought about walking around the house nude. Being nude was such a natural thing for Alex, and his roommates never commented on if they liked it or not so as far as he was concerned it was fair game? Hell, he could probably walk around with a boner and no one would even notice.

His roommates pretty much kept to themselves much like Alex did. Maybe that is why they all got along so well. It didn't matter; it was his house. That's probably a shitty attitude to have, but it's true. All three of his roommates were Tulsa University law students; Carrie and Seth lived mostly off student loans and part time jobs. John, however, who had been with him the longest, was a trust fund baby. Mom and dad paid for most everything, which Alex didn't mind at all because the rent was always paid on time. He knew there was an end in sight when you had students live with you; at least you hoped they would graduate at some point.

Alex moved into the house when his mother was admitted to a nursing home and not able to take care of it. Alex didn't get over to see her as much as she would like, but seeing her like that is hard for him.

Growing up in Tulsa had been a real trip for Alex. He was so different from his classmates and often was taunted for these differences. He never fit in at school and was often considered an outcast. His father left when he was a child; he didn't have many memories of him. His mother did the best she could for him, but was always a bit distant. She was a decent mother who always made sure he had what he needed, but she was just distant most of the time. His father's leaving took a toll on her that she never quite recovered.

11

His last memory of his father was of him yelling at his mother, but it was hard to remember about what. Sometimes memories come to him. It seemed as if his father was yelling at her about Alex, and about how he wasn't going to stand by and watch this happen to his son. But the memory would pass and he would wonder if it was even real. And what would he have been talking about, "watch this happen to his son?"

Sometimes Alex would have dreams that included his mother and father, but they were always weird dreams. Some were about what seemed to be Wiccan practices; sometimes they seemed darker, black magic, satanic even. Alex not being raised on any religion but migrated towards Buddhist/Naturalist spirituality. He knew enough to know his dreams were not for the faint of heart. Many nights he would wake up dripping in sweat, muscles aching and often screaming out for help, but never quite remembered from what.

Alex's best friend Brandy was into the herbalist lifestyle. Brandy tried many herbal remedies, herbal charms, and steeped teas meant to help Alex sleep better, to not have these crazy, weird dreams, but nothing has helped so far. If anything, they only seemed to enhance the dreams, make them more intense. Alex had been meaning to tell her they just were not working, but he didn't want to hurt her feelings; he knew Brandy was only trying to help.

Hell, if he wanted to justify his occasional escapes via Brandon's quality stash, he could at least say when he is rolling he didn't feel like he dreamed much at all. Except last night, last night was a first. As foggy as the memories were, he was still trying to decipher if what he did remember were fact, drug-induced fantasies, or just more crazy dreams he can't ever figure out.

Alex jumped into the shower and let the water spray all over his face as he just stood there taking it all in. Standing under the hot water was soothing to Alex's body; his body was a bit sore from the previous night's events. Standing underneath the hot water always gave Alex some time to think, some clarity, some peace. After ten minutes of just letting his muscles soak in the heat, he finally grabbed the soap and started lathering up. To the outside world Alex may look like a "freak," but he was nothing of the sort. Alex took pride in his body, his cleanliness and made sure he always looked his best. Well, at least as good as a man considered to be Goth with a body full of tattoos could look to the outside world.

Most of the people that saw Alex fell in love with his striking looks, dark hair and even darker eyes. Then they would see the tattoos that ordained his body. Alex took pride in them and considered them works of art. They were in fact works of art. Some of the best artists in the world have helped create this full body masterpiece of tats. There were skeleton heads on his hips, bats and serpents on his arms, a zombie on his leg, and a rather large face coming from his back around his torso onto his stomach.

There were many more covering his body, and he is proud of every one of them. Alex could remember the first one he got. At sixteen, the image came to him in a dream. An ornate looking symbol, old world looking. So enthralled with it when he woke up, he sketched it out and went the next day and had it tattooed to his back, just below the neck, just as it was in his dream. Most of the tattoos came from his dreams. As far as Alex is concerned, that is what made them special; a gift from his own subconscious.

Alex threw on some clothes and ran out of his room, grabbing the car keys, heading out the door. He was pushing it to be on time, but knew his clients wouldn't mind. They were just excited to have come up with a way to surprise their daughter for her birthday.

As Alex made his way down the streets of Tulsa, he was thankful traffic wasn't as bad as it could have been. It seemed they were always doing road construction these days. On a good day, he could make it from his house to his tattoo studio, Blue Moon Tattoo, in less than fifteen minutes.

Chapter Three

Demetri paced around his room trying to wrap his head around what had happened the night before. However, the more he tried to explain it, the more it seemed unbelievable. The pain is a constant reminder of what happened in his dream, mirroring itself in the waking world, or were his powers growing to the point he is hurting himself now? There is a nagging in his brain; *this is either real or one of his dreams foretelling the future to come.* Either way, it didn't bode well for him. Demetri's thoughts went back to the first time he encountered what he felt was a ghost or spirit attack him, which was the same time he realized his life would never be the same.

Demetri grew up in a small rural farming community in Oklahoma. He was raised in nature and felt that's why he had such a big appreciation for all things natural. Superstitions ran deep in rural communities, some coming across as old wives' tales, others in natural remedies, and some just downright mystical. There was a huge Native American community all around where he grew up in Braggs, and some of their traditions ran just as deep today as they had hundreds of years ago.

Demetri proudly came from a long line of farmers and ranchers. His family had a huge garden just outside of his grandparent's house in which the family grew tomatoes, corn, peas, carrots, lettuce, peppers, okra, cantaloupe, and watermelons. They had a large apple, peach, and pear orchard in the back part of his grandparent's yard behind the house, just before one of the barbed wire fences leading out to the cattle pastures. His grandmother would make the most delicious fried pies and could make some of the best jellies and jams from the fruit. His favorite was the plum jelly she would make from the random plum trees on the property. There are pecan orchards deep in the pasture, which he found comforting to be around, and he spent many hours playing there.

Growing up in the "country" as they called it instilled many good and bad qualities to his personality, but the good out-weighed the bad. His family, including his grandfather and uncles, raised cattle, horses, pigs, chickens, and other farm animals.

They grew their alfalfa and each summer they would all gather in the hay fields to haul hay bales back to the barns. It was a yearly tradition. Demetri started helping at a young age when his grandfather would let him drive the truck in the hay fields since he wasn't quite old enough to heft the bales onto the trucks. Even before he was able to drive the truck by himself, his grandfather was letting him sit on his lap while he drove.

Things started to change for Demetri when he had his first experience with his powers at age ten. He used to play out in the pastures and wooded areas of their land. There was a mid-wife named Mertyl, who lived on his grandparent's land, who even helped deliver his father and two uncles. She had died years before his birth, but her abandoned home and barn still stood down by a stream. The house, dilapidated and uninhabitable, still rested on its original foundation, which made Demetri and his cousins more than happy. Their imagination had transformed the ruined house into an amazing place to be.

The barn had weathered time and elements, making it a perfect a place for them to play. Demetri and his cousins ended up making the barn a clubhouse; it was a two-sided barn, small, with one side for a horse and the other for hay. There were piles of coal around the property; Demetri and the others didn't realize coal was used for heat back in the day, so they would assume it added to their wealth. As kids, there wasn't much they lacked in imagination. Kids today don't connect with nature like he and his cousins had.

He would often play there pretending it was his home. He would spend hours losing track of time in the process. He often got in trouble for not keeping in touch with his parents while down there, coming back at dusk after being gone all day. Even though, it was on their land, it was still a large place where one could easily get lost from the crowd of a large family.

It was his tenth birthday and still early in the day. He didn't have to be back home until his birthday party at six when all his cousins and other family members would get together. He was playing down at Mertyl's old place pretending to be a witch. The characters he assumed changed all the time, but they, usually, had something to do with the supernatural or some horror movie he would sneak out of bed to watch.

He stood outside, feeling nature around him; he was aware of the darkness in the far background of the sky and knew a storm was heading his way. Demetri, still stuck in the innocence of his youth, taunted the storm. Concentrating hard on getting it to focus on him so he could fight back as he stood with his arms stretched out to his sides, head leaned back looking up into the sky. He yelled out, "I command you; I summon you to send forth the winds."

To his delight the winds picked up a bit. Feeling the wind start to whip around him, blow through his hair, only enhanced the realness of what was supposed to be a make-believe play session.

"I command you to send forth lightning," he yelled with all his might, concentrating hard on controlling the lightening. Once again, to his delight, the skies started to light up with a flash of lightening followed by the roll of thunder. As all of these started to come into play time, as if on his command, Demetri's confidence grew in the character he had chosen for the day.

Arms still outstretched to his sides, his face looking up to the sky, he started to laugh. He was having so much fun and truly felt himself a witch at that moment controlling the elements around him. Then the storm got real. Lightening hit the big willow tree by the pond only 100 feet away from where he was standing. The loudness of it; the shocking, amazing awe of it combined with the boom of thunder following knocked him backwards onto the ground.

That pretty much did it for role play that day. He knew he didn't have time to run back home since the rain was already starting to trickle down so he ran into Mertyl's abandoned house which he had done so many times in the past. Only this time it felt different. This time he didn't feel alone in the house. It wasn't a big house, only a large room for the kitchen, dining room, and sitting room with a small bedroom in the back. The outhouse used back in the day had long been torn down but the house was never built with a bathroom. The house was dark due to no electricity and the darkness from the storm passing over, which left him feeling uncomfortable. The lightening and the thunder only added to his unease, he found himself letting his nerves get the best of him.

The shadows in the room were playing tricks on him as the house lit up with lightening and at times he felt he could see someone in the room with him. Of course, he knew this couldn't be true. Even at ten, he knew things like this didn't happen. The most he had to be afraid of was his mother for not making it home before the storm hit.

But as the storm grew more intense and the display of lightening and the subsequent boom of thunder continued its assault, Demetri started to see a dark form in the corner at first. Then he would see it coming near him and as the lightening would lay itself out across the sky lighting up the room, he would no longer see the dark form. But as quick as the light would dissipate, the dark form would make its way back into his line of vision. He was getting scared by this and was starting to think he was not just seeing trickster shadows, but rather a ghost like he would see in the horror movies he watched. His nerves were on edge and his heart was racing.

There was a noise coming from the kitchen sink. It was a subtle shaking at first, then became intense; a rumbling filled the room as the whole counter and sink rattled about. He cautiously made his way towards it, the wood floor creaking with each step he took towards the sink. In the blink of an eye, the counter top and the sink itself were in the air headed directly towards him. Demetri, shocked and scared, fell backwards on the floor and raised his hands up in the air as if to protect himself from the oncoming counter top screamed loudly, "NO!"

To his amazement, he felt an energy, a powerful calming release leaving his body. The counter top and sink, nearly two feet from crushing his body went flying backwards with such force, the counter top shattered into pieces.

He laid on the floor of the house in awe, in disbelief, and confusion. He knew the power came from him. He knew his instinct to protect himself had kicked in, but how did he do such a feat. Trying not to press his luck on what might have been in the house with him or what might have caused something to attack him; he opted to face the rain.

He bolted out of the house and ran in the rain all the way home to find his worried mother pacing on the front porch of their home. He knew from the scowl on her face he would be grounded, but he had never before been so happy to be grounded by his mother.

That was the day Demetri knew things would never be the same again and, quite frankly, he didn't know if he would want a normal life.

Chapter Four

Gina Long was busy that Sunday morning combing through book after book trying to find out anything she could about psychic dreams; levitation within dreams, and using dreams to foretell future things to come. Gina owned a rare herbal store as well as a New Age type book store. You could get books from Wiccan 101 to advanced potions books, almost any type of religion, self-help, to even books on astrology. Along with books and herbs you could get crystals, incense, Tarot cards, and Ouija boards. Gina wanted her store to be the one stop shopping experience for anything rare. It was a progressive store, especially since it happened to be in the heart of the Bible belt.

The store was laid out nicely, at least Gina thought so. There were two entrances into the building; one from the front where customers would come into the store and one from the back, which came into the living quarters where Gina resided. The main store was laid out basically in one room with the books lined up on racks or stacked on tables; there were display cases for the crystals and other items like the Tarot cards. In one corner there was a herb station where she had large apothecary jars filled with natural herbs from around the world, along with scales in which to weigh and bag the herbs you chose.

Her favorite part of the place was the reading room. It was a room where there were tables set up so people could read from a selected book to see if they liked it or not. Gina didn't mind for people to hang out and read in the room. There were computers set up in the room in which one could do some research if needed. There were a few restrictions on the public computers mainly so people didn't use them for watching porn and such as they truly were meant for researching all things Wicca.

The back was separated by a sturdy door and lock. This was where Gina lived, slept, and ate. It was a great setup. There were two bedrooms, a living room, kitchen, dining room, bathroom, and small library, but Gina preferred the reading room in the store. It had plenty of storage space, even its own basement. Gina felt lucky to find this place. It was almost 3,000 square feet and a find like this in the Brookside area of Tulsa was not easy to do. The bookstore itself was just about 1,500 square feet. Gina loved it here and was so happy to be doing what she was passionate about and to be able to live in the back was just an added bonus.

Gina had known long ago this was her calling. Gina was a practicing witch and a quite gifted one. She knew how difficult it was to find everything needed to practice her craft. So Gina opened up her own place so she and every other person out there looking for something different from the norm in Tulsa would have a place to go. She had opened The Mind's Eye - New Age Book and Supply Store in Brookside about five years prior. She was happy to be able to make a living at something she truly believed in and gave her the freedom to practice her craft as much as she wanted. The location was perfect and the energy in the area was truly charged for a witch like herself.

She was most proud of her own extremely rare book collection in the library, which wasn't open to the public. The store was a nice place and for Gina being only twenty-five-years-old, she felt pride for what she accomplished. She never forgets how this all came to her though and what a loss it was at the time. Gina's grandmother passed away from breast cancer and left Gina a sizeable life insurance policy in which Gina invested a chunk of the money into opening the store. It was almost a tribute to her beautiful grandmother's legacy as she was a witch as well.

Things were much easier today for a practicing witch than they were back in her mother's and grandmother's day. Back when her grandmother was Gina's age, she had to make sure no one knew what she was doing for fear of attack. She could have been killed by ignorant people who didn't seem to have the ability to understand.

Today, people were more accepting of different practices and religions, although there are still some haters out in the world. But for the most part, people left her alone. Even ingredients were easier to come by because of the internet. The internet has made a large world much smaller. Gina tries to make her store a place where anyone would feel accepted and a place where you can find anything you need, especially for witches.

Her best friend, Demetri, called her this morning in a panic talking about his all too real sounding dream and about the bruising he woke up with as well as the voices he was hearing. She was struggling with what this all meant. She grew up with him in Braggs and was well aware of his rare and special gifts and when Demetri was scared of something, Gina knew she needed to take it seriously.

Gina first became aware of Demetri's gifts when she happened to stumble upon him moving a desk with his mind in an empty room after school one day. They must have been in the sixth or seventh grade but when she walked up on him and saw what he was doing she let out a gasp. Startled, Demetri turned to see who had caught him and accidentally shoved her up against the door using his mind.

"Why would you sneak up on me? Are you spying on me?" He yelled at her, more out of fear of being caught.

"I wasn't spying on you. I just walked by and saw you moving the desk with your mind," she said to him in utter awe and amazement. "I have never met anyone who is telekinetic before."

"Tele what?" He blushed, not knowing what she was talking about. "I didn't do that."

21

"You don't have to worry about me telling anyone, I promise. I will even pinky-swear on it." Gina tried to make him feel at ease. "Besides, you just slammed me up against the door with your mind. That is so totally cool."

"You think so?" He wondered what she would do.

"Listen, I will tell you a secret too, but you have to swear to not tell anyone, even your parents. I could get in major trouble for telling you." She offered, wanting him to accept her olive branch.

"I promise I won't tell anyone. Pinky swear." Demetri said, curious about what was to be revealed to him.

"My family comes from a long line of witches. My mom was one, my grandmother is and even I will one day be a witch like them."

"Bullshit," he blurted. "You are pulling my leg."

"No, I'm not. I'm dead serious." Gina said, seeing his eyes turn from disbelief to belief.

Back then he was just learning about his powers and didn't have the control he did now. Once she saw his display of powers she knew she was going to come clean with him about her family. Her instincts about him were spot on. They were inseparable ever since.

It has been amazing watching his powers grow over the years. He has developed a more psychic connection and on occasion can actually talk to the other side, to those who have passed on. Over the past few years, he developed an ability in which his dreams have been able to tell the future. He is truly a gifted and talented psychic and some might say male witch. Demetri would disagree with the witch part even though he has been known to cast a spell or two; even dabble in potions with Gina.

Gina's gift developed over the years. It was purely a fascination thing in the beginning, watching her mother and her grandmother with their craft. She loved going into the woods with them and collecting fresh herbs and ingredients needed for their potions. People talked about them around town as the odd family. But those same people would always come running to her grandmother's door when someone was

22

hurt or sick and conventional medicines did not seem to be healing their loved ones. They would make a pact with the devil to get a "natural" remedy from the local witch. At least that was what the word around town was when someone would come to her grandmother for help.

Gina would learn the craft by helping them with their potions and reading in the *Book of Shadows*. It wasn't until her mother's death when Gina was eight when she experienced her first real taste of power. Her grandmother explained to her when her mother passed away her abilities came to Gina, as had their ancestors in the past. But Gina would still have to learn what they were and learn how to control them, because she could definitely testify these powers didn't come with a manual. The closest thing to a manual she had was her mother's Book of Shadows which was passed down to her. Over the years, her grandmother's guidance helped her to learn the craft and most importantly, to respect the craft.

Demetri and Gina had a strong bond, not only were they best friends, but they basically had to learn to use their own powers and what that consisted of together. Much like best friends going through puberty together, they had to deal with much more than hormones racing through their bodies.

Gina never was jealous of Demetri's powers; yes they were amazing gifts, but she was thankful for her own. She felt a connection to the earth that rivaled any other sensation a person could have. The universe, at times, felt as if it was screaming out through her, but what an amazing feeling.

Gina was shaken from her thoughts as she heard the bell chime of the store's door being opened. Customers were her livelihood, or at least her store's livelihood. Gina enjoyed helping people learn more about themselves and loved when experienced, gifted people came into the store and she had what they were searching for. If she didn't, she would definitely find it for them. To Gina's surprise, it was Demetri walking through the door. He didn't look his usual dapper self; there was a look of worry in his eyes Gina had not seen since they were kids.

23

Demetri came rushing over to Gina and gave her a hug as he usually did. When he leaned back from the hug, she could see the hand print on his neck. It definitely looked better than the picture he texted earlier. But this was still a bad situation and they had to get to the bottom of it before it escalated further.

Chapter Five

Charles Wilson was a man of discipline and structure. It was Monday, August 12th, and for the most part it was a typical morning, other than the fact it was his birthday. Charles would get up each morning at 4:00 a.m. He would put on his jogging gear and be out the door of his Riverside Drive and Denver area condo by 4:30 a.m. for his morning jog. Charles loved this time of the morning when there were few cars on the road; the sky was still dark with the night. When the weather was just right, he could hear birds singing an early morning song as he made his way down the jogging path that ran alongside Riverside Drive and the Arkansas River.

A typical jog for him would be leaving his home which was just north of 21st Street and Riverside Drive and jogging down to Interstate 44 before turning around and heading back. This gave him a good six miles of jogging. Once home, he would shower, shave, and read the morning paper while having his coffee. By 9:00 a.m., he was comfortably sitting in his office chair at the downtown Bank of America building. This was a morning ritual he had been doing for about three years.

Charles had lived in Tulsa all his life and loved the downtown feel. He graduated from Union High School at the top of his class. He went directly into the business/finance program at the University of Tulsa (TU) and landed his job as an investment banker with Bank of America before graduating. Charles was proud of the fact he had graduated

TU with honors. Life was really good and it seemed to just be getting better.

He had started dating this amazing girl, Tonya, whom he met at a jazz bar in the downtown Blue Dome District a few months ago and things seemed to be headed in a good direction. They had so much in common. Even though today was his birthday, Charles had a big night planned out already and wanted it to be filled with good food, wine, and romance. You only turned 25 once.

Charles was a good mile into his run and loved to see the lights from the Public Service of Oklahoma power plant sign play off the water of the river as he jogged along the path. There were always a few joggers on the path, but for the most part, he could always count on enjoying this time of his day alone. Not many people were out on the path at 4:30 a.m.

He was jogging along, making a mental list in his head of what he needed to accomplish today at the office. He had to get out a little early and head to the flower shop to get Tonya some flowers for the night. Charles was oblivious to the fact someone was coming towards him on the path. Had he seen this he would have always done the polite thing and moved over a bit. Before he knew what was happening, he ran right into another man who was jogging along this section of the path that was not well lit. It knocked Charles off his feet. It was like hitting a wall, a rock wall. Charles, winded and embarrassed, was quickly on his feet and offering his apologies to the man.

"I am so sorry, I didn't even see you coming," Charles said to the man. "Are you alright?"

The man just smiled at him and nodded his head indicating he was indeed alright, and was headed down the jogging path before Charles could say another word to him. This was a first for Charles, but it was a lesson learned, pay attention to the task at hand which was jogging.

Charles noticed the man had many tattoos and he was a bit envious. He wanted to get one for quite some time but didn't know if it would be acceptable in the corporate world and he wasn't one for making any waves for himself. If it

26

didn't fit neatly into his nice box of life he had created for himself, then he didn't force it. But he was turning twenty-five-years-old today, so maybe he would think about it again. What could one tattoo on the ankle or calf area hurt? It would always be covered up by his pant leg of his suit he wore to work each day.

Charles was once again caught by the beauty of the river at dawn with all the lights playing off the water from the surrounding buildings. He thought it one of the most beautiful areas of the city. He felt one day Tulsa would make an even bigger mark on the tourism industry once they started the planned projects to beautify the river and its proximity to downtown. There had been proposals on past election ballots to approve a tax increase for river projects, but it did not pass. Other cities had done it and were reaping the rewards of a booming tourism industry. He felt confident Tulsa was headed in the right direction.

Charles heard someone jogging up behind him and moved over to the edge of the path, but the person kept pace behind him. Before Charles could do anything, he felt a painful blow to the back of his head and felt dizzy and nauseous and he knew he was going down; he was passing out. Charles hit the ground near the Quik Trip Park around 41st Street and Riverside Drive.

When Charles awoke it was still dark and he felt a burning, wet feeling on his chest. As the fogginess in his head started to fade he realized he was tied to a tree, nude, not far from the park. There was a piece of duct tape over his mouth so screaming was out of the question. As he looked down, he could make out a carving into his chest of some sort, but could not make out what it was exactly. Blood was dripping down his chest onto his stomach and down his legs. The wounds were deep. Panic set in and he was hoping whoever had done this was gone and the worst was over.

Charles started to struggle to free his hands from the backside of the tree but found the duct tape around his wrist tightly in place. *What's going on? Who had done this and why?* So many thoughts were going through his mind and none of them made sense to him.

Charles' hope of getting free faded quickly and his heart started racing even more as he saw a man approaching him with a stone looking knife. As he neared him, Charles could make out this was the same man he had collided with on the jogging path earlier. *Was the man that mad he would do this?* As the man was standing closer to Charles, even in the darkness there was enough light to see he had curious looking tattoos on his body.

The man was chanting something in a language Charles had never heard before. As his mind tried to make sense of it, all he could really think was, *oh shit, I am going to die.*

"Ego immolans primus animam Bastiquil," was the last thing Charles heard the man chanting, which Charles knew either way wasn't good for him. The man rushed him and drove the knife into Charles's chest, directly into the center of the carving.

"I have sacrificed the first soul to Bastiquil," the man yelled.

Charles felt a searing pain and then a panic as the air was cut off from him. Thoughts of Tonya faded in and out of his head and the life they could have had together but will no longer have the chance as he knew he had been dealt a deadly blow to the chest. He could no longer breathe. As his lungs filled up with blood, his life was slipping away, fading quickly. The last thing he heard before he took his last breath was the man telling him his death would help bring about the destruction of the world.

Charles was startled when he found himself standing next to the tree looking at his own body, tied up, blood stained, and dead. He couldn't help but look upon himself with fear and dread. He could still see the man who had taken his life and it appeared his work was not quite finished. The man was chanting still, making scribbles in the dirt on the ground with what looked like Charles' blood. As the man worked feverishly to complete his task, Charles was expecting a white light to appear, an angel, or something. But, nothing like that happened.

The man finished his chanting and his scribbling in the dirt, got up smiling at Charles' dead body and walked over to the jogging path and took off running. He looked like any other jogger along the path Charles encountered each and every morning.

Charles was standing there, confused and baffled. The scribbles on the ground began to light up, but it wasn't light. It was almost a look of fire outlining the symbols drawn on the ground. They began to morph and move around eerily as one would expect in a dream. Charles knew he wasn't dreaming. Then he could hear the sounds of dogs barking in the background, but not just any dogs, it was the sound of large dogs and they were getting closer. Charles' instinct was to run but as he tried he found he was not able to move. Was he bound to his body, or had the man done something more than just kill him?

The dirt started giving way where the symbols had been drawn. At first it was a spinning of dirt and sand, and then it started to fall within itself. The hole it was making was beginning to brighten up, making a fiery pit. A large paw, larger than Charles' head reached up from the pit and then another. Then a large, enormous demon hound, much larger than a grizzly bear, made its way out of the ground. Its jaws were filled with teeth as big as any of Charles' fingers and bloody looking drool falling from its mouth. Another hound just as big and fierce as the last made its way out of the pit. Both hounds were circling around Charles and snapping at him. Charles unable to run could do nothing but stand there and hope this was not happening; hope this was not what he thought it was. He had led a good life, he was a decent man so why didn't this seem like angels were coming for him? Why did it feel like he was being led to the gates of hell?

All at once, both dogs jumped at Charles, one grabbing his leg and the other grabbing his arm and he was being dragged towards the pit. Charles screamed out in fear, in pain as the dogs bit into his soul and all he could feel was his

29

soul burning. As they made their way to the pit, it opened up just enough for them to jump into it with Charles in tow.

It was done, he was gone. His earthly body was still tied to the tree, bereft of life, but his soul was somewhere no one would ever find again. The hole had already closed up and all that was left were symbols drawn onto the ground. The blood used to draw them disappeared.

Chapter Six

Alex woke from his dream screaming. It was early Monday morning and the sun had yet to make its mark on the earth. The birds outside were starting to sing so it must be getting close to dawn. As he worked on calming himself down and telling himself he was fine, it was just another dream, Alex looked over at the clock on the nightstand. It was only 5:15 a.m.

These dreams were getting more and more intense and were feeling undeniable. There must be some real shit going on in his head to be having such night terrors. But they all seemed so real, with purpose, with intent and he was being given front row seats for a viewing he wished he had nothing to do with.

Lately, he had been experiencing a burning sensation on the back of his neck, right where he had gotten his first tattoo. Maybe that was why he kept seeing the tattooed symbol in his dreams.

Alex got up out of bed and walked into the bathroom flipping on the light. He stopped to look at himself in the mirror, to make sure he wasn't still dreaming. But as he looked at himself in the mirror he realized he looked as shitty as he felt. His eyes were getting dark circles around them. Man, what he would pay to get a good night's sleep.

Leaving the mirror, he walked over to the toilet where he stood taking his morning leak. As he was standing there, he started having flashbacks of the dream he had just experienced. They came in waves, one image after the other hitting his brain like a ton of bricks. They were so intense they knocked him off his feet and he fell backwards onto the floor knocking his head on the wall. He screamed which wasn't so much from the fall but more from the pain in his head caused by the wave of flashes hitting his brain like a strobe light.

As he lay there on the floor trying to keep a grip on reality he didn't even realize John had come into the bathroom. "Alex, dude, I heard a noise and you screaming, you alright man?" John asked. He looked Alex up and down as if he were seeing some nude, drunken, homeless guy lying on the bathroom floor. "Dude, you pissed all over yourself," John said stating the obvious.

Pissing on himself was really the last of what was on Alex's mind at the moment. "Can you help me up John?" Alex said trying to reach his arm up towards John. "Can you help me into the shower?"

John rushed over to Alex and helped him to his feet. John was a good guy and was in top notch shape and had no trouble getting Alex to his feet and into the shower. "Thanks, man, I'm good from here. I appreciate your help," said Alex.

"Okay buddy, if you need anything just yell and I'll come running," John said turning and heading out of the room.

Alex turned on the water of the shower and jumped a little as the cold water hit his body causing his muscles to spasm a bit but felt comfort when the cool water transitioned to warm then to hot. Alex allowed himself to sink to the floor of the shower, sitting knees pulled up to his chest, arms wrapped around his legs and his forehead lying on the top of his knees. Even though it was a bit hotter than he typically liked, he didn't care. He was glad to have something hurting him other than the pain he was feeling in his head.

The flashbacks from his dream had stopped when John entered the bathroom although Alex didn't put it together until just now. Man, Alex thought, I must be losing my damn mind.

Alex sat on the floor of the shower for another thirty minutes until he could feel the hot water starting to fade. Alex struggled to his feet, steadied himself, and dried off as he went to the kitchen where he started making coffee. There was always something about coffee he could depend upon. It is 6:15 a.m. and it seemed as if the entire day had happened in the past hour.

Alex sat silently in his thoughts until he was brought back by the beeping of the coffee maker alerting him that his morning caffeine was ready. Alex walked over and poured himself an extra-large cup. He is going to need it today.

Walking into the common area of the house, the TV room, Alex sat down on the couch and took a sip of his coffee. Grabbing the remote off the coffee table, he turned on the huge 72" flat screen TV. Flipping through the channels, Alex found himself stopping on one particular channel. As he sat there watching a Breaking News report on Channel 2 News, his hands began to tremble a bit. Alex had to put both hands on the coffee mug before he realized it wasn't helping, so he decided to put the coffee mug down on the table before he made the second mess of the morning.

What was unfolding on TV, in front of his eyes, Alex only wished was a dream. What the hell was going on here? His head started to ache again and his hands were shaking uncontrollably.

"This is Kathy Reed coming to you live with breaking news from the Riverside Drive and 41st Street vicinity. A yet unidentified male was found dead, nude, and duct taped to a tree close to the Arkansas River today apparently in what some are saying is a cult type ritual sacrifice. The police are still on the scene and have yet to release any names and minimal details, but sources say the male had a carving on his chest. The knife was still inside the man's chest when he was found earlier this morning," the reporter stated. "We will continue to bring you details as they unfold."

As Alex's dream was unfolding in front of him on the morning news, his stomach began to rumble; he became nauseous and ran back to his bathroom where he proceeded to throw up. *How could I have known this, how could I have dreamed this?* It was a night terror, just like the numerous ones he has had in the past. But this was not a night terror, this was really happening.

Who was this man Alex had dreamed about, and why would he dream about his brutal murder?

Chapter Seven

Alex had to get some answers. There had to be a reason he was dreaming all of these strange and brutal dreams. *Why am I dreaming about a man being murdered? From the timing of it, it appears the man had been murdered at the exact same time he was dreaming about it.*

Alex jumped into the shower again this time to get ready for the day. This was going to be a day to remember, he could feel it. As the hot water rolled down his body, his thoughts were on this man running along Riverside Drive and how his life had been plucked from him so brutally. Alex really couldn't go to the cops because, of course, it was a dumbass move to run into a police station and tell them "I dreamed about the guy murdered this morning on Riverside Drive." Alex may as well walk in there and say he had done it himself.

No, that wasn't the answer. He would head out and see if he could find some information, someone who could help him make sense of all this.

As the water continued to hit Alex's body and roll downward to the drain, he became completely aware of his inaugural tattoo. The symbol on his lower neck was still slightly burning and the hot water was not helping. Nothing in his world is making sense to him at this moment.

Maybe Brandy could make some sense out of this? Maybe she knew someone or somewhere he could go to get some answers. Brandy was one of the smartest women he knew, not just book smart, but street smart too. She was a tough cookie if ever there was one. Alex trusted Brandy with his life and she had on more than one occasion shown him she trusted him too.

When Alex finished his shower he called Brandy and they set up a time to meet for breakfast in Brookside. Alex loved this part of town. It was hip, cool, and culturally sound. That is why he had put in his tattoo studio in Brookside. Anyone who was cool in Tulsa was frequented this area. It is made up of restaurants, bars, shopping stores, and art galleries on Peoria Avenue.

Brandy had told him she would meet him at 9:30 a.m. and it was just after eight so he had some time to kill. Alex decided he needed to get some air. Grabbing his car keys he climbed into his black 1968 Shelby GT500, revved up the gas, and quickly took off down the road.

Already in Brookside at the Morning Café twenty minutes before Brandy arrived, Alex had ordered himself a triple shot espresso iced latte, nonfat milk and had ordered Brandy her green tea she always had.

"Hey love, you look like shit," Brandy said leaning over to give him a kiss on the cheek. "Another bad night of dreams?"

"You have no idea," Alex said with a look in his eyes so serious it made Brandy instantly uncomfortable. "Have you been watching the morning news?"

"I heard something on the radio on the drive over about a killing on Riverside Drive," Brandy said looking closely at Alex. "Poor guy was tied up and stabbed to death."

"What I'm about to tell you seems so crazy," Alex said. Reaching for his iced latte as his hands started shaking a little. "I want you to bear with me because I'm beginning to think I might be crazy."

Brandy was eyeing Alex with anticipation and fear. He didn't seem quite on his game this morning. Maybe the stress of not getting any sleep has finally made him snap.

"The murder in the park this morning," Alex started but found the words hard to get out. It seemed like eternity before he started again and he could tell Brandy was hanging on his every word. "I dreamed the entire murder and I think it was at the exact time it was happening," Alex blurted out as he scanned Brandy for her reaction.

"Hold on a minute Alex. How the hell could that be," Brandy said all the while thinking to herself *Alex truly has snapped.*

"I have no fucking idea how that could happen. I don't know if it was a psychic connection, spiritual connection, or just bad ass timing, but it happened Brandy and I need you, of all people, to believe me," Alex pleaded with her.

"Alex, I'm always here for you and we will figure this out, I promise," Brandy calmly said to Alex trying to get him to relax a bit. "Are you sure the news wasn't broadcasting on the television and maybe you just heard it in the background as you dreamed?"

"I would bet my life on it Brandy. I didn't even have the TV on," Alex said finally realizing he truly had dreamed this poor guy's murder. Alex didn't know why yet, but he was determined to figure it out. Maybe there was something in the dream he could remember about the killer.

Chapter Eight

Brandy Helmsworth had not always been a beautiful girl, but she was used to getting what she wanted. She learned this from an early age, she could ask anything of her parents or even her grandparents and it would happen. The only child of Ralph and Gerty Helmsworth, a family originally from England, they opted to raise their only daughter to be an atheist.

Why her family ended up in Kansas, Brandy will never truly know. They were tight lipped about things and when she would bring up the move to Kansas, they would shut her down by saying, "Brandy, we live for the future, not the past, so why must you bring up hurtful things from the past." This was always enough to make Brandy feel guilty and shut her up at the same time.

Brandy was always authentically curious as a child, always reading, always paying attention in class, especially science, which fascinated her. She was considered a geek growing up; she was taller than most girls in her class and a little lanky. She didn't have to deal with bullying too much. When the local pretty, popular girl thought she would attempt to keep her in check, Brandy just hauled off and smacked her right in the nose. She was expelled from school for three days, but it put an end to the girl's reign of terror before it even started. She didn't condone violence, but she believed in protecting yourself and your loved ones.

Brandy would go on to become the pretty girl in school. When puberty hit, she grew into her body. She was tall at five-feet, eleven inches, with long flowing blond hair, blue eyes, and the most beautiful smile. She had brains, which for many were a deadly and often intimidating combination. When you are pretty and smart many people become extremely jealous, rather quickly. Some men loved it and some truly hated it, but it didn't matter to her. She was her own individual and no one had any power over her but herself.

When she graduated high school and decided to leave Kansas, to go on to bigger and brighter things, she settled on attending college at the University of Oklahoma in Norman. She had a full ride, due to graduating valedictorian from high school and scoring high on her SAT's. Brandy ended up with a degree in chemistry and landed a nice paying job in Tulsa where she now works for a petroleum company.

When she moved to Tulsa a few years ago, she met Alex. She would be lying if she said there were not some sparks between them and they have fooled around on occasion, but for the most part they both concluded they were much better friends than they were lovers. But, neither of them were the type of person that needed someone in their lives to make them whole. They were great companions and if they ever so desired they were there for each other sexually. It was a perfect setup, FWB, friends with benefits. Although it had been some time since they had used the benefits card of their friendship; for the most part they were both self-sufficient and both beautiful people who could have whomever they wanted, when they wanted.

People seemed to be drawn to Alex and Brandy, men and woman, and both seemed to be equally as enthralled with his tattoos as they were with her long legs and blue eyes. But one cannot dismiss the pure natural beauty of Alex; those dark eyes of his were just mysterious enough they drew in everyone he met, well, most everyone.

Alex was the one who gave Brandy her first tattoo and it was actually how they first met. Brandy went into Blue Moon Tattoo to have "Knowledge is Power" tattooed on her right ankle. She was so nervous when she walked in, but Alex had a way about him of diffusing her nerves and making her completely trust him. He had her laughing during the most painful parts and they were inseparable ever since.

When Brandy's parents both died in a car wreck last year, it was Alex who was there for her. He went with her to the funeral and helped her go through her parent's things and stayed with her to settle things with their will and estate. They didn't have much, but had left everything to Brandy. If it were not for Alex and his strong heart and even stronger arms, she might not have made it through it herself.

To this day she will never understand how the wreck even happened. The police were chalking it up to faulty break lines. She knew her father and knew he took impeccable care of their car and instilled that in her by saying, "a car cost too much money not to take care of it."

The police report said they were driving in the rain and hydroplaned and when the brakes failed, they were unable to stop themselves from driving off the bridge into a surging river. Their bodies were found days later when the rain and water receded enough for them to dredge the river and send divers in to find the car, which still had her parent's bodies in it.

They skipped a formal funeral and just had a graveside service. This was more for Brandy's sake than anything else. She knew they would not have wanted a big church funeral as they had never attended church her entire life. Brandy holds to the belief science was the spark of life, not religion.

Even through these night terror episodes she would stand by him and help him figure it out. Brandy held her faith in science, in the here and now, what she could touch and see and she would use every resource she had, every contact she has developed to help Alex.

Chapter Nine

Alex and Brandy pulled into the parking lot, parked, got out of their cars and headed into the store. As they came into the store, the doors chimed to let the owner know someone was there. The smell of incense and candles filled the room and their noses with a somewhat powerful but pleasing smell. It was only seconds later a beautiful red headed woman came walking out of the back of the store and greeted them warmly. "Hello, welcome to The Mind's Eye, my name is Gina," she said smiling at Brandy and Alex genuinely. "How can I help you?"

Brandy started talking first. "Hello, we are here trying to get some information on dreams. My friend is having some intense night terrors and we are trying to find anything that might help him understand the cause of them and what we can do to make them stop."

"I see," said Gina, "night terror, which is known as a sleep terror occur during the slow wave sleep or the arousal from the deep sleep. There is lots of research on this, and it's thought to have happened back in ancient times as well. It wasn't until the research of rapid eye movement that they were able to tell a night terror from a regular nightmare. What kind of dreams are you having?"

Alex watched as Brandy looked at the girl intently, hanging on her every word.

"Oh, I get that," Brandy stated. "I am a scientist who specializes in…"

Brandy was cut short by Alex as he began talking over her.

"I'm the friend she is referring to who is having the night terrors, and believe me they are a terror," Alex said looking directly into Gina's eyes. There was something about her he was drawn to. There seemed to be so much knowledge behind those big beautiful green eyes. There was energy, an aura about her he felt connected to instantly. "I need your help as these dreams seem to be intensifying and I feel as if I am beginning to unravel a bit trying to decide on what is real and what is quite frankly dream world."

"Well, I have a book for almost everything you could possibly want or need to understand. I'm sure we can find something," she said smiling compassionately at him. "I just need to know what type of dreams we are dealing with so I can narrow the search."

Feeling he could trust what was behind those green eyes, relaxed and wanted to open up to her. But how did he tell a complete stranger he was dreaming about killing people and the last one he dreamed about he woke up, and saw it on the morning news. If he were being told this by someone he would probably pick up the phone and dial 911, but he just couldn't shake the feeling he was safe with her.

"I have been having these dreams where I think I am witnessing people being killed. Their deaths seem to be ritualistic killings," he said still looking into her eyes for any reaction she may be having to this revelation.

"Well, how horrible for you," Gina said sincerely. "Let me look into some books I have in my personal collection and I will let you two start over here in the dream section. My best friend is having similar problems with his dreams so I have already been doing some research."

Alex looked at Gina with hope in his eyes, feeling more comfortable knowing at least someone else could be having the same experiences he did with his dreams.

Brandy and Alex followed her over to the dream section of the bookshelves. They began scanning the shelves for titles while Gina went into the back part of the store to begin looking at her vast collection of books. As she scanned them, her mind began to think about the man in the store and his many tattoos. He was a gorgeous man, no doubt, and his tattoos added such an intrigue to him. The lady he was with, she was a beauty as well. Gina had been with many people over the years and seemed to be leaning more towards girls lately. But she had to admit if either one or both of them asked her to play she would be all over it.

Gina started mentally chastising herself for even considering such an option and told herself, *these people are here for her help and all you can do is fantasize about getting them both in bed. Real professional Gina,* kept going through her mind. But there was something about this man, something about his eyes, his smile, his tattoos that all called out to her.

As she read through the books she had out from the research she had been doing for Demetri, she realized she needed more information. Grabbing one of the books and heading back out into the store Gina was shocked when the door chimes went off and looking up she found the store empty again.

Gina was a little dumbfounded and more than a little curious about the two. Walking over to the counter, she laid the book down and looked over towards the register. To her surprise she saw a hand written note laying there. Picking it up she began to read it:

> *Forgive our abrupt departure I'm feeling a bit silly about this entire thing and don't wish to waste anymore of your time. Thanks for your help. I hope our paths cross again soon.*
> *Alex*

Gina closed the book and picked up the note to read again. How strange, yet quaint, it all seemed. Looking at his handwriting she couldn't help but be taken aback by the sheer beauty of it, the old world style of his handwriting. He was clearly an artistic man for sure. Gina's thoughts were interrupted as the door chimes went off and she looked up half hoping to see him walk through the door again. She smiled at the young pair of teenagers walking into the store. "Welcome to The Mind's Eye, please let me know if I can be of assistance to you."

Chapter Ten

Demetri was restless and needing some action. He was in between job assignments right now and had a lot of time on his hands. What he did for work, well most would never believe and that was okay, they didn't have to. It wasn't something you would find him posting at the Tulsa chapter of the Better Business Bureau.

Demetri loved what he did; it paid him handsomely and allowed him to work on perfecting his powers. He was what some would call a supernatural bounty hunter, but he took precautions to ensure no one got hurt, but that wasn't always possible. He actually would consider himself more of a supernatural private detective. When someone found themselves in trouble, their spouse or child was being attacked or had been attacked by the supernatural, he would come in and make sure everything turned out in the best possible manner. This depended on what the call was. Sometimes it was too late and someone was either dead or was turned into a supernatural creature. A job was a job and like it or not, it paid him enough that he was not hurting for money.

Demetri knew the supernatural world was one in which not everything is as it appears to be. There were families who have a long lineage of supernatural beings like the werewolves. Then there were others, some innocent and some not, which get turned into one of these many creatures. He didn't want to hurt anyone, especially innocent people who happened to be in the wrong place, at the wrong time. But he also wouldn't allow someone to just run rampant, killing at will and wreaking havoc. This was what he did; he tried to keep a balance between the supernatural and the human world. One where, even though it might sound weird, they could all coexist.

He had called Gina earlier to see if she would have any interest in meeting him tonight and to his surprise she said yes. He never really knew when she would say yes, most of the time she was busy with research for customers or making potions and such. He was glad she had said yes because he needed to blow off some steam and she tended to be a grounding source for him.

They had agreed to meet at The Other Side at 10:00 p.m., a Goth/fetish bar just east of downtown in an old warehouse around 4th Street and Elgin Avenue. There was no advertising for it so the bar was solely a word of mouth type place due its unique clientele. It was definitely not a club you would hear about on the radio station.

It had windows high on the second floor, but they were blackened out and with no windows on the first floor it helped create a dark atmosphere which was both good and bad. A car ramp remained from when the warehouse was originally built that went to the second floor. It had a large garage style door installed at the top of the ramp the club would sometimes leave open when the weather was nice.

One could get lost in there but had to take heed of the uncertain dangers. Not only was it a hangout for the Gothic and punksters, it is known to be frequented by the underworld. There were many that had heard the rumors this was a place where vampires, witches, and occasionally, werewolves hung out. They would come here to try and get a glimpse of the dark ones and most had high hopes of being chosen by the vampires to be their cocktail, their blood donor for the night.

Although few outside of the underworld knew about him, Demetri roamed around in the day with people being oblivious to what he was capable of doing. There were not many humans that knew and a vast majority of underworldlings feared him, even though he tried to keep to himself as long as nothing major happened. Demetri tried to blend in as much as possible and thought these creatures of the underworld had a purpose in this life or they would not have been created or come into existence. But there had been times when some of them would start to draw too much attention to themselves, typically newly turned ones and he would have to step in and set things right. This wasn't a pleasant thing for him to do, but he deemed it a necessary evil for the better good.

As he made his way up to the door, the bouncer quickly removed the velvet rope for him and ushered him inside. He was well known here and they actually enjoyed him being around just in case something did break out they couldn't handle. There wasn't much that surprised Demetri and he often felt like an outsider in his normal life. He felt comfortable around this crowd even though for many they would be considered the freaks of the human race, the perverts, and the rejects. But for Demetri, he felt more at ease here than most places.

The owner of The Other Side and most of the people of the underworld knew about him and stayed out of his way. But, even the ones who didn't know him always took notice. Demetri was a strikingly good looking man, high statured at six-foot three, slim but muscular frame, naturally-curly sandy-blond hair, brown eyes. He wasn't clean shaven tonight so he had some scruff on his chiseled face, which only enhanced his good looks. He was wearing his usual, tight-fitting black leather pants that left nothing to the imagination; a form-fitting low cut black V-neck t-shirt and black leather boots.

Heads were turning all over the room as he entered the club and walked to the bar. Demetri didn't drink much, mostly because he didn't like the way it made you feel the next day, but more than that, he always liked to be in control of his powers. It was better this way so no one would get hurt.

He could hear them talking about him, hear their thoughts when he allowed them inside his head. Unless he was extremely bored or on the hunt, he liked to keep them as far out of his head as possible. Walking up to the bar, he ordered a shot of whiskey, turned his back to the bar and leaned against it. Scanning the main room to see who was there, he could make out a few familiar faces, some human, some not so much. For the most part everyone seemed to be in a semi-peaceful mood. Peace could quickly change into chaos, at a moment's notice, when you have a clientele made up of humans and the ones who hunt humans for prey. The underworld had to learn to evolve and adapt their eating habits if they wanted to be included in this modern world today. Some still kept to the darkness, to the basement called The Underside, but that was more by choice than necessity.

The Other Side was made up of multiple rooms and was three stories if you counted The Underside. Not many were brave enough to go down into the basement and from what Demetri had seen from the few times he had been down there it was best for most not to. It was a feeding ground for the willing humans who gave themselves over as donors to be fed upon, and it was a place where some fetishes were played out.

The Underside or the basement, a lurid, dark place with some strobe lighting, smaller rooms with doors, and the crowd brought down by sheer fearlessness or extreme naivety. It could be a place where someone's dreams came true or nightmares come to life. If the greater Tulsa population found out what went on in those rooms in the basement, the place would probably be shut down or burned down.

Of course, the main floor wasn't a well-lit place either but it did have more lighting than the basement. One could deduct with the practices going on down in the basement, it is probably best kept in the darkness.

Everywhere Demetri scanned he was seeing people in more leather than he was in, some wearing much less, well a whole lot less. Some of the more extreme outfits were better left to the imagination.

One guy, with a shaved head and a red beard, was looking especially hot in his skin tight black vinyl pants, black vinyl tank trimmed in white and knee high black leather boots.

48

Another man was wearing black leather chaps with a black leather jock strap, leather biker boots, with no shirt on, but he did have some dog tags around his neck. One girl had on a black bra, with a tiny black vinyl skirt, webbed stockings and a black thong under the skirt. Her skirt kept rising up as she would bend over to pick up her cocktail off of the coffee table.

Demetri could go on and on about outfits, but it didn't matter, he loved it all. He loved their uniqueness, their fearlessness, their rebellion to public rules and norms. He had to applaud anyone who stood up for themselves and just lived their life on their terms. As long they are not hurting anyone else, who the hell cares, and if they do care, then seriously, they need to get a damn life.

Chapter Eleven

Demetri didn't mind bringing Gina here because he knew she was more than capable of taking care of herself. She would often get upset with him when he tried to step in. Gina is a strong, powerful witch and loved letting people know it, especially the ones who step out of line with her.

Demetri was always amazed Tulsa had such a huge Gothic presence especially for it being in the Bible belt. But once he had learned about his powers, then about ghosts, spirits, witches, vampires, and werewolves, a little Goth didn't seem like such a big deal anymore. Being here with this entire diverse group of people it actually made him feel at home, sometimes. Yes, he knew it was a weird statement, but let's face it nothing in his world was normal.

Demetri was just starting to get a little worried about Gina when he looked up and saw this red headed beauty with a side pony tail walking towards him. All decked out in a leather outfit that rivaled his own, she strode across the floor turning heads. She was a beautiful woman and full of powerful energy and it showed. Walking up to Demetri, she stood on her tiptoes to give him a hug and peck on the cheek. She was always affectionate with him and he loved it.

"So where is my drink hot shot," she said smiling at Demetri.

"Give her whatever she wants Ricky," he said to the bartender.

"Give me what he is having," She winked at the bartender who knew she could hold her own with the best of them. The bartender slid a shot of whiskey to Gina. She raised it toward Demetri smiling until he finally held his up too and with a clink of their glasses they both downed the shot in one gulp slamming the shot glass down on the bar.

Just then, a loud commotion broke out next to them. When Demetri opened up his mind to hear their thoughts, he could tell it was two alpha males arguing about a submissive young male. The young man was dressed in leather shorts, a leather tank top and was wearing a leather dog mask. It seemed the submissive pup wasn't being so submissive to his dominant male and had attracted the attention of another master seeking to dominate.

Before anyone could even think about stepping in to calm things down, the current master of the young male kicked the youngling in the stomach smashing him into a wall about five feet away. He hit the wall so hard a picture came crashing down on his head, shattering the glass everywhere. The boy was out cold.

Then the two men took after each other with the intent of only one of them walking out of the bar. They were swinging fists at each other, grabbing at clothes, and blood was already flying everywhere, which wasn't a good thing with vampires lurking nearby.

Demetri and Gina looked at each other for a split second then both took off in different directions, Gina to check on the boy and Demetri to see about breaking up this fight before someone really got hurt.

As Demetri hustled over to the fight, he tried to put a hand between the two when the dominant master swung at his face with incredible force. Sidestepping the blow, barely, he summoned his energy and focused it on the man, with just a wave of his hand sent him flying backwards until he fell on his backside. He wasn't injured, but his pride was greatly inflamed.

While all this was going on Gina was trying to help the young boy who was lying passed out on the floor. *Thank the universe he is alive. This would have been an ugly experience for everyone if the cops had to be called.* Removing the leather dog mask and laying her hands on the boy's forehead Gina went deep into almost a meditative state trying to get inside the boy's mind. With a few bursts of energy moving through Gina into the boy's brain, he slowly started opening his eyes. As he did, he was looking at Gina with confusion on his face; all of the sudden a look of fear began to form in his eyes, then on his face. The young boy saw something behind her and began to scream. Gina turned just in time to see the alpha male master coming at them both with such rage on his face that it took Gina by surprise.

The enraged man grabbed Gina by the shoulders, lifted her up off the ground and slung her to the side and behind him. He was instantly on top of the boy, hitting his face with one fist after the other. The boy's face was bleeding from the blows he was sustaining from his angry master.

Gina looking around as she gained control of her footing again saw Demetri was in the depths of battle with the other angry man who was not about to let this one go without a fight. Gina had only seconds to react before the man bludgeoned the young boy to death. Running over, Gina drew on all the energy around her and laid her hands on both sides of his head. As she did so, she let forth a ball of energy into the man's head, which made him instantly go rigid, as if hit by a tazer; then he collapsed on the floor.

Demetri finally tired of the bullshit, and tired of holding back, sent the man flying up against the wall behind him where he held him suspended in the air. The shock on the man's face was priceless. Demetri loved when he could take a cocky male down a few notches. What seemed like forever had only been a few seconds, but finally the bouncers who were well equipped to handle situations like this made their way up to Demetri and Gina. It wasn't that the bouncers were not aware of the commotion. The size of the place, the crowd of people, and the fact this had taken place so quickly made it seem as if it took longer to reach them.

"We'll take it from here," said the bouncers.

Demetri breathing heavily let the man slide down the wall slowly until he was apprehended by the bouncers and led out of the club. The medic, who was always on duty due to the nature of their clientele, was already working on the boy with blood oozing out of the gashes on his face from the man's powerful fists. Two bouncers carried out the man Gina had sidelined.

Gina and Demetri made their way over to the bar and ordered another shot of whiskey. "This one's on the house," the bartender said to both.

"How the hell did you do that to the man?" Demetri asked looking at her with admiration.

"Oh, I didn't realize you noticed," said Gina, then remembering even when Demetri isn't looking directly at you he is still looking at you. "I don't know how it happened. I have been working with the energy around and within me lately, and then when I was able to bring the boy out of his unconscious state, I thought why can't I send someone there too. I guess it was adrenaline," she said smiling coyly.

"Well, here's to adrenaline," Demetri said raising his shot of whiskey in the air. "And here's to you Gina, my kickass witch of a friend."

They clinked shot glasses then downed the contents. Laying the shot glasses on the bar in front of them she turned and looked at him. "Let's get the hell out of here before we get into any more trouble," she said laughing softly.

He agreed and they headed towards the door.

"By the way," she said. "I never did get to tell you about what happened at the store today. Kind of odd and weird."

"Let's grab some coffee and breakfast and you can tell me all about it," Demetri said putting his arm around her shoulders as they walked out the front door into the night filled sky.

Behind them in the bar, everyone was clambering on about the events having just transpired and about the humans with remarkable strength and magic.

Chapter Twelve

A few blocks down at Fifth Street Diner, a hole in the wall corner cafe, where they loved to eat, Demetri and Gina were eating their usual. Eggs over easy, country potatoes, bacon, and sausage with a side of biscuits and gravy. They had sat in silence for the most part, both absorbing the evening's events and both feeling tired from the exertion of energy and quite frankly because it was 2:00 a.m.

The smell of bacon and ham filled the tiny diner as did the smell of coffee that had been on the burners for way too long. However, when the waitress brought the coffee pot around to fill their cups, neither of them bothered to turn her down. At this point, caffeine was caffeine. Not much conversation could be heard around the diner since the rush of traffic from when they first arrived had started to filter out already leaving only a few remaining guests. The most prominent sound was the squeaking sound of the waitress' orthopedic shoes. She flitted around the room filling coffee, pulling empty plates, cleaning off already abandoned tables, and leaving tickets at the tables where people still sat. The squeak was a welcome, although annoying sound in the room. It was most likely due to the grease and film layering the floor in the kitchen which attached itself to the bottom of her shoes. It squeaked as each foot lifted, then came back in contact with the floor. Gina and Demetri both just looked at each other and smiled.

Demetri was the first to break the long silence.

"So Willow," Demetri teased her as he did often making reference to the witch from the teenage vampire television show, "when did this new power of yours manifest itself?"

"I told you, I have been exploring and playing with energies, which surrounds us every day, everywhere," Gina told him with a slight smirk on her face. "I have found through meditation I have been able to tap into and harness the energy flowing around me naturally."

"And you don't think it was important enough to tell me," he probed.

"I didn't, because I had never been able to do what I did before tonight. I'm still not sure how it happened other than to say adrenaline," she said firmly but not convincingly. "I saw the boy laying there passed out and hurt, possibly dead, and I went into reaction mode."

"Well, I am highly impressed. It is a most welcome addition to our little club we have of ever evolving powers," Demetri smiled at her as he took a sip of his ever so slightly burnt coffee. "I'm thrilled to see you have another ability, another weapon to arm yourself with. This world we live in is changing so quickly and getting more and more dangerous, and I feel relieved to know you can and do take care of things yourself. I will always be here for you, but I know I can't always be everywhere."

"Demetrius Marcus are you getting all sentimental and mushy on me," she prodded at him. "If I have told you once, I have told you a million times I can take care of myself. Since we were little, I have been taking care of myself. Yes, it is nice to have you around with your remarkable, super hero strength," she teased him, "but I think I've done enough to earn your respect and your trust. I'll be just fine."

"I know, I know," he said. "I just worry about the fact that both of our abilities are changing and evolving. Some have yet to be proven if they are a danger to us and others," he said slipping off into deep thought.

"So this beautiful man and woman came into the store today," she said to him, as he stared at her vacantly. "Are you listening to me Demetri?"

Demetri as if waking from a deep daydream looked at Gina with a confused look then quickly righted himself. "I'm sorry," he said, "what was that?"

"I was saying a beautiful woman and man came into the store today," Gina said a little more excited.

"Well, considering where your store is located, that isn't surprising," he said playing with her again; knowing Brookside was an area for young, attractive yuppies.

"These two were different," she said somewhat drifting off into her thoughts of the encounter.

"How so," asked Demetri? He could tell she wanted to tell him more and he tried to respect her wishes of not invading her mind unless it was absolutely necessary and life threatening.

"They came in looking for some answers on some dreams he had been having, more like night terrors," she said hoping to raise his interest.

"Well, considering what there is to be afraid of these days, I'm not surprised more people are not having nightmares," Demetri said matter-of-factly.

Ignoring him, she continued on. "He was having these dreams where he was witnessing people being killed in ritualistic killings. These dreams are dominating his nights to the point he can't sleep," she said wondering why he wasn't a little more sympathetic since he too had been having such bad dreams. "Doesn't that sound familiar?"

"So what did you end up doing for him?" he asked feigning interest.

"That's the weird part of it. I was back in my personal library looking through the books I had been researching for what happened to you in your last dream when I realized I needed to ask him some more questions. I walked out and they were gone," she said once again drifting off into her thoughts.

Demetri was eyeing her and curiously wondering what she was so deep in thought about, but didn't want to invade her head to find out. "So why is that so weird," he pushed trying to get her to reveal what she was thinking.

"I don't know, there was a connection of sorts, with him and the girl, but more so with him. It was on a deep level, energy, a spiritual level," Gina said remembering his eyes, those dark eyes.

Gina pulled out the note he had written her and handed it over to Demetri to read.

"Well sounds like he was either pulling one over on you or got cold feet and ran out the door," he stated after reading the note.

Feeling a little annoyed at Demetri and a little silly herself she stated, "Well it was something about the look in his eyes. There was desperation, a plea for help and his friend seemed genuinely concerned about him as well."

Demetri knowing how sensitive Gina was to other peoples energies, plights, and challenges didn't want to kid her anymore about it. She was concerned about him and that was one of the many things he loved her for. Gina had a huge heart and cared for people and their pain.

"Well, maybe he just needed some more time to think it over. He will most likely come back when he can get up the courage to tell you the truth about it," he said trying to offer some solace.

"Do you really think so?" she asked.

"Why not, you are the most qualified person I know who can possibly help him," Demetri said smiling. "So why wouldn't he come back and ask for your help?"

Gina smiled at Demetri and placed the note back into her pocket. There was just something about this man Alex, something about his eyes. He was afraid of something and his energy was putting off the same vibe as well. She hoped he came back and allowed her to at least try to help him.

Chapter Thirteen

Victor Von Helsberg prided himself on his attention to detail. He was a man who took life seriously and he was a stickler for details. Victor was a strikingly good looking, sexy man with a chiseled face and he used every inch of himself to seduce, manipulate, and get what he wanted. Standing at six feet, two inches, he was a brick house, working out every day, training every day for his cause, his entire purpose in this life. He had bulging arms, a huge chest, six pack abs, huge thighs, a round muscular ass; he was a machine, a machine trained to kill. He was covered in tattoos, some for fun, but most had a meaning, a story of his purpose in life.

Victor was a man of conviction and believed in dying for his cause. When he was told to come to Tulsa to prepare the way for the great one, for their master to enter this world he didn't hesitate. He packed his bag, boarded a flight from Germany and headed directly to Tulsa.

He had been here for over a month. It had been plenty of time to set up residence in a home near downtown, one with enough room and space for him to work. Most important, big enough no one would hear the screams and pleas for help from his sexual conquests. He always had a huge sexual drive, ever since he was a teenager. His experimentation with sex and his naturally dark personality soon shown him he liked control, liked to dominate, terrify, and shock. It didn't take much to get someone to come with him, he was a sexy man, and he rarely had to force, lure or drug someone to go with him. They came to him willingly, most of the time.

Victor liked things rough and he liked control. He had a little too much roughness last night as the girl lying on the floor of his basement could attest. He liked to toy with them, liked to make them suffer, humiliate them so they would be good and ready when they met his master. She didn't seem to be able to keep up with him. She died before he could even finish with her. This was the third one this week and he was just getting warmed up. He didn't really care if it was a woman or a man, they all served his needs. Ever since he got the message to come to Tulsa he was on high alert and sexually charged.

He didn't have much longer to wait though and the anticipation of meeting his master was almost more than Victor could bare, but one would never know it. He kept in full control of his emotions at all times, well most of the time as the bodies downstairs would surely try to disprove. He would be labeled an out of control monster, a brutal beast, but the truth is, he is very much in control and knows exactly what he is doing. It wasn't his fault these weaklings could not keep up with him.

August 20, 2013, the date the world would remember for an eternity. His master's birth into this world would be something of legend. People will fall before him on bended knees and hail him as their master or they will all perish. It didn't really matter to Victor either way. He had been obedient all of his life to his master. The Balashon didn't put up with anything but obedience. If you stepped out of line for an instant, you were dead.

Victor had been called to eliminate many of his colleagues and he did so with a clean conscience. Some start out loyal and brave, then they falter, they lose their way. But there is no room for these people within the Balashon.

Balashonian roots went back thousands of years. The Balashon has headquarters on all corners of the earth and employs an army of people just like Victor, an army of believers. They go to great lengths to cover their tracks and make sure they are still considered an extinct society. Even though they have been around since before the Free Masons were formed, the subject matter that interests them would not be taken well in this or any other century. So the members of Balashon lay low and immerse themselves into today's societies. Some are CEO's of banks; others are Fortune 500 business owners. Others are like Victor, an assassin, a trained killer who will protect the society first, then its members as long as they conform to the ways of their master. Many of them are members of the Free Masons today, infiltrating them so they can keep up their cover.

With such big connections all over the globe, it isn't hard for Victor or his associates to blend in when they arrive in a new city. It's also not hard for them to find housing, supplies, weapons, or even artifacts needed for a particular job. This one job he is on will be the biggest and grandest of them all.

Even though the Balashon was thought to be extinct, it still has enemies. Some who suspected it was still around wrote tell-all books about it, but who in their right mind would believe such a story! Hell, if the Masons could get away with what they have done through the years and still protect the secret they hold, then the Balashon is no different in that respect.

Victor felt much pride and honor in the fact that he was chosen to come to Tulsa. He was selected to watch the vessel and to be the one to offer the sacrifices needed to bring his master to this earthly realm. His destiny is at hand and he welcomes it with open arms. Victor had to make sure everything went according to plan. The vessel had to be kept safe until the blue moon fell upon them and the sacrifices had to be given at just the right times. The Balashon had tried a few times during the last few millenniums to raise the master and failed, but this time Victor would make sure they succeeded. Victor was ready to die for the cause, die to protect the vessel if he had to.

The first sacrifice had been easy to find and it only took a few days of staking him out to learn his routine.

60

Charles Wilson had been a predictable man; a man easily stalked and he never even knew it. It was like hunting prey, the ones who were predictable were the easiest to catch and kill. The ones who were unpredictable were more of a challenge. Had it not been one of the most important times in the history of the Balashon, Victor would not have minded the challenge of catching and sacrificing an unpredictable bird of prey. But they had to keep on schedule, they had to be super careful not to draw more attention to themselves than they would anyway. A ritual sacrifice is not easily hidden and it is one people love to hear the most about. The news was still going on and on about it.

It was a special honor to be able to deliver the first sacrifice for the master's arrival. The look on the man's face as he realized he was not escaping was just about more than Victor could handle. He was going to die and there was nothing he was able to do about it. It was a satisfying experience and a somewhat sexual one too. When Hell opened up to claim the sacrifice, Victor stopped jogging just long enough to see the first glimpse of the hounds. It was the most gratifying thing he has done in his life so far, and there were many things in Victor's life he was proud of.

Just two more sacrifices to go and then he would prep the vessel right before the blue moon filled the sky. Then his master would come and he would be made whole again, he would be given the honor of being in the master's army, maybe even one of his most trusted leaders.

Victor smiled to himself as he sharpened the knife preparing to go down into the basement to dispose of the body lying dead on the floor. He had to admit, the Balashon had some pretty decked out places around the world and this one in Tulsa was no exception. There was a pit in the deepest part of the basement of the house he was residing in. A pit where he was able to dump the bodies of the ones who were unfortunate enough to walk through the front doors either voluntarily or involuntarily. Either way didn't matter to Victor because they never made it out.

Chapter Fourteen

It wasn't that Alex didn't want help from the girl at the bookstore; it was just the more he thought about it, the more he realized he sounded stark raving mad. But something inside him knew he wasn't. Something was wrong on a major scale and he was afraid to even clue Brandy in on the extent of what was happening to him and what he was feeling. And the voice keeps talking to him, the voice in his dreams, in his waking thoughts, in his subconscious thoughts. If there were just a way for him to talk to someone, anyone who would keep an open mind, he would feel a lot better about this.

Maybe a good night out on the town was what he needed. He was feeling overwhelmed, overworked, and extremely tired, but there was this underlying charge of energy keeping him going. He definitely needed this, the question was where, with whom, and whether it would involve a call to Brandon or not.

Alex paced around the house picking up odds and ends. He had really been ignoring the place lately and it was showing. He was almost finished with laundry; he had vacuumed the carpets and mopped the floors. He took bleach to the bathroom and scrubbed down the shower, stool, and sink. To say he was restless was an understatement. He was freaking crawling out of his own skin.

He was lucky to have such good staff at the shop he could take some time off today. Alex did not have a lot of private bookings and he was able to rearrange the bookings he had originally scheduled for another day. The walk-ins would be taken care of by his staff. He had some of the best staff in the greater Tulsa area, maybe even the state of Oklahoma.

Maybe a quick swim in the backyard pool would clear his head, so Alex put the cleaning materials away. Alex removed his tank top and immediately felt the heat of the hot Oklahoma sun beaming down on his chest. It felt amazing. He removed his shorts and underwear and walked over to the edge of the pool and dove in. The water was an instant revitalizing sensation for his body and his mind.

Alex began to do laps in the pool and he could feel himself starting to let his mind go. Making his way down the length of the pool he started to feel his body tense up, his nerve endings felt like the water was actually starting to burn a bit. Alex opened his eyes with his face in the water to see what could only have been a vision as it appeared at the bottom of the pool and was somewhat blurry from the water. The vision was of a dark, almost black form of a creature with wings. He was startled at first and took in a bit of water. He immediately began hacking as he lifted his head out of the water. Clearing his lungs he quickly placed his head back under, knowing he should get out of the pool, but let curiosity get the best of him.

"Alex, I'm coming for you," the blurry vision said. Alex already knew this was the same voice that had been speaking to him, the same one that speaks to him in his dreams and in the bathroom that one morning.

"Why fight it Alex, you are going to set me free," the voice said as if it were trying to calm him down from an already frightened state. "Your destiny lies with mine Alex and when our destinies collide, we will set this earth ablaze."

He again took in some water and began hacking the water up trying to clear his lungs. Gasping for air, he made his way to the edge of the pool and hoisted himself up onto the side, lying on his back until his breathing calmed down enough so he could think.

It was in that moment he made a decision. He decided he had to get some help, but not of the mental kind, but of a

Wiccan kind. If he could not trust a "self-proclaimed witch" who he instantly felt a connection with, then who could he trust with his crazy ass story.

Alex rushed into the house and made his way to the bathroom. He turned on the shower and let it heat up for a minute before stepping in and placing his body underneath the water. Lathering up his body with soap and his hair with shampoo, he then rinsed, turned off the shower and grabbed a towel off the rack. He ran the towel through his hair, then he ran it over his body, drying it free of the remaining water which dripped from his body.

He walked from the bathroom into his bedroom closet. Walking over to his denim stack, he grabbed a pair of Levis and stepped into them, pulling them up to his waist and buttoning them. Then he found a tank top pulling it over his head and down his chest until it was in place. Sliding his feet into his flip flops, he ran his hand through his hair. He walked out of his bedroom into the side hall where a credenza set against the wall, next to the door leading into the garage. Grabbing his car keys and opening the door, he hit the garage door opener, jumped into his car and quickly backed out of the garage heading down the street towards The Mind's Eye. It was time he and a cute little red haired witch became more acquainted.

Chapter Fifteen

Gina was pleasantly surprised to see the handsome young man with the tattoos walk into her store. She had secretly been hoping he would come back. Gina couldn't help but think, *how beautiful he looks in his white tank top with his tattoos exposed. Those luscious looking plump pink lips, dark eyes that make me melt and perfect olive skin.* She could see the outline of pistols tattooed on his chest beneath his tank top. This man truly loved tattoos.

His aura was a little off today. He had some nervous energy exuding from him. As he walked up to her, he smiled genuinely and offered his hand. To his surprise he was excited about seeing her too.

"Hello, my name is Alex. I would like to ask your forgiveness for rushing out of here the other day without anything but a note left behind," he said shaking her hand. "That was a pretty lame move on my part."

"No need for apologies," Gina offered realizing she was hanging onto his hand a little longer than she probably should be. Letting his hand go she smiled back at him and said "my name is Gina, this is my store."

"It's a great honor to meet you," he said to her with a coy smile. "I believe I owe you an explanation."

Alex started from the beginning, laying it all out on the table for her to absorb. He included the dream about the murder on Riverside Drive, the voice in the bathroom afterwards, and about what had just happened earlier in the pool. She was listening intently and making a few notes as she did so. He explained why he had left so abruptly the other day, stressing that he realized she might have thought he had something to do with the murder since he had so much information. Some of the details still hadn't been released by the Tulsa Police Department at that time.

She was thinking to herself, *what an amazing story and how terrified Alex must be right now.* She felt honored in the fact he had come to her for help and she felt he was telling her the truth, or at least what he believed to be the truth. Dreams were tricky to decipher at times and could lead one down the wrong path, but they can be prophetic as well.

When he finished his story he held her gaze trying to decide if she believed him, or thought him crazy and was going to call the cops; he was looking for any kind of sign.

She looked at him, smiled, reached over and laid her hand on top of his hand. "I am not quite sure what all of this means just yet, but I promise you we will find out what is happening to you and hopefully figure out why as well."

At that moment, he could have reached over and hugged her but he just sat there in silence as his eyes filled up with tears. He was so happy someone believed him and he must be totally exhausted because he didn't get emotional like this, but there was something about this girl that he felt safe around her. He believed her when she said she wanted to help him find out what was going on and he already felt himself wanting to trust her.

Wiping the tears from his eyes, he righted himself up in the chair at the bar table and said "thank you for believing me and thank you for your offer to help. I'm not one who, usually, asks for help like this. I can honestly say nothing like this has ever happened to me before. I'm skirting new territory here and I need someone with a lot more experience than I possess."

"Like I said, we will get to the bottom of this," Gina reassured.

"Can I ask a huge favor of you? I know I'm a stranger asking this, but can we keep this between us. At least until we are able to come to some conclusions other than I am crazy and out of my mind," Alex looked at her pleadingly.

"Of course, we can, I take my business very seriously. I'm going to assume you figured out that I am a practicing witch since you came in here confiding all of this info to me," she asked.

"Yes I knew, but I felt a connection with you. I felt if anyone was going to be able to help me figure this out, it was you," he said looking at her with hope.

"Well, I do a lot of freelancing outside of just owning a book and herbal store. I like it when my clients feel they can trust me," she said rather matter-of-factly, but with humility.

Alex was already grateful he had decided to come back to Gina for help. He felt a weight had been lifted off of his chest just by saying it out loud to someone else.

"Tell me about your tattoos," she asked him somewhat catching him off guard.

Regaining his composure quickly, he replied. "Well, I own a tattoo shop called Blue Moon Tattoo's here in Brookside."

"Oh, yes, I've seen it right down the street," she said happy to have known about his place.

"I got my first tattoo when I was sixteen-years-old and I never really stopped," he said becoming somewhat introspective. "Come to think of it, my first tattoo came to me in a dream and I snuck out and had it tattooed on my lower neck."

"Seems like even back then your dreams were playing a big role in your life," she stated. "Do you mind if I take a look at your first tattoo?"

"Not at all," he said while removing his shirt.

Gina must have been blushing because she felt the heat rising in the room and Alex was quick to take notice.

"Oh, I'm so sorry," he started. "I guess sometimes I don't stop long enough to consider my surroundings." He made movements as if to put his shirt back on.

"No, no, it's okay. I was just taken off guard for a moment," she said smiling and trying to play it off even though she could still feel herself blush. "It's just a shirt, not your entire outfit you're taking off."

"Can you show me?" Gina asked.

"Sure, come here behind me," Alex said guiding Gina to where she was standing directly behind him. "You see the one in black, it looks like a symbol."

"This one here?" She asked as she placed her finger on it.

"Yes, that's it," he said knowing exactly where she was touching.

Immediately she got a flash of violence and manipulation from touching the tattoo. She immediately removed her hand as if she had received an electrical shock.

"Is something wrong?" He asked her feeling her hand remove quickly from his neck.

"Where did you say you came up with this tattoo? In a dream?" Gina asked concern filling her voice.

"Yes, I dreamed about the symbol and immediately felt connected with it. I drew it on a piece of paper the size I wanted it and went the next day and I had it tattooed on my neck. Why?" Alex asked wondering what the problem was.

Gina had a million things going through her mind and none she liked. "Are you sure you had not seen this symbol somewhere other than your dreams, like a book, a movie, anything?"

"I'm pretty sure the first time was in my dream," Alex stated starting to not even trust his own thoughts now. "Why?"

"I don't want you to freak out, but when I touched your tattoo, I immediately got a charge from it. Some major vibes of violence and manipulation," she said to him in a calm voice trying to make sure she didn't get him worked up. But she was trying to keep herself calm too.

"Almost every tattoo on my body has come to me through dreams," he looked at her with wide eyes as he swallowed down his nervousness.

Trying not to jump the gun on this one Gina's mind was working overtime trying to get a grasp on this. It was way too soon to come to any conclusions, but she feared when they did it wouldn't be a good one. She had learned to trust her instincts a long time ago and this time, in this moment, her instincts were on high alert.

"Alex, we have to stay calm and take this one tattoo at a time. I'm not sure what the actual tattoos with pictures will tell us, but we can definitely work with symbols and writing," Gina tried to offer comfort. "I'm pleased you came back to talk to me, I had been thinking about why you would bail on me so quickly but you just never really know about people. I'm so glad you trust me with this."

"So what is the next step, how do we go about this?" Alex asked looking half defeated.

She knew it would take some time to research all of this, so she had a thought and hoped he would go for it.

"I'm going to need to get some pictures of your tattoos so I will have them while I do my research," she probed, looking at him to see if she could gauge his reaction. "Do you mind?"

He stood up without hesitation and walked towards her as she led him into her private library where her camera was placed.

She turned the camera on and prepared to take pictures. When she turned around, she let out an audible gasp when she found him standing in the room nude, not a single piece of clothing on.

"What are you doing," Gina asked trying again to keep her voice calm but knowing that she was not doing a good job at it.

"I'm sorry, but if you are going to take pictures of my tattoos that are a result of a dream then you will need to see all of them," Alex said matter of factly. "One thing you should know about me is I don't have a shy bone in my body. We are born nude and we live our life trying to cover it up from then on. I just don't see the point," he said smiling at her.

Getting herself in check, she regained her composure while taking in a deep breath to steady herself, she moved toward him with the camera. "Let's get to it then," she said.

69

Gina began snapping pictures of Alex, first as a whole body shot from the front, sides, and back, and then she began to get closer to his individual tattoos to take the pictures. But even his individual tattoos seemed to run into another one. She took almost fifty pictures of him until finally she came to one she had been trying to not look at, but could not help but see it out of the corner of her eye.

"Um, I'm going to need to get a picture of your tattoo on your penis," Gina said knowing she was turning red. "It looks to me like it is Latin or something, but it is definitely an inscription of some sort."

He spread his legs apart to almost shoulder width, held out his arms and looked at her and smiled. "It's all yours; take as many as you need."

Gina cautiously walked closer to Alex and began taking pictures of the wording tattooed on his penis. As she zoomed in, she could make out a much smaller symbol of the tattoo within the writing.

He eyed her closely as she took the pictures, noticing she seemed a little perplexed by the tattoo. "You need some help with it?" he asked her. "I can move it around if you need to get better angles?"

She couldn't help but burst out laughing. As soon as she did, Alex joined in. It was a much-needed break from the tension that was building in the room.

"I think I got what I needed," she said still laughing softly.

"I hope I don't find these scattered all over the internet," joking with her.

Gina smiled at him. "Let's not forget who came to whom for help here. Hey, by the way, why do you have the same symbol of your original tattoo on your penis?"

Looking at her with a puzzled look, he replied "I don't know what you mean."

Gina walked over to Alex and pulled the picture up on the digital display monitor of the camera. She could tell by the baffled look on his face he did not know it had been placed within the wording.

"What the fuck, I never noticed that," he stated extremely disturbed as he looked at the picture on the camera. "My mind is spinning right now; this is so fucked up."

"Listen, I am going to get started on this right away. Try not to stress too much," she said trying to offer him some comfort and hope, but thinking if he was anything like her, he was going to worry until they had some answers.

"Rather easy for you to say. You don't have a ghost or whatever speaking to you and you are not having night terrors that are obviously coming true. I won't rest comfortably until I know why this is happening and that I had nothing to do with that man's death."

Chapter Sixteen

Victor sat in his black SUV with tinted windows sharpening his hunting knife and watching intently as Alex came walking out of the shop. "Looks like the vessel has went and made friends with a witch," Victor whispered. This is an unfortunate turn of events but still not one he couldn't handle. He's not about to let anyone get in the way of him fulfilling his destiny.

One evening when Alex had heavily sedated himself and was home alone, Victor broke into his home and placed a tracker/bug into Alex's phone and car while he was passed out. There was not anything he could do without Victor knowing about it first.

As Alex climbed into his car and sped away, Victor sat in his SUV watching the blinking dot of Alex's vehicle on the GPS. He decided it was high time he pays this little witch a visit. There was nothing wrong with checking out the competition as they say.

Victor climbed out of the SUV and slowly made his way across the street until he was at the store entrance. Grabbing the door handle, he turned the knob and slowly pushed the door open. Stepping inside, he heard a bell chime which he thought was to alert the owner, in this case the witch that someone was here. *Not a bad idea since there could be people who might be coming into your store to stalk and kill you,* he thought as he chuckled to himself at his quick wit. Intelligent, funny, sexy, and a world-class killer; Victor was quite the catch. It was too bad for everyone else that he wasn't the hunted, but rather the hunter.

Much to Victor's anticipation, the witch came walking in from another room to greet him. She was a looker, long red hair, nice pale skin, and a beautiful face. Victor had run across many a witch in his day, but none quite as lovely as this one. He may have to play with this one a little harder since she was a witch. She might be able to keep up with his stamina.

"Hello and welcome to The Mind's Eye," Gina said to Victor with a warm, friendly smile. "Is there anything I can help you with this evening?"

He looked up at her and gave her a broad smile from the book rack he was standing behind. He just smiled at her for a few seconds then just when Gina was starting to wonder if the guy was on something he said, "I'm looking for some books on demonology."

"What a fascinating subject," she offered trying to make the guest feel at ease and catching what seemed like a slight German accent from him. "Is there something in particular you are looking for or just a general book regarding it?"

"What do you have regarding, say, possession?" he asked toying with her a little.

"Well, what I would have would be over here in the occult section of the store," she said as she tried to lead the man over to the area where the demonology books were located.

She couldn't help but notice what an attractive man he was. Tall, huge muscles, dark hair, and a massive energy radiating from him, but she couldn't quite tell what she was reading from it. He had such a strong body, it could well have been his confidence she reacted to or it could be something totally separate. All she could really tell was it was intense.

Victor had no problem noticing the witch eyeing him and trying to get a read on him, but he was well trained in how to control his energy and at not letting someone invade his head. She could look all she wanted, but she would get nothing from him without using her words.

73

"Let's see what I have here," she said trying to refocus on the task at hand. She bent over to scan some labels on the books and he was not at all disappointed in the view.

This one would be fun to play with he thought. Feeling the steel knives against his legs as he walked around, watching, stalking, and giving him a charge of sexual desire. He thought of the witch tied up, nude, and begging him to stop. He knew this one would last longer than the others. But, as with all of them, she, too, would fade from the torture and her body would give out. It didn't matter to him as long as he got what he needed.

Grabbing all the books she could find on the shelves regarding possession and demonology, she took the books and led him over to a table where she laid the books and pulled out a chair for him to take a seat if he so desired.

"No need," he said to her in his German accent. "I will take them all."

"Oh, okay, great," Gina said happy she was able to help him out and get a nice sale out of it too. "Let me take these over to the register and ring them up."

Grabbing the books, Gina walked over to the register with Victor trailing closely behind.

He couldn't take his mind off of the knives rubbing his thighs and how he wanted so much to use them on this young witch and hear her beg him to stop.

"Your total is $364.74," she said as she began to bag up the books. "Will you be charging that today sir?"

Victor stood there looking at her for what seemed like an eternity to Gina then he finally answered. "No, it will be cash."

Taking out a fold of one hundred dollar bills, he peeled four of them off and handed them to her.

After making change for him, she handed him his bag and asked him if there was anything else she could help him with.

"Well, I'm new to town and could really use a tour guide," he said to her smiling, "any chances of you showing me around the town?"

Gina glanced at him and was again struck by how stunningly handsome he was. "I make it a policy to never go out with someone I don't know. I do appreciate your business though and hope you will come again."

He was staring into her eyes for a few seconds as he leaned just a little over the counter and said, "well if I come back a second time I will no longer be a stranger and then I will not take no for an answer."

Victor leaned back from the counter, grabbed his bag, winked at Gina, then turned and walked out the door.

Chapter Seventeen

Demetri stepped into the shower and let the warm water run down his body. He eased his head under the spray of the water and let the sensation of it ease his troubled mind. There had been so much going on lately he really hadn't taken a whole lot of time to relax. He had been combing the city looking for answers to the Riverside Drive killing. He hoped in the meantime to find out what had actually happened in his dream. What caused him to levitate, to be thrown up against a wall and to end up with a hand print in the exact spot where he had felt the power of the man in his dreams hold onto his neck?

Lathering up his body, he thought about just letting it all go for the night. Gina had agreed to meet him at The Other Side so they should be able to have some fun, maybe dance away some stress, and possibly take a shot or two. He may even try his luck down in the basement and see what was happening there.

Rinsing off the soap and giving his hair one last run under the shower he flicked his head back letting some of the water splash away. Grabbing a towel, he stepped out of the shower to dry off his wet body. Running the towel all over he made a few extra passes across his cock and balls because he didn't want them to be wet with the outfit he had picked out for the night. Demetri didn't like to wear underwear so it was a commando leather night.

Running his fingers through his sandy-blond curly locks of hair, he decided it was best to put it up into a ponytail. His hair wasn't too long, but he could get it into a small version of one. He put some eyeliner on which made his eyes look even fiercer and then he giggled to himself remembering how Gina would tease him about it.

"Oh, I see you have your mangara on," Gina would say teasing him.

"It's not 'mangara' Gina, because I'm not putting it on my lashes," Demetri would reply back each time. "Besides, there is no 'g' in mascara."

They would both crack up at the joke and laugh sometimes until his eyeliner would run a bit.

Demetri walked over to his bed where he had his clothes already laid out and pulled on his boot socks. He then picked up the tight fitting leather pants and put one foot in at a time and pulled the pants up over his ass. Putting on a long sleeve gray t-shirt, he tucked it into his pants. He then pulled on a black t-shirt with a pig's face on it along with the word "SQUEAL" under it which he also tucked into his pants. Buttoning the top button, he put his leather belt on. Pulling on his high leather boots he tucked his pants legs into his boots and grabbed his black baseball cap and walked into the bathroom. He placed the hat on his head and made sure his ponytail was through the back of the hat.

Feeling sexy in his leather outfit, Demetri paced around the house a bit until he decided to head over to Gina's instead of waiting for her to call him to pick her up.

Not too far away, Alex was placing into his mouth a pill he got from Brandon. It was supposed to be a mix between ecstasy and acid. He was feeling the need to disconnect for the evening. He didn't want to be in his current reality, so he decided he would alter it the best way he knew how.

Feeling sexy and feeling the need for some fun, Alex decided he would fade into the crowd at The Other Side. Wanting to alter himself altogether, he decided on an outfit he had not worn in a long time. Although it would hide him somewhat, anyone who knew him and his tattoos would not be fooled by his hiding behind the suit.

Never the less, he was decked out in all leather. He had his leather pants on, biker boots, leather belt with his belt buckle that read "Cocky," a leather armband on each bicep, leather gloves, a leather biker hat, and sunglasses. He opted to not wear a shirt because, well just because. He was winging the night and he was hoping it would turn out to be an exciting one. Alex had already placed a call to the taxi company and was impatiently waiting for the cab to arrive. He was hoping to get to the bar before his trip set in. He was relieved when he heard the honking of the cab signaling its arrival and his night of fun was just beginning.

Victor Von Helsberg was just finishing getting ready himself. He knew he would be out tonight when he listened in on the vessel's call to the drug dealer. He was going to have to eventually gut this dealer if Alex kept this up because even with Victor watching over him, the vessel could easily end up hurting himself one of these wild nights. But, that wasn't going to happen on Victor's watch.

It wasn't his first time there, and Victor felt extremely at ease at this club the vessel frequented. It seemed to be in line with his sexual impulses and he quite enjoyed being able to spend some time in the basement teasing, taunting, and sometimes hurting the willing participants. There he could indulge in his extreme fetish side, but he had to be careful and make sure no one died even though he wanted to make it the last time for some. But, that is what he had his place for.

Victor had some sexual thoughts about the witch as well. She had dominated his thoughts all day long. He wondered if she would be out tonight and if he would be able to talk her into coming back to his place. He really needed to keep a close eye on her and find out just to what extent her powers were or if she was just a want-to-be witch. Hell, anyone can call themselves a witch anymore, but only a few could actually pull off the magic. He needed to make sure about her, this Gina, because he didn't need any surprises from her if and when he got her home. What was he saying, if, of course, she would come home with him, it was just a matter of when.

Victor was admiring himself in the mirror, flexing his muscles. He liked his outfit pick for the night. No one would be able to see his face and those needy little fuckers in the basement, both male and female, would be crawling on hands and knees trying to get him to dominate them. Maybe he would and maybe he wouldn't. It would all be determined by the vessel.

Victor took one last look at himself in the mirror. Yes, he had chosen wisely. He had on tight vinyl pants which showed off every muscle he had in his legs and was complimentary to his crotch. He had on elbow length vinyl gloves, no shirt, and topped it off with a vinyl gas mask. The mask had big round glass eye holes and a place around the mouth and nose area which extended outward for a breathing tube to be attached. The freaks were going to eat him up. Or, better yet, maybe he was going to eat them alive.

Chapter Eighteen

Alex could feel the effects of the pill starting to set in on the drive to the bar. He could tell by the way the street lights and the lights on the cars passing started to leave trails of light behind them. The lights inside the cab were starting to take on a life of their own. Alex was thinking it was about time. He needed to forget about everything, if only for tonight. Tonight was just going to be about fun, guilty pleasure, and maybe some sexual pleasure too if the night so demands.

The cab pulled up to the curb to the front door of The Other Side even though there was no sign indicating it was a bar. It was another way to protect the privacy of their clientele. Tonight, Alex appreciated the privacy more than he ever had before. There was another entrance, one on the second floor. Alex didn't know what it had been before the club bought the place. It was a unique old warehouse.

Paying the cab fare, Alex exited the vehicle and walked up to the door where two burly men stood watch at the front entrance. After showing them his identification, they opened the door for him and told him to have a great time. Alex planned to do just that, he wasn't going to let anyone or anything stop him from having a great trip.

As Alex walked through the front door, he was greeted by a nice surprise. The black lighting, usually, made everything a little more distorted, but right now it was really making things visually stunning. The pounding, pulsing sound of the loud music coming from the speakers was hitting his body like a vibrating machine. Making his hearing an erotic experience in itself, while the vibrations of the music danced all over his body.

Alex walked over to the bar and ordered bottled water for now. He may have something stronger later, but for now, he wanted to soak in the sensations hitting his mind and body.

As the DJ played one of his favorite Nine Inch Nails songs, he felt his body take over as he found himself walking towards the dance floor. It was still early and even though there were quite a few people here, there would be tons more later in the night.

Alex was standing in the middle of the dance floor, alone, but that didn't bother him. He started dancing and moving his body to the beat of the music. His arms started moving from his sides by his thighs, up his waist to his chest and landed on his face. He was rubbing and touching himself all over, making love with the song and the trip he was on.

People all around were watching him, watching a beautiful, tattooed man, basically having sex with himself on the dance floor. It was not in a crude kind of way but in a sexual, seductive way. It was obvious he was into what was happening at the moment and quite obvious he didn't have a care in the world. He could have been in the bar alone and he would not have cared. It was about the music, the beat, the sensation of all things sensual coming together for him.

He was so into what he was experiencing he didn't see the man in the vinyl pants with the vinyl gas mask making his way onto the dance floor. He made his way towards him, arriving at the point where he was dancing, he positioned himself behind Alex.

Victor reached from behind and began rubbing his hands all over Alex's chest and abdomen. He spent some time concentrating on Alex's nipples, rubbing them, playing with them, pinching them, teasing them until his head leaned back towards Victor and he was moaning with pure pleasure. He was so into the immediate erotic pulses being sent through his body he didn't even open his eyes to see who was behind him.

He didn't care as long as they didn't stop what they were doing.

Victor moved in closer, thrusting his crotch up against Alex and began moving in the same rhythm and motions. This was an intense overload of electric sensations creeping all through his body. He was in love with this feeling and he was so happy this man was helping his cause. He knew it was a man too, not by the hands moving over his body, but by the hard crotch he felt behind him moving along with him. He didn't care; this was ecstasy.

He had no clue Victor had slipped a miniature tracking device on his leather arm band which would transmit the distance he was from Victor's phone hidden in his boot. If found, it was such a plain looking device no one would have an idea what it was and, most likely, throw it in the trash.

As the song started winding down and the last beats of it were bringing the climax of their dance to an end, he still kept moving to the beat and still kept his eyes closed. He didn't care to know who this man was, the night was young. He hoped everyone he came into contact with, male or female was going to bring him as much pleasure as this man did by just rubbing himself against his backside and chest.

He had loved it when the man made contact with his nipples as it was another electrifying shock that instead of running body wide ran directly to his cock. Alex didn't care if people saw his hard cock, he loved it and he was looking forward to a night filled with many more experiences like this. When the song ended, Alex turned to say something to the man, but found himself, once again, standing alone on the dance floor with no man in sight. Maybe he had imagined it. Stranger things have happened.

Another song came on and he found himself caught up in this one like he had the last one. This time more people made their way to the dance floor and Alex could tell the night was just getting fun.

Chapter Nineteen

Demetri was pacing around Gina's place while she was finishing getting ready. He loved Gina like a sister, but sometimes she took forever to get ready. He focused on some books she had laid out on the table in her reading room and began to look through them. There was some about dreams, some about ancient symbols, and others on telekinesis.

He loved the way she always tried to take care of him. Even when he wasn't, she was always on the lookout for an answer. He had been so preoccupied with the ritual slaying on Riverside Drive he completely forgot about Gina offering to help.

"Hey, how is the dream research coming? Any ideas yet about what might have caused the levitation and handprint on my neck?" Demetri yelled to her.

"As for yours," she said, "I have to dig really deep into psychic abilities and their impact on dreams. The fact is we don't know enough about your powers and their limitations or lack of limitations to make an educated conclusion. We are going to have to dive into what others have been through and hopefully come across something similar to yours."

"What do you mean 'as for yours?'" Demetri asked her sounding a little curious and a whole lot jealous. "Are you two-timing me?"

"Two-timing? Never, you know you're the one I love, however….." Gina said to him jokingly. "I do have another case I am working on, but until I get the all clear from my client, I would like to stick to the confidentiality aspect of my work," she said. "And you know, if I could tell you, I would. It may come down to me having to ask for your help on this one, but not just yet."

He decided to let it go for now. He respected her for being such a stickler for client confidentiality and to tell the truth; there were a great many things that he didn't always tell her. Most of the time, it's because he would worry her more than divulge or break anyone's confidentiality.

"Let's get a move on girl," Demetri yelled. "We have some dancing to catch up on."

Gina came walking out of her bedroom wearing a form-fitting, green vinyl tank style dress and it really played well with her green eyes and set her red hair apart as the best accessory. He was always amazed at what a beautiful woman she was. She was his best friend and confidant, but to top it all off, she was fun!

They hopped into Demetri's Jeep and headed for The Other Side. This was going to be a fun-filled night.

Chapter Twenty

Alex felt in the height of his trip and so far so good. It felt fucking great! He had been wandering around the first and second floors of the club checking out the different areas, dance floors, and people. The people and the music were making this a damn good night!

He thought about the collision of the gothic world that came here versus the fetish world and where those two came together and where they separated. There were clichés here, as there were in any bar. Watching the interaction, the conversations, the body language, the touching, kissing, and movements of the dance of courtship, seduction, and sometimes just friendships had his mind deeply involved in this place.

The people on the upper floors had been a pleasure to watch and enjoy. Their movements had tantalized his mind, his vision, and had helped send him into somewhat of a trance at times as if their body movements were hypnotizing him into a world where everything felt so good. The touch of anything felt like it was the first touch, the first time the connection between hand and mind was made. Whatever Brandon had given him was definitely working its magic.

The people frequenting the first and second floors for the most part kept to themselves, some out of safety and fear of what happened in the basement and some out of pure ignorance. What went on in the basement was not for the faint of heart. It had been a long time since Alex had been down in the basement. But, feeling a reckless need, reckless abandon, he hoped the basement would make him forget; make him feel disconnected or maybe even connected to something he could comprehend.

Alex soon found himself standing at the top of the stairs leading to the basement. The music on the first floor was drowning out most of everything he thought he heard coming from The Underside. Every once in a while he thought he could hear a scream, a loud moan, people begging, people crying. He could feel a breeze coming up the staircase and there was a smell in the air, a smell he could not quite put a name to, but he felt he had smelled it before.

Removing his sunglasses, Alex took the first step downward. Descending into a darker world and with each step he could feel the happiness he was experiencing upstairs slowly start to slip away and he felt fear start to creep up inside him. Why was he doing this? Why didn't he turn around? The answer was clear even though he didn't want to accept it. He was looking for something here, something now, which could grab a hold of him and make him realize there are worse things to fear than a dream. He needed to feel in control, not in the dream world.

The lighting in the stairwell was not great, but the steps were each outlined with a strip of lighting which made it somewhat easier to guide yourself downward, down into the darkness, the unknown. Alex had been down here a few times before, but never while he was tripping. Each time had been a different experience. This time he felt he saw things clearer than ever before. Some would argue he was just experiencing a deranged sense of bullshit, of something brought on by drug-induced stupor, not a sense of reality. But for now, this felt intensely real, senses heightened, adrenaline pumping through his body, ready for the next heightened state of consciousness.

As Alex cautiously made his way down the winding stairwell, he was on high alert and extremely nervous. He had his hand on the railing letting it be his guide. He was startled when his hand brushed up against another's hand sending him immediately into flight mode, but he held on, wanting to see, wanting to experience something new. When Alex eased around to where he was standing in front of the person in the stairwell, he could make out he was wearing nothing but a black leather thong, boots, and a leather mask.

The mask is what caught Alex's attention. It was a black leather mask formed to the head and neck through rivets and stitching, with two eye slots and holes where the nostrils would be so that whoever wore it could get some air. The mask was so detailed, so intricate; it had a strap going over the top which fastened with silver buckles and straps over the ears on each side of his head. Down the forehead to the bridge of the nose, a narrow leather piece stitched to form a Y around the nose with rivets along the cheeks. Additional buckles and clasps tightened two leather straps across the mouth making it almost impossible for the person to talk. As Alex looked into the eyes behind the mask, he could hear moaning coming from under the mask.

There was a leather part of the mask covering his neck with a zipper which ran up the front. Alex reached up to the man standing there, realizing he was tied by his hands to the railing of the stairs. He grabbed the zipper on the neck and eased it upward towards the man's chin. Peeling back a side of the leather mask, he could see blood running down the man's neck. There were teeth marks on his neck, flesh torn, and blood oozing slowly out of the marks.

He backed away, unsure of what to make of this. He panicked, unsure and really wondering if this was a good idea or not, but he kept moving down, deeper into the stairwell hoping he would make it to the basement soon. His nerves were starting to take over and it was not a good thing to happen when you are tripping.

To Alex's relief he felt the basement floor under his feet. What did the basement hold for him, pleasure or horror? Alex was hoping it was pleasure.

Chapter Twenty-One

Demetri and Gina were singing loudly to a song playing on the radio as they pulled into the parking lot of The Other Side. It looked like it was going to be a packed place tonight. They found a parking spot in the back corner of the lot and hopping out of the Jeep they headed through the lot and to the front door. The two bouncers shook Demetri's hand and welcomed him to the club.

Walking in they were hit by the sounds of people laughing, music blaring and just an overall good energy. People were having fun and it was exactly what the two of them were looking for tonight, fun.

They walked up to the bar where their favorite bartender, Ricky, was working and both ordered a shot of Jack Daniel's. Asking Ricky to start him a tab, Demetri handed over his credit card and they picked up their shot glasses, clinked the glasses together and downed the shots at the same time.

They were both feeling sexy tonight and it must have shown in their confidence because they were being eyed by everyone. Demetri liked it immensely. It had been a while since he had sex with anyone other than himself so this may just turn into a fun evening. He had a fire burning inside of him and he needed a release.

They were playing some great music tonight and feeling it take over, he grabbed a hold of Gina and led her to the dance floor. They joined in with the already existing crowd of people dancing and moving to the music, some were dancing individually and others pumping and grinding on someone else. The lights were coming on and off, changing colors with the beat of the music which played nicely off everyone's dark leather and vinyl clothing. The crowd was really moving and loving the music. The energy coming off each body was electrifying.

They were sweating before the song even finished. Demetri loved dancing with Gina because she knew the exact way he loved to dance. Sometimes with her and sometimes without, but they each seemed to be in perfect sync with each other because they were both having a great time. He was getting into this next song, loving the hard beat and lyrics. It was a hard, yet sexual song and that was exactly the way it was making him feel.

Gina opted to head over to the bar for another shot. When Ricky placed it down in front of her, he said, "That gentleman in the gas mask at the end of the bar has bought this one for you."

"Who is it?" Gina leaned in closer to the bar to better hear Ricky.

"The guy in the gas mask at the end of the bar bought this," Ricky said a little louder than before.

Gina smiled at the man, raised the shot in salute and thanked him and in return he nodded his approval at her. She took the shot and slammed it back laying the glass on the bar. Turning to thank the man again, she looked over at the end of the bar to find he was no longer there.

Gina, thinking nothing of it, turned and headed back onto the dance floor where she made her way over to Demetri, who was busy putting on a show for everyone around him. He was really into the song. She smiled at him thinking how she was so fortunate to have him in her life.

Gina started getting into the song herself and was dancing once again. She was really having fun and loving all the energy. She glanced up and caught a glimpse of the man that bought her a shot just a few minutes ago. He was standing against the wall not too far from the basement door entrance. She was so curious as to whom this man was and looking him up and down she noticed he was rubbing his crotch and looking right in her direction. Inwardly she was wondering if she should be flattered or repulsed but she could not deny he had a gorgeous body. He was a muscular, built man, but you could not make out his face due to the mask. Something about him felt familiar too, but she couldn't quite place where she knew him from.

True to fashion for the evening, when she looked up again she saw him disappearing down the stairs to the basement. Did he want her to follow him? She had never been down there before, even though she knew Demetri had been. Demetri had begged her one time before to never go down there alone, it wasn't as safe as some made it seem. She promised him then she would not, but today she had to admit, she was curious as hell who this man was.

Chapter Twenty-Two

Alex had no clue he was covertly being followed by the overly charged Victor. It wouldn't have mattered if he knew because he would have thought it was someone who was interested in approaching for sexual favors. He probably would have found his body something he would not have been able to turn down. But Victor was not going to allow such a thing to happen. He was keeping a safe distance from him and sticking to the darkness where he was well-hidden.

Alex was somewhat lost in the dark basement with occasional flickering lights and every so often, at timed intervals, strobe lights would start flashing. This was an intentional effect the owners thought gave The Underside more appeal. He wasn't really paying attention to what was going on or where he was going. His fascination laid with these little rooms down here. There seems to be hundreds of rooms which seemed to go on forever.

There was a characteristic of this place filling him with excitement, the voyeuristic side, which had been building up since he had arrived at the bar. But, there was a nervousness nagging at him, telling him this dark place was not for him, not tonight.

Some people didn't mind if you stopped and watched them because they would leave the doors open to the rooms and others would have them shut or shut them in your face as you stopped to watch.

Alex stumbled upon a room where the light was off but as he stopped at the open doorway the light overhead started blinking and he was able to make out someone on the floor of the room. He could hear chains and identify the person was in all vinyl head to toe, even their hands chained to the walls were covered with black vinyl gloves. There was a mouth gag securely covering the face much like the one on the man in the stairway.

As the light flashed on and off, Alex could see he was sprawled out, with his legs chained to the floor. He must have been abandoned for the time being by his master and laid out for display. As with the one in the stairway, this mask had riveted holes where the nostrils would have been, but had a different style of eye slots. These were not actual any eye sockets, but rather an arrangement of holes punched into the vinyl as if to give the person tied up many different small views of what was happening in front of him.

He was actually quite eerie looking and it appeared as if his eyes were glowing behind the holes punched into the mask. Alex thought to himself, *even though it appears real, remember, you are tripping and it most likely was just an effect of the drugs.*

Moving on to the next room, he found it empty and decided to stop for a minute to rest and try to collect his thoughts. He set back onto the extended bench thinking back on the man chained in the stairway. Someone had taken a bite out of his neck and the man was bleeding. Alex assumed it was a punishment a master inflicted on his property, but man what a fucking harsh way to learn a lesson.

And what was up with those glowing eyes of the man chained to the floor of the room a few doors down? What was going on down here? There is some sick twisted shit going on. No wonder they run this place by word of mouth only with no advertising. This is one thing you wouldn't want the evening news to be broadcasting.

The strobes lights had started again and it was really messing with his vision. Looking up at the doorway, Alex was startled to see a man standing there. He stood feet shoulder width apart, wearing black leather boots, leather pants, black leather vest, and a whip held out in front of him. The man had a thick hairy chest and a dark beard. There was something commanding about him, something that demanded respect.

"So boy, are you ready for your punishment?" The man started smacking the sides of the doorway with the whip.

"Um, uh, what's going on?" Alex stammered at the man.

"I said are you ready for your punishment, boy?" The man cited in a firmer tone this time.

"Hey man, I'm sorry if I got your room," Alex tried to say, but the man was already approaching him with the whip raised ready to strike him.

Alex raised his arms up instinctively to protect himself and to his surprise the man suddenly went flying backwards into the hallway. The lights had stopped flashing, so all Alex could rely on was his hearing, because his vision was gone until the lights started flickering or the strobe light started flashing again.

He heard the man with the whip screaming out in pain and Alex was wondering what the hell was happening. It sounded like someone was trying to kill him.

"This is freaking the shit out of me," Alex said out loud more to himself but loud enough for someone else to hear.

He struggled to get up off the bench, trying to collect his balance. His heart was racing, his senses on high alert. He could still hear the man screaming in the distance, but it sounded as if it was gradually getting further and further away as if he was being dragged away kicking and screaming. Then there was silence.

Alex was standing in the frame of the door to the room, in which he was just lying on the bench, looking both ways down the hallway, but was not able to see anything. Darkness was not a good thing at this moment. He was scared, completely overwhelmed, and tripping his balls off. This was crazy. Things were taking a seriously bad turn as he struggled to keep control of himself and not let this spiral in a bad direction.

Alex crept back out in the hallway and slowly felt his way down the corridor in which the man was dragged away. As he inched passed rooms on each side of him, he would look cautiously inside to see if anyone else were down here with him. The flickering lights started again and it wasn't but a few minutes later the strobe lights started again. The strobe lights were messing with his head and vision, but they were a blessing, because it gave him the ability to see more than just the darkness present without them. It was the darkness in the basement that seemed to be more alive than the actual people down here.

He had heard things and seen things in this club, but he had never been this deep into the basement especially while being this deep into a drug-induced mind-altering experience. But he was wondering if everything down here was alive or not.

He arrived in a room where the lights were still flickering. He saw a man lying face down on a makeshift bed, layered in what looked like white linen sheets. His legs were bound by chains to the foot of the bed and his arms bound in chains behind his back. All he had on was a jock strap slightly pulled down under his butt cheeks. The man lying there heard him and turned his head toward Alex and he was trying to say something, but as he tried to listen, he noticed the man's eyes were glowing like the guy earlier.

Alex stepped backward until he backed into the door on the opposite side of the hallway. Turning quickly to look at what he bumped into, he was facing the door to the room across the hall. He was seeing flashes of a woman and a man in what looked like a passionate make out session. They heard him standing there and the woman looked up from where she had been kissing on the man's neck and smiled at Alex. She spoke to him, inviting him to join. He could see blood dripping from the woman's mouth, and her teeth, they appeared to be razor sharp.

He took off running down the corridor trying to get as far away from these people, if that is what they really were. Reaching the end of the hallway, his happiness was short lived when he saw two directions he could go. Right or left? He noticed the room to his right actually had a light, not just a flickering light or strobe lighting. Alex made his way towards the room and quickly realized it was a unisex restroom.

When he walked into the restroom, he was more confused than he had been out in the hallway. There were five urinals against the far wall and standing at the urinals were five horses pissing. But how could that be? His trip was definitely taking a bad turn. Now he was seeing animals in restrooms and they are standing upright pissing.

Four of the five horses were black, and the fifth one was white with some black spots. The white horse was standing in between them leaving two black horses on each side. But, was the white horse a female horse? One of the black horses had a white mane and white tail. They were bridled up and looked like they were adorned with leather straps. Was the white horse in the middle wearing high heels? *What the fuck was going on?*

Alex tried to wrap his brain around what he was experiencing, but that wasn't going to help him make any sense of this. Then he began to focus on the horses and began to realize they were actually people dressed up like horses. Four men dressed like black horses with a horse mask placed over their heads and they were pissing at the urinals. The white horse was a woman, in black high heeled boots, a black body corset and black leather type underwear with a white horse tail hanging from the back of it. She must have been the dominate one and the four others were part of her herd.

Just when Alex thought he could not take anymore. He realized he needed reality to come back to his world, the white horse lady turned her head towards him but still stood in a stance as if she was pissing in the urinal.

"Why do you fight destiny Alex?" The white horse lady said to him but in a man's voice. He recognized the voice immediately as the one haunting his dreams and his waking hours. "We are destined to unite, to conquer, to destroy."

Alex turned and ran from the room heading down the hallway hoping to find his way back out of this hell he currently found himself in. This night was a total and utter nightmare. He felt as if he wasn't ever going to make it out of this maze of a basement. It was dark, there were people being tortured down here, there were creatures with glowing eyes and talking horses. Alex just kept running. As he started to see a glimmer of light up ahead, he found himself falling quickly onto his stomach, hitting his head slightly on the ground.

Alex let out a painful gasp, as the fall almost took his breath away. He knew he tripped over something or someone lying in the hallway. Alex began feeling around in the dark trying to find what it was he had tripped over. His hand landed on something lying on the floor. He immediately knew it was leather and as he started running his hand over it, he was sure what he was feeling was a leather whip and it was a little wet, a little sticky. Was this the same whip the man was trying to use on him earlier?

Why was it laying here on the floor? It wasn't as big as whatever he felt he had tripped over. Just then the lights in the room next to him started to flicker and Alex could see what he had tripped over was indeed the man who had tried to attack him with a whip. But he lay on the floor with his head in the center of a pool of blood and his eyes wide open. It was as if he was staring past Alex's eyes and directly into his soul, but what was staring back at him was a soulless body of a man; a dead man.

Alex began screaming and calling for help, but help was not coming, nor was the end of this hellish nightmare of a night. Alex could not believe he was laying here next to a dead man, a man who had just a few minutes earlier tried to dominate him. *Did this man deserve this?*

As he sat there looking at the man, giving up on anyone coming to help him, Alex started to think, *I'm never going to get out of here. I am going to die down here just like this man. No one's coming to help and no one knows I'm down here. I hadn't even told Brandy I was coming to the club tonight, let alone thinking about coming down into this basement.*

If Alex was a part of any organized religion, he knew this was the time he would have started praying for divine intervention. *It was too late, wasn't it? No one was going to listen to a man who had chosen years ago to not believe in a God who would allow horrible things like this happen to people.*

Alex was once again startled from his thoughts. He could hear something down the hallway. "Help, help me please," Alex begged in a soft voice almost afraid to see who or what was coming.

Then he started to make out shapes where the darkness started to blend with the flickering lights. It was a woman and a man, both on their hands and knees scurrying wildly and unusually fast towards him and the dead man beside him. He could hear them hissing as they neared. The man looked as if he were crawling towards him on the side of the wall; but how could that be? They were so sinister looking, showing razor sharp teeth and glowing eyes as their hisses took on a more moaning tone. *They are going to kill me,* Alex thought to himself. *This is it. I am going to die down here.* As they were just feet away from the dead man's body, Alex closed his eyes in preparation for what he knew was coming.

Just then, he felt hands on both of his arms and he started to scream as he was lifted from the floor to his feet in one full, powerful swoop.

"Run," said a voice to him, "run now!"

Alex opened his eyes to see the man in a black vinyl gas mask telling him to run. Alex did as he was told to do and took off running.

He could hear hissing, moaning voices of a man and woman and the scuffling sounds of what appeared to be a fight. *Was this man fighting for my life? Why was he doing this for me?*

Alex felt a sense of guilt leaving the man behind who had saved him from whatever was down there. But when he found the stairs leading up to the first floor, the guilt quickly gave way to a feeling of gratitude. Tears filled his eyes as he climbed up the stairs, climbing towards the music, climbing towards life.

Chapter Twenty-Three

Gina was moving on the dance floor as her favorite song blasted through the speakers. As she was soaking in each note, each lyric, she couldn't help but smile to herself. Demetri was right; she was having a great night. She had a nice little buzz going on, not too much, just enough.

She was eyeing the crowd as well; she loved to people watch. There were all types here and each one had their own unique individual style, a flair for the dramatic. They were all wonderful in her opinion. She loved people who were true to themselves, people who stepped outside of their comfort zones and sought out something more, demanded respect, demanded to be seen and heard.

Gina was a longtime advocate for equal rights. She believed in equality for all. Gay and straight alike deserved to be happy; to experience all life had to offer. It was this richness in diversity that made life so wonderful, made everything seems so much more.

Man she loved this song.

Just as it was starting to get into the last parts of the song, she noticed Alex coming up out of the basement. He had a terrified look on his face and was desperately trying to make his way towards the door.

She rushed off the dance floor navigating her way through the crowd until she was just feet away from him.

"Alex," Gina yelled trying to speak above the music and the noise, but not having any luck getting his attention.

She rushed forward touching her hand to his shoulder, "Alex, are you okay?"

Alex turned quickly with his fist clenched ready to strike her, then through his tears realized it was Gina. He started to stammer in an attempt to say something then collapsed in her arms sobbing. She held him for a few seconds then tried to get him to tell her what was wrong.

As he struggled to find his words, he realized he didn't even know where to begin. "Dead," he said in her ear, his voice trembling.

"Who is dead?" she asked timidly, starting to feel a sense of dread and fear creep in. Something has him scared; his energy was off the charts.

"So many, dead, down there," Alex stammered as he was shaking and wiping at the tears on his face. "There are creatures down there, killing people, eating people."

"Alex, calm down, okay," she pleaded with him. "You are not making any sense right now."

Alex was shaking his head back and forth, agitated and wanting out of this place. Just as he tried to break free from her arms, his body went rigid, his back arched, his head went back slightly, and his legs went limp. Instead of falling to the floor, he began to rise slowly off the floor. Gina's arms fell to her side as she stared at him, fearful for him. *What was happening to him?*

Alex then went flying backwards until he slammed up against the wall, two feet off the ground, suspended in the air. He let out a painful scream as Gina gasped in horror.

"You," Gina heard a familiar voice over the noise of the club. "Who the hell are you?"

She turned to see Demetri, his face contorted in anger, in fear. She had seen him like this only a few other times in the history of knowing him and it wasn't good.

"Demetri, what are you doing?" Gina yelled at him as she rushed over to Demetri. "He wasn't hurting me, I'm fine."

"I know you," Demetri said to him, ignoring Gina. He slowly walked towards him, his arm outstretched in front of him, surging with the energy he was using to suspend Alex from the floor. "You are the man from my dreams, the one who tried to hurt me, who left this mark on my neck."

Gina and Alex's faces both showed a look of surprise.

"Demetri, stop this," she yelled at him. "I know this man. This is Alex, the man I was telling you about; the man who came into the store."

"Tell me how you did it," Demetri said to him standing just a few feet away from him.

Gina was desperately trying to get Demetri's attention but was having no luck. Grabbing at his arms, waving her hands in front of his face, she tried to break his focus away from Alex. This is crazy; he was out of control.

They were starting to draw a large crowd now. Some who saw when Alex was lifted off the floor and smashed into the wall. Others who were noticing the commotion because a man was floating up against a wall, two feet off the floor as if he were a hanging piece of human artwork.

Just then, the crowd parted from behind Demetri, as people were being flung to the sides as Victor made his way through them towards Demetri. Victor grabbed him and sent him flying backwards sliding across the floor and rolling to a stop. Dazed, he lay there for a few seconds trying to make out what had just happened.

Alex fell to the floor the instant Demetri's concentration broke.

Alex was stunned, confused and once again grateful to whomever this man was that kept showing up to save him. He wasn't sure who he was or why he was helping, but he was thankful.

Alex made his way back onto his feet about the same time Demetri did. Demetri was eyeing Alex and the man who had sent him tumbling across the floor.

Gina was already moving at Victor, fists clenched and swinging at his head. He caught her fist in his, midair, her small hand fitting into his large one as he pushed backwards on it sending her flailing onto the floor roughly.

Demetri became enraged at this, stretched out both arms and focused all his energy sending Victor and the fleeing

Alex off their feet once again smashing them onto the wall where Alex had previously been suspended.

Gina lay on the floor, not believing what she was seeing. This was so out of control. *How could her best friend and the man she had sworn to help find answers to his night terrors be connected? It just didn't make any sense.* Her attention turned back to Demetri and Alex. If she didn't do something, Demetri could, and possibly would, kill Alex.

To everyone's surprise, the man in the gas mask started to fight back. It was subtle at first; with a strong push against the wall he was using some incredible strength to free himself. Leaning into the energy Demetri was using to hold him back, he started with one foot forward, then another until he was moving slowing but steadily towards Demetri.

This man, Gina thought, *was showing some amazing strength.*

To Demetri's surprise, he found himself having to make a choice between the man who had tortured him in his dreams and the man who was fighting back.

To the delight of Gina and the dismay of Demetri, he let Alex fall to the ground. It took everything he had inside of him to do it. He wanted answers from this man in his dreams, but right now there was a more dangerous threat to him, one that was obviously able to fight back against Demetri and his powers.

The man in the mask yelled out to Alex, "Get the fuck out of here. Now!"

Alex decided it was in his best interest. He didn't know who this other man was either, but he was displaying some powerful shit which Alex had not seen before in real life, he thought this was stuff in movies, not reality. Alex turned and headed out the door, taking one look back at Gina before disappearing into the night.

Demetri, refocusing his energy, started concentrating on Victor who was moving towards him, as if he were pushing a brick wall backwards. Victor was strong, but Demetri knew he was stronger. Summoning all the strength he could spare he focused it all on Victor. It seemed to be working as the Victor's feet started to slide backwards.

But that was short lived, as he once again found his footing and was taking one step at a time moving forward towards Demetri. Demetri seeing a barstool out of the corner of his eye moved one hand towards it and with the wave of his hand sent the barstool hurling across the room smashing it against Victor's body. As it struck him, it was shattered into pieces and he was knocked off his feet, falling to the ground and sliding backwards from the energy Demetri was still hitting him with. Victor was back against the wall, on the ground this time.

Gina was watching this power struggle between both men; this was something new, something she had not seen before. As she looked at Demetri, she noticed a small flow of blood coming from the left nostril. This battle was taking its toll on him and if she didn't do something to help him, he might be in trouble. Gina was trying to get in Demetri's head, trying to get him to tap into her energy. *Let me help you! Accept this energy and use it on this man.* She mentally said to him.

Demetri let go for a second and fell to one knee. The man in the mask feeling the energy dissipate around him let out a yell of anger. He was on his feet headed directly for Demetri. Before Demetri could act, Victor was on him throwing Demetri to the ground, smashing his fist into Demetri's face one blow after another.

Gina shocked at this, ran towards them calling upon the energies within and around her. As she reached them, she used her energy by laying hands on both sides of Victor's head. She let the energy pulse inside his brain, temporarily throwing him off balance, and obviously pissing him off even more. He yelled out once again in a scream coming from deep within, a warrior yell. Swinging his arm backwards, he struck Gina sending her stumbling many feet, stunned and dazed by the force of it.

This was just the moment Demetri needed to take control again as he placed his foot against the Victor's chest and with all his might sent the him backwards until he fell on his ass. He was up in a flash and headed towards Demetri.

Demetri, not wasting any time, up on his feet refocusing his energy towards him, this time was hitting him with one burst after the other. He finally started to give way to this and Demetri went in for the kill. Throwing one last burst of energy at him, which almost took Demetri's breath away, he went flying backwards at a speed which shocked everyone. This time when Victor hit the wall he didn't just stop there, he went through it landing in the corridor where the entrance to the bar was.

Demetri fell to his knees, blood still dripping from his nose and a gash along his eyebrow from the forceful blows the man had delivered to him. Gina ran over to Demetri as he was struggling to get on his feet again and helped him up. They both walked together towards the entrance of the bar. To their surprise, the man was not there. All that was there was the remains of a wall where there was now a hole.

Who the fuck was this man, Demetri thought to himself? He had not seen anyone to date who could force their way through his powers, fight back at him and leave him this damned drained. Demetri felt he had not seen the last of this man either, which made him a bit happy as his ego was a bit bruised along with his face.

Demetri and Gina stepped out into the night air, both breathing heavily, both feeling the beating their bodies just took and both needing to sit for a minute to collect their thoughts.

They sat down on the sidewalk with their back up against the building in silence for a few minutes; the only thing they could hear was the deep breathing coming from both. Inside, the bar was buzzing about what had just happened. It wasn't unusual for a fight to break out every now and then, but this one was epic. The underworld would be talking about it for some time to come. As the talk spread throughout the bar, there were many creatures who were overly pleased by this turn of events. Many were glad to see the bounty hunter meet his match! Some were only sorry the masked man was not able to finish him off.

Chapter Twenty-Four

Alex had run down Elgin Avenue for many blocks trying to get away from the bar and the people in it. Tired, frightened, and scared he was trying to make sense out of a senseless situation. *How could that man, the one with Gina, do the things he was capable of doing? How did Gina know him? Why was this masked man helping him? What the hell was going on down in that basement? Were those real people, or even worse were they dead, or were they vampires?*

These were all good questions, but there were no good answers coming to his mind about it. *Brandy was not going to believe any of this shit. Plus, she would tell him what an idiot he was to have gone down in the basement especially when he was not in his right mind.* Brandy was a woman of logic, the brain between the two of them, the scientist.

As Alex was running out of wind and energy, he slowed down to a walk. He had gone this far on adrenaline alone, but now he was starting to burn out. His chemical induced trip was starting to wear off. Now he was left with distorted thoughts, distorted images, and crazy mind blowing questions.

He had trusted Gina, told her everything that had happened to him and she wanted to help him, or he had thought she wanted to help him. He didn't know what he believed anymore. A man who could move things with his mind or his hand? He wasn't sure which one it was, but it was fucked up. He did recall Gina trying to get the man to stop, both men actually. He recalled that the masked man knocked her to the ground.

Alex was so deep into his own thoughts right now that he wasn't even aware he was being followed by a black SUV. It had been tailing him for blocks now, staying back far enough to not be seen or noticed.

Alex looked up to see a taxi dropping someone off at an older brick apartment building down on Elgin Avenue. As the person was getting out of the cab, he ran towards the cab waving his hand, trying to get the drivers attention. To his delight, it was waiting for him. He climbed into the back seat telling the driver where he lived. As the cab pulled away heading towards Alex's home, so did the black SUV.

The ride was quiet, except for the public radio station the driver had on. Alex was once again stuck in his thoughts. How was any of this possible? *How was this man able to move both Alex and the masked man up against a wall?* He was actually holding Alex in the air. *Maybe I was dreaming again, maybe I fell and hit my head in the bar. That would make perfect sense, or would it. Actually, none of this made any sense whatsoever.*

His hurting body told him none of this was a dream. In fact, many thoughts and memories of the night would haunt Alex for years to come. People had died down in that basement and he had not even called 911 to help them. To his defense, he was not in his right mind, the people were already dead, and he had to get the hell out of there before he had become another tally on the dead list. He kept telling himself someone would call the police, *someone would do the right thing; someone always did, didn't they?*

He felt drained. This was supposed to be a night of fun, a night of unwinding and letting go of the stress for one evening. He should have gone to a meditation retreat instead of a self-induced chemical high he thought to himself trying to decide if he wanted to cry or laugh.

As the taxi pulled into Alex's driveway, he was brought back from his thoughts by the taxi driver telling him the fare would be $20.55. Alex handed him $25.00 and thanked him as he got out of the cab. He closed the door to the cab and walked towards the front door of his home. Home, he couldn't think of a better place to be right now. Grabbing the lock box from behind a planter near the door, he entered the code and took the key to the front door out of the box. Opening the door, he placed the key back into the box returning the box back behind the planter.

All the while, Alex was oblivious to Victor watching this entire interaction from his SUV a few houses down with night vision binoculars. Victor was sure he had obtained the code and would test it later. You never know when it might come in handy. There would come a time within the next week when he would have to take the vessel into his custody in order to keep him safe while they prep him for the master to return. After all, this is the entire reason for his stay in Tulsa.

Alex entered his home and after the night he's had, Victor doubted he would be headed anywhere other than to bed. This was good for Victor because the time was quickly coming for the second sacrifice to be offered to the master, but right now, he needed some action, some sexual action. He needed to inflict some pain on someone.

It was probably not a smart idea for him to head back to the bar tonight, not after the display that just took place. He wouldn't be surprised if it had been shut down for the night. He had taken care of three hindrances that night at the bar. One was just a wannabe leather daddy looking to inflict some punishment on a willing man playing a boy, but he had picked the wrong boy to inflict his pain upon. Victor dragged him away quickly from the vessels room, dragged him down the tunnel and around the corner before sticking a knife into his jugular with lightning precision. The man bled out quickly.

The other two he was not overly concerned with. They were dead before Victor even laid a hand on them. Not all vampires were unruly bottom feeders, but these two had to be dealt with as they were in the throes of a feeding frenzy and had their sights set on the vessel. Once again, bad fucking choice on their part. They may have been vampires, but they were young worked up ones so they were not as easily dealt with as the others; still, they were no match for Victor. He had taken down bigger and deadlier creatures than these two vamps.

Once Alex was safely running towards the stairs, Victor grabbed the first vampire from behind, placing his hand under her chin pulling her back close to his body while spinning the both of them towards the male vampire. With one sweeping move of his free arm, he slashed the throat of the male vamp with his hunting knife exposing a huge gash in his neck where blood immediately started flowing. The male vampire grabbed at his own neck, trying to stop the flow of blood, trying to stop his impending death. He fell to the floor trying to hiss, trying to yell, but Victor had expert precision with his blade, cutting hard and deep into the vampire's windpipe.

Immediately, Victor turned his attention to the female vampire who he had pulled close to him still holding her from under her chin. He reached his other hand up with the speed that rivaled any vampire and snapped the neck of the female vampire. As she fell to the ground, immobilized, he bent down wiping his bloody knife off on the clothes of the male vampire. Then Victor stood up, walked over to the male vampire raising his foot in the air and quickly bringing it down onto the side of the vampire's head, smashing it open with one forceful, heavy blow. Walking over to the female vampire, Victor proceeded to do the same to her.

There was always the threat of regeneration from these supernatural beasts, since they were demonically made. This, however, took time when they were severely damaged. By the time they are found, taken away and disposed of, there would be no chance of coming back from the destruction that was just bestowed upon them.

He then made his way up to the main floor where he encountered a most remarkable specimen of a man. He was powerful beyond anything Victor had seen in years and he did not give admiration easily. Human's rarely impressed him, but this male witch didn't even know his own power, Victor had read about men of this witches kind in the journals of the

Balashon and had even encountered a few in the past. Though small in number, every so often, one born in a generation possess many remarkable powers, deadly powers. Typically they are quickly identified and disposed of if the Balashon were not able to recruit them. *Why hadn't this one been taken care of? Why hadn't Victor been warned about him?* This was an interesting turn of events, one that Victor would have to take more seriously. This male witch would not stop what was going to come. His master would be here soon, and if the witch got in the way, Victor would deal with him. If the master were here, he would crush him.

The fact that the witch had turned his attention to the vessel was not a good thing at all. No, this was not good. Victor would have to keep a much closer eye on the vessel. Any complications to the time line would not, could not be tolerated. When the time comes, Victor's sole responsibility lie in making sure the master's arrival into this realm was not met with any interruptions. It's going to happen, one way or another.

Chapter Twenty-Five

At 2:00 a.m., when Brandy got a call from John, Alex's roommate, she didn't think twice about jumping into her car and driving right over to Alex's place. She could tell by John's voice that Alex must be in bad shape. Brandy had sworn to always be there for Alex no matter what, just as he had sworn the same to her.

When she arrived at his house, she found John on the front porch, pacing nervously, not knowing what to do. Typically, she would have used her own key to open the front door and let herself inside, but with John out on the porch, the door was already unlocked.

"I don't know what is going on with him lately, but some strange shit has been happening. He's losing it, I think he's mental," John said in a worried voice. "He was going on and on about how some man at the bar made him levitate by just using his mind and how he was attacked by monsters and then some man in a leather mask saved him. I mean mental, right?"

"You did the right thing by calling me. Try not to worry too much. I will see what I can do," Brandy said as she laid a hand on his shoulder trying to give him comfort.

When Brandy entered the house, she found a trail of what she could only assume to be Alex's clothes leading to his bedroom. Boots stood in the front end of the hallway, leather pants laid mid-way with a hat and arms bands at the base of his bedroom door. She knew him well enough to know that whatever happened, he would probably be curled up under the covers of his bed, nude and clutching a pillow.

True to fashion, as she walked into his room he was just as she expected. The bedroom lamp on his nightstand was the only light in the room turned on. As she approached the bed, she could see him shaking under the covers. She walked over to the side of the bed, crawled onto it, lying on her side facing Alex.

"Hey sweetness, how are you?" Brandy asked him softly as she reached over putting a hand on his cheek.

Alex just stared at her, his eyes wide, body shaking.

"Why don't you tell me what happened tonight?" She said to him trying to get him to give her some reaction. When she received none, she really began to worry.

"Alex, sweetheart, I'm going to go make you some hot tea and then we are going to have a long chat about what happened." She told him, in a commanding, take charge way.

As she got out of bed, she made her way into the kitchen. There she filled the tea kettle, turning the knob on the gas stove until the flame burned high and placed the pot onto the flame. Walking over to the cabinet, Brandy reached up and brought down two tea cups and two saucers. Placing each cup onto its saucer she walked over to the tea canister and took out two prepackaged bags of green tea. She placed them into the tea cups waiting for the tea kettle to whistle.

As she stood there, she couldn't take her mind off of Alex, the scared look in his eyes, his body shaking, and the strange story that John had told her. *Where is John? He must have calmed down enough that he was able to go back to bed.* Now that she was paying attention, she could hear the TV playing in his room. If she needed him, she knew where to find him.

Just then, the tea kettle whistled; she turned off the gas burner, the flame went away with a pop as it went out. Brandy removed the kettle from the burner. She then turned to walk over to where the tea cups were, to her surprise, her very big surprise, she found Alex standing behind her in the middle of the kitchen next to the island.

"Alex, you scared me half to death," Brandy said as she steadied herself thinking how grateful she was to have not burned herself or Alex with the tea kettle. "What are you doing in here? I was going to bring the tea to you in bed." She walked past him to the tea cups and poured the hot water into the cups. She turned and walked back over to the stove placing the tea kettle back onto the burner.

Walking over to Alex, she embraced him and gave him a long hug which he did not return as he would have in his normal way. He just stood there, body limp, almost lifeless.

"Come on, let's get you back in bed," Brandy said. She turned him around by placing her hands on his shoulders, gently leading him back to his bed where she placed him under the covers. Fluffing his pillows up so that he could sit up in the bed, Brandy turned to go back into the kitchen to retrieve the tea.

When she got back to Alex's bedroom, she was relieved to see him still in bed, propped up on two pillows looking at her. She walked over to his nightstand placing a cup and saucer down for him and then walked around the bed to the empty side where she had been laying before. Brandy crawled in under the covers and leaned over to Alex. She placed her right arm around his back pulling him close to her so that she was, in fact, hugging him. She just laid there with him listening to him breathe, listening to the quiet house.

It didn't take too long, maybe twenty minutes, before Alex started to calm down, to stop shaking, and relax his body into hers. They continued to lay there like this for another fifteen minutes or so.

To her delight, she heard the sweetest sound she had thought she had ever heard. It was Alex talking to her. "Thank you for coming over here," he said.

She pulled him tightly to her. "I can't think of anywhere else I would rather be," she said to him as she turned her head to kiss him on the forehead. "I do have to say though that I think our tea has gotten cold." There was complete silence for a few seconds then both of them started laughing at the same time. "So what do you say, want to tell me what happened tonight?"

As he leaned up from her hug, he looked at her with big eyes. "I don't think you will believe me if I tell you."

"Why don't you let me be the judge of what I will or will not believe, Alex Rogers," she said to him in a tone that he knew not to mess with.

As they both started sipping on their cold tea, he began to tell her about the night and its many events. She tried to remain a calming force for him as he told his story, but as he continued on with it, she had to keep reminding herself to remain calm and not get excited. She didn't want to upset Alex any more than he already was. But if truth be told, she was freaking out a bit. She knew him well and she knew him well enough to know that whether or not what he was telling was truth or fiction. He believed it to be true and she believed in Alex. She had no other choice; at least she felt that she didn't, than to believe what he was telling her. Brandy knew what she had to do. She would have to pay Gina a visit at her store. She was going to get to the bottom of this before anything else happened to him.

Chapter Twenty-Six

Demetri and Gina both could agree on one thing, they didn't want anything to eat. They were exhausted, nauseous, and confused as hell. They were both a little aggravated with the other, but neither knew where to start. As they sit at their favorite booth at the Fifth Street Diner, they were feeling the aches and pains of the night's events settling into their bodies. They had been beaten and bruised. This was definitely one for the books.

As they sat drinking the burnt tasting coffee they both looked up at each other at the same time. They both knew it was a coincidence because they did not feel the other probing into their minds.

"Okay, what the hell happened tonight?" Gina asked Demetri.

"I was going to ask you the same question. How do you know the man with the tattoos and why were you protecting him?" He shot back.

"I told you at the bar that it was the man who had come to the store asking for my help about his night terrors. And he has a name, it's Alex." She glared back. "Why the hell would you come out attacking him like that anyway Demetri? You knew he wasn't hurting me."

"I knew nothing of the sort, G," he said to her. "All I know is that man, Alex, is involved somehow in the dream I had and the mark that was left on my neck."

"I get that, but I told you he wasn't hurting me. I saw him coming up from the basement and he looked terrified, so I went over to him to see if I could help. I had no idea how in shock he was or how you were going to react. I don't want to fight with you. Can't you see that you and Alex are both looking for the same thing? You both want answers to the dreams that you both seem connected to."

"Well, I don't recall him having any marks on him after the dreams or being thrown up against any walls after the dream," Demetri tried to rationalize.

"Oh, and you would know what state he was in after the dreams, how?" She snapped at him. "The only time I know of him being thrown up against a wall is when you threw him up against one at the bar earlier."

"So all of this tonight is my fault?" Demetri said getting angrier.

"No, that is not what I'm saying, I'm saying things got way out of control expeditiously before anyone had a chance to explain," she said reaching over the table and grabbing his hand. "I have always, always had your back as you have had mine. Tonight was no different, I was ready to take on that man that came out of nowhere and attacked you, the one that was wearing the mask."

"Speaking of the psycho gas mask freak," Demetri said relaxing a bit. "What the fuck was up with him?"

"I'm not sure, but he was a strong son of a bitch. He tossed me around like a rag doll," she said thinking back on the night's events. "Now that I think about it, he was watching me most of the night. He bought me a drink at the bar, but wouldn't come near me, just told the bartender to give it to me. Then when we were on the dance floor I saw him standing by the basement door entrance, watching me dance. He was rubbing his crotch, looking at me, and then he turned and disappeared down into the basement. The next time I saw him was when he tossed everyone aside in the crowd to get to you."

"That is interesting. That man was a beast, but a human beast at that. He had supernatural strength. Did you see him pushing his way towards me through my own power surge?" He asked, still surprised and a little in awe of the guy.

"I did see that and if you ask me, it wasn't just by happenstance that he was there," she added. "This man watched me all night, and then when you attacked Alex, he comes to Alex's rescue? It just doesn't make any sense, but there is too much in common to ignore. We have a new player in town, one that is strong enough to take you on."

"He was definitely a strong one, but let's not forget who got the better of whom in the end," he said letting his ego bow up a little at her last statement.

"I'm just saying, don't underestimate him. I have never, ever seen anyone human, be able to do what he did to you tonight," Gina said with worry in her voice. She could not get that nagging suspicion out of her head that he, meaning the masked man, was familiar to her somehow. But it was completely lost on her at the moment.

"Thelma," Demetri called to the waitress. "Can you top us off over here?" Demetri smiled holding up his coffee cup.

Chapter Twenty-Seven

Victor rounded the corner to his current lodging and pressed the button for the front gates to open. The gates were heavy wrought iron, with metal lions adorning them and an eight foot stone fence with wrought iron adornment on the top that went all around the palatial estate. There was a long driveway once you entered through the gates that led up to the actual house that was owned by the Balashon. The house was secluded and took up an entire city block. It was located near the Philbrook Museum. Victor had been to the museum in his first days in Tulsa. He was a lover of art, how could he not be living in such splendor for the better part of his life?

On occasion, he would be forced into hiding or his trailing of someone would lead him outside of the finer things in life, but Victor was born with a love of art. The darker the art, the more he loved it.

As he drove up towards the house, he was always struck by its beauty. It was built back in the oil baron days of Tulsa's history, and one of those barons just happened to be a member of the Balashon. The architecture was exquisite. It was like looking at one of the castles in Europe. The exterior was made mostly of stone and concrete, but the intricacies of the house were something that you would not see in this part of the world, except maybe in older catholic churches. There were high arches, tall glass windows where the arches of the windows were beveled leading up to the arch. There were large tower-like structures that shot up from the sides of the house, almost like bell towers or watch towers.

The estate itself was an immense immaculate maze of greenery and shrubbery, beautiful rose gardens and had an amazingly large pool in the back. There was a six car garage off to the back side of the large house that connected through a closed-in tunnel that was made of glass. The inside was even more beautiful than the outside. It had lush decorations, priceless art and artifacts from around the globe, and a dungeon in the basement that would make anyone with a fetish for this kind of kink wet.

As Victor drove around to the garage and waited for the garage door to open, he was still stuck on the night's events. He could not believe the power exuding from the male witch. He was a beautiful male witch at that too. But he still didn't have command of all of his powers yet, which could work in Victor's favor. If he had been in full command of his powers, he and the vessel may not have left that bar alive. Yes, it was time to get to know the players in this game a little better, actually a whole lot better.

Pulling into the garage he could hear the girl beside him starting to rouse a little. He didn't have a hard time finding someone from the bar walking down the street, obviously someone who lived not far from the club. Without his mask on, he used his good looks and charm as a spider would use a web, to lure an unsuspecting prey into a trap they would never leave alive. This girl was no different.

He had pulled the SUV beside her, rolled down the window, and began a conversation. In less than a minute she was walking around the side of the vehicle, jumping into the passenger seat. He rolled up his tinted window and turned to the girl.

"What a beautiful lady you are. Such lovely eyes, plump lips, and smooth skin," he said to the girl as he ran his fingers across her forearm seducing her with his eyes, his words, and his German accent.

As the girl geared up for a kiss leaning in towards him, lips puckered, eyes closed, Victor lashed out with a brutal thrust of his fist to her head, knocking her unconscious. He smiled at the ease of it all and began to whistle to himself as he drove back to the estate.

Safely in the garage, Victor reached over the girl and opened up the glove compartment. With the girl waking up, he needed to go ahead and take some precautions. He pulled out a roll of gray duct tape and began to wrap it around the girl's wrists, making sure that it was tight and secure. When her wrists were secure, he pushed the button to the garage door and it closed behind them.

Victor got out of the SUV shutting his door and walked around to the side where the girl was sitting. He opened the door and as she was attempting to look at him through half opened eyes, moaning slightly, he scooped her up and hefted her over his right shoulder. He slammed the door to the vehicle shut and headed out the door through the garage and started walking through the glass paned tunnel that led from the garage to the house. Once he made it to the house, he opened the door and with the girl still straddled over his shoulder he punched in the numbers to the security system.

He entered the house and immediately turned around and activated the security system. Once that was done, he quickly turned and made his way to the basement door. What waited down there was a growing delight in his mind. If the girl knew what was about to happen, she would probably be struggling to get free, that is if she weren't still groggy from him smashing her face. He couldn't help that just thinking about what he was going to do to her was making his cock grow hard.

He was in the basement, the lights were on, but dim and everywhere he looked he saw a sexual playground. He loved his sexual dungeon, his sexual prison. There had never been a place that Victor had been sent that wasn't equipped with something that he could use to fulfill his sexual fantasies, his sexual fetishes, sexual needs.

The girl was wide awake now, with a ball gag in her mouth, attached around her head with a leather strap and

119

clasp. She was confused, scared, and her eyes were franticly searching the room looking from one piece of equipment to the next. Some she may have known what they were; others he was sure she had never seen before, nor had she ever thought something like that existed. As luck would have it, she would get to try one or two of them tonight. As her eyes continued to search the room, she finally landed on Victor. He was standing in the corner of the basement room, one foot propped behind him against the stone wall which was helping to steady him as he leaned back onto the wall. He was just watching her, taking it all in.

The girl began to plead with him, but it was an incomprehensible audible mess when she tried to talk. It sounded more like moaning than it did actual words. As he pushed away from the wall with his foot and started to walk towards her, she began to get more agitated, more animated. She was in a sling, with her hands bound by leather straps to the chains that ran up directly off the side of her head. Her feet were elevated upward, legs spread, feet bound by leather straps to the chains that ran upward at that end of the sling. She soon realized what was happening to her. What he was planning on doing and even though she would have willingly done this with him, the fact that he had chosen to take her forcefully was what was scaring her the most. If he was capable of this, what else was he capable of?

He had stripped her nude before putting her in the sling, so she laid there exposed. As he came closer to her, she could see that he too was nude, his cock hard, huge and standing out before him. He had on high leather boots that came up to his knees, but nothing else. There was a black tarp laid out beneath her spread at least fifteen feet in each direction. She was aware of the knife he was sliding his fingers up and down on the non-sharpened side of the blade as he approached her, smiling, and happy.

Once he was standing on the tarp, looking at her, he had the most unusual look on his face. It was a look of conquest, one of winning, but what was the prize? She soon found out her answer when he walked alongside her standing next to her face. He thrust out with the blade quickly slashing at her left cheek, splitting it open. A trail of warm blood streamed down her face as she let out a muted-yell of pain due to the gag. He then ran the blade alongside her left arm starting at the shoulder muscle. Slowly, but deeply, he inserted the blade pulling it upward along the outside of the arm almost to the wrist, avoiding any major arteries, but making blood spill out from the incision.

She again wailed in pain and wiggled around in the sling which made the sling rock back and forth. He reached over and grabbed her by the throat, leaning down close to her face; she could feel his warm breath against her face. "He tried to hurt me tonight, but he did not succeed," he was speaking out loud, looking at her while he did, but not really talking to her.

She was confused and wondering what the hell he was talking about, but the pain was so intense and he was squeezing off the air from her body by his tightly wrapped hand around her neck. "He tried to harm the vessel too, but I stopped him as I always do. I have stopped many people and I will continue to stop them. My master will rise in all his glory and take this world, take the pesky, insignificant people like you. The ones who are weak and defenseless, but even the strong will not be a match for him. So take solace in the fact that you will be relieved of your life tonight. You don't have to bear witness in the flesh; your soul will feed all of those hungry souls burning in hell. Demons hungry for more, just waiting to be fed, to grow stronger, to rise from the depths of the closed off realm that will soon be open."

The girl looked at him with her eyes wide, her face turning blue from the loss of oxygen, and then he loosened his grip on her. He turned, walking alongside the sling and as he passed her left leg, he let the blade slide across her thigh, almost as if an afterthought, but cutting her still. She again let out a yell of pain, wiggling around, trying to search for any sign of getting out of this sling, out of this room, and to safety. With each wiggle, each movement, she began to realize that she was securely bound and was going nowhere unless he allowed it.

He was standing positioned between her legs and as he stood there looking at her, the most angered, fierce look came over him. He laid the knife down on her belly, wrapped his arms around both of her legs and pulled her towards him as his raging hard cock slid into her. She was overcome with so much pain from his entry into her, the cuts from the knives, the blow to the head she had received in the car, and the choking of her throat. She tried not to focus on this, to hope this experience was just a dream, an atrocious dream. With each thrust into her, she became cognizant of the realness of what was happening to her. He was a large man and he had a large cock. She was trying to keep her wits about her, but it wasn't working, she was starting to give into the pain, the real never ending pain that was being inflicted on her.

Victor thrust at her wildly, and with purpose. He was turned on by the red-headed witch. He was frustrated, mad, humiliated by the male witch, and turned on by him as well. It should be one of them in this sling, taking his pain, taking his cock. Before he was finished with his duty in Tulsa, he may well have a chance to make them a part of his playground. But for the time being, this girl would do.

As he continued to thrust faster and deeper, his mind kept going back to the male witch, his powers, and his anger toward the vessel. As Victor looked down at the girl, he saw the image of the male witch lying there instead, the ball gag over his mouth. He saw the male witch's face, arms, and legs bleeding from the cuts and taking the brunt of Victor's thrusts deep inside. Victor was turned on but exacerbated, so much, in fact, that he reached over, grabbed the knife, and slammed it deep inside the abdomen of the male witch. But as he did so, he heard the gasp of a woman, the pain of the woman, the woman he had grabbed off the street. As he came to a stop, and the sling slowed in its motion, he looked down and saw the wide-eyed girl, no longer seeing the male witch laying there. It was the girl, looking upwards at him, and then she looked down again at the knife that was deep inside her stomach.

She lay there for a few seconds feeling the pain, but as the seconds continued, she began to feel nothing, to become groggy. She felt tired and wanted to drift off to sleep for a few minutes. The pain in her arm, leg, and cheek were starting to subside: yes, it was sleep she wanted. But, again, as she looked at the knife buried into her, she knew that it was not sleep coming for her, but rather death. Death by the hands of this beautiful, sick, deranged man who showed no remorse, but rather a sense of pride. As she took her last breath, that was the last image that she saw as well, the image of the man who killed her standing over her smiling with pride, smiling at his handiwork. Then she was gone.

Chapter Twenty-Eight

It was Wednesday morning and Brandy was going on almost no sleep. She had stopped at the Starbucks down the street from Alex's house and ordered herself a latte with a triple shot of espresso. There was one thing on her agenda for today and it was getting some answers as to what happened to Alex.

When Brandy was looking at him this morning as he slept soundly, she was in shock at the number of bruises that were starting to form on his body. Maybe there was some truth to what he experienced?

Brandy saw the sign of the shop she was looking for and turned into the parking lot. She jumped out of her vehicle, shutting and locking the door behind her. As she made her way to the store's front entrance, she found that she had another ten minutes before the store opened at 10:00 a.m. This was fine with Brandy as she needed to down some more of the latte that she ordered. She was still running on fumes from the previous night and if confronting Gina on what had actually happened to Alex would help her piece things together, then a confrontation it was going to be.

Something clearly happened to him and it was so traumatic that it took a long time for him to even tell her the story. He was shaking uncontrollably when she arrived at his house last night. His roommate, John, was upset over the entire thing. When she talked to him this morning, he had filled her in on some of the other things that he had experienced with Alex. It all was leading up to something big, she just couldn't figure out what.

The time moved ever so slowly as she kept looking at her watch while pacing in front of the doorway. She was somewhat relieved when she heard the lock on the door turn and saw the open sign light up in the window. Brandy took a deep breath and proceeded to enter the bookstore. The bell chimed just as it had when she was here with Alex and she saw Gina turning around with a smile to greet her. There was a look of familiarity on Gina's face as she looked at Brandy.

"Good morning and welcome to The Mind's Eye," Gina said to her. "How can I help you?"

Brandy walked over to Gina and extended her hand in an offering of respect. Gina took her hand and shook it. "My name is Brandy, I was in the other day with my friend, Alex, and we were looking for books on dreams."

Gina's smile faded slightly for a minute remembering who this woman was but in an instant she recovered herself. "Oh yes, I remember. I'm glad to see you. Have you seen Alex? How is he?"

"Well for starters, you can tell me what happened to Alex last night? I found him curled up in his bed, shaking, unable to speak, half scared out of his mind. He was talking about creatures in basements, dead people, and being thrown up against the wall by one of your friends, who only used his mind to do it?" Brandy said in one full breath wanting to get it all out.

"So you have seen Alex." She asked. "Is he okay?"

"Does it sound like what I described to you is okay?" Brandy lashed out at her. "I need some answers and I need them now. What kind of trouble did Alex get into last night, how much of his story is real, and how are you involved in all this?"

Gina, looking at Brandy seriously for a long pause finally said, "Come with me into the reading room where we can sit and talk."

Brandy reluctantly followed Gina more out of curiosity than anything, because Brandy's instincts were telling her to run, to get the hell out of there.

"You should listen to your instincts more," Gina said to Brandy, taking her a little by surprise. "Our instincts are a basic, mind memory recollection, sometimes called a gut instinct for a reason; your gut gets butterflies and your fight or flight mode kicks in. But I'm not going to hurt you and I'm not the enemy. I have been trying to help Alex find out what has been going on with his night terrors, the voices that he is hearing. He seeks answers as to why he would dream about someone's murder as it was happening."

Brandy was taking all this in, looking Gina up and down trying to figure out if she was telling her the truth.

"Whether you believe me or not doesn't really matter at this moment, what matters is how can we help him?" She said taking Brandy again by surprise.

Brandy was a bit taken aback and started to say "How the hell are you doing that? I was just…"

"Thinking it?" Gina finished her sentence. "I am a witch, Brandy, and not a bad one. I am blessed with many gifts and mind reading happens to be one that I can typically do, although it doesn't always work on everyone. Some people have a natural gift for masking their thoughts while others have learned to develop the masking as they have found a need for it."

"I'm speechless," Brandy said, fidgeting a little in her chair. "I honestly don't know what to say."

"It's okay, I understand. It takes some people an entire lifetime to believe while there are some who seek us out," she offered in an attempt to make her feel better.

"What has all of this got to do with Alex?"

"Well, that is the million dollar question, not to make light of the situation and I sure wish I had an answer for you. I'm still working on that. Alex came back to the store after you left yesterday and he told me everything. All I know right now is something is happening to Alex and whatever it is, it crossed paths with my friend Demetri last night, and, who knows, maybe even before last night."

Brandy seemed to be understanding this, soaking in the new information, but still extremely cautious. Her main priority was protecting Alex and she was still on the fence as to whether she was friend or foe.

"Alex mentioned something about a guy that kept showing up; helping him out of most of the situations he kept finding himself in. He mentioned that the guy was in a gas mask, is that your friend?" She was trying to get more information out of her, but hell, if the witch could read her mind, then she already knew why she was here.

"Well, he is not my friend, but yes, that guy was definitely the man of the hour both in a good and bad way," Gina added. "I want you to know, my friend, Demetri, was acting out of fear. I think somehow their dreams are connected and in one of them Alex was the catalyst in Demetri's dream that was hurting him. He even woke up from the dream, midair, being thrown against his bedroom wall, and walked away with a handprint burned onto his neck."

"Holy fuck," she said. "Excuse my language but this shit is getting way too real and way too sci-fi for my taste. What do you think is going on?"

Gina thought long and hard before answering, struggling between what she should keep confidential and what she should share. Alex had come back to her for a reason, but from what Gina was reading from her and her energy, she felt that Brandy was truly here to help. "I think that he has somehow gotten mixed up into something evil, his tattoos have hidden symbols in them, and his dreams are of domination and torture, of killing and of future human decimation. I fear that he may be caught up in something that he doesn't even realize. I was hoping to be able to talk to him about his past, his family, their beginnings, and their transgressions."

"I'm fucking freaking out here," Brandy said in a slightly broken voice. "To think that he has been labeled for something that has brought these powerful individuals his way, powerful individuals that have hurt him, scared him, and could kill him! How do we help him? How do we protect him?"

"I don't want anything bad to happen to him either. Unless we get the truth of the matter from him or whoever has put him down this path, I'm afraid that there may not be too much we can do for him," Gina said firmly.

"Listen, there is something you should probably know about Alex. I believe he was on some sort of chemical induced high, on some drug," She told Gina. She hoped that divulging this did not get her in trouble with Alex, but she was willing to risk it if it would help figure out what was going on.

"That would make perfect sense as to why he was unable to make the connections between what was real and what was probably a hallucination from the drugs. But, I will add there is some freaky shit that goes on down in the basement of that bar. Not too many people go down there as a novice and come back up. You have to know what you are doing and what the stakes are. If you go down there, you are risking not coming out alive. Most people who frequent it are people who are into the fetish world, or the supernatural world," Gina said probing her reaction to her last statement.

"What do you mean supernatural?" She said a little cautious and a whole lot suspicious.

"Wow, you are just getting thrown into this whole thing. The things you have heard about on television all these years, read in books, or saw in movies, most of them are real." Gina tried to start out the conversation slow and ease into it.

"Okay, that's vague, what are you referring to as being real?" Brandy questioned further.

"I'm talking about witches, ghosts, vampires, werewolves, good and evil, psychics, and telekinesis. It's all real, and that is just what we know of so far. The world, as you know, is such an amazing and mysterious place, one we are getting to know and it has so many wondrous things yet to find." She was saying to her, who looked at Gina with wide eyes and a semi smirk on her face.

"Are you telling me that Alex was correct about that basement, that these creatures were actually killing and eating people down there? Is that what you are trying to tell me?" Brandy was asking sounding somewhat on the defense.

"Look, I get it. It's a lot to take in and I don't expect you to believe me solely on this, because I know that would take a great deal of faith in a person you just met. But I am not trying to hurt him; I'm trying to help him. What I think happened to Alex, he was high on drugs when he went down there and he ran into some newly made vampires. Vampires who were a little out of control and they attacked him," she told her, trying to make a calculated guess as to what really did happen.

"I'm speechless; I don't know what to say. I don't know if you are one crazy ass woman or telling me the truth?" Brandy said honestly.

"I get it and its okay," Gina offered. "We both want the same for Alex and that is to help him, but for me to help him, I need for you to know who all the players are in this game. I need you to help me to get Alex to let me help him. I know he and Demetri didn't get off on the right foot, but Demetri really is a good man and is knee deep into whatever Alex has gotten involved in as well. Demetri was just scared and confused when he first saw him; he was the man who hurt Demetri in his dream."

"Let's just say that I believe you and I'm not really admitting that I do, just yet," Brandy questioned. "How do we go about helping someone who is seeing himself kill people in his dreams? Who is the guy in the gas mask? And who is this person Alex claims is talking to him even when he is awake?"

"I don't have an answer to any of those questions, but I can tell you I'm honestly working on it. I want to help Alex, but what scares me the most is that I have a feeling, and I'm honestly going on a gut feeling here. Alex has inadvertently been involved in this for a lifetime and doesn't even realize it," Gina said thinking back to the tattoos with all of the ancient symbolism in them. If Alex didn't ask for those to be in the tattoos then that means that someone took the liberty of adding something, more than once, to Alex's body in a permanent way.

Brandy was looking perplexed and deep in thought. She wasn't sure what she was going to do. How she was going to help Alex. What she did know, is that if what Gina was saying was true about the supernatural world, then she was way out of her league here. *How is she supposed to defend Alex from some supernatural being?*

"Well, I'm hoping that you will trust me to help you with that," Gina said catching the last part of her thoughts. "My friend and I, have been trying to find a balance for some time in the supernatural world. We have been studying it and trying to keep some semblance of order in what is sometimes an extremely chaotic hidden world."

"What do you mean?" Brandy asked.

"I don't know how to say it other than to be a hundred percent honest with you. Demetri is unique in that he is a gifted male witch. When I say gifted, I truly mean that. He is one of the most powerful witches I have ever met, even though he doesn't really consider himself a witch," Gina stated, with Brandy looking at her with a cautious eye.

"Demetri is able to move things with his mind, he is able to hear people's thoughts, much like me in that aspect, but I'm not able to move things with my mind. Both of our powers are still evolving, still being shown to us and we are both students in this supernatural world classroom and learning the rules as we go along," Gina tried to explain to her.

"Well, I have a question for you then. How are you and your friend, going to help Alex if he doesn't trust Alex, and Alex doesn't trust him?" Brandy asked in a quiet, but direct voice.

"I can talk to him, he will listen to me. Let's not forget, he is just as involved in this as Alex is. By helping Alex, he in turn is helping himself," Gina said, trying to reassure her that all would be okay.

"What can I do to help?" Brandy questioned.

"Get Alex to come back here to talk to me and once I have earned his trust back, I will invite Demetri to join us," Gina said to her, who didn't look reassured.

"If I bring him here and something happens to him, I will hurt you," Brandy warned.

"I would expect nothing less from Alex's best friend," Gina said smiling at her in a friendly way. "He is lucky to have you in his corner."

Brandy gathered herself and bid farewell to Gina. She would go back to Alex's to check on him and see if he was still sleeping it off or if he was up. She wasn't sure what to make of everything she had just heard, but there was something in Gina's voice, some conviction that drove her statements that Brandy couldn't ignore. She believed in what she was saying that much Brandy knew. If there was something or someone out there, trying to hurt Alex, she had no choice but to trust the witch to help him. Taking a deep breath, letting it out, she got into her car and started the drive back to Alex's.

Chapter Twenty-Nine

Demetri was a person who could function on little to no sleep; he could be totally charged and ready to go with about four hours of sleep. This morning was no different, but he was charged by the thought of a new player in town, extremely powerful, but not a supernatural creature. He sensed something about the masked man that was of a supernatural source, some kind of energy, some kind of push that was driving him. Demetri wasn't able to get into his thoughts last night because things happened so quickly. He was pretty damn sure this man was more than equipped to block any mind reading Demetri could throw at him.

The masked man's ability to stand up and walk through Demetri's energy force was something that just had never been accomplished before by a human being. He had been up against some powerful vampires that had been able to challenge him in the same way the man had. We are talking old vampires; some had been around for hundreds of years.

Then there was the guy from his dream bugging him today too. How could it be a coincidence that he ended up in Gina's store asking her for help? He didn't believe in coincidence, he didn't have that luxury. Things like that happen for a reason and that reason has to be the dream connection. Somehow, someway he and this man, Alex, were connected psychically. The how they were connected and why they were connected was exactly what was driving him bonkers.

He had been having so much fun hanging out with Gina last night and had worked up a sweat on the dance floor. Then all of a sudden Alex appeared out of nowhere and the night quickly turned from fun to hellish. He will admit that he may have overreacted by attacking Alex, but one had to admit he had good reason to believe he was a threat. He had been in the dream where he had woke up levitating before being thrown against the wall and let's not forget the hand mark on his neck. This fellow had been the one in the dream calling the shots. He had been the one that had attacked Demetri and had caused all the deaths of the supernatural creatures that were in the dream. Was this a foretelling, a psychic dream that was a warning of things to come.

Demetri had never even seen Alex before, unless he had seen him at the club and just not paid any attention. But he had to admit, that if he had been at the club before, he probably would have remembered him. He was a stunning man, a beautiful man covered with tattoos. There was something about him that is intensely sexual.

What the fuck am I thinking? This is a man who for the most part should be considered a threat to me and maybe even Gina. But then there was Gina, who believed in Alex, and felt that he was telling the truth; that he was caught up in something out of his control. Ugh, he was so frustrated.

Yes, Demetri was extremely frustrated and wanted some answers. He had way too much coffee already this morning and was already making a second pot when his cell phone started to ring. He picked it up and looked at it, *Gina, finally someone to talk to.*

"Hey G, what's up?" Demetri answered the phone.

"Good morning my dearest, how are you doing? Did you get any rest?" She asked, already knowing the answer.

"Um, what do you think?"

"Yes, that is what I thought. Well listen, the reason I'm calling is about last night and what happened," she started the conversation to see if it would tell her where his head was.

"I'm listening," he said in an almost too still of a voice that made her a little nervous, but she prompted onward.

133

"I had a visit this morning from a friend of Alex's, Brandy, the one who had originally come to the shop with him the first time I met him. She had lots of questions and is worried about him," Gina said.

"So, what did you tell her?" Demetri asked his voice still not where she would like it to be.

"I told her the truth Demetri, I told her everything that I know," Gina said.

"Are you freaking kidding me G? You tell a complete stranger about me, you and God knows what else?" He yelled into the phone inflamed.

"Look Demetri, I'm not an amateur at this. I got a feel for her. I read her mind to find out where she was really coming from and she was sincerely worried about Alex and wants to help figure out what is going on," Gina shot back at him.

"Well, you are not just playing with your life G; you are putting many lives in the hands of a complete stranger. Are you willing to live with that?" Demetri asked.

"When have I ever put your life in any danger, on a purposeful level? I have always tried to protect you, build you up, and support your every decision even when I didn't always agree with it. So for you to now question my loyalty and trustworthiness like this just flat ass pisses me off," Gina shot back to him in a hurt, but angry voice.

Demetri realizing that like last night, he may have jumped the gun a bit on this one and decided he had better back track. He hadn't heard her upset, this hurt in a long time. "Listen G, I'm sorry. You know I trust you. I'm just stressed out and worried about what is going on here. I don't think it's a coincidence that he came into your store that he had this man with supernatural strength protecting him. I'm just worried and you know it isn't like me to worry so much about something. Usually, I face it head on, but this one G, I just don't know about."

"Well, I'm sorry too for putting all of your dirty laundry out for a stranger to see, but I truly feel that she wants to help," she said softening.

There was a long pause on the line, and then Gina spoke again. "Why don't you come by the store, but before you do, grab me something to eat, anything actually. I'm starving. When you get here, I will read your cards and see if maybe the universe can give us some help on what is going on?"

"I think that sounds like a good idea. Listen, I'm really sorry for losing it like that, last night and today. You know I love you and I trust you; don't you?" He probed.

"I love you too, you freak show," Gina laughed into the phone.

Demetri smiled as he hung up the phone, grabbed his keys, and was out the door.

Chapter Thirty

Gina was happy to see him walking in with food in his hands and a smile on his face, even though battered and bruised from the night's events. He seemed as if he was no longer angry with her and for that she was thankful. Gina did not feel like spending the afternoon arguing with him. They needed to have a serious talk and get down to the business at hand.

Demetri walked over to Gina and gave her a kiss on the cheek. She loved how affectionate he was. Maybe being in touch with his emotions, the softer side of him was what made him such a gifted witch. It was truly possible because one has to be open to every possibility to be able to truly tap into great power. He was such a person and she knew that he had more power than any other witch she knew, living or deceased.

Often times, he would work with her on charging and cleansing crystals, meditating with her, learning to become one with the universe. She truly believes that it has helped him greatly to be at peace with himself and some of the demons of his past. He used to be quite the hellion. He was always getting into trouble when they were younger, not intentionally, but rather out of curiosity. He had a natural curiosity for things unknown, unseen. He had always been drawn to the supernatural side of the universe.

Through meditation, he had learned to calm himself, to clear his mind, and with that stillness, he was able to make his first contact with the other side. She remembered how excited he was to be able to communicate with the spirit. With further practice, he developed the ability to tap into other people's thoughts. Gina had learned that many years ago with the help of her grandmother.

What he was capable of no one knew yet. He was a brilliant witch thus far, but she knew that he had much more in store. It would probably be a continuous evolution of powers. She knew herself, having absorbed her families' Wiccan powers upon their deaths, had more power that she too had yet to tap into. It was a game of learning, of waiting, and of anticipation. They were still young; they had a long life ahead of them. So far it had been fairly adventurous, but she could feel, could sense somehow that they had just brushed the surface of what was to come.

As he was eating, he peered over at the center of the table and picked up a picture that was lying on top of a stack of pictures. "Hey, what's this?" He asked.

Gina knowing she couldn't avoid him or lie to him as he had always been able to tell when she was honest with him. "It's a picture of the symbol that is tattooed on the back of his neck?"

"Interesting," Demetri stated casually. "Does he worship the devil?"

"Why would you say such a thing?" Gina said flustered while grabbing the picture from his hands. "And, no, he doesn't worship the devil any more than you do."

He let it go for now, but found it quite interesting indeed. There was a nagging in his gut telling him he needed to keep an eye out on this one.

After they had finished eating, she told him that she wanted to read his cards. Tarot was a practice of reading what one's energy was putting out, it wasn't a foretelling of the future, per se', but more of where you stand at this moment. Demetri always agreed to let her read him when she asked. She often wondered if it was more of an indulgence on his part because he loved her so much he didn't want to hurt her feelings. You see, just because he was a witch, it by no means meant that he used all of the practices that a typical Wiccan would use.

Gina spent a few minutes burning some sage, smudging as it was called, cleansing the area around the reading room. This was probably her favorite room in the entire store. It had such a wonderful energy about it, people got lost in there while reading books, people opened themselves up to magical worlds in there, to new experiences, new hopes and dreams. It was exactly the type of place that she had hoped to build when she opened the store.

After finishing the smudging ritual, she put four candles on the table, two to the left and two to the right. She was seated on one side of the table with Demetri directly across from her. The candles were on each side of them. She had lit some incense which contained frankincense and myrrh. As she closed her eyes, concentrating on clearing her mind, silencing her thoughts, she begins to focus on the candles. An image of all four candles formed in her mind and as she sank deeper into the silence, she began to picture that the candles, one by one, would ignite. As he sat watching Gina, watching her prepare, he smiled proudly when he saw each candle, one at a time, ignite with fire, a soft burning flame to the wick.

"Clear your mind. Try to focus your thoughts on the here and now." She told him, giving him a few minutes to concentrate on the task at hand.

She then handed him the deck of tarot cards and asked him shuffle the deck. As he held the cards in one hand, he would grab some of the stack and quickly placed them forward, backward, and in the middle in an attempt to shuffle the large deck of cards. He had thought about using his powers to shuffle the cards but didn't want to unduly influence them.

He laid the deck down in front of him and looked at her.

"Now close your eyes and think of a question. When you have a question in your mind, I want you to reach out and cut the deck of cards," Gina instructed.

138

He had his eyes closed as he thought carefully about what he wanted, no, needed this reading to reveal to him. There were so many things he could ask, but what was really playing on his mind was what the overall meaning of the dream he had was? *Was it about an internal struggle for him or was there an evil coming that he should be prepared for?*

Taking in a deep breath, eyes still closed, he focused on his question. *Reveal to me whether or not I will be able to handle what is coming in the very near future.* Once he had cut the deck she took the stack and laid out three cards, left to right on the table in front of her.

As Gina grabbed the first card and turned it over it revealed The Tower, which is regarding the past. She didn't look surprised at all to see this card turned over. She began to explain the possible meaning of it.

"The Tower represents the struggle within us all, the positive and the negative, the reality of self, versus what we don't want to see in ourselves. Sometimes wisdom and enlightenment come easily like a calm wind. For most wisdom is blocked, building ever so slightly upon itself, wanting to free itself, manifest itself until there is nothing left. It comes crashing onto us as would water from a breaking dam drowning everything in its path, including the person with whom the wisdom was intended. The Tower card is about energy, it is closely related to The Death card because of its destructive power." Gina kept speaking trying to reveal what the card's function is and trying to get the meaning to reveal itself.

"One has to be open to change, to accept that sometimes things we were told, deep-rooted familial beliefs become outdated. Instead of hanging onto them with clenched fists, we need to be more open to the possibility of change. We can't allow ourselves to hold out for something or someone as our only means of security, we must allow ourselves to be open to the power and energy of the soul and the mind. We must realize that they hold far greater power and wisdom than any one physical object. For when we believe that the object gives us power, gives us wisdom and strength, we allow ourselves to build a foundation that is not sturdy enough to hold us up. It will collapse upon itself when the weight of the falsehoods come crashing down upon us."

"The lesson to be learned here is that when we accept this fall that we are vulnerable, not invincible, we are shown the true wisdom and power of our soul and mind. But for most people, they would see this as a negative that the world was against them and not truly encapsulate the gift that is being shown here. When we allow the fall of the Tower, when we truly accept it for what it is and the lesson is learned, we allow our ego to go with it. We allow our true power and our wisdom to flood our lives, to make us into a better human being." Gina said, looking at him, watching his face, his emotions as he took all this in.

As she reached for the middle card, she turned it over to reveal The Devil card. They looked at each other and then back at the card. Considering that the previous card was regarding ego and building up of emotions, it wasn't totally surprising to Gina this card showed up, but she could see his growing uneasiness, yet trudged onward.

"Well," she started, "The Devil card is a commonly misunderstood card as it refers to the negativity each person has in their own body and soul. People like to blame the Devil when something bad happens or when someone does something so horrible, but this card is more about what was intrinsically inside one's self. The first card, The Tower, was about not letting ego interfere with us learning life's lessons. It was about us gaining wisdom. Well, The Devil card, tries to hide that wisdom from us, it wants to pervert that wisdom, show us something that isn't actually wisdom at all. It lets it manifest within our soul, lets it devour us like a malignant cancer eating away at us. When you allow this cancer to take hold, you are allowing your inner Devil, your negativity, to take hold of every aspect of your life. You allow your powers, your intuition, and your control to be bound to the darkness, to become a force of evil."

140

Gina was watching him as she explained the possible meaning behind the card; she could sense that he was inwardly bothered by it.

"Demetri, the good thing about this, just like the first card, is that the power lies within you. You control your own destiny. You control your choices and whether you will be used for a force of good or a force of evil. Lots of times when this card shows up in someone's reading, it is because they feel they are not in control of their life. There is a loss of hope or in one's own abilities. Since this card showed up in the present, I think that it could give meaning about what happened last night, someone challenged you, someone strong, and he appeared to be human. I think that bothers you because you have not met someone in a long time that you couldn't beat; this has maybe bruised your ego a bit. This is a perfect time for a life lesson, to not take your powers for granted. Sometimes there will be times of victory and sometimes there will be times of defeat. The fact that you keep getting back up to fight again, and you keep looking for the good in all beings, human or supernatural, is a wonderful trait. Don't let last night knock you off your path Demetri, but rather let it remind you we all have moments when we doubt ourselves. Know that inside you are good, there is heart, and there is compassion."

Gina waited to see what reaction he had to this before she went on, but she saw no significant change. His brow was still raised slightly, still stern looking.

"Let's see what the last one has to say," he prompted her on.

Gina nodded and decided that he was as ready as he was going to be for the next one. She was just hoping that it wasn't something horrific. Clearing her mind she brought herself back to a centeredness of spirit and calm. She reached over the table and turned the third card. The third card represents the future. She took a deep breath inward when she turned over The Magician.

Gina thought about this turn of events. She thought about the previous two cards, their possible meanings and

141

what has happened over the past week. Gina then proceeded to explain the meaning and significance of this card, even though she wasn't sure if it meant what she was inwardly thinking or not.

"The Magician, which is a representation of the number one, an infinite number, is a powerful card in itself. He can transform himself; manipulate the basic elements of nature and life. His powers are believed to be of a divine nature that he is a conduit for a higher power that commands the entire earth. The Magician is a master of illusion, his powers coming from outside of himself and he is defenseless without them. Maybe, because in your dream Alex was able to defeat you and your powers were useless against him. You felt a basic need to lash out at him when you first saw him at the club last night?" She was making a statement, not really expecting him to answer back.

When he just nodded at her and didn't respond she continued on. "If one were to look at modern depictions of a Magician, you will, usually, find one or more symbols of infinity. The snake eating its tail and the horizontal figure-eight being some of the most common, which lends one to believe in his limitless powers. One of the most impressive things about the Magician is that even if his worldly powers are taken away or destroyed, he will never truly be defenseless. Because he has will, which can never be contained or destroyed? The Magician is both positive and negative; he builds and he destroys. He knows what has to be done and why. Wishing is not enough; one must decide to make things change. He is a force of creation and destruction, with wisdom and confidence he can be a powerful force for good. You are what you set your mind to be."

Gina looked at him and saw his deep introspection, lost in thought. "I think the message here, especially regarding your future is that as long as you act out of true wisdom, not out of ego, your future is limitless. You can be whatever you want to be. Your greatest power is you."

Demetri looked up at her and smiled at her in a sincere, heartfelt way. He had an emotional look about him

142

and she truly felt for him at that moment. "My grandfather always told me, no matter what I did in life, no matter what path life took me down, to never forget to be humble. Never let another man lead me down a path I knew wasn't right," he said, his eyes watery, but not yet crying. "So if I understand the cards correctly, in the past I have been driven by ego, but by letting that go I am letting in true wisdom?"

Gina nodded her head in agreement. "That is what I took from it as well."

"As for my present, I am going to be tested and tempted, between good and evil. A seduction game, of what is right and what is wrong. If I stay strong, remember I have the power to make up my own mind, and then no matter how big the temptation, I can come out on the other side a stronger, whole person?" He summarized his understanding of the card and once again Gina nodded her head in agreement.

"As for the future, there are going to be forces at play that will allow me to tap into truly great power, we still have much yet to uncover. But instead of it being truly about the power, it becomes more about my will power. How I will handle the conflicts that are coming and I think we both know that there is something coming?" He stated staring at the cards that lay out before him.

"You amaze me," Gina stated. "Your understanding of yourself is outstanding. You were raised in a good, wholesome family, one that worked hard and understood sacrifice. You remember your family values and yes, you have had opportunities to be ego driven, to be seduced by your own ego, but I have never seen that. You always come from your core family values and a belief that people are inherently good, that a particular thing happens for reason, that all life is fragile and has meaning."

He was looking at her and was truly moved by how well his best friend knew him. She knew his family and knew what truly great people they were. "So what's next?" He asked. "Where do we go from here Willow?"

Just as the last word left his lips, the flames of the candles shot up at least a foot burning brighter and hotter than they ever should have. Demetri's eyes were wide with amazement and he looked at Gina, who was equally in awe. "That is some trick; how are you doing it?" He asked her.

"It's not me. I am not doing that," she said in a cracking voice.

The air in the room became dense, warm and as they watched the flames burn hotter and brighter. They saw the candles were starting to burn down faster, the wax of the candles spilling over onto the table.

Then a voice came forth, as if from the flames themselves. "My dear boy, I have told you that the time is coming near, the wait will soon be over. You are destined for greatness; you will be a warrior among men, a leader of hell's army. Angels will fear you and all of earth shall know your name as you stand by my side."

They were both on their feet backing away from the table where the candles were still burning hotter than a furnace at this moment. "Who the hell are you and what do you want with me?" Demetri asked the voice, wishing he had a face to put it with.

"I have told you before, I am not of your realm, but I am everything. I am your fear, your desires, your wants and needs; I can make everything you ever desired come true. With you by my side we will rule earth together, you being the second most powerful being next to me," the voice said.

"Who are you? Why won't you answer me?" He asked of the voice.

"You know who I am; it's just that your mind hasn't connected with the memory of your soul. We have actually fought together, side by side, more than three thousand years ago and we will do it again, this time without failure, without defeat. You are at the most powerful stage you have ever been with your powers in millenniums and I am growing stronger as well. Together we shall defeat all who stand before us, who do not kneel before us," the voice was saying. "The forces are at work to reunite us and it will be a glorious day. When your Blue Moon is full in the sky, you will know me again. You will

144

remember our strength together. You will remember the name Bastiquil."

As the voice said the name, Bastiquil, out loud, Demetri fell to the ground, broken flashes of memories flooding his mind. He saw an ancient world long ago, a world where it felt evil ruled, where bodies were piled high, the war was raging. He saw images of a beautiful man, one that had a powerful command about him, a powerful presence. The man walked the earth, as if a king, but with the wave of his hand people were falling dead. Demetri's body shook and convulsed with these memories flooding his brain. Gina was at his side trying to help him, to hold his body still while it continued to convulse.

"That's right, remember, remember it all, and remember me." Bastiquil continued his assault on Demetri.

As he lay there, memory after memory hit his brain, some were almost too painful to watch, but he was not in control. He was still in the ancient world, watching the beautiful man wreaking havoc on the people and there was another man walking just slightly behind him, but still with him. He was a familiar man to Demetri, but how could that be? Demetri knew that these images were of thousands of years ago. This voice was playing tricks on him; he was trying to get him to believe in something that wasn't truly there to remember.

"Demetri, even I can't make you remember something that isn't already there. I told you, your soul contains the memories, the brain is just the conduit in which the connection is made for you," the voice said reasoning.

As the assault of images flashed on, Bastiquil said the name "Zamaranum" and at that moment, Demetri could make out that the familiar man was actually him. He suddenly felt the connection; he felt the oneness with Zamaranum. Tears were streaming down his cheeks as he remembered. As they continued to overwhelm him, he begins to struggle, he screamed out in pain, in anger, in frustration. Then, just as quickly as they came to him, they were gone.

145

He lay on the floor, Gina at his side, his head pounding, his heart racing. He felt that he had a complete grasp of the meaning of the Tarot card reading. It was telling him of this moment in time, the past him. This voice was his temptation and it was a strong one, and the future, this Blue Moon that the voice referred to would be his triumph or his undoing.

The flames were gone, as were the candles. They had melted down to nothing other than wax spilled on the table. He felt himself get nauseous. He wanted to throw up, wanted to be sick because it would feel much better than having these thoughts, these memories of a time long gone in his head. This couldn't be happening, but he knew that it was. The dream, everything was starting to come together. It still made no sense, but he at least saw a correlation in them now.

Things were set in motion the voice had told him. One thing Demetri knew, one thing he felt deep within, is that this thing that is coming was not coming in peace. He was destruction, he was evil, and he was from the depths of hell. Bastiquil, yes the name sounded familiar to him now, but it was a memory of the past, of thousands of years ago. How could that be? How could he make that connection in this time, in this age?

He knew that this was real. He felt it, deep inside him he knew the voice, Bastiquil, was telling the truth. He was coming, he was a force of great power and evil and he wanted Demetri to join him once again, to reclaim a time long ago when they ruled the land. But was it actually a ruling of the land, or was it an annihilation?

In the distance, he could make out another voice, another familiar voice calling to him. It was getting closer to him, yelling his name, telling him to wake up. He then realized that it was Gina. She was holding him in her arms on the floor, crying, trying to get him to open his eyes to wake up. He then saw her, looking at him, holding him. She begins to smile through the tears and leaning down, she kissed his forehead.

"Please tell me you are okay?" She was pleading with him.

"Other than this splitting headache and a voice that was over three thousand years old wanting to have a family reunion with me, I'm great." He smiled at her, trying to make light of the situation.

"You scared the shit out of me. I thought this thing had taken you, was trying to possess you." She said picturing in her head the images of Demetri flailing around on the floor, grabbing his head, screaming in pain all the while candles bursting with flames. She was convinced it was demonic possession or, at the very least, he was having a seizure that was lasting way too damned long.

"Well, I don't think you are far from the truth. He definitely wants me alright. Seems like we may have a bit of history together."

"History, what are you talking about?" She said in a panicked voice. "You know he can't be trusted. He was more than likely lying to you."

"Well, I can tell you that, yes, he can't be trusted, but I don't think he was lying," He said to her in a reflective voice. "Help me up and I will tell you what I saw."

Chapter Thirty-One

Demetri was in the Jeep driving towards Kansas City, Missouri, just a few short hours after his Tarot reading. He had a bad feeling about what he had seen. It appeared so real to him and even though he knew he lived his life by the truth and that anything is possible, he was still struggling. He was struggling with the fact that he has a soul that has crossed millenniums, one that has been reincarnated over and over for this special moment in time, for the rebirth of this Bastiquil.

The images he had seen were so damn real, he even felt the emotions, the power that came with them. People feared this Bastiquil, but for some reason Demetri did not, at least in the visions he hadn't. *So what could all this mean? Was his soul a time traveler, a soul destined to be aligned with this man, this demon of destruction? Why had he felt so comfortable with him? He had almost felt some sort of love for him in the visions.*

Poor Gina, she had been left behind to find whatever research she could on Bastiquil. He wasn't quite sure what type of information, if any, she would find about a three-thousand-year-old tyrant. A demon, which lived off the killing of innocent people who would not conform to his will. There was that word again, will. The cards had talked about Demetri's will that he would have to choose between the good and evil, the right and wrong. He felt he had been doing this all of his life and like anyone else in life, he had made mistakes. For the most part he tried to be the best man he could be, the man his father and grandfather would be proud of.

Passing Joplin, Demetri had already merged onto Hwy 71 headed to Kansas City. Demetri was always stunned to see how a town like Joplin had already rebuilt itself from the devastation and destruction that was brought down upon it by the tornados of 2011. There was a huge hospital that was being built just off of Interstate 44 that was close to being finished. The perseverance and strength of the human race was astounding.

It was about 7:00 p.m. and Demetri was deep in thought. He loved this drive. There was such green, lush foliage of pastures with windbreaks of trees followed by more open pasture. All of which would typically be well on its way to turning brownish by the August heat and drought of the summers past, but this summer had been much milder. It had rained a lot and the temperatures only reached over 100 degrees a couple of times in July. The farmers in this region of the country were unusually lucky.

The miles of this road were lined with farmhouse after farmhouse with old rustic barns and the occasional pond or a random windmill. It reminded him so much of home, not his Tulsa home, but his hometown of Braggs. Demetri loved seeing all the old silos and old barns that were still left on some of the farms along the road. It took him back to his youth, when he and his cousin Deanna would play at their great-grandfathers farm which had many silos. They would sneak into them when they were near empty, some grain still lining the bottoms. Looking upwards inside them was a spooky experience, but even at a young age, Demetri was drawn to the thrill of being scared, of believing in ghosts, witches, and other creatures of the night.

Deanna and Demetri would often laugh and run around in the silo when they would see mice running around under the grain. There wasn't that initial scare for them that most people had of mice. They were creatures put on this earth for a reason. Maybe it was a childhood thing and when you grow into adulthood you have less tolerance for things such as mice, but while they were young, they loved most things. Of course, things like snakes and scorpions were not some of Demetri's favorite things. Man, he remembered the numerous scorpion stings he received as a child growing up in the country. Living in a brick home, scorpions loved the coolness, the darkness brick and rock brought to the foundation of a home, the earth underneath it.

Deanna and Demetri had been close growing up and yet somehow they had let life and time distance them, but he still remembered her fondly. They would run into each other from time to time at reunions or the Christmas breakfast that were annual events for his family. Demetri made every effort to attend these events when he was in town and not traveling. He wanted to keep as much of a connection with his family as possible. He loves his family and cherishes the strong connection with them.

Demetri passed a green sign along the road that said Kansas City was just 49 miles ahead. He was so deep in thought that he didn't even realize that he had been clocked by a police officer who was behind him now with lights flashing. Demetri pulled over to the side of the road, pulled out his driver's license, insurance verification card, and vehicle registration knowing that the police officer would ask for them anyway. The police officer approached the passenger's side of the Jeep and indeed did ask for them. The officer asked him if he had realized he was going eleven miles over the speed limit. Instead of making up excuses, he just apologized to the officer and said he would slow it down. It seems they were doing a project where an airplane was clocking the drivers and radioing down the speed of the car as police officers were pulling over cars one after the other.

Man, he thought, it won't be long till we will be clocked by satellites telling us we are driving too fast. The officer was a nice man and informed him of something he didn't know about Missouri law. One cannot drive in the left-hand lane unless you are passing another vehicle and according to the plane he was driving in the left lane for some time and not passing a vehicle. He laughed to himself, which he shouldn't have because he should have been paying more attention to what was happening around him, but he didn't even realize that he was in the left lane. Of course, he received a citation and a warning to slow down. He smiled at the police officer and bid him a good day. Then he was off again on his right lane drive to Kansas City.

His thoughts turned to an old friend of his. Adalrik Ostergaard, Aldrik for short, was a longtime friend of Demetri's. They had met years ago when Demetri was tracking down a rogue vampire who was on a killing spree. He had come upon Aldrik in Kansas City during this particular job and there was an instant connection. He had, in fact, helped Demetri track down the vampire, but in the end he had not wanted him to kill the young vampire, but to let him deal with it instead. Demetri had not argued with him about it, but felt a strong respect for the man. He was so composed, so eloquent, so wise that he was more in awe of him and did not feel the need to challenge him.

Adalrik Ostergaard was born March 26, 484 AD. At fifteen-hundred-plus-years-old, he was the oldest vampire that Demetri has yet to come across. He was a wise, beautiful man. He was Nordic and was born in a small fishing community in Sweden that made their living by fishing the Baltic Sea. He was a striking man with small, crisp features, a strong Nordic look to him, especially his profile. He had a rusty blond color to his hair. His body was surprisingly chiseled, with the striations of his muscles, his veins showing slightly through his tight skin. He had a broad chest, tight small waist, and muscular arms. His eyes must have been naturally blue, but now they glowed a beautiful blue color one could get lost in. He had to have been in top notch shape when he died and been reborn a vampire. Aldrik walked this world for fifteen hundred years looking the same, never changing.

He called Aldrik to ask him if he was available and still in Kansas City; Aldrik has always been more than gracious about receiving his call and had told him he was more than welcome to come. One didn't want to surprise a vampire with a drop-in visit, especially one that is as old and powerful as

Aldrik. Even as old as he was, he was still such a modern man but yet full of tradition. He loved technology, loved music, loved to watch and be around people. Demetri believed that is why he was so drawn to Kansas City; it was so full of life and culture. When he would visit Aldrik, he always met him in the same place each time. It was in the Crown Plaza shopping district. He loved to walk around watching the people and he often would go up into one of the many towers that the buildings in the area had around them and watch people for hours. He had hearing like no other and could hear even the quietest of conversations on the streets below.

He lived in a penthouse condo in Townsend Place, which overlooked Crown Plaza, buying out the entire top floor which consisted of four condos and renovating them into one place. It ended up being around a ten-thousand square foot immaculate place, full of world art, and of course, tinted windows. The man is extremely wealthy and even though Demetri felt he had come by his money legitimately, he never asked where it came from, quite honestly, he didn't care. After fifteen hundred years, you would think a person would have earned some decent money; at least that should be one of the perks of being quasi-immortal.

Demetri knew Aldrik was a brilliant man and a business man. When he had stayed overnight with him on past occasions, he would often find Aldrik up at night, sitting at his office chair in his study trading stocks on the computer. Aldrik told him it kept him in touch with life, the pulse of life. Business and industry was something that Aldrik has witnessed firsthand boom from small at first into a massive expansion of growth, taking over the world. Now business and industry is even in outer space. He often wondered what Aldrik thoughts on such matters and he hoped one day they could have that conversation to hear his point of view.

Chapter Thirty-Two

Gina's mind was racing as she continued to read over the notes that she had written down from Demetri's recanting of the visions he saw. She truly thought he was having a seizure or something. It was scary shit. This was truly mind blowing, but the more she thought about it, the more it started to make a little sense. He was one of, if not the most powerful witches she had ever encountered. His powers could be linked to his soul. If his soul has reincarnated for at least three thousand years, it is no wonder he is able to do the things he is capable of doing.

This Bastiquil was a curious turn of events. He and Demetri ruled over the land over three thousand years ago? Bastiquil wanted to rejoin Demetri to reclaim what they had lost so many years ago; she tried to wrap her brain around it. *Think outside of the box*, she told herself. Find this Bastiquil and you will find the answer. Google searches turned up little. Bastiquil is a mythical creature that people from olden times believed in. There was no real hard evidence recorded, or at least none that Google could find. *She was missing something here. What was it? Think Gina, think. The Book of Shadows, maybe, just maybe it would have something. If not her mothers, then maybe her grandmother's would have something?* But, just as she had feared, it turned up nothing. Frustrated, she yelled out, letting her frustration go by expressing her anger out loud, to herself and to the universe.

Refocus yourself, center yourself, stop thinking about it being Demetri and think about how you would go about helping someone else in this situation. He had gone to talk to Aldrik to see if he would be of some use. She didn't like the idea of him leaving, they needed to be together, to protect each other, but she knew he needed to go there to talk to him. She let it go, put it out of her mind. She decided to switch gears.

Where was the link to Alex? There had to be something that linked the two. As she was running various scenarios through her head, she started to make additional notes. The notes she had taken when Alex had been in were intriguing as he too had been visited by a man showing him visions. This could not be a coincidence; it was so close to what Demetri was talking about. *But what could Bastiquil want with Alex? He was very clear in what he said to Demetri, he wanted to remake what they had all those millennium ago.* As she was thinking, she wrote down Bastiquil's name on the center of a piece of paper. Then she wrote Demetri's name to the left just below it and Alex's name to the right just below it.

Bastiquil was the common denominator, but what was the question? What was the purpose of all of this? What was the end game? She was missing it; it felt like it was staring her right in the face and she just wasn't seeing it. "Come on, do your thing. Help these boys figure this out, before they end up killing each other," she said out loud.

Both had been having dreams, both had been visited by Bastiquil, who may or may not be a ghost, a demon even. If it was a ghost that would be so much easier to deal with, but if it ended up being a demon, well that was another story.

As Gina was thinking, she was getting more and more frustrated by the minute. It was late, and she was exhausted. She put another pot of coffee on and made this one strong, jet fuel as Demetri's grandmother called it. She laughed to herself at this. She was delirious, tired, and extremely frustrated. As she was waiting for the coffee to finish brewing, she was thinking about connections. Were the three of them all connected? She was scribbling on the notebook paper hoping to come up with a clue to something, anything.

She heard the coffee maker on the counter shut off indicating that her jet fuel coffee was ready. As she looked down at the paper, her mouth dropped open. *Shit*, she thought. *Is that it? Could it be that?* Gina felt like she had finally been given a glimmer of hope and it was all from frustrated scribbling, doodling on a piece of paper. When she looked at it, she was thinking to herself why she hadn't thought of this before. While she was scribbling on the paper, frustrated, looking for answers to this, her subconscious was busy at work, behind the scenes trying to help and it paid off. When she looked at the paper, she was looking at the symbol, the one she had seen twice now. Alex had it tattooed on the back of his neck and it was secretly embedded into the tattoo on his penis.

Gina started to think back on the pictures she had taken of Alex and his tattoos. She pulled them up on the computer after inserting the flash drive she had saved them on. One by one they begin to pop up on the computer, tattoo after tattoo. They were beautifully done, so detailed, so intricate, he was so beautiful. *Geez Gina, stop that; you need to be helping this man not lusting after him.*

Gina pulled up the tattoo of the symbol on Alex's neck. It was definitely an old world looking symbol, something you would see in Egyptian hieroglyphics, something on the inside walls of the pyramids. She clicked on the picture and hit the print button and started printing the symbol. As she waited, she decided to pull up the other image. She searched through the pictures, once again, she found herself blushing, chastising herself for lusting after this man when he had come to her for help. *He was so damn gorgeous.*

She was looking at the pictures of the tattoo on his penis. This one, in particular, that she knew when magnified almost two hundred percent, would show the symbol much better than the other views. When the other image finished printing, she went ahead and printed this one. She picked up the image of the symbol from his neck and was pondering over it. This was the answer, she knew it. Deep within her gut, she knew if she could find the meaning of it, the answer to

155

what this symbol was, then she would be closer to being able to figure out what Bastiquil was up to. *Why he was, doing this and how are we going to stop him?*

Gina then had another thought. She remembered something she had written in her notes when Alex was there. Flipping through them, she came to the page that she was looking for. *"Yes, here it is,"* she thought to herself. Alex had said he had not done all of his tattoos himself, but he did say that he had dreamed most of them. Some he had inked himself, but the others were done at the hands of someone else.

Gina went back to the computer and began to click on the various images of the tattoos she had taken of Alex. As she did, she enlarged them all by two hundred percent. She began to move them around on the screen of the computer, searching, looking for any sign of that symbol. It didn't take long to find it. There it was embedded into the pupil of the giant troll looking creature that was tattooed on his side and part of his abdomen. She clicked on that section to print it out. Then she moved on to the next tattoo. One after the other she begins to find the symbol in every tattoo, subtlety hidden within the tattoos, but there none the less.

Gina was frantically printing image after image. There were just a few tattoos on Alex that she was not able to find any sign of the symbol and she logically deduced that those had been the ones Alex had done himself. Gina was getting an overwhelmingly bad feeling. *There was a huge deception going on here. Someone had deliberately put these into his tattoos. Why though, what was the reasoning and who? This had to be it. This had to be the answer. Alex had dreamed the first one and the hidden versions had been put into his other tattoos without his knowledge. Someone had deliberately put them there. Why would someone do that? It had to be the meaning of the symbol.*

The original symbol on Alex's neck was the best picture, the clearest. She pulled it back up on the computer and opened up a search application, one that would search the internet for any picture or symbol that was selected. It went through many databases that are compiled around the world.

She felt that if anything was going to give a link to the answers of what was going on with Alex and Demetri it would be this symbol and the meaning behind it. Gina could recognize some of the individual symbols within the tattoo, but she didn't have a clue as to the meaning of the compilation of symbols. She selected the picture, uploaded it into the search engine and pressed enter.

The computer went into search mode and hundreds of pictures started flashing through the filter of the program. She decided to get up and grab that coffee that she had brewed just awhile ago. She definitely needed it as she felt this was going to be a long night.

Chapter Thirty-Three

The sun had almost fully disappeared as Demetri made his way into Kansas City. The city was lit up with the night lights of a bustling city. As he exited onto Swope Avenue headed towards the Plaza, he was starting to get an excited feeling. It had been a while since he had seen Aldrik and he was starting to get that feeling he always got around him. It felt like a high school crush or meeting your favorite rock star for the first time. But he knew that it would be like it always was, they would pick up where they left off, like there had been no time or distance between them.

As he turned onto Main Street, headed towards Broadway Street and 46th Street where the Townsend Place condos were located, he drove past the Cheesecake Factory and just happened to look up at the tower. It was the highlight feature of the building across the street, the one he knew Aldrik liked to frequent. He could nonchalantly be above the crowd, watching and listening but still far enough away that he wasn't in the mix of the crowd. He was not surprised at all when he looked up and saw Aldrik in the tower, looking down his way. He had never been able to get anything over on Aldrik.

He was thinking to himself as he was trying to find a spot to park his Jeep. *There was something comforting in knowing there was a man, ancient and powerful, as powerful as he was and who cared for him the way Aldrik did.*

Aldrik had offered to turn him into a vampire once and he had politely turned him down. There was a slight appeal with the immortality gig, especially with someone as wonderful as Aldrik. But he wasn't sure he was ready to die, even if it was to be reborn into a new creature, one with powers like his own, but different as well. He wasn't even sure if he would have his same powers if he were turned. There was so much uncertainty about it. He was just not ready to entertain the thought, but he knew Aldrik would ask him again when the time was right. The only thing he didn't know was if he would take him up on it the next time he offered.

As he parked the Jeep, locked the door, and headed down the sidewalk towards the tower where he knew Aldrik was waiting for him, the nerves disappeared as excitement set in. The stress of the past week melted away and all he could think of was that wonderful, amazing man that stood up in the tower, watching, waiting for him. Demetri made his way to the back entrance of the building, back where there were no prying eyes. With little effort, he concentrated on the dead bolt lock on the gate and with a flick of his wrist it turned and unlocked. He rushed inside and quickly locked the gate back behind him.

Running up the flight of stairs to the second floor while staying clear of the restaurant that leased part of the second floor, he found the place in the ceiling where there was a spot cut out for a pull-down attic ladder. Within a few minutes, he was crawling out the window in the attic, onto the ceramic tiled rooftop. Using his hand to steady himself, he walked up to the tower where he saw Aldrik standing there, looking at him.

His smile brightened as he laid eyes upon Aldrik. He was as beautiful as he remembered him being. As he stepped inside the tower, he was face to face with Aldrik. Not missing a beat, Aldrik grabbed him by the waist and pulled him close. Reaching up and placing a hand behind his neck, Aldrik pulled him into a kiss, one that he didn't realize he had been longing for since the last time he had seen Aldrik.

159

There was no denying the love between the two men, the common respect, and the safety of each other's arms. When he was with him, he felt as if the world melted away and all that was left was the two of them. He was used to being a strong, independent man, but when it came to Aldrik, he knew that he was his weakness. Actually, make that one of his three weaknesses. His family was one, Gina was the second, and Aldrik was the third.

As he stood there lost in the kiss of this beautiful man, he could think of nothing else. The world disappeared and all that mattered at that moment was this man and this kiss. Demetri held nothing back, he kissed him with a passion, with love, feeling his tongue touch his, sucking on Aldrik's bottom lip. It was in this moment that he knew he could stay with this man forever.

Forever had a tricky way of catching up with you too. He had come here in a panic. To see if this man, this vampire who was the oldest one he had met to date, could offer him any insight into what was happening to him back in Tulsa. Outside of Gina, Aldrik was the closest person to him and he trusted him with supernatural matters completely. His heart was another matter.

As he tried to speak, to tell Aldrik why he had come, he was surprised when Aldrik put his finger to Demetri's lips and shook his head. He was signaling to him that he wasn't ready for conversation. He knew if Aldrik had wanted to, he could have swept himself and Demetri from that tower to his penthouse condo in a matter of seconds. Aldrik was always one that played on the side of caution when it came to humans. He tried to not use his powers in such a manner that could be seen by the regular public. Aldrik liked his life here in Kansas City and didn't want to do anything that would jeopardize it.

As they made their way down to the street much in the same fashion that he had gotten up there, Aldrik continued his hold on Demetri. He held his hand the entire walk to the condo. When they were in the elevator on the way up to his penthouse, Aldrik once again was kissing his lips.

He could not believe that he still felt this way about this man. He hadn't even gotten a full sentence out yet, but here he was entering Aldrik's condo, kissing his lips, holding his hand. The troubles of the past week, the attack the previous night, meant nothing at this moment. The only thing that mattered was this man before him, this beautiful man, this man that had such a hold on him like no other before.

Aldrik led him into his huge master bedroom that had an oversized four poster bed; it must have been custom made since it was far larger than a king size bed. Aldrik began to take off his clothes, one piece at a time, looking at him as if he were the last person on earth. But it was a look of pure longing, of caring. He had no fear of Aldrik, he trusted him with his life. Even when he had turned down Aldrik when he offered to turn him into a vampire so that they could spend an eternity together, he still had no fear of him. It wasn't what you would think either, yes, if he needed to protect himself from Aldrik he would be able to do it, but it was a much deeper understanding between the two of them. They both held a mutual respect for the other, both compelling men and both equally passionate for the other.

When Aldrik stood before him, clothes lying on the floor, he eased himself up onto the bed, crawling up onto it backwards, never taking his eyes off him. He lay on the bed, his nude tight body exposed, and his cock hard and longing for Demetri to join him on the bed. Vampires may be creatures of the night, considered the undead, but the misconception that they are cold blooded killers with no room for love and compassion was incorrect. They are able to love more so than any human because they feel with all their senses on high alert at all times.

Demetri hadn't realized just how much he had missed him until he saw him, exposed, longing for Demetri, showing him the passion he still held for him. He didn't care what anyone thought about this, not even Gina. He was as worthy as anyone else to have love, passion, longing, and sex in his life as the next person.

He started to remove his own clothing. When he was fully unclothed, he climbed up onto the bed and laid himself across Aldrik's body. He began kissing him again, their tongues touching, their lips sucking on the others. Their hands were moving over each other's body, exploring, feeling, getting to know the others body again. It was just seconds till their hard cocks were touching each other's, both showing their love and passion for the other, both powerful in their own right.

Demetri's lips were kissing their way down Aldrik's neck. His tongue made a trail down to his nipples, where he flicked his tongue playfully over them making him moan with pleasure, and causing him to arch his back up off the bed as if he had just shocked him. Both were in pure ecstasy and both wanted so much to please the other.

He continued his journey down Aldrik's body until he had made his way to his cock. He ran his tongue over the length of it, lingering at the head of his cock. Aldrik once again was moaning in ecstasy. He took him in his mouth and began to suck on him, slowly at first then faster as he was fueled on by the moaning he heard from Aldrik. He could not help but want this man, he was a Nordic beauty, he was passionate, he was caring, he was here with him now, moaning in pleasure at his attention to him.

He felt the need, the desire to have him now. With his feet on the floor, he pulled Aldrik by the legs until he was positioned at the edge of the bed. His feet firmly planted on Demetri's chest. As he lubed himself up he was looking in Aldrik's eyes, watching him as he knew that he was anticipating his next move and he did not disappoint him.

As he entered him, Aldrik let out a gasp of pure pleasure. He pushed with his feet on Demetri's chest but held firmly to his hands so he was not pushed away, but rather pulled further inside him. He began to thrust himself into him slowly at first, then faster as the moans of both encouraged him on.

He reached down and grabbed a hold of Aldrik's thighs, pulling on them as he continued to pump his cock deep inside him. Aldrik's hands clinched the comforter on the bed, his head pressed into the mattress each time he entered him again. He knew he wasn't going to last much longer as he could feel the buildup of the pleasure taking over his body. He pulled out his cock when he realized that he was going to shoot his load. As he continued to stroke his own cock he shot his load all over Aldrik's stomach, some hitting his chest.

Aldrik sat up slightly, grabbing his neck as he pulled him into his kiss. Even though, Aldrik has the ability to ejaculate, he most often did not. He was more about the intimacy of the act, the bodies interacting, and the minds working in unison. As he collapsed on top of Aldrik, panting, out of breath, he laid his head on Aldrik's shoulder, so happy to be this close to him. Their chests were breathing together, heaving at the same time, neither one cared about the mess that lay between them. It was a labor of love, the result of unbridled passion for each other.

"I have missed you so much," Demetri said

"As I have missed you too beautiful one."

"I didn't realize just how much I missed you, until I saw you. It was as if all of my worries and troubles just disappeared, even if for just a little while," Demetri said into his ear, still breathing hard.

"Demetri, my love, if I can do that for you then I am a happy man," Aldrik said. "But I fear that this will be a short-lived reprieve for you. You look as if you have taken a beating, my love." Aldrik said as he looked at his bruised face. "I gathered from your call and from you now that this visit is of grave importance for you."

"I wish I could say that it wasn't, but I would be lying to you. I'm here for your help, your guidance. I fear that you are the only one that can help me?" Demetri said.

As he took advantage of being in Aldrik's strong embrace, he begins to recount the events of the past week. Aldrik listened to him without interruption, his concern growing as he told the details of what has happened.

Aldrik's fingertips were rubbing through Demetri's hair as he listened intently, trying to comfort him, to reassure him as he kept talking.

Chapter Thirty-Four

Victor had long been planning this evening, the way it would go, and the way it needed to be done just right. He expected no interruptions as it was almost midnight and the park was closed to the public at this hour. There was a sign on the gate that stated that the park closed at 11:00 p.m., but that didn't keep Victor out. If you want to make sure no one got into the park after hours, then you need to make sure that one can't easily bypass the gate by going up onto the curb and around the gate. Sure you had the random visitors that came, especially the young teenagers out looking for a place to lose their virginity. He hoped he didn't have to deal with anything out of the ordinary like that. He didn't like killing kids, only if it was a direct order from the Council or if they were stupid enough to interfere with what he was doing or even see from afar.

Victor had an eye like a hawk and impressive hearing so if someone were watching him, he, usually, knew about it. Plus, he was meticulous about his research, his Intel before doing a project so that he could avoid any unfortunate scenarios that would have to be 'cleaned up'.

He had chosen the two deliberately. They were a married couple, Bill and Claudia, no children yet, but they had only been married a year. Today, August 14, their one-year anniversary, they will be given the greatest gift of all; no other anniversary present could match this one. They get to be the

165

second feeding of his master; they will both join him for eternity on this day of their one-year anniversary.

It wasn't hard for Victor to find a couple that was wed on the day he needed to offer up the sacrifice. He visited the public records at the Tulsa County Courthouse and the Tulsa World, the local newspaper, for couples that were married on that day. He didn't spend too much time getting their routine down. After he followed them, he realized they had no security system in their home. He waited till they were both at work, broke into their house, without them knowing, of course, and planted a few bugs around the house. He quickly knew the time and place that they were going to be spending their evening celebrating their beloved one-year anniversary. Such an ordinary looking couple too. His master would be so happy with them and it would add to Victor's satisfaction as well. Anything he could do to make the master happy and his transition back into this realm made Victor intoxicated.

The area around Woodward Park was the perfect place for the sacrificial offering. It was dark, deserted at night. The park is protected by a locked gate at night. He had chosen the perfect place that was well off the path from the bridge in the park, one that had a sturdy tree in which to hold his two offerings.

They lived in a wooded area outside of Tulsa, in a suburban area still under development. He had parked his SUV off the road and lay in a ditch awaiting their approach in their vehicle. He had chosen a silencer for a gun for a couple of reasons. Out here in the open area, he didn't want a loud bang going off and echoing far enough that someone heard it and called the cops. He didn't want the couple to hear the gun and call the cops either. So as he lay waiting, patiently as a lion stalking its prey, he was soon rewarded with the lights of a vehicle. He had night vision goggles on and knew that it was them by the shape of the car and he was able to identify two people in the car.

As they approached, they were going about forty miles per hour. As they were getting ready to pass by him, he fired one shot and it landed perfectly where he aimed. The car went out of control as the back passenger side tire blew out from the gun shot.

Bill and Claudia were shocked by the turn of events. She let out a yell thinking they were going to run off the road and crash into the ditch. Bill tried to remain calm and remember the steps to go through when you had a tire blow out. He was tapping at the brakes, trying hard not to panic and slam on them as the car slowly decelerated and then he pulled off to the side of the road. He let out a sigh of relief that they were both okay. He then began to curse inwardly at the construction people in the area that were building a housing addition just a little further down the road from where they had built their house. He was sure that some nails had fallen off their truck as they drove like mad men down the one lane road.

They were discussing where the spare tire was located. Victor, who was decked out in all black, quickly and stealthily ran back to his SUV, gun and night vision goggles put away in his backpack which was thrown over his shoulder. He had to get to them before any good Samaritans came by to offer the couple any help with their tire. After all, it was Victor who planned to play that role. He removed his black jacket to reveal a blue Oklahoma City Thunder t-shirt, one that he had found at a local gas station. They were an NBA basketball team which was a big deal Victor gathered since the team recently moved to Oklahoma. Everyone seemed to be crazy about them and Victor laughed to himself when he heard the catch phrase "Thunder Up!" Americans were so funny that way.

Victor made it back to the SUV within a minute of his shooting out the tire. With his Thunder t-shirt on to help make the couple feel more at ease, Victor turned the ignition to the SUV, turned on the lights. He started down the dirt road that he had pulled onto to hide his vehicle. When he reached the main road, he made a right turn onto a one lane road and made his way down to the stranded couple. They were both standing outside of the car. The man looking in the trunk for what Victor figured to be a spare tire and the lady was standing by the flat tire with her arms folded over her chest as if upset by the whole ordeal.

Victor pulled in behind them with his lights still on and proceeded to get out of the SUV. As he came around to where the couple was standing he said, "Bad luck with the flat tire."

The man quickly said "yeah, we had a blowout. Damned construction people don't clean up after themselves letting nails and debris fall off their trucks everywhere."

"A nail you say; how interesting. Can I offer you some help? He said to the distressed couple.

"Just having your lights from your truck mister will be a great help. I will try and get this changed quickly," Bill was saying.

As Bill was digging in the trunk to get the spare tire out of its compartment, Victor walked over to him laying his arm on his shoulder.

"Let me give you a hand," Victor stated as Bill turned around and he quickly slammed his fist into Bill's face sending him to the ground out cold.

Claudia was in shock at first then she started to scream. As she attempted to turn and run away from Victor, he was quickly upon her. Grabbing her from behind with his bicep of his right arm, securely under her chin using the forearm of his left arm to squeeze his right arm tightly until it was cutting off her air supply until she became faint and passed out. Victor was not trying to kill them, well not yet at least. He just needed them incapacitated while he tied them up and transported them to the park where he intended to offer them as a sacrifice.

He had nothing against these two people in particular, as he had nothing against the first sacrifice. Truth be told, it had less to do with the people being sacrificed and more to do with the significance of the dates. He did as he was told to do. Certain details and rituals were laid out for him, but how he did it and whom he chose was left up to him as long as it fit the date preselected by the Balashon.

168

Victor had them both tied up, hands restrained behind their backs, duct tape over their mouths. He had taken the extra time while they were both out cold to go ahead and tie their feet together. He bound their lower legs and feet by securely wrapping a thick rope around their ankles six times and tying it off into a metal clasp which he would use later when he got them to the park. He had taken all their clothes off of them while they were out, so they lay bound, unconscious and nude, which was the way that the first sacrifice had met his master.

As Victor drove towards his destination, he could not help but fantasize. He fantasized about what his life will be like when he stood beside the master as he comes into this realm to reclaim it once again as he had three thousand years before. This time he would not be banished. This time there would be no old world magic around that could hurt the master, disarm him. These witches today were more about earthly peace, herbal gardening, and dancing nude at summer solstice instead of practicing the dark magic of the days of old. Wiccan and Paganism has had resurgence in the past couple of years. There were not too many great witches, true witches left that had the blood line to draw upon the ancient mystical magic it would take to even make the master wince.

Most of the true, great witches were burned at the stake during the Salem witch hunts and the witch hunts that took place before that in Europe. The world would be a much better place if they would do another cleanse of the witches; just eradicate them all.

Victor was getting excited now that he was nearing the park. He was getting charged up, both mentally and sexually. He had always gotten a sexual charge out of killing and he made no apologies for the hard cock that he had in his pants. In fact, he was rubbing his hardness through his pants right now. This was going to be a great night.

Victor turned off of 21st Street onto Peoria Avenue, and then he quickly made a left hand turn into the park entrance. He previously checked the park at night to make sure that there were no gates that were locked. He had been here a few times to clock what needed to be done and what might happen that could throw a kink into his plans. But, each time, he had successfully completed his dry runs. He was confident in his ability to get this completed in the time frame he needed to. This was a special night, a special sacrifice, and he was going to make sure that he followed through with his plan in its entirety.

He pulled his SUV into a preselected location, one that was sure to not draw any attention even if security or police were to drive through. He parked, turned off the ignition and pulled on his black jacket and black hat. He needed to be as stealth as possible. Yes, he could have done this deep in the country, far away from prying eyes. But, he knew he could do this where the sacrifice could be done in its proper ritual style and still keep the flair of his own killing style intact. He loved that people were still talking about the first kill on Riverside Drive, the rumors flying in the newspapers and the local television stations. There was a fear developing in the city over his first kill and he knew that it would blow up to serial killer level when they find these two from tonight.

The papers would really eat up the fact that this was a married couple on their first-year anniversary and they were taken just down the road from their home. The method and way they would be killed will have this town talking for years to come.

As he stepped out of the SUV, he walked around and opened the back door. The man and woman were both laying in the back side by side, both awake and crying. Their mouths being duct taped, all you could hear from them were loud murmurs which were more than likely pleas for help, for mercy, which, normally, Victor would have loved to hear but not in this setting. They can cry all they want; they were being sacrificed to the most wonderful master, one that would enjoy their souls for an eternity.

He grabbed the man out of the SUV first, throwing him over his shoulder. Shutting the door behind him so the woman couldn't get out and he started walking the man to the tree he had picked out already. He had taken the time prior to this night to come and put two pulley systems up onto the sturdiest limb he was able to find. When he reached the tree, he laid the man on the ground. He hurriedly shimmied up the tree a bit where he had laid the two ropes, hidden them from sight, away from nosey prying eyes. Letting them both fall down to the ground they were basically ready for the couple. Each rope had already been placed through the pulley that was anchored up in the limb and on the end of each rope there was a clamp tied on.

Dragging the man over to the rope, he made quick work of snapping the clamp to the metal clasp that was tied to the man's feet. He started pulling on the other end of the rope and as the slack was taken out, the rope became taut. The man's legs were the first to be lifted off the ground, then his butt, then the rest of his body. His head dragged for a slight second on the ground before being heaved up to where he was barely hanging upside down about a foot above the ground. Victor tied off the rope around the base of the tree making sure that it was secure and tight.

Victor then turned and headed back to the SUV to get the woman out. She was still crying and screaming from underneath the duct tape. The murmuring was irritating to Victor because he would very much like to hear what she had to say. It fueled him on when they begged. Victor grabbed her and placed her over his shoulder as he had her husband a few minutes ago. Grabbing his black bag from the back, he placed it over his other shoulder, then shutting the door he started out into the wooded area making his way to the tree. When he got there, he laid the woman on the ground with a thud. As she looked upwards she started to struggle and make louder noises as she saw her husband upside down, naked, bound and scared hanging from the tree limb. It was very dark, but she could still make him out in the darkness and she could tell that his whimpering was filled with fear and pain.

Victor took the other rope and hooked the clamp from the hanging rope to the metal clasp that was attached to the rope that bound the woman's legs and feet. Grabbing the loose end of the rope, he hoisted the lady up in the same

171

fashion as he had her husband. He tied her rope off around the base of the tree as well. As he tied them off they hung just a foot off the ground and about two feet from each other. The struggling they did was making them spin around. Each time they spun around and were facing each other, even though it was for just a second, it sent them both into another round of crying, muffled screams, and whimpers.

Victor was still good on time and as he was getting into his bag to start preparing for the ritual, he began reciting to himself in the ancient language of his master. It was one that was lost to most of today's society, but one that the Balashon had kept records of and had taught to the highest-ranking members of each generation including their best assassins like Victor. When they were preparing a sacrifice to their master they wanted to speak to him in his language, the one that he had used when he walked in this realm.

This chanting, talking in this foreign language, got the attention of both the woman and the man. They listened closely to him as if he was going to relay some valuable piece of information to them that might save their lives. It wasn't going to. It was going to bring about their gruesome and horrific death and even more horrific fate for their souls. They had stopped struggling which made them finally stop swinging around and the noise had stopped as well.

When Victor brought out the ceremonial knife and started using it to draw symbols in the ground beneath them, they both started squirming around again making the ropes swing a bit. They were whimpering and making noises again. As they flailed about, the man's head made contact with Victor's face banging it pretty hard. This infuriated Victor and he quickly reached out punching the man in the face, dazing him into silence. The lady went into a raging fit and Victor reached over and punched her hard in the face as well leaving her as dazed as it had her husband. With stillness and silence back upon them, Victor began chanting again and drawing symbols in the ground beneath them.

Once he finished with that, he turned his attention back to the couple. Squatting down, he grabbed the man behind the neck with his left hand. With his right hand, he took the knife and began to carve the symbol that was on the ground into the man's flesh on his forehead. This met with resistance from the man, but Victor had such a death grip on the man's neck that even though he struggled against him, it was to no avail.

When Victor was finished with the man, he turned his attention to the dazed woman. Grabbing her as he did the man he carved a symbol into her forehead. It was the ancient symbol, the one that had not been seen outside of the Balashon until the first sacrifice. The symbol used to bind their souls to this spot until the hell hounds came to take them away. This same symbol is carved into the ground in four different sections within a circle, each one facing north, east, south and west. The symbol in the middle of the circle was the symbol that represented his master, Bastiquil.

After he had finished with the woman they were both ready, both prepped for the sacrifice to begin. Victor, on bended knees before the couple, just on the outside of the circle began chanting again. This time it had more of a ceremonial feel to it. The couple could not understand a thing he was saying, but it progressively got more intense, more guttural. As Victor was chanting louder, harder, and faster, he reached out with a flash of speed he slit the throats of both. Their blood spilled out of their neck, moving down their chin, mouth, cheeks, and over their scared, bugged-out eyes, filling their hair on their heads until finally spilling over into the circle and onto the symbols that lay below them. As it did this Victor kept chanting until they took their last gurgle of breath as their bodies go limp from the loss of blood and eventual death.

As their bodies hung there, dead, their spirits were standing beside their dead bodies, confused, stuck, and not able to move on. They were able to see each other, and their spirits clung to one another, but they were not able to move from this spot. They both knew they were dead, they could see their bodies, their throats cut, the blood everywhere. This is not what Bill or Claudia expected death to be like, but

173

neither of them had truly thought much about dying, let alone being killed together and so brutally. The fact that they were stuck, unable to move from this place was another frightful thought that they were both experiencing. Why this was happening to them was still a mystery.

The man who had just killed them was still chanting away, until the symbols on the ground began to light up. At first a filtered light, as if a spotlight were shining upward from the dirt below. But then the light changed into a more burning look, as if flames were shooting upward from the symbols.

The dirt started giving way where the symbols that were lit up had been drawn. At first it was a spinning of dirt and sand, and then it started to fall within itself. The hole it was making was beginning to brighten up, making a fiery pit. There was a large roar that their spiritual forms heard from within the pit and both kept clinging to each other knowing what their fate was, but not really grasping a full understanding of it. Then a large paw, reached up from the pit and then another. A gigantic hell hound, larger than anything they had ever seen made its way out of the ground. Its jaws were filled with teeth, as big as great white shark teeth, with red bloody drool falling from its mouth. Behind that one, another hound just as big and fierce made its way out of the pit.

They were screaming loudly, but the only ones that could hear them were the hell-hounds and their murderer. Victor could hear them and see them because he was mystically linked to this death due to the ritual he had performed. Once they were gone he would no longer have that connection, but until then, he stood back and enjoyed the show.

The hounds circled the couple until they had them pushed up near the hole's edge. Then both hounds simultaneously leaped at them, each grabbing one of them with their large mouths and pulling them into the hole's entrance, into the fiery pit that lay below. What was awaiting them when they got there was something far worse than the death they just experienced. His master was going to feast well tonight.

The hole closed in on itself sealing the couple and their fates behind it. The bodies of Claudia and Bill, void of soul, were still hanging from the tree limb. Victor smiled with pride as he gathered up his items that he had used for the ritual and quickly made his way back to his vehicle. Once inside, he made his way out of the park and back onto Peoria Avenue. There was nothing left linking him to the couple whose bodies still hang in the still night of the park. He had succeeded in his second sacrifice to his master. One more to go, then his master would join him here. His master would rule this world once again.

Chapter Thirty-Five

Alex was already awake when he had received the phone call from Gina. He had been woke up by a nightmarish dream of a couple, hanging upside down from a tree in a park with their throats slit. Blood was everywhere and their souls were being dragged to hell by some huge beasts he hoped he would never encounter. These dreams were so vivid, so real that it made him start to second guess his belief in heaven and hell, in the afterlife. His tattoo on his neck burned again, itching as it often did after he dreamed of others deaths.

He was half listening to Gina when she called, frantically telling him something about his tattoos and how she had found a common thread between them. He had thought the only common thread was that he had dreamed their shapes before getting them tattooed on his body. But, it seems that there may be another.

Gina had asked him if he was able to meet with her at the bookstore. She had apologized profusely to him about what had happened at the club with her friend and explained that she had talked with Demetri about how he had acted and he felt remorseful for what he had done. Gina had reassured him that Demetri was not going to be at the shop when he got there as he was in Kansas City trying to get some answers as to what was going on.

It was 1:30 a.m. and he didn't think that he would be getting back to sleep anytime soon so he had told her that he would definitely come meet her.

Alex took a quick shower after he hung up the phone, just to get some perspective and to wake himself up. He had been tired most of the day as the previous night's events had taken quite a toll on him.

Even though he had been frightened by her and her friend, he believed her apology and believed in her. He knew she wanted to help him and he still believed if anyone could help, it would be Gina. So he had put on some clothes, grabbed a coffee to go, and took off to meet her at the store.

When he got there, the door was locked as she had long since been closed for the day. He knocked on it a couple of times until he saw a light turn on and Gina come walking towards the door. She turned the lock on the door and opened it for him.

As he walked inside, she cautiously walked up to him and asked if she could give him a hug. He hesitated only for a second then leaned into her hug. "I'm so happy you could make it," she said. "I thought after everything that went down that you would never speak to me again."

"Well, believe me; I was totally freaked out by everything that happened. But to be totally honest with you, what had happened with your friend Demetri was just the icing on the cake that had been baking all night," Alex said to her. "I can't even begin to explain to you the horrors of what happened down in that basement. If it were not for that man in the mask, I would have never made it out alive."

"Speaking of him, who is he?" She asked hoping he wasn't offended by her question. "I am not saying I'm not happy that he helped you, but why is he protecting you so fiercely?"

"Well, those are questions that I don't have an answer. I don't know who he is or why he saved me. But, let's not forget, he saved me from your friend, too," Alex shot back at her feeling the need to defend himself.

"Listen, I'm not by any means defending what he did to you," she said to him knowing that he was a bit hurt by her previous question. "I will say that he acted out of fear and lack of information."

177

"And what does he have to be afraid of me for?" Alex questioned.

"Demetri claims to have never met you before that night and as I have gathered, you are claiming the same?" Gina asked.

"This is true," Alex stated curiously.

"Well, Demetri dreamed about you a few weeks ago and in the dream you were trying to kill him. He described you down to the details of some of your most hidden tattoos." Gina said, trying to explain where his head was at when he attacked Alex. "When he woke up he was floating in the air and then was slammed into the wall of his bedroom. He even had a handprint burned into his neck where he claims that you held him in the air by only using your mind."

"Well let me just say, I think he has us confused. The last I knew, and I have intimate details on the matter, he was the one that held all the cards in that market," Alex said, somewhat defensively and somewhat kidding trying to lighten the mood a bit. He really liked her and didn't want to argue with her.

"Well, that's my whole point I'm trying to make to both of you boys. You are both drawn together by your dreams, and your dreams are what is attacking you both," Gina was trying to explain her theory to him.

"I don't know if I buy that. I mean how can he have dreamed about me in such detail and why haven't I dreamed about him?" Alex asked pointedly.

"What if you did dream about him, but you just don't remember it?"

"Okay, you have lost me," Alex said.

"Please don't get upset when I tell you this, okay?" Gina asked. He nodded that he would not.

"Your friend, Brandy, came by to see me today and she was disturbed and agitated," Gina started to tell Alex. He was visibly disturbed by this and stood up and started pacing the room. "Hey, remember now, you said you were not going to get upset."

"I remember," Alex said trying to stay calm. "It just pisses me off she would come to you without telling me. She called to check on me, but never told me she came here."

"Well, she told me about the types of drugs that you use. When you take mind altering drugs, you open yourself up to many possibilities. You run the risk of opening yourself up to a magical portal, one that links you to the other side, the spiritual side." She was explaining to him while trying to gauge his level of anger. She hated to betray Brandy's trust, but she had to take a risk here if she was going to be able to help Alex figure this out.

Alex stopped his pacing and turned to look at her. "What do you mean I open myself up to the spiritual side?"

"There have been many world religions that have practiced within a mind altering state of being so that they could make a connection with the other side. One of the most common ones and close to home is the Native American practice of using peyote." She was watching him as she spoke.

"I'm Native American, a member of the Cherokee Nation Tribe," Alex said, not in defense of himself, but more for a knowledge reason.

"Well, this is good to know. That may mean you have a stronger connection to the dream world than you think," Gina said. She was finally feeling like they were getting somewhere, he was opening up to her, starting to trust her.

She then asked him if he would hear her out before he said anything further on the subject. She wanted to inform him of what she had found and what she was still trying to find out. She had another favor to ask of him, but it would require that he go out on a limb with her; it would require that he trust her.

Gina went on to explain, she had been trying to figure out the connections between what was happening to Demetri and what was happening to Alex. She briefly explained about the tarot reading she had given to Demetri and the incident afterward. It had gotten her to think about Alex and about his connection to his tattoos. The fact that he had dreamed each of his tattoos held great significance which could not be

179

ignored. She explained to him, it had been lingering on her mind. The fact the symbol on his neck, the very first one he had dreamed about, was hidden within his other tattoos, or at least the ones he hadn't tattooed on himself.

He was listening intently and getting a bit nervous in the process. She pulled out the pictures that she had printed explaining to him that some of them had been blown up so he was able to see the symbol embedded in the tattoo. She was willing to show him which tattoos they belonged to, if he wasn't able to tell. He was in awe at the pictures, he could not fathom how anyone could have betrayed him like this. He lived by the ethical standard that you give the customer what they asked for and you didn't take any artistic freedom with it unless it was expressly consented to in writing before you started. Alex's mind was going nonstop and Gina had been concentrating hard to not listen in to his thoughts but, was getting a little nervous and was thinking about breaking her own rule.

"Okay, I'm sorry; this is just a little freaky for me. I trusted these people to do my tattoos, to follow the exact drawing that I had given to them. The fact that they added what I thought was my own design in them is not only wrong, it's fucking creepy," he said frustrated and upset.

She explained that it went a little deeper than that, actually, a whole lot deeper. Gina explained that she decided to do a search on the symbol that he had tattooed on his neck especially since it kept appearing in his other tattoos. Alex was anxiously waiting for her to reveal the efforts of her search. Her hesitation was that she wanted to ask him a question, but somewhat feared to; she wanted to ask if he could have unknowingly drawn the symbols himself as he was sketching out the drawings? She had learned how powerful the brain could be at blocking out what we may not want to know. She decided it best not to go down that path just yet.

She told him that, at first, it didn't turn up anything, but that she had a feeling, a gut feeling, that there was more to this story than what they both knew. She decided to email the symbol to Dr. Vance, a professor she knew who worked at a local theological seminary college that dealt with ancient symbols and their meanings. She forewarned Alex that he was probably not going to like what he was about to hear which made him that much more apprehensive and fidgety.

She told him about the professor emailing her back right away to explain that the symbol was from a long lost civilization thought to be a myth only. The symbol referred to a ruling king in those days over three thousand years ago; his name was Bastiquil. He was thought to be a tyrant, a mystical ruler who relied heavily on magic and killed anyone who dare defy him. There was not much evidence around, actually none to support if it was a real story. There was more evidence to support it being a story one passes down to children at bedtime, to make them behave, to keep them in check if you will. Some even thought it was more demonic than mystical. This raised more questions than it offered answers so Gina had picked up the phone and called Dr. Vance's office and to her surprise, Dr. Vance answered.

"Hello, Dr. Vance, I'm so glad to catch you. This is Gina and I was just reading your email and was curious if you had a few minutes to clarify some things for me?"

"Sure, I would be more than happy to help you any way I can," the professor said.

"Well, I was able to decipher some of the symbols within the tattoo such as the symbol for infinity and immortality. I understand what the serpent represents, but in your email you said the symbol was from a lost civilization, thought to be a myth only?" Gina posed the question.

"Yes, I did. There is little mention of it in the history books which tends to lead most to believe it is more myth and not reality, but this is where it gets interesting. You find more about this ruler, this Bastiquil, in references like The Book of the Dead and books regarding satanic history. So if one were to think, if this ruler was truly as bad and evil as one is led to believe, then would you want him in your history books? Yes, I know in today's day and age we write about our evil rulers like Hitler and such. But, back then, when an entire civilization was almost demolished due to a demonic ruler, things were different. They would not have wanted this to be passed on as their history." The doctor was explaining to Gina.

"So it is of your opinion that Bastiquil did exist and that it has been swept under the historical rug, so to speak, instead of being written down in the records."

"That is an exceptional way of looking at it. But, I must tell you, there are some theologians whom I have spoken with that would say Bastiquil was not a demon from hell because hell doesn't exist. But, rather, he is a being from a rip in time, a veil between worlds, a wormhole, so to speak. That was how he disappeared without a trace as well as most, if not all, of that civilization." Dr. Vance explained.

"So what would you make of it if I told you the symbol I sent you in the email was actually something someone dreamed about when they were sixteen years old and then had it tattooed on the back of their neck?"

"I would say that this child had been given access to some books that he or she should never have been allowed to read."

"Well, what if I told you he hadn't been exposed to it, that he has tattoos all over his body he dreamed of in the same manner. We are now finding that inside those tattoos, the artist who did them added a smaller version of the symbol that is hidden within the larger tattoo."

"I would say that someone is playing a precarious game with your friend's life, actually his very soul," the professor warned. "You need to stay as far away from this as you can because it can lead to nowhere good Gina."

"Well, I'm afraid I'm too deep into this to stop now, but I do thank you for your guidance and knowledge." Gina sincerely said.

"You are most welcome child, but please do be careful. You are messing in ancient mysticism that can be treacherous. I will be thinking of you and will let you know if I find out anything else regarding this matter." Dr. Vance said to Gina as she said goodbye and hung up the phone.

What really bothered Gina is what had happened to Demetri, not only in a dream and the mentioning of three

182

thousand years ago, but in his visions after the tarot reading that referred to this Bastiquil. The implications of this are undeniable. Demetri and Alex were both being contacted by Bastiquil, but for what purpose was unsure. Gina relayed all of the conversation that she had with Dr. Vance to Alex, who was looking at her as if she were insane.

Gina realized that Demetri and Alex were going to have to work together in order to figure this out. They were going to have to put the past behind them so they could figure out their future.

"Do you have any idea how absurd this all sounds?"

"Actually I do, but I am accustomed to people thinking that things that come from a witch are absurd, but you are going to have to trust me here Alex," she pleaded with him. "I can't protect you, nor can I help you if you don't trust me."

He listened to her and took this all in. He was definitely being stalked by something that was trying to make contact with him. He had no idea what this masked man's game was or what his next move was. Hell, he didn't even know if he could expect him to be there the next time to protect him when the shit hit the fan. But he didn't intend to be down in the basement anytime in the near future. Then there were the tattoos, in which people that he knew had betrayed him. They had deliberately altered his tattoo to put that symbol in there which obviously is a symbol to a blood – thirsty tyrant that may or may not have lived three thousand years ago. He was pacing still when she spoke.

"I know I have not done enough to earn your trust, but I want you to know I'm fully on board. We are going to figure this out, one way or another." Gina said, meaning every word and he felt her true meaning.

"Do you have any whiskey?"

"Do I have whiskey? What kind of girl do you take me for?" She kidded him. "Of course I have whiskey. Give me a moment and I will grab a bottle and some shot glasses."

He continued his pacing around the room stopping occasionally to look at the pictures that she had showed him.

How could he be involved in what has turned out to seem like a huge secret plot against him? He really honestly didn't know who he could trust anymore. Alex's thoughts went back to the argument that his parents had before his dad walked out of their life for good. His dad had said that he wasn't going to stay around and be a part of this. *A part of what?* Alex was asking himself. Although Gina raised many more questions in Alex's mind, she brought him closer to some possible answers, answers he hasn't had in a long time.

As she came back into the room, she placed the bottle of Jack Daniels on the table with the two shot glasses and filled them both full. She handed one to Alex then grabbed the other for herself and said "here's to trusting." Alex smiled and clinked her glass as they both tipped their heads back and downed the whiskey. It was such a welcome burn.

"I have one more favor to ask of you Alex," Gina said to him hoping that he would indulge her.

"What would that be?" Alex asked of her. "Do you want to tell me that I have a long lost psycho brother that I never knew about?"

They both started laughing at his attempt to lighten the mood of the room.

"I would like to know if you would allow me the opportunity to see if I can make a connection with your tattoo on your neck. I know it may sound weird, but if there is any energy there, any connection that is being sent out because of it, I might just be able to tap into it." Gina said trying to make her case.

"I would be honored to allow you to connect with me," Alex said to her looking at her seriously. His eyes making contact with hers as she quickly looked away and tried to make herself look busy by gathering two chairs together, placing them to where they were facing each other.

Alex removed his shirt so that she would have full access to his tattoo. "So you want me facing you?"

"Yes, if you don't mind? I think it will be easier to make the connection if our mind's eyes are facing each other."

184

she said, but hoping that she didn't just lose him in Wiccan verbiage.

"Oh, okay, I get that," he said placing himself in the chair across from her.

Gina sat down in the seat in front of him and shaking her hands and arms to her side to release any negative energy she began trying to focus her mind on the task at hand. She leaned her head in toward him so that their foreheads were touching each other. He felt very close to her at this moment as she explained to him that she was trying to make a connection between both of their third eyes. He couldn't help but feel the intimacy of the situation here, but tried to remain as professional as possible.

She then reached back with both of her hands to his tattoo on the back of his neck, the symbol, the very first tattoo. She began to concentrate on the symbol and on Alex. She tried to picture him at sixteen years old and him dreaming about this tattoo and then going out to have it inked on. She tried to imagine what he must have been feeling when he did it, the joy of a new tattoo, the sneaking out so that he wouldn't get caught, and stopped by his mother.

She was trying everything she had to make that connection to this symbol. Then she decided to take another route, she moved her hands up to each side of his temples. Concentrating hard on not hurting him, she light sent pulses of energy into his brain, trying to force it to reveal to her the meaning. This felt much different than the first time she touched his tattoo and received a shocking flash, she only wished she would have stayed with it and explored more then.

What Gina got back was the feeling that she was being blocked by something or someone powerful. It didn't feel like he was the one blocking her. She kept trying to make the connection, but each time she tried, she was blocked. She leaned her forehead back to his, not in an attempt at a connection, but more in frustration.

He felt a real connection with her at this moment and decided to act upon it. She leaned into him, their faces touching at the forehead and nose. He leaned in just a bit more and kissed her on the lips, softly at first to test the waters. When he did not find any resistance from her, he reached up and placed his hand behind her neck and pulled her into his kiss. He kissed her passionately and with intent. Their lips were locked in a lingering kiss, their tongues touching. He was in pure heaven right now and it was all due to this beautiful red headed witch named Gina. She was magical he knew, but this kiss was even more magical.

As they were kissing more intensely, Gina reached up and ran her fingers over his bare chest. She loved his body, his tattoos and his dark features. He was definitely the type of guy she would go for if she wasn't into girls, but she had to say this felt right at this moment and she wasn't doing anything to stop it.

As they were busy getting to know each other's kiss, Victor had been at the window watching from outside. When he found out that the vessel was on the move, he had to go and make sure that he was safe. He was relieved to find out that the male witch was nowhere to be found. He was also just a little jealous of the vessel for getting what he had wanted since the first day he laid eyes upon the witch; he had been wanting a shot at her. However, it looked like this was going to be the vessel's lucky night; so be it.

"Would you like to go to the bedroom?" Gina whispered into Alex's ear.

Not hesitating, he stood up, grabbed her hand and let her lead him to the bedroom. Reaching the door and walking through it, he reached over and lifted her shirt up and over her head, revealing firm breasts. She unbuttoned her jeans and let them and her panties slide down her legs to the floor.

Both falling onto the bed, they kissed each other, felt each other, and fulfilled a sense of longing they both needed.

As they continued their exploration of each other, she sucked on his bottom lip and then moved back to kissing his mouth and sucking on his tongue. He reached over and placed his hand down between her thighs. She moaned in pleasure as he felt the warm moisture on his hands and let his finger enter her. As he continued his pleasuring of her with one hand, the other found her breast, where he cupped gently, sucking on it before moving to the other. He nibbled at her breast until she begged for him to take her.

His tattooed cock erect and ready, now urged him on relentlessly. Climbing between her, he parted her legs running his hands down her white, soft flesh. Aiming his cock, he eased it inside her as she moaned in pleasure, arching her back to give him all access to her. Grabbing her thighs he pulled her closer to him as he pumped his hardness inside of her.

On his knees, scooping her up off the bed, his cock still inside of her, he brought her up close to him and pressed his tongue into her mouth while fondling her breast. Using his thighs as leverage, she bounced up and down on him, turned on by the sheer electricity of the experience. He could feel himself building up in momentum and excitement. He sucked on her lips as he exploded inside of her as she too matched his orgasm with her own. They were moaning in unison until their bodies relaxed and he drew his cock out of her.

Falling onto the bed, both euphoric, but still trying to catch their breath, they both knew without words, this is just as it appeared, sex. No commitments, no proper words to be exchanged, just two people who needed the interaction, the physical touch, and connection with someone else. They both had smiles on their faces as they lay on the bed deep in their own thoughts.

Chapter Thirty-Six

Demetri lay sleeping, his head resting on Aldrik's chest. He had his arm around Demetri's shoulder as he ran his arm up and down Demetri's back, thinking about all the things that he had told him. It was nearing dawn, although he had tinted windows in all the rooms of his penthouse, he still pressed the button on the bedside table and all of the curtains in the entire condo started to close. This was a daily ritual for him as it is well known that vampires and the sun don't mix well.

He was well-versed on Demetri and his powers. He knew that there was so much more in Demetri that he had still yet to discover. He was a good man, with a great heart and Aldrik had faith enough in Demetri that he would always strive to do what is best for himself, his loved ones, and the world in general.

He was much like Aldrik in that he was one of life's gentle mutations, but the difference lay in the way that these mutations came about. He was born with them, probably passed down from generations of people with power. Every so often one like Demetri would get a super dose of the mutation and become one of the most powerful people on this planet. He was glad that Demetri had a good soul striving to do well, to be the best man he possibly could be.

As for Aldrik, his mutation was brought on by violence, by a bite on the neck and the painful transformation began, that ended with his death and then his rebirth into this world as a vampire. There were many, many myths and legends surrounding vampires and what will and will not kill them and he found them all quite funny. People think that holy water will burn them; well, it doesn't. People think that a stake to the heart will kill them, well, it doesn't; but it sure hurts like hell. There are two proven methods to kill a vampire; one is by beheading and the second is sunlight. He made sure to avoid the second one at all cost and as for the first, well he just made sure that he was the most skilled fighter that walked into a fight. The only other way to avoid being beheaded was avoiding the fight altogether, which wasn't always possible.

Vampires do not need sleep like humans do. Yes, when they have exerted themselves or need to regenerate or heal from an injury, they need rest, but for the most part, they are awake. With that being said, fifteen hundred years is a long time to be awake, to think, to hear things, and to read up on things.

This one particular problem of Demetri's had him concerned. From everything that he had told him, it seemed like there was a reason for worry. *Why would this spirit or demon be making contact with Demetri, showing him visions of a world long gone?* These visions included Demetri fighting alongside Bastiquil over three thousand years ago; of course, it was not the Demetri that lay sleeping beside him, but a version of him, a piece of his soul. *Why resurface now? This Alex person that he had mentioned had to be the key to all this. Why else would Demetri be dreaming about him being able to beat Demetri in battle? Why would these two have connecting dreams if not for a common purpose that has yet to be revealed to either of them?*

Bastiquil was a name of legend, of myth. He was believed to not be real. Even back in Aldrik's early days, no one believed that he was real and back then superstition ran rampant. There was something that they were all missing here. Such brilliant minds pondering the same questions yet all missing the answer.

Demetri stirred in his sleep, he held him close for he feared that he may be having a bad dream. As he held him,

Demetri's eyes opened and looked upward to his face he said "good morning beautiful."

He smiled at him and said, "Good morning to you as well my love. Close your eyes and try to get some more rest."

"I would much rather look at you," Demetri said as he leaned up just enough to give him a kiss. Aldrik did not stop this as he was so happy to see him and had waited so long to get these sweet kisses.

"I must confess to you, I have laid here most of the night contemplating your current predicament and all of its possible meanings," Aldrik stated. "I am concerned for your safety. Even though, it goes against your very nature, you must proceed with caution. Promise me?"

Demetri smiled to himself, listening to this beautiful man. Aldrik was correct in that typically he would charge into the face of danger, not heed caution to it. As Aldrik talked to him, he was hearing that Aldrik cared for him. He didn't want anything to happen to him. This meant so much to him, as he knew, felt in his heart that he loved this man and always would. He has never felt this way for anyone in his life and he wished that there were easier ways for them to be together other than him have to die to do so. This made Demetri somewhat sad, he reached around his abdomen and held him tightly with his head still resting on his chest.

"You still have not answered me," Aldrik said, rubbing his fingers into his curly locks.

"I will be as cautious as the investigation will allow of me. I cannot back off finding the truth because of the danger. I am in danger all the time." Demetri said, breathing his warm breath onto his cool skin.

Aldrik, in problem-solving mode, began to question him about the many ideas he had rambling in his head. He asked him about the dream again, the one where he had woke floating mid-air then was slammed into his bedroom wall.

"Can you rule out, with absolute certainty that you and your growing powers did not do this to yourself? That you didn't cause the burn mark on your neck? Maybe somewhere,

190

deep within your subconscious, you have the ability to inflict this type of pain on yourself."

"The thought has crossed my mind, but come on Aldrik. The handprint, the details about Alex, a man I have never met before, and the detailed dreams? So no, I don't think I did this to myself."

"Okay, the Alex thing aside, you feel with the utmost confidence your powers did not inflict this on you in your dream state?"

Thinking for a moment before answering, Demetri stated, "Yes, I am fully certain of it."

"What about his man, Charles Wilson, who was sacrificed by the river? Why do you think there is a connection to his death and what you are going through now?"

Demetri explained to him that there were similarities that he had just found out and hadn't even shared with Gina yet.

"When I was at Gina's the other day, I happened to see the symbol tattooed on the neck of Alex. It was on a picture she had taken of him. Something about it just struck me as odd, something in my gut. So I followed my hunch and it paid off." Demetri explained, continuing on with his story. "I went down to the police station, hanging out, blending into the scene at the station. I was just waiting, mind open, trying to get a read on the detective working the Riverside Drive murder. It took a while, but I finally connected with him. I was able to tap into his brain and uncover the symbols which had been carved into the chest of Charles Wilson. The symbols had also been carved into the ground near Charles body, including the one tattooed onto the back of Alex's neck. You can think what you want, but to me, that isn't a coincidence."

"No, I would have to agree with you. There is a definite connection between this man, Alex, and the murdered man, Charles." Aldrik said, already deep into his thoughts. "What if this Alex truly does not know why this is happening to him? What if he is a pawn of whatever source this voice, this entity that showed you the visions and he doesn't even realize it? Are you willing to kill a man who just may be innocent?"

"Are you kidding me?" Demetri said, raising his head from his chest. "Are you seriously picking Alex's side?

"Hold on there. I am by no means picking his side over yours. I am merely playing devil's advocate, pardon the pun, if you will. I just want you to be sure you are weighing all of the information equally. You know in your line of work that there are innocents all of the time who get sucked up into this supernatural world of ours." Aldrik stated, trying to put Demetri's fears at ease. "If there is ever a side to pick Demetri, it will always be yours."

"I'm sorry," he said, laying his head down once again to Aldrik's chest. "This all has me so stressed out. I know you are on my side; I don't even know why I said it." Demetri felt bad about his reaction, but knew Aldrik had a point.

He had not considered that Alex was a pawn being used, but it would go with what Alex and Gina have been saying all along. *But if he is innocent and doesn't know anything, then where does that leave them?*

"What about this masked man at The Other Side? Were you able to get anything from scanning his mind?"

"That is the weirdest fucking thing about it. I couldn't get anything from him. His mind was blocked from me," Demetri stated, thinking back on the battle. "You would not believe the amount of energy it took just to hold the man back. He was walking towards me through my own energy field. He was strong, Aldrik, with a supernatural drive to him, but he was human."

To this, his ego was a bit bruised. He remembered the tarot reading and what it had said about him being ego driven. He didn't want to be ego driven, he wanted to be driven by what was right, not by greed or ego.

"Tell me about the incident which happened after the tarot reading, where you were introduced to this Bastiquil and shown visions where you both ruled the land thousands of years before my birth," Aldrik asked, curious to hear more.

"What I got from it was a feeling that it was me with Bastiquil, but I looked entirely different," Demetri explained. "I felt it was my soul and that is what Bastiquil had insinuated as well. So what I took from this was that at some point we were both overthrown and killed. Somehow, my soul has continued to be reborn from thousands of years ago waiting for the day that Bastiquil and myself would be reunited and once again rule this world."

"I am curious as to why you would give any credence to what this Bastiquil had to say anyway? If he is demonic, he is conniving and manipulative."

Demetri became quiet and thoughtful.

"I guess it has to do with what I feel when these visions are happening. I feel something deep, deep within my soul, almost like a memory. Even though, it wasn't my face on the man ruling beside Bastiquil, I could feel the connection with my soul in his body." He said, reflective. "It was more of my soul recognizing itself, than anything else."

To this Aldrik just took it all in and pondered it for a moment.

"Do you think the soul recognition could be a trick bestowed upon you by the demon?"

"No," Demetri quickly stated. "The feeling was too real. The visions resonated with something deep within, even though I had no memory of seeing these before."

Aldrik was thinking about this and had a thought. "It is like the Dalai Lama. Each time one of the Dalai Lama's pass on, their soul is reincarnated and the monks seek out the boys that they believe could possibly be the Dalai Lama reincarnate. They give them some simple tests, one of which is they lay a few items out in front of each boy. Personal items, with only one of them being the actual personal item of the previous Dalai Lama. When one of the boys picks the correct item, he is named Dalai Lama and whisked off to a Buddhist camp where he is intensively trained to be the next spiritual leader for Buddhism." Aldrik explained all of this to him, which he knew mostly, but didn't interrupt Aldrik. "I know we don't have any past items we can use to help identify the truth, but what about past life meditation?"

Aldrik had heard of some who have successfully completed it. It is an extremely intense meditation, one that can be nearly impossible to accomplish. Sometimes even a little dangerous if people go in with a preconceived notion of what they want to find, will find just what they asked for, which is not the intention of this practice. The intent is to go into a spiritual realm with no preconceived ideas of what you are expecting, but to go in with a clear mind and open heart and let the past reveal itself to you. He believed with Demetri's powers and mind control he would have a greater advantage of success than most others who have tried it and failed miserably or just came out of the meditative session more confused.

Demetri was a little apprehensive at first, but the more he thought about it, the more he realized that it just might work. He asked Aldrik what his thoughts on whether a person had been able to travel back over three thousand years in this meditative trance. To this Aldrik clearly stated no, that he knew of no one that even attempted such a feat as that. But Aldrik had faith that he could do this if he went in with the correct mindset and proper intentions.

Aldrik looked over at him and said, "Your phone has been going off for some time now, but I didn't want to wake you since you were sleeping so soundly and peacefully."

"My phone, I didn't hear anything?" Demetri stated.

"That is because it is in the entryway on the credenza by the front door with your keys. I have most excellent hearing in case you have forgotten," Aldrik smiled at him, who had gotten so caught up in this entire situation that he had forgotten.

Demetri reached over and gave him a kiss then crawled out of bed and walked towards the entryway. Aldrik admired the sight of his perfect nude body as he walked out of the room. When he reached the phone, he was a bit surprised and concerned that he had at least fifteen missed calls from Gina and five voicemails from her. As he played back the messages, his surprise turned to fear, then to surprise and back again.

Gina's first message was telling him about Alex coming by and the link between the tattoos and the symbol being embedded in them. She was convinced that he was being used for some reason but wasn't quite sure what. She had begged him to call her back.

Then the next message was about what her search of the symbol turned up and he wasn't going to like it at all. It was a symbol of demonic origins dealing with the demon Bastiquil. To this his heart sank as he realized that there was something deep inside him that he had already known, but was in denial about it.

The next two messages were more recent and they were telling him that there had been two more murders that night in Woodward Park, a married couple who were strung up to a tree with their throats slit. It was all over the news. They are now claiming that there is a ritualistic serial killer on the loose. Gina was begging him to call her back.

The fifth and final message was of Gina telling him that he needed to come home. That she needed his help, his guidance. That Alex had just revealed to her he had dreamed about the killing of a couple just before he had come over and that they were both freaking out about it. She was stating that there had to be a link with the symbol and Bastiquil. What she feared is that Bastiquil was going to use Alex as a way to get back into this world, to cross realms and take possession of him. That was the only thing that made sense to her. She had been thinking about this ever since her conversation with Dr. Vance. If Dr. Vance was correct and Bastiquil did exist at one point and he was a magical being, maybe even a demonic being, then he would have the means and knowledge to get back into this world. Gina begged him to call her when he got this message and worried that she hadn't heard back from him by now.

Demetri pushed redial on his phone and she picked it up on the first ring. "Demetri, where in the hell are you?" Gina asked him frantically. "Are you okay?"

"I am with Aldrik in Kansas City and, yes, I am okay. What the hell is going on back there? Why are you with Alex? And what do you know about these new killings?" Demetri fired off the questions one by one at her.

"Demetri I think all hell is getting ready to break loose. I can feel it, something is coming. There have been too many signs pointing towards it. Alex came over last night and I went over the pictures where someone had embedded symbols of his tattoo on his neck, but on a smaller scale, where he would not even be able to see it. I only saw it because I magnified it by two hundred percent." Gina said.

"I am going to ask you a question and I want you to be very careful in how you answer it. Is he there with you now?"

"No!"

"How do you know that he isn't the one that killed that couple in the park? How do you know that the killer isn't there with you now?" Demetri asked her pointedly. "You could have a killer in your home right now."

"Would you please give me some fucking credit? I am not a bumbling idiot! I don't for one minute think that he killed those people; I do, however, think that he is being used in some fashion that is going to put his life in danger."

"Then why didn't he tell you right away about the dream of the couple? Why did he wait until you saw it on the news?"

"What would you do if you came over here and I told you that ninety percent of the tattoos on your body, which you dreamed of before you got them, were actually put on you with hidden demonic symbols?" Gina asked. "Would you be in the right frame of mind? Would you just be forthcoming with the information that you dream about people's deaths as they were happening? Probably not!"

"I just want you to be careful. I don't trust him at all," Demetri stated.

"Well, I do, and if you trust me then you are going to have to get over whatever it is you think he might have done and trust that I am right on this one. We need your help, not

196

your resistance." Gina told him, who was starting to once again feel bad for doubting her. She never ever doubted him and he just kept on doing it to her lately. This whole thing is such a mess that it has everyone on edge.

"I'm sorry, I really am. I am just so worried about you, me, and what is happening. I would die if anything happened to you," Demetri said, which softened her from the anger she was feeling towards him.

"I feel the same about you and that is why I try to always be there to have your back. You are always in some dangerous situations and I fear that one day I am not going to be there and something will happen to you."

"Well, today isn't going to be that day," Demetri stated.

"Was Aldrik able to offer any help with this riddle we are dealing with?"

"Aldrik had lots of good advice that I will tell you all about when I get back. Right now it sounds like I need to be there, so let me say my goodbyes and get on the road."

"Okay, be safe and I love you Demetri," Gina said to him as he smiled to himself.

"Love you too, G."

As he made his way back into the bedroom where Aldrik was awaiting him, he knew that he didn't need to tell Aldrik what all was said, because he knew that he had heard everything. With super vampire hearing, he was able to hear their conversation.

"Sounds like you have your hands full back in Tulsa," Aldrik said to him as he stood up from the bed and walked over to Demetri taking him in his arms.

"Yes, I am going to have to head back right away," Demetri said as he closed his eyes for a moment and just took in the sweet embrace that he was being given.

"I wish that you could stay longer, Demetri. I feel that I don't see you as much as I would like to," Aldrik said as he was hugging him tightly.

"I feel the same way, but right now I am needed back home," he stated, a little lost in this embrace and this

197

confession of Aldrik's. He would like nothing better than to stay with him, to be here with him; hell, he would love for him to come back to Tulsa with him, but he would never ask that of Aldrik.

As if reading his mind, Aldrik stated, "Demetri, you know that if you ever need me, all you have to do is ask and I will be there."

"And I love you for that Aldrik," he said as he leaned down and kissed his lips. "Now I have to head out and see if I can get to the bottom of this mystery."

"Demetri, don't discount the past life meditation; it may just offer you some clues that could be of use to you," Aldrik said to him as he watched him get dressed.

Demetri smiled at him as he finished putting on his clothes and pulled on his leather boots. Not wanting to say goodbye and definitely not wanting to leave, he said simply, "Until I see you again, my friend, my love."

Aldrik gave him one last kiss and watched him head out of the bedroom to the front door of the condo. Then he was gone.

Chapter Thirty-Seven

When Gina got off the phone with Demetri, she was thrilled to hear he was coming home right away. This new information not only about the murders but about Alex dreaming about them was especially interesting and worrisome. This was going to take all of their combined efforts to figure this out. One thing she was completely sure of was that Alex was not involved in an intentional way, but he was inadvertently a witness to these horrible murders through his dreams.

The fact that his tattoos included smaller versions of the symbol on his neck, and they were believed to be linked to a demon named Bastiquil, who may or may not have ruled three thousand years ago with Demetri's soul. This could not all be just a coincidence. This was getting far too real for comfort.

Demetri called Gina on the drive back and had filled Gina in on Aldrik's thoughts about the situation. He told her about the stories Aldrik had been told about Bastiquil as a child before he was turned into a vampire. These were supposed to be stories to keep children from being bad. From everything Gina was beginning to piece together, she was leaning towards the unthinkable possibility Bastiquil may actually be making an attempt at coming back to this realm. *Could this actually be real?*

Demetri informed her of his discovering that the symbol tattooed on Alex's neck was found on the body of the first victim, Charles, and drawn on the ground near the body. This could be the reason that Alex is dreaming about these murders. If this were the case, then logic would have it that they will find these same symbols on the bodies of the couple that was murdered in Woodward Park last night. She shuddered at the thought and wondered just where they needed to go from here.

Alex had left a little bit ago as he had to open the tattoo shop. He had a guy call in sick today who was supposed to do it so he kissed her, telling her what a wonderful time he had last night and that he would call her later. She had enjoyed it as well.

She dreaded the thought of having to talk to Demetri about it. She wasn't afraid of what he would say, but more of what he might do to Alex. Gina would have to just get him to see Alex was as much a victim in this as he was.

She knew she had a little time before he made it back home to Tulsa and decided that she was so wrapped up in all that was happening she had lost her centeredness. She needed to reconnect with the earth, with the spiritual world, with the four corners. She needed some time to meditate. Gina set about getting the room ready for her to do a cleansing on herself. She took a white candle, a black candle, and a green candle and set them out. She knew that she would need a lot of help with this so she took some myrrh out and lit it. Concentrating on the three candles before her she imagined the three wicks with flame and as she concentrated she felt the energy leaving her body and in her mind she saw the candle wicks light up with a flame. She knew she had been successful because she could smell the soot from the candles as they were burning.

Reaching deep inside herself, she attempted to remain as calm and peaceful as she could until her mind finally started to settle down and relax. She could feel herself starting to drift into a meditative state. She was becoming one with her surroundings and she was connecting with her chi. She liked to manipulate the energy, move it around, and control it. This was a practice she had been doing for years and as the years had gone by she was learning to control the energy around her much easier even when she was not in a meditative trance. This is how she had learned to send energy jolts into the minds of others, sending them into almost a reboot of sorts.

Gina knew that her mother and grandmother would be so proud of the witch that she was becoming. She was so into the craft and promoting it as a good practice and showing people the inner witch that we all have in us. It was about energy, elements, and nature. One had to believe in their ability to control some situations and realize when some things were out of their control.

Gina caught herself thinking again and quickly identified the source and worked to shut it down. She needed to be thought free, one with the energy around her. As she sank deeper again, she began to send out mental thoughts that she was seeking answers to. She was asking the universe about what she was missing in this entire situation, what was something that she needed to know so that she could get a better grasp on the situation. As she threw the question out to the universe, she allowed herself to be calm again, to let her mind go, let it sink deeper into the trance that she was finding herself surrendering to.

As she was sitting there, cross-legged on a pillow on the floor, an image started to come to her. At first she was thinking it was a light ball, an energy source revealing itself. As she maintained control of the trance, she realized that it was actually a full moon, but a different type of moon; it was a blue moon. This had so many implications that Gina tried hard to not give into all the thoughts that were fighting so hard to come to the surface. As she watched this moon, this blue moon, she saw it come to its peak height in the sky, she saw the underworld come out and revel in it. She saw Demetri and Alex under the blue moon. There lay the connection. This is it, the break they had been waiting for.

Gina found herself falling out the trance and back to reality. She quickly jumped up from the floor and made her way to the computer. She typed into the search engine to identify when the next blue moon would be. To her amazement, it turned up as being this month, less than a week away. *How the hell did she miss this?* She was a witch who operated on the elements, the universe and its alignments.

Gina was reading an excerpt from the Huffington Post about the blue moon which is due on August 20, 2013. It is not only the Blue Moon; it is the Full Sturgeon Moon, the Full Red Moon, the Green Corn Moon, and the Grain Moon. *This is going to be one fucking powerful full moon. How the fuck could I have missed this? This was not like me.*

The energy surrounding this moon would make magic at its all-time powerful, and could make it possible for this Bastiquil to make a move. *My god, what was going on? Is a three-thousand-year-old demon that walked the earth and is actually probably thousands of years older than that, going to try and break through the realms in less than a week? It is the only thing that makes sense.*

How would she get Demetri and Alex to first of all believe her and secondly to get them to work together to make sure that if she were right, that it didn't happen? This would not be a good thing.

Gina decided to give Demetri a call on his way home and talk to him more about the situation and about what she had seen in her meditative trance. To her surprise, he was actually listening to what she had to say and not being judgmental. But, as she was telling him about the full blue moon that was quickly approaching she had a sudden realization; Alex's tattoo parlor was called Blue Moon Tattoo. In a game they seemed to be caught up in, this seemed too surreal to be anything but another sign. She didn't think for one minute that it was just coincidental.

She decided to give Alex a call after she hung up with Demetri. When he answered the phone, he told her he had just finished with the customer.

She told him that she had a question for him. "Fire away," Alex said to her.

"How did you come up with the name Blue Moon Tattoo?"

"Well, I have always been fascinated with full moons, but if I was to be totally honest with you, I had a dream that I

202

named it that, so I did," his voice trailing off slightly, as he realized that his dreams had once again played a huge role in the decisions in his life.

"Alex, we need to talk. Can you come over when you get off work? Demetri may be back by then and I really need you two men to meet and get on the same page."

He was more than a little worried about the prospect of meeting up with a guy who has the power to lift him off the ground with his mind and slam him up against a wall. But he had to admit that he really, truly trusted Gina so he told her sure, he would meet them.

"Alex, thank you so much. I will make sure Demetri is on his best behavior."

She then placed another call to Demetri and told him what she had set up. She warned him within an inch of his life that he had better come in to this with an open mind and his guns holstered, not out and blazing. Much to her surprise, he had done it again, he told her that he was willing to meet with him and see what he had to say.

Chapter Thirty-Eight

Victor had been on edge for most of the morning. As soon as the news hit he had been getting phone call after phone call from some pretty important members of the Balashon asking him what he was thinking making such a spectacle out of the sacrifices. They were saying such things as it should have been done in privacy, where no one could have found out. That he was drawing unneeded attention to their work and was running the risk of being caught.

What they didn't know about Victor or what they have chosen to forget is that he makes no mistakes; he knew what he was doing. The scare that was in the city right now was creating a paranoia that was charging the air. The scene was going to be ripe for when their master came. He would tell Victor what a wonderful job he had done and bestow upon him the honor of being a general in his army. He would fight to the death for the master and he didn't care what these pansies from the Balashon thought. It was Victor who was here making the calls on the sacrifices, making sure they were ones that the master could feast upon that the master would love.

He knew that once the master arrived, things would be different. No longer would he take orders from the billionaire members of the Balashon, but rather from the most powerful force of nature that ever walked this earth. He would rule them all as he had the last time. They would bow at the master's feet, wash his feet, even lick his feet if the master so

204

desired. They quickly forgot that if not for the master's love and support they wouldn't be in the powerful positions they were now.

He continued to pace the huge library that was in the house. He had made the right call on this sacrifice just as he had on the first one and for that he offered no apologies. He would only apologize if the master so demanded it of him. But careful thought and planning was put into each one so he knew that the master would understand that, know that as he devoured their souls and he used them as fuel for his homecoming day.

Victor had picked out three possibilities for the third sacrifice. Even though, he only needed one of them, it would make him honored and proud to be able to give the master all three. These three selections would be what the vessel needed to be broken enough for the master to take over, to take root inside him, to cast him aside, and rule through him. There was already one that was offering to be a sacrifice, which is good, a willing sacrifice is a just and righteous one and will be accepted by the master as the others had. The pomp and circumstance of being able to offer up three gifts as the third sacrifice just was too rich to pass up.

He continued to pace, to plot, to plan. Well aware of the vessels actions the night before, he knew he had gone to the witch after the second sacrifice and spent the night with the witch. That was okay though, even the vessel deserved to be able to get some sexual relief once in a while. He had to admit that he would have really enjoyed the red headed witch servicing him after such a ripe and erotic kill last night, but he would have his opportunity. The gap is quickly closing in on the time to reap the last offerings to the master and he is going to make sure that he had his way with the witch before she was given over.

As for the male witch, he might try to stop him but he was not afraid of him. He had almost bested him in direct battle with the witch using almost full capacity of his powers and still he had proven his strength, his determination, and his willingness to do what was needed. What the male witch didn't realize is Victor is willing to die for his cause. The third sacrifice would be offered up because there was an army of men just like Victor waiting in the wings to step in at any moment to finish what needed to be done for the master's arrival.

He prayed daily to the master and he prayed now for the master to be proud of him to accept his offerings with the intent they were given. He wanted so badly to hear from the master himself, but that is coming and coming quickly. Less than a week away from his master's arrival. This gave him such pleasure, he found he was growing hard at just the thought of it.

He had found a willing victim last night as he was driving back from the park. He had made a slight detour on the way back and went through an area of town where he knew that some prostitutes worked the streets. One had really stuck out to him, because of his likeness to the male witch. He hadn't planned on bringing a male back with him. He had intended on bringing a female whore back, but the male whore favored the male witch so much, he found himself determined to have him, even if force was needed to take him. But that was not necessary because the male whore climbed into the SUV willingly. He was a pretty boy who didn't need to be whoring himself out, but what did Victor care, if the boy wanted to whore, let him. This would be his last trick he turned; actually the trick would be on him.

As he drove back to the compound, he had told the boy to service him. He was still hard from the kill as he, usually, was for hours after, and the boy did not hesitate to oblige his client's wishes. He gave him such good mouth service on the drive back. He let the whore walk into the house, let him gaze upon the splendor of it, of the richness and decadence of it. The boy's eyes filled with amazement and he knew what the boy was thinking, what they all thought before he started to fill them with terror. The boy thought maybe, just maybe this was his shot. That this man would fall deeply in love with him after this one night of sex and whisk him off the streets and out of the bonds of prostitution. Oh, how wrong they all were. He had one goal and one goal only and that was to fulfill his destiny to his master.

So this boy, this whore, like so many before him would soon find out there were so many horrors on this earth, so many pains to be inflicted on a person, they would eventually beg for death. They would beg for him to end their miserable lives.

He had used the boy for hours when he arrived home with him. At first he had thought he had lucked out. Then the boy saw the basement, the dungeon-like area full of sex slings and bondage equipment, he thought he had found a man that was just kinky, who had a fetish, and a role he wanted the boy to play. The little male whore had told him that it would cost him extra for the role play, especially if he wanted him to get into the sling or any of the other equipment. He just smiled at him, stroking his own cock proudly, telling the boy to name his price.

The boy then smiled with joy when he agreed to his terms, but he had no idea that he had no intention of paying up, that he would never leave this dungeon alive or in one piece.

But the boy was resilient; he had lasted a long time. He had put him through the ringer and still the boy held on. He wasn't in his right mind at the moment because his pain threshold had been surpassed, but he had held out longer than any of the others.

Victor had gone upstairs leaving the boy in a wooden stockade, one that made into a bench. He had the little whore straddling the bench. His crotch and stomach were facing the bench, his legs hanging from each side. His head and arms were locked down into the stockade which was a little higher than the bench itself so the boy was forced to stand slightly or he would risk more pain and injury to his head and neck.

Victor paced the library, raging with anger from the annoying calls from people he had admired for so long, his thoughts went back to the boy downstairs, the one whom all of this rage was getting ready to be focused towards. The boy has been taking a beating for each call Victor received this day.

He would take all that Victor had to give him. If he survived, he might get to rest until the next time he was ready to play. He had his doubts that he would last this go around. He had some pain he was ready to inflict. His cock grew hard with the thought of it.

Walking down the stairs to the basement, he could feel the rush of blood to his cock. He was pumped and ready for this. As he entered the basement, he made his way to the dungeon where the male whore was still strapped into the wooden stockade. He could tell that the whore was starting to give out as his legs were starting to quiver and falter. The boy let out a moan of pain each time his legs gave out because it was putting such a strain on his neck. The intense pain he felt left him numb and detached. The torture he had endured just hours before had been almost too much for him to bear, he was praying for help, for someone to save him, then he was praying for death. This man was a brutal beast and he knew that he was not going to get out of here alive.

As the boy's eyes opened just enough to see Victor coming towards him, he tried to speak with what little voice he had left, but it came out as a garbled whisper. "Please just kill me, don't hurt me anymore," the boy pleaded with him.

As he approached him, he reached out and punched the boy in the face. "Shut the fuck up boy or I will keep you alive down here forever."

The boy let out a weak scream as the pain ricocheted throughout his body, his face tingling with the pain that Victor's fist had just inflicted. There was blood dripping from his mouth and off his lips. His mouth was so dry that he didn't have the saliva that one typically would have to mix with the blood. He verbally assaulted the boy, calling him a whore, a weak sex slave to be used for his pleasure then left to die from his injuries. He made sure that the boy knew there would be injuries, more than he had already received.

The boy started to cry and again was begging Victor to just kill him. He was begging in a hoarse whisper of a voice. He just laughed and told the boy, "shut the fuck up before I get the knives out and continue to teach you a lesson."

The boy quickly stopped crying, pushing it back, pushing it deeply inward so that he would not know that he was crying. The one thing he did want him to know is that he wanted to die. He wanted this to end.

He took a bullwhip out of the armoire that was opposite the head of the stockade. He held the bullwhip out behind him, swinging it back and forth, cracking it behind the boy to make him wince in anticipation of an impending connection of the leather with his skin. As he was tensing up, he was using more and more of his already spent energy from trying to hold himself up so that his neck was not being stretched out in pain. But then the boy got an idea, if he just threw himself downward onto the bench it just might break his neck so that he didn't need to beg him anymore to kill him. He could finally take that out of his hands.

As the boy threw himself down, it hurt like hell but did not achieve the intended result. He was alive, neck unbroken, and could hear the crack of the bullwhip as it was in the air heading towards his backside. As it made contact with his back, it broke the skin, blood flying from the impact and his hoarse voice found some new life as he let out a yell from the pain that he was feeling. "You sadistic fucker," the boy yelled at him as the whip was once again in the air cracking as it made contact with is back again. The blood from the tears in the skin on his back was flowing down his back, across his ass cheeks, with some even in his ass crack, and running down his legs.

Victor finally took the whip and wrapped it around the boy's neck, pulling it tight as the air was being kept from his lungs and the blood was unable to enter or leave his brain. His face started to turn red and as he entered him from behind he was not even able to let out a hint of a yell of pain due to the lack of oxygen and blood, but the tears were rolling down his face. He knew that this was it. He was in immense pain, but this was going to be the time that he would die. He finally found the way he was going to take this boy from this earth.

As Victor plunged deep inside him, the face of the boy was turning from red to purple. He was starting to struggle, as

209

was natural when your body was put into survival mode even though the boy wanted to die.

"You are a nasty, bitch, whore of a boy who needs a man to teach you your place on this earth," Victor yelled at the boy, as he plunged deeper into him and pulled on the bull whip tighter and tighter. Just when the boy was starting to drift into unconsciousness Victor dropped the bullwhip and continued to pound the boy's ass with his cock. He was wearing the straps around the thighs of his legs that held his daggers. Reaching down to the sides of his thighs, he pulled out both daggers. With an insult to the boy, he held both daggers up and out to his side then swiftly brought them down driving into each side of the boy's rib cage, puncturing his lungs.

The boy could do nothing but gurgle as his lungs were filling up with blood. He could feel the drowning sensation and lack of air. He was grateful in a way as he no longer was going to be subjected to the cruelty of this monster; he would finally die and be done. Victor pulled out both blades as he continued to pound on the boy from behind. He then proceeded to plunge the knives back into the boy's sides, pulling them out and driving them back in until the boy was limp, hanging there by his neck and his arms.

He pulled himself out of the boy and looked down proudly. He could think nothing other than another piece of trash was off the streets and he had some fun taking out his frustration of the male witch. He wished that witch was the one laying here on this bench dead to the world. Soon he would have his chance; soon they would all feel his daggers.

Chapter Thirty-Nine

Demetri arrived back in Tulsa around noon and went directly to Gina's. He was excited to see her and to hear about the new information that she had found. He pulled into the parking lot of Gina's place and made his way around the side of the building to the back parking lot where there was an entrance to her living quarters. He used his key to let himself in knowing that she would probably be in the front of the store since it was business hours.

He went directly to the bathroom as he had to take a leak. He had been holding it since right after he passed through Joplin and he felt like he was about to explode. When he was finished, he came out of the bathroom and was standing in Gina's bedroom and he suddenly realized she had not been alone last night. If she had been alone, she would have done something completely out of character, which was to undo the other side of the bed and use those pillows. Unless she was having company sleep over, she didn't bother to undo the other side of the bed, she just didn't. He had an idea what had gone down here and he wasn't sure how he felt about it. He knew though, that she was a grown woman and that she wouldn't have agreed with what he had done the night before so he had better tread lightly.

As he grabbed a pastry off the counter in the kitchen area, he decided to head out to the sales floor where Gina was. Eating the Danish along the way he was wondering if Aldrik was thinking about him? He wondered if Aldrik was already missing him like he was missing Aldrik. He knew that it couldn't work between the two as he was not ready to be turned. He didn't know if he ever would be ready, but still that didn't stop how he felt about him, how he wished things had been different.

When he found her on the sales floor, he walked up behind her without her knowing and poked her in the side. She jumped letting out a scream which scared the two customers that were in the store. She turned to see him and slapped him on the arm before hugging his neck and telling him that she was so glad he was home. She turned and apologized to the two customers for her best friend's ill-timed antics. They both smiled as if they understood and went about their shopping.

"When did you get back?"

"Literally, just a few minutes ago," Demetri told her. "I let myself in through the back, took a leak and grabbed a pastry off the kitchen counter. I'm starving."

"Aldrik didn't offer to feed you?" She asked him a little sarcastically.

Demetri looked at her with wide eyes thinking, *girl two can play that game.*

"I am surprised you had any left to offer me. I figured that you would have fed Alex before he left here this morning," he shot back at her as she looked at him with guilty wide eyes.

"You are a total asshole Demetrius Marcus," she told him. "Did you get into my head?"

Laughing at her, he said, "I didn't have to, I could tell by your bed that someone had been here, but you just confirmed who it was."

Gina began to laugh as she knew she couldn't get anything past her best friend. They were like that. Both very observant, down to the slightest of details; an extra indentation in a throw pillow, a magazine out of place, just things they both knew about themselves and the other that would alert them that something was up. There was some

212

comfort in that knowledge as well as complete and utter frustration.

"So what's up with a double murder in the park?" He asked her as the two customers looked up again overhearing what he had asked and both having a fearful look about them. All of Tulsa and the surrounding towns were on edge as they were calling the murderer a serial killer in the press. Actually they were calling him the 'Cult Killer', saying it was a ritual killing, one that would be used to sacrifice an offering to the devil. It had slowed business down for her as people were nervous about getting out and about being seen going into a store that had even a remote connection to what some would think occult.

"All I really know is that it happened sometime around midnight, it was a married couple, celebrating their first-year anniversary. They were grabbed from their car just down the road from their home. They were taken to Woodward Park which is where they were found early this morning, hanging upside down from a tree with their throats cut," she explained in a quiet voice so that she didn't further alarm the customers.

"Do you know if there is a connection yet between the couple and the first man who was killed?"

"If there is, other than Alex dreaming about them, the police department hasn't let that out yet. Come over here to the reading room I want to show you something," she said as she grabbed his hand pulling him along. "Look at these pictures of his tattoos and see if you can see the hidden symbol in them?"

As he was checking out the pictures, she had to head to the cash register as there was a customer who was ready to pay for her purchase. He was looking at the pictures closely. He noticed the symbols were well hidden, some barely noticeable to the eye and some that would not be noticeable at all had it not been for the fact that they were blown up so big. He did stop and stare a bit at the picture she had taken of the tattoo of Alex's cock. He had to admit that it was impressive, both the tattoo and the cock. *Maybe this guy, Alex, was telling the truth. I mean if you are going to deliberately put hidden symbols in your*

213

tats, why hide them? Especially when no one would know what they mean if they truly were from an ancient past language that is lost to this day and age.

He was looking at the other information she had on the table as well. She had printed out information about the upcoming blue moon. This will be a multiple of different types of moons, making it one of the rarest of its kind, not seen for many centuries again. If there ever was going to be a magical convergence of astrological importance, this was it. This would be the time to attempt to bring someone into this world that had long been gone. And if he really were a demon, Demetri could only guess that he would be a powerful one. Especially if he had the ability to communicate with Alex and himself when he wasn't even a part of this realm yet. This wasn't sounding like it was going to be a fun week. He really wished that Aldrik was here to help him with this.

"So what do you make of all this so far?"

"I think we are screwed and need to run for the hills," he said half joking and half serious.

"I've never seen anything scare you before and I don't want to start now," Gina said as she looked at him seriously.

"I'm not going anywhere until we figure this out, but I fear that we are running out of time. I think you are on to something with this blue moon concept," Demetri said to her as he held up the printed materials he was just looking at.

As Gina geared up to tell Demetri something else, she took a deep breath and let it out as she began to speak. "I want you to listen to me and listen well. I have invited Alex over here for lunch hoping that you would be back so we could all sit down and discuss this like the adults we are."

"And what pray tell am I supposed to be listening to?" He asked her with a coy smile.

"You attacked him in the bar and slammed him into the wall," she said to him with a raised voice.

"Well, if you count dreams, he attacked me first," he said looking upward instead of at Gina.

"Demetrius Marcus, I will only say this one time. I believe in my heart of hearts that he is innocent in this.

Everything in me is saying this. I think someone is using him and has been using him for years now, but to what end I am not sure yet. So I expect you to treat him with respect, to apologize to him and to listen to him if he has something to add to this," she said to him sternly. "Am I making myself clear mister?"

"Oh, yes ma'am, loud and clear," he said to her as he pointed towards the customer that was looking at them weirdly. Gina just realized that she must have been raising her voice. The customer decided it was time to leave before anything broke out and headed out the front door of the shop. She was a little relieved to see her go as she was still a little nervous about getting Demetri and Alex in the same room together.

Gina jumped a bit as her cell phone started ringing. She thought to herself, *get ahold of yourself Gina, you're too anxious.* As she looked at the screen of the phone, she saw it was Alex calling.

"Hey Alex," she said as she answered the phone. "How are you?"

"I'm good," he said. "I'm in the parking lot and just wanted to know if it was safe to come in."

"Yes it is safe to come in," Gina said looking once again sternly at Demetri. "Demetri is here and we're ready to sit down and talk."

"Okay, I will be right in."

She once again made Demetri swear to be on his best behavior and he said that he would be. Both looked up as the bell chime sounded and Alex came walking into the store carrying a box of pizza and a two liter of soda.

He walked in with the best look of confidence he could muster up and walked up to Gina and kissed her on the cheek. He set the pizza and soda down on the table and looked over at Demetri. He stuck his hand out to Demetri in an attempt to shake his hand. "I think we got off on the wrong foot last time, so to speak," he said. "My name is Alex."

215

Demetri looked at Gina, who was eyeing him closely and then he looked back at Alex, taking his hand and shaking it. "Yes about that, I wanted to apologize for my impulsive behavior at the bar. It seems we have a lot in common and a lot to talk about."

"It would appear so," Alex said.

Chapter Forty

Gina grabbed three glasses out of the kitchen and placed ice in them. Demetri and Alex were sizing each other up. Demetri knew that he had spent the night here with Gina, but wondered if Alex knew where he had been last night. *Surely, Gina wouldn't have told him about that. Would she?*

Gina returned to the reading room where she placed the glasses down on the table. Turning to head back into the kitchen to get some plates, she said, "You boys are playing nicely aren't you?"

Demetri turned to her and smiled saying, "Of course we are, do you think we are Neanderthals that would go around slamming people into walls?" He laughed a bit, but then realized he was the only one laughing. "Too soon?" Demetri said to Alex and Gina who both looked at each other.

Gina broke the awkwardness by saying, "I would never think of you as capable of reaching the category of Neanderthal, Demetri."

All three of them remained silent then burst out laughing. This helped to lighten the mood of the room. Gina was gone and back in a flash with the plates as Alex was opening the box of pizza placing it in the middle of them so they could all reach it easily.

"So I have a question for you Alex? That is if you don't mind me asking?"

"No, not at all; I will do my best to answer it," Alex said smiling.

"I actually have a ton of questions for you but will start with the tattoos. You had no idea that someone was putting symbols in your tattoos that you didn't ask for and that was identical to your tattoo on the back of your neck?" Demetri asked him with a puzzled look.

Alex had thought about his answer before he began to speak. He wanted to be completely honest with them, but he knew that he had to win over Demetri so that he would help him and because he meant so much to Gina. Getting up from the chair where he was sitting at the table, he began to unbutton his shirt which got inquisitive, yet puzzled looks from both Gina and Demetri. As he walked up to Demetri, he opened up his shirt to show the face of the troll that was on his stomach. The tattoo came from around his back and ended with the face on his stomach.

"Look at the face on this troll. Look really closely. Now look into the pupil of its eye. Can you see the symbol just by looking at it?" Alex asked him trying to prove a point.

"Actually, no I can't. Point taken," Demetri said. "I guess I just thought, you being a tattoo artist, an owner of a tattoo shop, you would know if something was askew. But, it is minuscule and I know G had to blow it up to even see it."

"Yes, I don't think there was anyone more shocked than myself to find out that I had been deceived by people I thought I could trust," he said looking sad for a moment then returning his gaze back to them.

"So you knew the people doing all of your tattoos?" Demetri asked him.

"Yes, I knew every one of them. I hired most of them and the ones that I didn't, were always begging me to let them be the ones to do my next tattoo. I guess, I know why now," he said with a hint of bitterness.

Demetri had the pictures of Alex's tattoos spread out on the left side of him on the table looking at them while he was eating a slice of pizza.

"So G tells me that you dreamed about all of the tattoos that you have on you that contain the symbol? Is that correct?"

"Yes, you are correct."

"You seem to have some pretty intense dreams," Demetri said changing the subject slightly. "What is it that you feel when you are having the dreams of the people who have been murdered?"

Alex was a little taken aback with his bluntness, but had told himself that he was going to answer him honestly. "Well, I felt their fear, but I felt it from a standpoint more of a watching aspect, as if I were there, but just watching all of this being played out."

Demetri was thinking about his answer and felt that he was sincere. "Well, that actually sucks. That you would have to watch something so sadistic, so brutal and that you can't even tell the police about it for fear of them thinking you had something to do with it."

Gina and Alex both nodded in agreement.

Alex then became distant, reflective for a moment. She caught this and reached over and put a hand on his arm. "Are you okay, Alex?" She said to him.

"I told myself that I was going to be totally honest with both of you with whatever question you asked me, but there is something that I haven't told you. Something that has been in both dreams of the murdered victims," he said looking frightened at the moment.

Demetri leaned forward so he could better hear him, and Gina turned in her chair so she was facing him. "You can tell us anything, I hope you know that? We are all in this together and if we are going to figure it out, we have to have all the information," she said to him.

"During the dreams, I can feel what they are feeling, as far as emotions, and some of the pain associated with those emotions, but there is something else. I never actually see the face of the murderer. He does some writing on the ground of some symbols. My neck tattoo being one of them and carves them into the flesh of the people," he said his eyes tearing up a little.

"Oh my god, that is horrible that you have to witness this," Gina said thoughtfully.

"Well, I think it's more horrible for the people it's happening too, but please go on," Demetri said prompting him to continue with his story.

He continued on. "The murderer is chanting something as he is carving these symbols in the ground and in the victim's flesh. Chanting in another language and it feels as if I should know what he is saying, but I don't. As he is chanting, the symbols that he has drawn in the ground become like flames, then the ground starts to give way and opens up to a fiery pit. This next part is going to sound so far off the fucking wall, but then these huge, gigantic dog-like creatures come out of the hole. They circle the souls of these victims and then attack them, dragging them into the burning pit. The souls of those people are screaming as they are dragged down into what must be hell."

He was getting emotional as he recalled the latest dream he had the night before. He grabbed the glass with the soda and took a sip. He was looking at them to see if they believed what he was saying. He was looking for any sign that they understood what he was trying so desperately to explain to them.

"So what you are saying is that these people are being killed as a sacrifice to either Satan or this demon Bastiquil?" Demetri asked.

"I believe so," he stated relieved that Demetri was thinking along the same lines as he was.

"So let me get this straight," Gina said trying to wrap her head around all of this. "Tulsa has a serial killer that is sacrificing people and sending them to hell? Is this what you are saying? Because if this is true, then we have bigger things to worry about then how you two are linked together by some dream. I mean, come on. It's one thing to think the symbol tattooed on the back of your neck was regarding a demon, but it's another thing if someone is actually in Tulsa killing people as an offering to this demon."

"What else could it mean?" Alex questioned. "I felt their fear as they were attacked by the beasts and then dragged into that pit. When the ground closed behind them, the connection or whatever I had to the victims in the dream was lost. They were gone."

Demetri thought about all this for a moment as they all sat in silence, no one knowing really what to say. He had to admit there was something happening here, something supernatural, one that had people on edge, afraid. For the most part, he felt that this is what was wanted by people who go on serial killing sprees like this. They want to make people scared, scared to go out at night, scared to leave their homes, scared to say hello to their neighbor. But this was what Demetri was here for, to fight those who would cause this type of chaos. He was here to make sure that the supernatural world stayed in line as much as possible. To make sure it wasn't spilling over into a perfect, sublime ignorance most of the human race chose to keep themselves in.

But that was okay, because you take away a person's hope and faith and they are left with panic and despair. Panic and despair were never a good thing for the city to be in. People started doing crazy things like marshal law, shooting the paper boy because he was too close to their home, robbing, and pillaging. No, Demetri thought it was best that some people were kept in the dark, allowed to believe in the best of the human race, there were no supernatural beings out there that can hurt them, that life on white picket fence lane was just glorious and fabulous.

He brought himself back to this moment, back to the conversation at hand. There had been such a long period of silence that both Gina and Alex jumped a bit in their chairs when he spoke. "So the dream I had about you Alex, the one where you were able to lift me in the air with your mind, able to command your tattoos to attack, able to kill off an entire army of witches, vampires, and werewolves by just instructing your tattoos to do it. Let's talk about that dream?" Demetri said bringing them all back to the conversation at hand and making Gina a little nervous in the process. She wasn't sure where he would take this conversation and she was sure that things were going fairly well between them.

"Well, I'm not sure how much help I would be since I don't remember having a dream like that before?" Alex stated, being truthful with him.

"You were this all powerful being, one that had the entire underworld of Tulsa shaking in their boots, scared of their own shadows. You were chasing me down Riverside Drive, telling me that we were destined to be together that it was three thousand years in the making. You had said that when the moon was blue that you would return and we would once again rule the earth or destroy it if the humans chose not to bow down." He was trying to get a reaction out of Alex, to see if he recalled any of this.

"I'm sorry Demetri, but I don't know what you are referring to. I will admit to partaking in some, mind altering drugs lately and sometimes I get to a point where when I wake up I don't even remember anything about the night before."

"What the fuck G, you want to date some drug addict?"

"Well, first of all, drug addict is a little harsh; I don't do this every day and I only do it to escape from all these dreams haunting my sleeping hours. As for Gina, let's not bring her choices into this. It's me that you are mad at, not her," Alex shot back at him, doing his best to stand his ground without provoking. He didn't like to hear her being put down.

"Demetri, we have discussed this many times before and I will only say this one more time. I am a big girl, who can make my own decisions and I can take care of myself. I love that you want to protect me, but you have to let me live my life on my terms, not yours. I don't owe you an explanation about anything, but I will say Alex and I are both consenting adults and what may or may not have happened is none of your concern. It was a moment in time between two adults and to answer your earlier question, no we are not dating." She told him, who knew that he had gone too far. She knew that Demetri was still frustrated that he was holding onto his "I don't remember anything about your dream" card. Which if truth be told, he may not. This may have been just Demetri's dream and his alone. It's not like Demetri has been dreaming the same dreams that Alex has.

"I apologize to both of you; that was a low blow. I am just frustrated as I know you both are too. I think that we have to just go with what we know and keep looking for answers. My dream felt foreshadowing, almost apocalyptic. I felt like it was telling me something, as had the visions I had after the tarot reading, which I'm sure you have already filled him in on?"

She nodded in agreement that she had told Alex. She figured that wasn't going to sit well with Demetri either, but to her surprise he kept moving on.

"In my dream, although it looked like Alex, it was not Alex, but rather some supernatural being who was able to match and beat every power that I had; I wasn't even in control of my powers. He said that we would be together again, when the moon was full and blue. Well, we know that time is coming up quickly; next week in fact. We know that Alex has been shown visions in his dreams, actual events taking place at the same time they are happening. We also know they are linked by the same symbol on the back of Alex's neck, the symbol of Bastiquil, believed to be a demon of hell. There is a serial killer running around Tulsa killing people, using that symbol. These souls are being devoured by beasts from what can only be assumed is hell and taken away down into the pit. We know that someone is protecting Alex and has not revealed his true self to anyone. We know he was flirting with you Gina the other night. We don't know if he is just a Good Samaritan in disguise or if maybe, he is the actual killer. We do know people have deceived Alex for most of his adult life by hiding that symbol within the majority of his tattoos. Tattoos that Alex just happened to dream up each and every one of them before having them tattooed on his body." Demetri was summarizing the known. "Am I missing anything?"

Alex sat there for a few seconds taking in all that was said and having a hard time believing it, but unable to deny the realness of everything that has happened thus far. "There is

223

another thing; my tattoo shop is named Blue Moon Tattoo."
Alex offered as Demetri just smirked at him. "I got the name
through…."

"Let me guess, a dream?" Demetri interrupted him in
an almost sarcastic tone.

"Yes." Alex nodded.

"Alex is a victim here as well. Everything that you just
summarized is what we know or think we know to be true.
But one thing that I know is, whether you want to believe it or
not, is that Alex is innocent in all of this. He is a pawn just like
you, a chess piece being pulled across a big game board for
someone else's pleasure. But I'm not going to let anything
happen to the two of you. We will figure this out and we will
stop it." She said trying to motivate the two. She turned her
attention to Demetri. "This is what we do, isn't it? Help the
innocent, stop the big bad evil?"

He looked up at her and for the first time in a long
time, she wasn't sure what he was thinking. She could, usually,
judge by his expressions, but he just looked blank to her. "G
people are dying, either for Alex, myself, or both. We have to
stop this at all costs, but we still don't know who the other
major stakeholders are in this game. We are still looking for a
lead as to who is in charge of this master plan."

"Well, I think we all know that we have to try and find
out who this mystery masked man is and I fear he isn't a
Good Samaritan either. I fear that he is one of the key players
that you just referred to, but to what end game he is playing
towards, I can only imagine?"

"Well G, you are the intuitive one here; you are a
witch, one with the earth. You have got to have an idea or
thought of what the end game is?" Demetri said to her, almost
pleading for a lead.

"If I were to guess, the end game is the resurrection of
this demon Bastiquil, next week when the moon is full and
blue. It is one of the most powerful full moons we have had in
centuries and if anyone were going to try and pull something
off like this, then that would be the time. A time when the veil
between worlds would be at its thinnest." She said to them

224

both, not knowing if it is what they wanted to hear, but knowing that is what she believed was happening.

"So if we were to go off of my dream alone, then is it safe to say that they plan on planting this Bastiquil into Alex's ready-made body?" Demetri asked of her as Alex's eyes widened in surprise.

"Well, as much as I hate the idea of it, I have to say it is the only explanation that makes any real sense here," she said as she placed a hand on Alex's already heavy shoulders. He felt as if he had just been dealt a sucker punch.

"So I just sit here and wait for this blue moon to come along so that a demon can kick me out of my own body and take it for himself?"

"Well, hopefully, we will have some better information before then, a better plan of action," She said to him trying to give him hope.

"Hopefully, isn't an encouraging word right now," he said as he sat in the chair looking defeated.

"Listen man, cheer up," Demetri said to him stepping in and trying to make things better as he saw that this was hurting Gina deeply. "I know you don't know me and I haven't been the nicest to you so far, so I get that you don't have a lot of trust in me. But one thing Gina can testify to is that I am one bad ass fucker who doesn't like to be messed with. I like it even less when my friends are messed with so I am not going to let any of this happen. I am going to stop this before it gets to the point of your body being possessed. We just have to figure out who the masked man is and what this Bastiquil needs to be able to enter this world."

Gina looked over at Demetri with the most grateful eyes. She loved him so much and that he would step up now with such a pep talk, a much-needed pep talk at that made her love him that much more. "He is right, together we are unstoppable. We can do anything," Gina said to Alex. "What do you think we should do first Demetri?"

Demetri looked at them both and with the most serious of faces said, "Well I have to travel backwards in time, three thousand years, and meet Bastiquil. I have to figure out what and who he was, what he has become, and what his weaknesses are?" He said to them both.

They both looked at him, but Alex was looking at him as if he had lost his mind.

"Are you saying you are going to time travel? Can you do that?" Alex asked of him, still looking at him as if he were an alien and not believing that those words had just come out of his mouth.

"In a manner of speaking, yes, I am," he said to them both. "Aldrik, a friend of mine in Kansas City, an astute man, told me that if I tried past life meditation that I might be able to make the connection."

"I know you trust Aldrik, but past life meditation, at least as far as what I know, it is used for going back a few hundred years, five hundred or maybe even a thousand at the most. But three thousand years, I don't know if that can be done?"

"I understand your concern," Demetri said. "But I would like to point out that people who have tried it in the past did not have the privilege of having my powers. They also did not have the most powerful female witch around to help supercharge me, my connection with this meditation technique, and the fact that we don't really have any other options right now. Do we?"

Gina was smiling at him at this moment, realizing what he was referring to and thinking to herself, *the two of us attempting this together just might work. If it doesn't, then we are all screwed.*

Chapter Forty-One

Alex told Gina that he had to go run some errands and check on the shop. She and Demetri were gearing up for Demetri to make this grand leap three thousand years into the past to meet Bastiquil. To see this demon in action, to see if she could find out how to kill the bastard. The truth was though that Alex needed some air, he needed to get out of there as it had gotten way too real and way too serious for him. If they were right, come next week a demon was going to make every attempt at taking control of his body. From the sounds of it, if Gina and Demetri fail, then he is done for.

He had no clue that Victor had been outside waiting this entire time, watching from afar as he had sat and had lunch with the two witches. Victor was seething that the vessel was being tarnished by the witch's energy, their plots, and plans. He wanted to cut the tongues out of both of the witches so that they would not be able to talk to the vessel again. Alex needed to be ready, to be prepared to take his master into himself. Victor had to take matters into his own hands; he knew it was ahead of schedule but drastic times as they say call for drastic measures.

Alex decided that he needed to see his mother, to hear her voice, to let it ground him, bring him back to reality. But a small piece of the reality was that he wanted a chance to say goodbye. This may be the last time that he would be able to see her. If something were to happen to him next week he didn't want her to think he just disappeared without a clue, without coming to see her first. He wasn't sure what he would say to her or if she would even understand him, but he had to try.

Alex climbed into his car and pulled out of the parking lot and onto Peoria Avenue. He was headed to Brookhaven Assisted Living Facility, a large home for people who were not able to live alone anymore. Those who either didn't have family to live with or the family didn't have the time or resources to help them. It was a beautiful place, a place that his mother had liked when they had first visited it together. She is considered young compared to most of the people there, but she had broken down mentally to the point where she was no longer capable of caring for herself. Alex had no other choice than to admit her there. He hated doing it but knew it was the best thing for her.

As he was driving across town, still unaware of the black SUV that was making all the same turns, kept about the same speed as he did, but just hung back a little so that he didn't alert Alex that he was being followed. If Victor was right, he was headed to his mother's facility and he was going to get the surprise of his life. Victor laughed to himself that he was able to predict what needed to be done and when. He was the perfect weapon, the perfect assassin. The Balashon had chosen the right man to clear the way for the master to arrive.

As he neared the home, he was getting nervous. He hadn't seen his mother in a few months and he was suddenly racked with guilt about it. What was her mental capacity going to be? What was he going to say to her? He hoped that she would be able to understand him, but there was a huge part of him that hoped she wouldn't. That she would be able to stay in perfect innocence of this entire situation. If anything were to happen to him, a part of him hoped that she never even remembered having a son so she wouldn't mourn him, miss him.

He pulled into the parking lot of Brookhaven and parked. As he did, the black SUV passed on by and went down the road before turning around and heading back to the

Brookhaven parking lot. He wanted to give Alex time to get inside so that he wouldn't see him.

As he made his way from the parking lot to the front entrance of the facility, he stopped for a minute and began taking deep breaths and telling himself that he could do this. He could say goodbye to his mother and leave her here not really knowing that he was saying goodbye, but rather just being a good son and coming to see how she was. He wasn't going to cry or break down. He would fight back any emotions that crept up so that he didn't scare or worry her.

Alex entered the front doors of Brookhaven and headed to the front desk. It was basically a routine check in. You had to write your name down, who you were seeing and your driver's license number on the sign in sheet. He had done it many times in the past so it was just second nature to him. He didn't even realize that there wasn't a nurse at the front desk. Usually this is where your ID was checked to make sure you are who you say you are and that you had the right to visit the patient. He just thought they must have been called away for a patient emergency; all he could think about was the task at hand, telling his mother goodbye.

Alex left the front desk making his way down the hallway to his mother's room. Sometimes when he got there she would be asleep, other times she would be sitting in her chair watching television but staring at it blankly, as if no one were home.

Alex got to her door and before he went through he again started taking deep breaths trying to calm himself down from the nerves that were creeping up inside of him. He knew exactly what he had to do; he just didn't want to do it. He didn't want to say goodbye to the lady who had given birth to him, who had raised and loved him the best that she knew how. She wasn't a perfect person, but she tried. When his father left them it had caused her irreparable damage, she never recovered from it. She tried, but as the years went by she slowly became less and less herself, less and less the mother she used to be.

As he put his hand on the door handle pushing it down he opened the door to walk inside only to find an elderly gentleman lying in the bed where his mother was supposed to be. The man looked over at him and waved hello. Alex waved back, confused, and leaned back to look at the number on the door again. It was his mother's room, but where the hell was she?

Racing out of the room he headed back to the nurse's desk in a panic. So many thoughts were racing through his head right now; *had she died, been taken to the hospital? They would have called him if any of that had happened, wouldn't they?* He was running down the hallway until he finally reached the nurse's desk. This time there was a nurse there. She could tell that he was upset and wondered if something had happened to one of the patients.

"Excuse me nurse, I just went to my mother's room and she was not there. Did she get moved to another room? Her name is Ella Rogers. She was in room 1190." He said to the nurse trying not to get too overly excited until he found out what was going on.

"I will look it up for you sir. Just a minute," the nurse said as she started typing away at her computer keyboard. "Do you have any identification on you?"

"Sure," Alex said digging into his back pocket and taking out his wallet. He opened up the black leather wallet that was fastened to his jeans belt loop by a chain and clasp and took out his driver's license and handed it over to the nurse. "So has something happened to my mother?"

"Sir, uh, Alex, I am showing that your mother was checked out yesterday," the nurse said to him nervously. She could tell by the man's face he didn't know this and was getting distraught by the second. *Why did this have to happen on my shift* she was thinking to herself?

"What the hell do you mean she was checked out of here yesterday? That is impossible. I am the only family she has and I have sole guardianship of her. I pay the bill to this place so you need to be telling me right now where my mother is," he said becoming irate.

230

The nurse was getting flustered and was looking through the computer trying to figure out what to tell the young man. Covered in tattoos and piercings, he had begun to make her feel spooked. She wasn't going to wait for him to get mad enough to do something to her. She reached under the counter and pushed the panic button alerting security, management, and the director of the facility that there was an issue.

"I'm waiting for an explanation," Alex said to the nurse.

"I have someone from management coming down to speak with you sir. They should be here any second," the nervous acting nurse said to him.

That is weird, I didn't see her call anyone. Maybe she had sent an email or instant message on the computer. Either way, Alex was glad to be able to speak to someone other than this lady so that he could find out where his mother was.

As he was standing there a few minutes went by, but it seemed like hours. He couldn't imagine how such a mix up could happen. As he was getting ready to ask the nurse how much longer it was going to be he heard someone quickly approaching from behind. As he turned around, he saw two armed security men, guns pulled and pointing at him telling him to put his hands in the air, screaming at him to do it now. Alex quickly figured out how the lady had alerted management of his situation. Putting his hands in the air, he turned his head slightly to look at the nurse who was quickly turning away from his scorned look he was giving her.

"Sir, what seems to be the problem here?" The security guards asked him as they checked him for weapons, not finding any.

As he started to tell them what was wrong, he saw a man dressed in an expensive looking business suit and tie approaching them. He had a concerned look on his face.

"The problem is that I went to see my mother only to find out that she was checked out of here yesterday. Which is a huge problem, considering I am her only family, I have sole

231

guardianship of her, and I didn't check her out of here," Alex said to the security guards and the man dressed in the suit.

"I'm deeply sorry that this has happened," the man in the suit said as he approached Alex and reached out his hand to shake his hand. "My name is Dr. Grant, Dr. Andrew Grant. Thank you Rick and Spencer, but those guns won't be necessary. I will take it from here."

"Are you sure Dr. Grant," the security guard named Rick asked him.

"I'm positive," he said to them as he turned and smiled sympathetically at Alex. "Please come with me to my office so we can get this figured out as quickly as possible."

Alex followed the doctor to his office in the administrative wing of the building which was on the first floor. As they entered his office, he offered Alex a seat in the leather chair that was facing his desk.

"I know you have already told the nurse your name and the name of your mother, but would you mind repeating it for me. Again, I apologize. I know this must be upsetting for you," the doctor said to him trying to calm him down. He had been trained in diffusing volatile situations. He knew the security guards would have followed him back to the office. It was protocol no matter what the doctor had told them, but it was so that their presence wasn't seen as a hostile position taken by the facility.

"My name is Alex Rogers, here is my driver's license. My mother's name is Ella Rogers who is supposed to be residing in room 1190 as she has been for years." he said to Dr. Grant, who was looking at him with a curious look on his face.

"I am aware of your mother. Her guardian came in yesterday and checked her out saying that she was going to be taken home where she would be receiving home health care," Dr. Grant said to him.

"That's impossible Dr. Grant, I am her guardian and I did not come here yesterday and check her out of here," Alex said, feeling as though he were going to be sick to his stomach. *What the hell was going on here?*

"Well, let me get her file and we can work on figuring this out," Dr. Grant said to him as he stepped into another room which was obviously where they kept the patient files. Alex was contemplating what could have happened and each time he came up with something it seemed just as implausible as the next thing. After what seemed like an eternity, but actually was only a few minutes, the doctor returned with a file in hands.

"Yes, Ella Rogers. It's right here. She was checked out by her guardian, Victor Rogers, her younger brother. It's all right here in the paperwork. Here is the file-stamped copy of the judge's order," the doctor showed him.

"Are you fucking kidding me? A younger brother; she doesn't have a younger brother. I am her only family and I have legal guardianship of my mother. I cannot believe that you turned my mother over to some stranger who is claiming to be her younger brother?" Alex said fuming, his voice rising slightly.

There was one knock on the door and the security guard, Ryan, poked his head in the door. "Everything okay in here boss?" Ryan asked.

"Yes, we are good Ryan, thank you."

But the truth was we were not fine, Alex thought to himself. *Nothing about this situation was fine.* He kept expecting to wake up and find out that this was just another one of his horrible dreams. But he knew that he was awake and that someone claiming to be his uncle had kidnapped his mother.

As Alex looked over the paperwork, he was getting sicker by the minute. It looked authentic, hell it could have been for all he knew, but he did know that there was at least one forgery on it, his own signature. Yes, it looked like his signature, but he sure as fuck didn't sign it.

"Dr. Grant, how can this happen? How can someone just walk in here, give you fake paperwork and you just let a man stroll out of here with my mother? My mother, damn you," Alex said almost to hysterics.

"Now wait a minute young man. We had this paperwork checked out for authenticity just like we do any other paperwork we receive. It met all the criteria. He showed us his identification, your mother seemed to respond to him, your signature matched the signature we had on file for you, and we had no reason to doubt its authenticity." The doctor said defending himself and the home. "It even says that she will be staying at your home."

"Well, I can assure you that I did not sign this, I have no uncle and my mother never showed up at my home. As for my mother responding to him, that is absurd as she hasn't responded to anyone in years. I will sue this place for all its worth if anything has happened to my mother," Alex said pointedly to the doctor. "And I will especially take pride in making sure you are removed from this position immediately," Alex said as he had his phone in his hand dialing a number.

"Who are you calling?" The doctor asked nervously, feeling sick himself.

"Yes, I have an emergency; my mother has been kidnapped from the Brookhaven Assisted Living Facility. I need a police officer here immediately," Alex said into the phone to the 911 response person while looking at the doctor in disgust. He could see the doctors face turning redder by the minute. After speaking for a few minutes with the response person, they had told Alex that the Tulsa Police Department (TPD) would be there within a few minutes. Alex had always respected the TPD as he felt they were doing a great job given the circumstances of the elected officials that they had to deal with. He felt if anyone could find her, they could.

Chapter Forty-Two

As Demetri and Gina prepared for the past life meditation, they both turned off their phones so there would be no interruptions. She had locked the door to the store and had put a sign on it saying "Temporarily Closed, Will Open Tomorrow Morning."

She had placed candles in a circle all around Demetri. She sprinkled salt around the circle, to help ward off any spirits that may try to tamper with the meditation. It will also help ward off any demons like Bastiquil that might try to unduly influence him during his silent, peaceful state of mind.

He was in the center of the circle sitting on a throw pillow on the floor, legs crossed, back fully upright, head relaxed, and looking forward. His eyes were closed and he chanted to himself. He has always done the chanting right before starting a meditation, to try and help get some of his other, many random thoughts, to silence themselves.

Gina had put on some incense and resin that contain mystical properties so that it might help aid in his long transportation to get back to his past life, three thousand years ago.

She tried to get her mind into a state of peace, where the energy of the earth was centered and focused on this one moment, this one task of getting him to cross millenniums of past lives. This is something that neither of them has tried to do before and it would require both of their skills, their energies and their powers to do this. She knew it would be a fantastic feat they were attempting and she was concerned about him. This was not just meditation, but rather a mental mind trip, where he would be letting his mind go, letting it move through the ether, thousands of years into the past.

What if something went wrong? What if he didn't come back or he came back different, changed? What if her enchantments and circle of safety wasn't enough to protect him from this demon Bastiquil making an attempt at him? What if it wasn't Demetri that came back? All of these thoughts and a million others were running through her mind. She had to get centered, had to focus if she was going to successfully help push him through this journey.

She would be doing just that, pushing him. They had decided she would let him get started, and then she would tap into his brain to see where he was at and what he was seeing. If he lingered too long, then she would push energy into his mind, a mental blast to boost his transport further along. They hoped that it would work, but neither could be a hundred percent sure. He had asked that she give him about thirty minutes before trying to tap into his mind to see if she could tell where he was.

As he started, he began by focusing on clearing his mind, concentrating on his breathing, thinking about nothing more than taking a breath in and letting it back out. He would take deep breaths in, concentrating on more diaphragmatic breathing. This allowed his diaphragm to expand and not his rib cage, which allowed for deeper breaths. This allowed him to reach a more relaxed state of mind and body.

As he began to feel his body slipping deeper and deeper, he pictured his soul, the essence of himself, the light of his being. He pictured it as a white light, one that was ever present and bright. Trying to keep it simple, he wanted to picture his soul as a round ball of white light. He attempted to make that white light find its past memories, the memories of not just this body that it inhabited now, but the bodies it inhabited over many lifetimes.

This was not proving to be of any use. The ball wasn't going anywhere. He started to concentrate again on the diaphragmatic breathing, letting it, and the sound, guide him along this journey, this path. He practiced this for about ten minutes visualizing the ball of white light and hearing and feeling nothing but his deep breathing.

Then out of nowhere he began to see images, moving images, almost like watching a movie being played back on the old time reels. He didn't know the faces he saw, but he began to get a feeling of recognition. He was feeling the connection of whom and what this was about. The soul was the one on this journey, not Demetri. He had to let go of thinking this was about him and let the soul see what it needed to see and to feel what it needed to feel.

As the images came quick and fast, he could see centuries pass, knowing it was just that, centuries, due to the nature of the scenery he was being shown. Wardrobes changed, locations changed, landscapes changed, homes changed, and so did the people.

In one scene he knew that he was a frontiersman, setting out on a remarkable journey. In another instant, he was on an old ship crossing the oceans but was in shackles, a prisoner. Then another image came to him and he was a beautiful girl getting dressed in her European decorated bedroom, with a headmistress trying to synch up her corset.

He had never really thought of the concept that a soul was an energy source, devoid of preconceived notions of gender, race, and time, really everything that the human brain finds itself contemplating on a daily basis. He was fascinated by this discovery.

Staying focused, he was now a man in what appeared to be the Middle Ages, where he seemed to be running for his life. Then just when he feared being caught, he found himself in a scene where he was a fisherman on a fishing boat off the coast of Sweden in what had to have been around 500 AD.

He was shocked and amazed to find himself working alongside what looked and felt like an adolescent Aldrik. They were pulling in fishing nets together as the winds blew hard and the waves of the sea crashed down hard on the boats. They were laughing and carrying on. *How could this be? I had known Aldrik when he was a teenager?* This was unreal, it was not possible, yet here he was staring him in the face. His soul had been soul mates with Aldrik. He had a new respect for that term, soul mate. He was just getting into seeing the interaction when it was ripped away and another image was trying to take form.

He hadn't even known what he was doing, but he used everything in his being to fight moving on, to go deeper into the other lives that he had lived before. He wanted to stay and see what his life had been like with Aldrik. He knew it was selfish, but he didn't care. When would he have this opportunity again?

Just as he was starting to get the image back of the fishing boat, he was hit by a surge of energy so powerful his mind went totally blank except for the ball of white light. This could have been nothing other than Gina tapping into his thoughts, pressing him onward in his journey, forcing him to leave behind a memory that he so wanted to remember.

If it had been left to him, he would have stayed as long as possible, but Gina had stepped in and did what he didn't have the willpower to do; to fight his inner selfishness. Yes, he wanted to learn more about the teenage Aldrik and what their relationship was like back then, but he was in this situation for a reason and that reason was Bastiquil. He had to concentrate on the task at hand. With Gina's help he was forced deeper into the past, working his way past his life with Aldrik.

Another flash brought him to a time where he was a witness in a crowd of people, all screaming and yelling. People were throwing things into the streets. What appeared in the vision next was unbelievable. This had to be a mistake. The man, wearing a crown of thorns on his head, with blood, dirt, and sweat rolling down his face came into view carrying a heavy-looking cross made of wood. He could not have been witness to such a cruel crime, could he? As the man neared him, his eyes darted over looking at the body that Demetri's soul inhabited and in those eyes he saw such love and compassion in them that it made him cry.

Whoever Demetri was back then had witnessed the persecution and sacrifice of Jesus and was brought to tears when Jesus looked his way.

Again, the image was ripped from him before he was finished with what he wanted to see, as the light was once again moving deeper, farther.

He felt another powerful surge of energy hit his brain and the ball of white light shot like a bullet speeding into the past. When he arrived at the destination where the image came to his mind, it seemed familiar, very close to home. He had seen this image before. It was of Bastiquil and standing beside him was the man who his spirit inhabited back then.

Of course, this man was being possessed by the demon Bastiquil, but he was still able to tell that this was a powerful man, one that was a leader, a privileged man of his time. Bastiquil called this male witch, whose spirit Demetri shared, by the name of Zamaranum. Bastiquil used the powers of Zamaranum, combined with his own, to create fear in the hearts of everyone in the land.

The people had one choice, bow down to Bastiquil or die. This was much of the same choice that he had given in Demetri's dream. Bastiquil was not a demon of complacency. He wasn't just satisfied with occupying a host body and destroying it from the inside out. No, this was an upper-level demon with tremendous powers that chose to surround himself with powerful allies.

He had the sense that he always had a source of power about him. That it was connected to his soul, but that it was the body that Demetri's soul occupied that determined the degree of his powers. It would appear from the images he sees in this time, Zamaranum is a powerful witch, even more powerful than Demetri is today. He was flinging people about without any movement of his body, just by thinking of it. He was able to set fire to people and send them flying hundreds of feet in the air.

One image showed Zamaranum and Bastiquil standing outside of a large stone house. At the command of Bastiquil, Zamaranum looked at the house as it lifted up hovering about ten feet from the ground below. Granted, there were still people inside the house, as Demetri was able to hear screams from inside of the house as it was hovering, then with no warning Zamaranum sent it falling to the ground. Upon impact, the house was decimated, lying in shambles and all who were inside dead.

At this Bastiquil laid his head back in the air, laughing at the destruction of the home and the deaths of all who were inside it, including children. Zamaranum did this willingly, without coercion, without the threat. At least, that was as it appeared and felt to Demetri as he watched the images playing out before him.

He had yet to see any of Bastiquil's powers, but he felt sure that it would come, that he would reveal himself and what he was capable of. There was too much evil, too much arrogance, not to reveal it. He was hoping to be able to see these images and figure out a way to stop him.

What he witnessed was not easy for him to watch or experience. Knowing that one had bad thoughts at times was one thing. Knowing that at one point in time, your soul had been a killing machine that laid waste to many a city and people, did not sit so well. He did not know it, due to being deep inside of his meditative trance, but a tear rolled down the side of his face. The knowledge and burden of what he was witnessing within these visions would haunt him till his dying day.

The image switched suddenly to Bastiquil being confronted at his palace by a powerful witch. This was even earlier than the images Demetri had just witnessed. The witch was calling him out on being possessed by demon spawn from the underworld, a dark, demented demon and she was trying to cast Bastiquil out of the body he possessed. Bastiquil, amused at this, let the woman carry on until the entire room was laughing at her. They were taunting her and yelling at her for accusing their beloved leader of being possessed.

Bastiquil quieted the crowd and asked to be left alone with just the witch and Zamaranum. The crowd, doing as asked of them, left the room, closing the huge doors behind them. Bastiquil then threatened the witch that if she didn't fall in line he would destroy her and her entire bloodline.

The witch, inflamed by this, exerted amazing strength and will, using only her mind picked up a large ceramic urn that lay to the side of his throne and sent it hurling through the air until it smashed into the body of Bastiquil. The urn broke into a thousand tiny pieces. When the witch saw that there was not a scratch on the human body of Bastiquil, she began calling forth the ancient powers of her ancestors to help her. To help her cast out the demon that lay in the body of this man.

The air in the room became dense and then a large gust of wind flung the doors open and sent dust flying into the room where the three of them were standing. Zamaranum started to head to the doors to shut them when Bastiquil looked over at him and shook his head at Zamaranum, for him to remain where he was.

Bastiquil stood up from his throne, lifted his arms in the air and the doors that were just flung open by the great winds were once again closed. The room was still again. The witch was not expecting such a display from the demon but was no less deterred from her course of action. She was still calling on the ancient bloodlines of the dead to come forth to help her battle this demon. At this, the metal weapons that adorned the walls were lifted off their resting spots and hovered in mid-air. With another command from the witch, the weapons were sailing at the body of Bastiquil. Only to be met with such force that they were bent and warped from the impact that they had when they hit Bastiquil's body.

The witch, although impressed with the demons powers, was not going to let this stand either. She had fought demons in the past and had successfully expelled them from the bodies they inhabited. Walking towards Bastiquil she was chanting an invocation, a spell. It appeared that it was starting to have an effect on Bastiquil as he was wincing in pain. As the witch neared Bastiquil he burst out with laughter placing the palms of his hands together as if in prayer, but not praying. He then lifted them upwards towards the vaulted

241

ceiling in the chamber. With this action the witch was stopped in her tracks, lifted off the ground until she was at least fifteen feet in the air. She was cursing at Bastiquil, hurling spells at him in an attempt to free herself.

Bastiquil had his eyes closed and his head bowed from the time he had put his palms together. He slowly opened his eyes, rolling them upwards until he was looking at the witch in the air with such evil, such distain in his eyes. Then he smiled slyly and with a sudden movement he pulled his palms apart from each other moving them out to his sides. With this action the witch's body exploded, skin, bones, blood, and all as it still hovered in the air. With a few spoken words from Bastiquil, the remaining urn from the other side of his throne was suddenly moved over until it was directly under the remains of the witch. The top of the urn was lifted and moved to the side, but still floated in the air. When Bastiquil lowered his arms to where they were flush with his legs the remains of the witch fell quickly and smoothly into the body of the urn. Once inside the lid was quickly put back in place as the urn slid back to the side of the throne from where it had come.

Chapter Forty-Three

As Alex was waiting for the police to finish questioning the doctor, he had been trying to reach Gina. The phone was immediately going to voicemail which was just adding to his agitation. He wasn't sure what was going on here at the home where his mother had been and he wasn't sure what was going on with Gina. He had tried reaching Brandy but has been unable to reach her as well. He really didn't know where to turn next.

He was pacing the hallway outside of Dr. Grant's office. This was just complete and utter bullshit he was thinking to himself. What was going on? His mother is missing, taken by someone pretending to be her younger brother and the staff here just hand her over. No phone calls to try and reach Alex to verify. The incompetence of this situation was starting to wear thin with him and he had to control himself as to not rush in the doctor's office and punch the man in the face. He screwed up, own it.

Finally, the two police officers that had been questioning the good doctor came walking out of Dr. Grant's office and came up to him. They handed him two business cards advising him that he needed to go home and they would be in contact as soon as they heard anything. They were going to be checking video footage from Brookhaven, from the traffic lights to see if they could come up with any pictures of the man who took his mother.

Alex wasn't thrilled with this advice, but he didn't know what else he could do until they called him. He didn't have a clue as to where to go to even start looking for this man and his mother. Greater Tulsa had a population of about 960,000 people and that is if they stayed within this area and had not gone someplace else. Why in the world would someone want his mother? She didn't have any money, she couldn't talk most of the time, and she suffered from dementia-like behaviors. This made about as much sense as everything else in his life right now.

Alex turned and headed out of the front doors that he had been so nervous to walk through earlier. He had come here with the intention of telling his mother goodbye. Even though, it would have been only ceremonial as she would probably not remember why he had even been here thirty minutes from the time he left. He didn't have that choice now; someone had made that for him. He couldn't even think about this Bastiquil and what he may or may not do to him. His mother was missing! *Am I supposed to go after my mother or am I supposed to stay the course and prepare to battle this Bastiquil? Why the hell wasn't anyone answering his calls?*

He had left Brandy and Gina numerous messages and neither of them were calling back. He was trying hard to not become hysterical as he walked to his car but the more he thought about it, the more he felt the weight and seriousness of the issues that lay ahead of him. As he got to his car, he was again oblivious to the fact that across the street, Victor was watching him safely from behind the wheel of the black SUV. As Alex pulled out of Brookhaven's parking lot and headed down the street, Victor pulled out a safe distance behind him and began to trail him.

Smiling smugly, Victor was so proud of himself. He had successfully gotten the vessel's mother out of her home and safely tucked away back at the Balashon mansion and had paid the vessel's best friend Brandy a visit. She had been quite the struggle. She put up a good fight. He was extremely impressed by her. She was in tip top shape and boy she was lean and mean, much like Victor himself.

Chapter Forty-Four

After Victor had gotten Alex's mother to the mansion, he then went over to Brandy's house. He knew her routine much like he knew the other players involved. It was getting close to the final sacrifice and from all of the calls that had been pouring in from other Balashon members he decided he needed a little insurance in case any other problems arose from the vessel.

Victor had easily let himself into Brandy's house, overriding her security system in a matter of seconds and then just lay patiently waiting for her to arrive home. It wasn't long until he was rewarded with the sound of her garage door opening. Victor was standing in her bedroom with the lights out patiently waiting for her. She must have stopped at the grocery store on the way home as he could hear the sounds of bags brushing up against the door as she walked into the house and put the bags on the kitchen counter. Walking over to the keypad for the alarm system, she punched in the code to disarm the alarm. She did not see that it had been set for staying inside the house. It wasn't something she would have even thought about on any given day.

Putting the items that she had gotten from the grocery store away, she then put the bags into a recycle bin and poured herself a glass of water. She drank the entire glass not realizing how thirsty she had been.

Setting the glass into the kitchen sink she turned to walk into her bedroom, but Victor had already made his way into her closet and behind her clothes that were hanging on the rack. Brandy flipped on the bedroom light and began to take her jewelry off, placing it on the dresser. Brandy lifted up her shirt pulling it over her head and tossing it on the bed. She then unbuttoned her jeans that she had on and pulled them down sliding her legs out of them. Using her right foot, she lifted the jeans off the ground, grabbing them with her hand and placed them onto her bed as well.

Brandy then walked over to her closet and opened up the door. Reaching in she grabbed at her robe, not realizing that Victor was leaning closely to her arm, smelling her skin, thinking thoughts about her that if she knew would make her shutter in disgust. Feeling her robe, Brandy grabbed it off its hook and laid it on the bed. With the closet door open, Victor had a clear visual of Brandy and her movements. Reaching behind her back, she unhooked her bra and slid her arms out of both sides of the bra, exposing her nice, but not overly large breasts. She then slid her panties down and stepped out of them. Brandy placed both the bra and the panties on the bed with the other pile of clothes she had just removed.

Grabbing her robe she headed into the bathroom as she turned on the light and hung her robe up onto the hook that was on the back of the door. Turning on the water to the shower, she let the water heat up as she put her hair into a ponytail and curled it around itself until it was in a bun. Walking over to the shower she felt of the water and feeling the warmth of the water she stepped into the shower sliding the glass door shut behind her.

As she was enjoying the heat of the water and letting it relax her body, she was unaware that Victor was out of her closet. He was standing on the bedroom side of her bathroom door, but where she couldn't see him but he could still see her through the slit where the door was hinged to the doorframe. He was rubbing his crotch as he watched Brandy in the shower. She was a masterpiece, and his erect cock was showing just how much appreciation he had for women with

246

discipline that treated their bodies like the works of art they are.

He could have easily grabbed her when she came into the house and had already been back to the mansion with her. Victor liked to stalk his prey, he liked to watch them, especially when they were so beautiful and they had no clue he was there. He loved the show anyway; she was rubbing the soap all over her body, into every crevice. As she rinsed the soap off, it appeared like she was posing for a shower commercial. She was stretching slightly in the shower, more than likely from the warmth of the water loosening up her muscles. Smart girl, she was going to need to be fully stretched out for what was in store for her.

As she appeared to be winding down with her shower, Victor made his way back into her closet. He waited for her to get out, dry off and come back into her bedroom where he was going to grab her and go.

Slipping her robe on, she returned to her bedroom, grabbing the dirty clothes she had just removed and placed them into the basket that was lying in the floor of her closet. As she was looking down she was struck by a curious thought. That looked like a pair of men's boots in her closet and just as her heart started to race, Victor came flying out pushing her onto the bed. Brandy screamed, but Victor quickly placed his hand over her mouth. He was reaching into his pocket to retrieve a syringe full of a sleep agent that would assist him in getting her quietly out of the house, but, she managed to get her knee in just the right position and slam it into his balls.

As strong as Victor was and as determined as he was, he was still a man and that fucking hurt like none other. He rolled off of her slightly, giving her the opportunity to jump up from the bed and try to flee from him. She started around the bed to go to the bedroom door and, hopefully, to the alarm system, but she was just a foot from the door when she felt the tension on her robe as she was pulled backwards into the arms of her assailant.

As Brandy tried to elbow him and kick backwards, she was virtually defenseless once he had her in his grasp. She had

247

never felt such force, such power before in a man. It was only seconds later she felt the jab of the needle as it entered her neck and immediately she was feeling woozy, feeling the sensation of impending sleep. Brandy went limp in Victor's arms, but he couldn't think of anything other than how much his balls were aching.

Laying her on the bed, he went to the alarm system, entered the numbers and opened the door leading out to the garage. Pushing the button to the second garage door, Victor waited until it was open to see if anyone was walking around outside. It was dark, at least he had that on his side, but he didn't want to take a risk at this point of anyone being able to identify him.

Walking out into the night, he pulled his SUV into the garage and shut the garage door. Going back into the house, he picked up Brandy and placed her over his shoulder. She was going to be out for hours so he knew that he didn't have to rush and he knew that no one was going to be coming over either. The vessel was too busy with Gina and that allowed Victor the opportunity to grab both his mother and his best friend. Putting Brandy into the back of the SUV, he walked back into the house and packed a bag full of her clothes and undergarments along with some toiletries. He may be an assassin, but he wasn't a monster. Before leaving, Victor entered in the code for the alarm, walked out into the garage and was quickly on his way back to the mansion. Yes, he had thought about having his way with her, but what fun was that when she was sleeping and unable to struggle? Hell, the struggle was ninety percent of the fun.

The memories that Victor had of grabbing the girl still brought a big smile to his face. He was sure that he would have no problems with the vessel, but, just in case, he had an insurance policy now. As Victor whistled a little German victory song, he thought to himself *life was great, but it was going to be extraordinary once the master arrived.*

Chapter Forty-Five

Gina couldn't help but worry about Demetri and what this was doing to him physically and mentally. The stress of being in a self-telling trance for so long gives one access to so much information and knowledge that you would, normally, never know about yourself. Your soul is capable of carrying the guilt of your past transgressions, but the current mind and body may not be.

Gina watched him carefully and had pushed him onward a couple of times when she was allowed in to see Demetri's progress. She was just as surprised as Demetri to see that he was with Aldrik even fifteen hundred years ago. Some paths and destinies are just meant to cross and keep crossing. The journey is part of the reward, part of the learning process that we go through during our time here, but the soul is eternal. It is everlasting, an energy source that keeps giving. Maybe that is why there have been so many different stories told about the fight between good and evil over control of the soul. It is an amazingly strong energy source.

As Demetri was under, she kept a careful watch on him. She didn't want to push him any more than she had to as she wasn't really sure of what it would do to him. So she kept watch, making sure nothing went wrong on this side, but in case something did go wrong, she would do her best to make sure that he is brought out intact. But even doing that would be a trial and error situation she wasn't sure Demetri's mind could take.

Meanwhile, Demetri was still within his vision of the throne room looking at this display of strength that Bastiquil had shown. He totally destroyed this powerful witch and did it as if it were child's play. He was not fazed by the physical objects that the witch had flung at him. The only thing that did seem to faze him was when the witch was chanting the spell at Bastiquil; he felt he should know what it was. The language was speaking to something deep within, but he wasn't sure if it was the current Demetri or Zamaranum that it was speaking to. He remembered the words the witch had spoken, but he didn't really understand them. It was a language that was long lost, or at least assumed to be. This was a witch from three thousand years ago who may well have been calling on magic that was considered ancient even back then.

What Demetri was sure of was; first, he had definitely dealt with Bastiquil before and it had been as an accomplice to his horrific crimes. Second, he and Bastiquil had wreaked havoc on this civilization all these years ago. Of course, Zamaranum was exerting so much more power than Demetri had in the current day and age. One thing he was learning, the soul carried with it amazing powers, but it took a body open to accepting these powers to be able to tap into them and wield them to their fullest.

Demetri was still hoping to be shown more in this vision. He was hoping he would be shown how Bastiquil was actually defeated. He had to have been defeated and sent back to the depths of hell for Bastiquil to be trying to claw his way back into this world. So far this trip has been informative in that he knew Bastiquil was one powerful demonic force, but Demetri has yet to be shown his one true weakness.

The image changed to Zamaranum and Bastiquil walking together through the city streets of Ur, in ancient Mesopotamian. As they walked through the crowds, the people parted in fear of them, fleeing to the safety of their homes. But there was no real safety in their homes, as Demetri was shown in the earlier image. When Zamaranum had taken a large stone home and demolished it with just a thought, he did so without regard for the human lives that were destroyed in the home.

Demetri didn't recognize this version of him, but the soul connection was undeniable. Yes, he recognized and acknowledged that, but the evil exuding from Zamaranum was such a foreign concept to him. Demetri had never thought of himself as a killing machine, a doer of demonic wishes, but the fact was, in this time in history, three thousand years in the past, he was a killer.

Bastiquil found pleasure, just as much pleasure as Zamaranum, that people were terrified of them. The people of this time feared with good reason, as many had witnessed Zamaranum and Bastiquil's displays of power. These were done to keep the people in line, to keep them from revolting.

Bastiquil had the men of this town building his palace, a great dwelling for living, and for the people to come to worship him. They were being led by a general, who Demetri could tell was possessed by a lower level demon. He drove them on, forcing the people to work through exhaustion, fatigue, hunger, and illness.

The palace being built was enormous, a palace worthy of a king, a pharaoh, a leader. It was made from the best stone and marble of the day. There were statutes being commissioned, artwork being made and brought in, gold and silver were being brought in to be stored in the depths of the palace. Bastiquil was a feared tyrant ruler and Demetri could tell this wasn't sitting well with Zamaranum. He felt a jealousy, a wanting, and a hunger for power, for all Bastiquil had acquired, but he kept this to himself, pondering what to do and when to act on it.

Bastiquil was telling Zamaranum he was planning a raid, an attack on the neighboring cities and countries. He wanted more and more and didn't want to stop until he had conquered every known nation. He wanted to rule the known world and then take on the unknown. He wanted it all and he wanted Zamaranum by his side. He wanted to conquer this together, to be one force, fighting and killing everyone who

251

would dare oppose them. They would either bow down at his feet or perish.

The images changed again and Demetri could tell he was pushed into the future a bit, as they were deep in battle. The forces of Bastiquil's army were taking the lands by storm, and laying waste to anyone and everyone that wouldn't surrender and serve the master Bastiquil. The men were not only plundering and pillaging the villages, but they were raping and killing innocent people. This didn't seem to bother Zamaranum, but Demetri was watching in disgust and horror.

What did bother Zamaranum was that all of this was being done by men that he had taught to fight, but were being led by Bastiquil. Zamaranum wasn't content with Bastiquil getting the glory and the honor of the kill. He wanted the glory, and he wanted the people and nations to bow down before him, to erect statues in his honor, to bring riches to lay down before his feet. As the bitterness and resentment grew, Zamaranum was plotting and waiting for the right time to make his move.

Demetri was watching the horror of these visions of the past and realized this is the moment he had been waiting for. Zamaranum was ready to battle Bastiquil. He was ready to take him on, one powerful being against another and he knew it would be to one of their deaths.

As they were feasting and taking refuge for the night in one of their conquered villages, Zamaranum was curious why Bastiquil had not joined the men in their victory celebration. He began looking for him and it didn't take long to find him. Bastiquil was in the bathing room of the nicest home they could find in the village. It was the home of a wealthy trader, who had long lived as one of the richest and most powerful men in the village. When Zamaranum walked into the bathing room, he saw that the owner of this home was sprawled out, hanging to the wall by knives forcefully shoved through the skin and bones of his hands and feet.

His daughters and sons were being forced to give Bastiquil a bath and forced to pleasure him as they did so. He was laughing at them as they cried and whimpered in their duty of pleasuring and washing him. They knew there was no fighting him so they did as they were told. They had witnessed their father's stance of authority and now their father was affixed to a stone wall, still alive, made to witness the desecration of his offspring.

Bastiquil was taking one of the daughters who he had found beautiful and was making her take extra special care of him. He had decided he would take this one with him on the road. She would become his concubine, his whore. He turned her away from him and laid his hand upon the back of her neck. As he did so, his hand made a glowing light and the girl let out a yell of pain as her siblings looked on in horror, her father whimpering as he watched this. When Bastiquil removed his hand, Demetri could see that he had burned a symbol onto the back of her neck, one that looked like the one Alex had tattooed onto the back of his neck.

Bastiquil then took the girl on the floor beside the bath, taking her intimately and forcefully. He went at her until he had successfully flooded her with his demon seed, telling her she would be his forever. Her offspring would be his offspring and she would give him a son, one to rule at his side, one that would carry on the bloodline for generations to come.

Just then something became clear to Demetri; this image had been shown to him for a reason. As hard as it was to watch, he knew now the connection to Alex. He knew what Bastiquil had in store for Alex; his dream was now made clear to him.

With this knowledge, the images begin to change once again. Zamaranum was confronting Bastiquil on his taking all the glory of the kills. He wanted to be given his share, he wanted to go his own way from Bastiquil, make his own mark on the world, without Bastiquil. At this, Bastiquil became enraged and began to shout obscenities at Zamaranum. He vowed if Zamaranum walked away from him it would be as a dead man. Zamaranum laughed, which further fueled Bastiquil's rage. Zamaranum, taking a stand of defiance to the great one, turned his back on him to walk away.

Bastiquil yelled out in rage as Zamaranum felt himself being lifted off the ground. Zamaranum knew this would be his attack on him and he was ready for it. In all his power and greatness Bastiquil was still predictable. Using his force, Zamaranum turned himself around mid-air so he was facing Bastiquil. He was laughing at Bastiquil, taunting him, telling him he would have to do better than this if he were going to make an example out of him. Zamaranum focused his strength on Bastiquil and with one push of his mind he knocked Bastiquil off his feet. He sent him flying backwards until he smashed into the wall behind him, knocking a hole where his backside hit the wall.

Bastiquil seethed with hate at this display of defiance. He ordered every man in the room to attack Zamaranum. As each man hesitated, Bastiquil screamed out in anger that if they did not do as they were told their wives and children would pay the ultimate price. The men hearing this and fearing for their families, one by one, charged Zamaranum and one by one they were all sent flying across the room just as Bastiquil had been flung.

Bastiquil bowed his head and clasped his hands together as he had done with the witch and began to raise the hands upward and with his rising hands Zamaranum went upward. Zamaranum knew the outcome of this and if he planned on walking away from this, he had to act now. Fighting back, Zamaranum began to focus all of his energy on Bastiquil. He thought of him rising up in the air, of his hands being bound together. He was forcing all of his energy, every power known to him on Bastiquil.

Demetri, monitored by Gina, was beginning to wear down. He was witnessing these images, but they were starting to take a toll on his body. Gina noticed his nose had started to bleed on one side, with blood starting to pool around his lips. This sent Gina into a panic mode as she raced to try and bring him back. He had been under for well over an hour and things must be getting heated. She tried to tap into his brain to see if she could tell where he was and if she could wake him from his meditative trance.

254

Bastiquil had begun to rise off of the ground and as he did, he opened his eyes wide looking directly at Zamaranum. He was staring at him with eyes that said "how dare you betray me, how dare you use your magic against me."

Zamaranum struggled, trying to loosen the hold Bastiquil had on him. Both men, or should it be said, the male witch and the demon, both pushed outward with all the power within them and sent each other flying backwards until they crashed into opposite walls. Zamaranum was up and on his feet, quickly concentrating on the ceiling above Bastiquil's head. He only had a second before Bastiquil would begin his assault again, so Zamaranum pushed hard with his energy and as the ceiling gave way it fell onto the demon below. Thousands of pounds of stone fell upon Bastiquil.

As Zamaranum caught his breath, he heard a rumble where the ceiling had just caved in on Bastiquil. The building started to shake and then the thousands of pounds of stone, which had fallen on Bastiquil, went flying in all directions as he stood up out of the middle of the rubble.

His face, inflamed with rage as he stood, body mangled, and half of the flesh missing from his face. As he struggled to right himself, Zamaranum didn't waste one second. Focusing his energy, he tried to hold onto the physical body Bastiquil was inhabiting, while focusing on the demon himself inside the body. He had never tried anything like this on such an upper-level demon. But, if it worked on a demon at all, it should either weaken him enough that he could kill the human form or at least knock the demon out of the body.

With all energy focused on Bastiquil, Zamaranum had contained the physical form and started his mental attack on the body trying to locate the demon. He closed his eyes so he could picture the demon; find him hiding within the body. Once he located him, he summoned all the energy he could from every source around and sent the demon who was screaming, flying out from within the body.

To both of their surprises, Zamaranum was able to knock him out of the physical body. Within a few seconds, the body Bastiquil had inhabited was crushed, sending it falling to the ground dead. It would not have survived anyway due to the damages it sustained from the stone ceiling unless Bastiquil made his way back into the body.

The demon floated in the air, a black vapor like material that loomed about in the form of a winged demonic creature, screaming insults at Zamaranum. The ground opened up below him, exposing a fiery pit where he was sucked back into the hell from which he had come.

As Zamaranum was standing there admiring the powerful witchcraft he had just worked, he was not paying attention to what was happening behind him. The young girl who Bastiquil had taken by the bath and who was impregnated with the baby of Bastiquil came up behind Zamaranum and sent a stone spear directly through his heart.

Zamaranum's eyes widened with confusion. He looked down at the spear as blood came flowing from his mouth. He dropped to his knees, realizing he had focused solely on the demon and had not thought about the demon's spawn growing inside of the young girl. As he fell face forward hitting the ground, moments from death, he realized he defeated his foe to inherit the kingdom, but instead, he was inheriting death. But even while he was dying, the powerful witch knew death was just the beginning. If he had learned anything, it was this.

As Gina continued to work on bringing Demetri back from his trance-like state, she was relieved and a taken off guard, as he woke up gasping for air. He fell forward, just as Zamaranum did in the vision, clutching at his heart, happy to find it was still intact. What an amazing journey that had been and what a terrible burden he would bear knowing what he now knew. They didn't have a moment to spare. They had to be prepared for the return of Bastiquil. Demetri was now convinced more than ever Bastiquil was going to make an attempt at resurrection. But he was going to be there to stop him, to fight him as he had all those thousands of years ago.

As he pushed himself back up onto his knees, he wiped his nose and realized he had been bleeding. Gina was talking to him, saying something, but all he could think about was the coming battle, the battle to save them and this planet. She handed him a glass of water and as he drank it, he was already making plans in his head.

As he looked at her, he said, "We need to get prepared for the evil that is coming. We are nowhere near ready to do battle with it."

She looked at him with surprised eyes and concern on her face.

"What did you see?" Gina asked as she helped Demetri to his feet.

He only shook his head, "We are not ready."

Chapter Forty-Six

It was Friday, August 16th, and Victor had just taken his guests, Ella and Brandy their morning breakfast. Neither were too happy with him, as he probably would not be either, but this was their situation for the moment and he had told them the rules. They were to be locked in their rooms and were not to try and escape. It was useless to try as the doors were reinforced and the windows were shatterproof and contained bars on the outside. Victor had made sure that they had some rooms retrofitted with security bars before he brought his guests here. You never know what you might have to do to get the vessel to cooperate.

Speaking of cooperating, he had only gotten both of them to settle down by telling them that if either of them tried to escape he would kill the vessel, Alex, as they knew him. This seemed to get their attention, or at least it got Brandy's.

The mother, she was a little bit crazy. She was withdrawn, didn't talk, and stared at him. He felt that there was something more behind her eyes than she was letting on. Victor could tell things about people's personalities, a part of the trade profession, and this lady was hiding something. As long as she cooperated he didn't care what it was. He had no problem with killing either or both of them, but it would be nice to have them as collateral if things went bad with the vessel.

He wasn't sure when they had started to arrive, but he was getting word that some of the higher ranking Balashon members were in Tulsa. This was not truly unexpected; after all, there is a major undertaking about to happen. They have been waiting for this to happen for three thousand years. When their master, Bastiquil, had been on this earth previously, his time was cut way too short. Victor would make sure that didn't happen again. The master would have free reign over this earth before it was all said and done. But, as with all things of grand scale, it would take time and patience.

When Victor had heard some of the other assassins of the Balashon had arrived in Tulsa, he wasn't a bit happy. If they thought they were going to come in at the last minute and steal his thunder, they had another thing coming. He would rip out anyone's throat that even attempted.

Victor had made sure there had been no evidence left at the scene of the crimes that would lead back to him. All three murders had gone off without a hitch, and the taking of the vessel's mother was such child's play. It didn't really take a rocket scientist to pull it off. Especially with Dr. Grant being a Balashon member. Forging a few documents and taking some heat from the vessel and the police was the least the good Dr. Grant could do for the master's arrival.

Then there was Brandy. Man was she feisty. He liked her a lot. There was nothing at her home that could lead to him or the Balashon. Hell, as far as anyone knew, the Balashon was as much of an urban legend as Bastiquil was thought to be.

Victor would have to keep a close watch from this point forward; an even closer watch than he had been. Word may have gotten back to the Balashon council there were two powerful witches in town who have befriended the vessel. Even with Victor keeping a close watch on them, he could not have predicted they would have joined up with the vessel, or that the female witch would be sleeping with the vessel. Once the master was here, he would take care of her, and if it so pleased the master, Victor would volunteer to do it for him.

With the master's big day looming near, it was of the utmost importance the vessel be procured and brought back to the mansion for safe keeping. At that point, he expected an entire team of guards to be swarming upon the mansion to safeguard the vessel. No one, not even the witches would be able to get past this team that Victor had personally selected. They were the best of the best and could take down almost anything that came their way.

He couldn't get it out of his head though, Alex, the vessel, was staying with the female witch. Maybe it was that old saying "safety in numbers." He thought, *of all of the times I've had the opportunity to just gut the witch, or snap her neck. So many possibilities, they were endless, but I hadn't for some reason? This is bothering the fuck out of me.*

What was it? Yes, she was a beauty, an object I have yet to dominate, but it's much more than that. Something about her has gotten under my skin. Deal with whatever emotions you feel because you can't allow them to interfere with the task at hand, nothing was more important than securing the master's safe return. The rewards of that return and the fact it had been because of Victor's careful planning mattered more than anything.

Tomorrow he was going to have to figure out a way to separate the vessel from the witches because he needed him to be here at the mansion, protected and safe. Victor was sure Alex would not feel that way about it, but Victor would explain to him what an important role he will play in all of this. Once he realizes he is the chosen one, the host body for the master's return, he will then see things differently.

Victor already knew the vessel had felt the master about him; lingering, waiting and Victor knew he had been visited by the master. The fact that this was even happening was more than enough proof Alex was the chosen vessel; he was the one bred and born for this task. The vessel was a direct descendant of Bastiquil himself. There was no greater honor that could be bestowed upon the vessel, than to take in Bastiquil, to let him take over his body, to use it at will.

Once he had secured the vessel and had him safely at the mansion, then they could begin preparing him for the arrival of Bastiquil, and for the blue moon. There was still lots that had to be done, but by that time, this mansion would be filled with high-ranking Balashon officials who were ready to complete the final sacrifice and rituals. This was an exciting time and the end of the old way was nearing and the beginning of the new world was upon them.

Victor busied himself by making sure he was ready. He sharpened his knives, got his other weapons ready. He even had guns ready for when the guards arrived so they would have the needed weapons, to patrol and protect the perimeter of the mansion. They were to shoot first, at the sign of any unexpected movement, and ask questions later.

Later today, the house staff who are employed by the Balashon would be arriving to get the house running smoothly. They would take care of the prisoners and prepare for the arrival of the Balashon dignitaries that would be staying with them. The mansion was large enough that everyone would be comfortable, safe, and ready to begin the final tasks needed to usher the master back into this world, back onto his throne.

Chapter Forty-Seven

Just two days earlier, Alex had come to the doors of the store not long after they had finished with Demetri's past life meditative experience. He came in all frantic, stating someone had taken off with his mother from the home where she was living. This caught both Gina and Demetri off guard. They were both drained from the past life meditation and Demetri had just finished cleaning up the blood from his nose.

It took a few minutes to get Alex to calm down long enough to tell them what was going on and why he was so upset. They knew it had something to do with his mother, but he was talking so fast and so incoherently; they just saw him in a panic.

Gina had taken him aside, set him down while making him a hot cup of tea as she tried to be a calming force for him. It did calm him down allowing him to formulate his words so he could explain to them what he knew about his mother's disappearance.

It appears someone went to a great deal of trouble to do it. They had forged paperwork, court documents, Judge's signatures and district court file stamps just to get at his mother. He could not think of anyone who would do such a thing, but he was on the verge of tears as he vowed to find out. Demetri and Gina offered their help in aiding to find her.

Gina, Demetri were reeling from Alex's news of his mother's kidnapping and his best friend Brandy's disappearance as well. This could not be a coincidence when they are almost on the eve of the blue moon. So much was happening that they were struggling to keep their sanity while trying to figure out who all the players were in this cat and mouse game they found themselves in. There was no evidence at the home where his mother was a resident nor was there any evidence at Brandy's home that would link them to the killer.

Demetri knew this was happening too closely to the upcoming blue moon, when Bastiquil would try his entry into this world again. There is no telling how many times in the last billions of years he has come and gone, but Demetri felt sure, he hadn't been back since their last encounter thousands of years ago.

Demetri was thinking about what he had seen. He had seen Bastiquil take this young girl, the daughter of a wealthy businessman in town, and impregnate her with his seed. She had been the one to kill the body that Demetri's soul had been in, once Zamaranum had vanquished Bastiquil. He knew it was probably a big leap here to make this assumption, but big leaps were all they had left. Alex had to be a descendant of that baby, born out of the sexual exchange between the girl and Bastiquil. She had birthed his child and over the years it and its offspring had survived.

If you thought about it, thousands of years of descendants, had to go through many wars, famine, disease, and world destruction. *The fact the line of descendants from Bastiquil's bastard child had survived, was absolutely amazing. How did this happen?* He knew that it could, but the chances were stacked against a young girl and her child. There were people loyal to Bastiquil back then, just as there had been people loyal to Zamaranum. Could the people loyal to Bastiquil have helped to raise this child, protect it, make sure that it birthed a child of its own, and so forth and so forth? The implications were staggering. Just thinking about it made him somewhat nauseous.

Demetri had not had time to process everything he had learned and everything it implied. He didn't have the luxury of remembering the vision where he had been on a fishing boat with Aldrik, laughing and working. They looked so happy, like they were the best of friends. *Focus Demetri, there will be time for this later,* he hoped, but right now there were more pressing problems they needed to face.

Out of pure desperation Alex was still trying to get in touch with Brandy, but the phone kept going right to voicemail. It wasn't like Brandy not to answer the phone. She at least would have called him back if she were not able to answer when he called. Alex had told Gina that he felt something was wrong that she didn't ever, in the years he had known her, not answer the phone. Gina had suggested that they all go together, Demetri included, to Brandy's home to see if maybe she was there and her phone was dead.

Gina didn't think it wise or prudent for them to split up now; things were getting too crazy and out of control. At some point, Gina is going to have to get the full low down on what Demetri had witnessed in his past life meditation.

As they all climbed into Demetri's Jeep and headed over to Brandy's place, Alex had an unsettling feeling of impending doom. He felt what he was going to find there, was going to rock his world, again.

As they arrived at Brandy's home, Alex jumped out of the back of the Jeep before Demetri had been able to completely stop. Gina yelled after him, but he was running up to the front door. Taking out his key chain, he used his spare key Brandy had given him.

"Brandy," he was yelling as he ran through the house looking for her, but hearing nothing but the sound of the alarm alerting him to enter a code. Alex quickly entered in the code to the alarm, as it was maddening to listen to the fucking beeping.

Alex continued his search for Brandy. "Brandy, are you here?"

As Demetri and Gina caught up with him, they could tell the house was empty. Heading into Brandy's bedroom, Alex was a little puzzled by the disheveled duvet on her bed and some items from her nightstand lying on the floor. His heart sank deep into the pit of his stomach and he felt he was going to throw up. Alex heard Demetri in the other room yell something.

"Hey guys," Demetri called out. "Brandy's vehicle is in the garage, but there is an empty spot on the other side. Does she own two cars?"

As Alex ran into the hallway near the kitchen, then into the garage, he was sure something was wrong. Brandy had been taken as well. "She is gone. There had been a struggle in her bedroom and this is her car here in the garage. She doesn't go anywhere without it." Alex's face was pale as the gravity of what was happening started to sink in.

"And, she doesn't own another car?" Demetri asked again.

"No," Alex said, as the word felt like it was being forced out of his mouth.

As Alex's mind was taking this all in, Gina was on the phone calling the Tulsa Police Department. As Gina reported what they knew so far, she was informed units were on their way and for them to try not to disrupt the scene any more than they have already. They were advised it would be best if they could wait outside.

As they were all three waiting, nerves on edge, they could hear the sirens of the police cars as they approached the house. Upon arrival they began by securing the area, getting statements from Gina, Alex, and Demetri as well as the neighbors. There wasn't a whole lot they could tell them other than what had happened to Alex's mother. Then Alex had been trying to get in touch with Brandy, her not answering her phone, and coming over here to find her car here, her bedroom amiss, and no sign of Brandy anywhere.

After a long wait, they were told they could leave after they gave their contact information to the detectives in charge. The detectives advised the three of them they might be needed down at police headquarters later for further questioning, but they would call if they needed anything else from them. A police officer told them if they had any questions or concerns they could call the detectives at the number provided on their business card. The officer assured Alex they were doing everything they could to find his mother, and now Brandy.

The officer had asked Alex to let them know if he came up with any ideas of who may have it in for him, or who might want to hurt him by coming through his loved ones. Alex didn't think they would appreciate hearing it could be some three-thousand-year-old demon hell bent on bringing destruction to the earth. After a moment's thought, Alex decided it was best to keep that little tidbit to himself.

Driving back to Gina's place seemed like a long trip. They all sat in silence as the night air that hit them, felt warm and almost sauna-like, with the top off of the Jeep. The summer nights in Tulsa, especially August summer nights, were known for their sauna-like feel, where you couldn't step outside without feeling the sweat starting to form on your face.

By the time they got back to Gina's they were all dripping in sweat, their brains drained, from either too much time travel to past lives or worry about missing loved ones. There was definitely not a lack of drama happening around this place.

"Alex, I'm sorry all of this is happening to you," Demetri said, trying to break the ice a little and offer an olive branch.

"Thanks. I appreciate all you are doing to try and help us figure this out. I know I am not your favorite person, but it does mean a lot you are trying to help me, help my mom and Brandy." He said to Demetri, as Gina smiled at the bonding going on here. She was proud of both of them for their attempts to reconcile.

"Well boys, I'm glad to see you both have put your differences behind you. I'm going to need the best of you both focused and ready to battle for our lives. I'm not sure what your mom and Brandy have to do with this yet Alex, but we will figure it out. If the universe is on our side, Brandy and Ella will be alive and well when we find them." Gina said trying to get them both refocused on the task at hand, which was figuring out what Bastiquil's end game was.

She knew Alex played a big part in this and she feared his mother's and Brandy's disappearance was a direct result of his involvement. If they were alive, which Gina questioned, they should show up if she scryed for them.

"Alex, do you happen to have any of your mother's items with you? A brush, preferably, that might contain some of her hair? I'm going to scry for them which is a kind of a Wiccan GPS locater. I use a crystal and a map along with something personal from the person I'm trying to locate. If they are around, the crystal should point to them on the map," she was explaining to him.

"I don't have anything on me, but I do believe I have some of my mother's things packed away at the house," he told her. "I'm sorry, but I don't have anything of Brandy's. Do you think they police will allow us back into the house? I would think not, at least until the investigation is completed."

Gina gave a coy smile as she pulled a brush out of her bag.

"Hey, that's Brandy's brush," Alex said, not knowing whether to smile or cry. "How did you get it?"

"It was lying on the counter when we arrived at Brandy's. I thought; why not grab it, just in case I need it later." She explained. "I guess it was witches intuition."

"That is awesome," Alex said to Gina. "So now all we need is to go to my home and get my mother's?"

Gina looked at Demetri and then at Alex. "I'm going to get started with Brandy's stuff. If you wouldn't mind going with him Demetri, so he would have some protection, I would greatly appreciate it."

Demetri was looking at her with a bitter look and said, "Who is going to protect you?"

"You know perfectly well that I can take care of myself Demetrius Marcus, so please just do this favor for me," Gina said to him with a little irritation.

"Fine," Demetri said to them both. "I guess it would make sense if the two people closest to you just disappeared without a trace, you would be the next likely target. Besides, if I am with you, then I stand a better chance at getting my hands on the person who is after you."

"Thanks, I think," Alex said to him as they grabbed their stuff and headed towards the door.

"Wait a minute, Demetri. Before you go, I want you to help me charge up this crystal so we know it is working at maximum performance."

He walked over to her and together they laid their hands over the crystal and sent energy waves into the crystal as it lit up with a glow. She smiled at this and now felt ready to get down to the business of finding the two women.

As they prepared to leave, Alex came up to Gina and gave her a big hug.

"I'm extremely grateful for your support and efforts in trying to find mom and Brandy," he said, tears welling up in his eyes. "I don't know what I would do if anything happened to them."

At this display of affection, Demetri rolled his eyes and said, "Come on Romeo before I change my mind."

As they walked out the door and climbed into Demetri's Jeep, he looked over at Alex. "Okay, I have one rule."

Alex nodded his head, waiting for Demetri to tell him what the one rule was.

"If the shit hits the fan, you fall back behind me and let me deal with it. Got it?" Demetri said to him waiting for a verbal answer. The head shaking wasn't going to cut it.

"Okay, okay, I got it. Shit hits the fan, I get behind you." He said to Demetri, who was ready to kick some ass.

Driving to his house did not take long, as he lived just down Peoria Avenue in a neighborhood just behind the Channel 2 News building. As they pulled into his driveway, they got out of the Jeep, cautiously walked up to the door. As he started to put the key in the door, it was suddenly opened from the inside. As his roommate, John, stood there, Demetri was already in strike mode and Alex had to quickly put his arm up in front of Demetri to stop him from blasting John across the house.

"Alex, I'm so glad to see you are okay," John said to him. "I have been worried sick."

"Yes, I'm sorry about that," Alex said to him. "It's been somewhat of a whirlwind and I haven't been in my right mind; I'm sorry for not keeping in touch with you better."

"Dude, as long as you are okay; that's all that matters," John said.

As they came through the doorway, he started down the hallway to his room where he was sure he had some of his mother's older things in his closet. As he searched through the closet, he found the box he was looking for. Within it were some old birthday cards, some old pictures, his mother's favorite mirror, and her silver brush and comb set. He knew it was here and he hoped it would help. He grabbed some fresh clothes out of the closet and threw those on.

While he was getting his things out of the bedroom, Demetri was standing in the kitchen with a healthy looking John. The guy looked like he worked out and took care of himself. He was an average looking guy, on the better side of average, actually, and seemed like a down to earth kind of guy.

Demetri quizzed him about what it was like living with Alex and his other roommates. John was accommodating to his questions. He liked it when things went according to plan and he was trying to get information out of John and he seemed more than happy to divulge. While he was sitting at the barstool with his back to the refrigerator, John asked him if he would care for a bottle of water. Demetri, actually quite parched from the hot summer days and nights, thanked John for his hospitality, and said yes to the bottle of water.

As John went over to the fridge and pulled out a bottle of water placing it on the granite counter top in front of Demetri, he reached into his pocket and pulled out a syringe. Quickly taking the top of it off, still standing behind Demetri, he jabbed the syringe into his neck, injecting the liquid.

Demetri never saw it coming; he had been disarmed by the good ole boy charm and had actually been enjoying

269

talking to John. As reality blurred and his senses went numb, he was thinking to himself, *how the hell did this kid get the better of me?* As he faded into unconsciousness, John helped him lay his head down on the granite island counter top.

Alex had made his way out of his room and was shocked to find John standing outside of the doorway to his room.

"John, you scared me. I wasn't expecting you." He said visibly startled.

"Really, oh I am sorry about that. I didn't mean to scare you. I thought that maybe you and I could have a little talk," John said to him as he pointed toward the living room.

As Alex walked that way he said, "I really don't have any time to waste John; I am trying to find my mother and Brandy."

"Oh, they are fine, or should I say they will be fine, as long as you and I have our little talk right here, right now. Take a seat," John said staring at him while pointing to the sofa.

Alex was spinning on the inside as he sat down on the sofa as John had asked. Had John just implied what he thought he had implied? Does John know something about his mother and Brandy? "What are you talking about John? What do you mean they are fine?"

"Just as I said to you, they are fine. They will continue to be fine as long as you do and say what I tell you to do," John said looking directly at him with cold steel eyes.

Alex had never seen him like this before and it was beginning to unnerve him. But it was clear that he knew more than he was telling.

"What do you know about my mother and Brandy?" He said standing up as he was starting to get pissed off.

"Sit the fuck down Alex or they will die just like our wonderful roommates did, just a few minutes ago," John said, allowing himself to get upset, then quickly turning that into a smile, which did nothing but make Alex think he was psychotic.

"John, what do you mean die like Carrie and Seth? What did you do John?" He said his voice cracking.

"Oh, I slit both of their throats with a butcher knife from the kitchen," John said still smiling.

"What? Why? What did they ever do to you John? Are you fucking kidding me right now? Demetri...," he started to scream, but John just laughed at him.

"Demetri will not be joining us, if you are referring to the handsome man that came with you? He is otherwise preoccupied." John said.

Alex was fuming, confused, screaming on the inside and didn't know what the hell to say to this crazy ass man who had obviously snapped. "Did you kill Demetri too?"

"No, he is taking a long nap and will not remember much when he wakes up. Nasty headache too I would assume." John said laughing to himself.

"What do you want John? What have I ever done to you to deserve this? What have any of us ever done to you to deserve this?" Alex said pleading to him.

"Actually, nothing yet, but you are going to," he said to him looking at him again with those cold eyes.

"What do you want from me John?"

"Actually, I am going to take you to your mother and Brandy."

"What, you know where they are?"

"Have I been talking to myself this whole time?" John said out loud. "If you come with me willingly, nothing will happen to you or them. If you resist, one or both of them will be tortured, wounded, or killed."

Alex stood up, looking at John with shock and fear in his eyes. His eyes actually started to tear up. "Please take me to them," Alex said, "I won't resist."

"You're a smart man, Alex, smart indeed," John said. "Hold out your arms so I can secure your hands. I know we have lived together for a long time, but I am not sure you are feeling all warm and fuzzy towards me. I think I would rather take my chances with your hands bound."

Alex did as he was told and reassured John he just wanted to see his mother and Brandy. He could not believe John had been in on the kidnapping, and just admitted to killing his other roommates Carrie and Seth. It was just sinking in what John said and he was just now feeling the weight of that news.

He hadn't even tried to find them, to see if they were still alive. But as he felt the knot of the rope tighten around his wrists, he knew it was too late to think about such things. He was on his way to see his mother and Brandy. He hoped John was right that Demetri was just out cold, that he would wake up and be okay. Alex knew when he did wake up and realized what had happened, he was going to be one pissed off witch. Heaven help John and whoever else is involved with this when Demetri and Gina find them.

John finished tying the knots to the rope around his wrists. He told him to relax, that it was going to get a little dark, but that if he was good he would be with his mother and Brandy in just a few minutes. As soon as John finished saying that, the lights went out as he felt a cloth sack come down over his head, obviously meant to keep him from seeing where they were going. He felt that it was being tightened around his neck, not enough to choke him or cut off his air, but tight enough that he wouldn't be able to take it off.

John led him out into the garage where there was a black SUV waiting for him, Opening the door to the back of the SUV, he had Alex lay down flat on his back and he shut the door behind him. John then walked around and climbed into the driver's seat where he pushed a button on the remote that he had in his pocket. The garage door started to open as he pushed the button. He turned the ignition and fired up the SUV and started backing out of the garage into the driveway. As he was clear of the garage door, he once again pressed the button on the remote and the garage door began to close.

He backed out into the street and headed toward the Balashon mansion. His many years stationed here, getting to know the vessel, getting to keep a watch out was almost at an end. He had done his job well, and his next duty was to deliver

Alex to a man named Victor, who did not know that he was anything more than Alex's roommate. He had no idea that he was Balashon or that there were actually many Balashon warriors who have been placed here for many years. All here, watching silently over the vessel as they all waited for this day to come, August 20, 2013. It was going to be a magical day, one that Tulsa would never forget, and one the world would never forget.

Yes, as he neared the Balashon mansion, the life that John had been playing so dutifully was washing away from him and his Balashon life was beginning again. It felt good to be back where he felt he belonged, alongside other Balashon warriors, awaiting the arrival of the master.

Chapter Forty-Eight

As Demetri began to wake up, his head was pounding and his memory was foggy. He struggled to remember where he was and why he was waking up sitting at the island counter, in a kitchen he didn't know. This couldn't be good. As he steadied himself enough to get on his feet, he struggled to focus, trying to remember.

When his head cleared enough for him to walk, he left the kitchen and made his way to the hallway. As he followed it, he realized it led into the living area with what looked like it might be bedrooms shooting off in different directions. The living area had double French doors that led out into the back yard. As he looked out the French doors, he saw a pool.

"Hello," he called out. "Is there anyone here?"

Nothing, no response at all, as he realized he was in the house alone. He decided to try the rooms off the other side of the living area. As he made his way into one of the rooms, he noticed it was immaculately neat, free of clutter, free of almost anything. It was as if the person who stayed in this room was temporary; hell, it may even be a guest room for all he knew.

As he left that room and went into one of the others, he immediately got a sense something wasn't right. He was hit by a feeling of loss, of sorrow, as if something horrible and tragic happened in this room. As he looked around he was searching for any clue that might lead him to figuring out why he was there. He would even take a ghost at this point to help him out.

He noticed the room had a bathroom attached, so he walked inside and turned the light on. Before he got a light switch flipped up and turned on, his nose was hit by the smell of death, the smell of fresh blood. As his eyes focused to the lights, he saw a girl, actually a woman, lying in the bathtub. It was as if she just sat down in it the wrong way with her legs hanging out of the tub, her throat cut from jugular to jugular. There was blood everywhere.

Demetri was so appalled at this, *why had this happened, how did he come to be at this place? Why couldn't he remember?* He backed out of the bathroom, out of the bedroom and made his way back into the hallway. He headed down to the third bedroom that was on this side of the house. As he walked inside of it, he got the same feeling of something not right, that something had gone horribly wrong here. But as he searched the room and the closet, making sure to not touch anything unnecessarily, he could not find anything in this room to support the feeling he was having.

Leaving the bedroom, he headed to the next door at the end of the hallway on this side of the house. If he were correct, it should be a bathroom. When he turned on the lights, he noticed his assumption of it being a bathroom was correct and he was right in thinking that something had been wrong in this young man's bedroom.

He too was sitting in the tub, same as the girl in the other bathroom, throat cut in the exact same way. Both of their eyes were wide open, bug-eyed almost as if they were begging for him to save them, but they were far from that now. They were both dead and he could do nothing for them.

Quickly making his way out of this hallway he headed toward the last room, on the side in which he had originally walked in. As he walked into the room something felt familiar about it. He knew he hadn't been there before, but he felt he knew the person who occupied this room, and owned this house.

When he made his way into the room, he saw a picture on the nightstand. As he approached it, he realized why it felt so familiar. It was Alex's room and he assumed by the tall blond in the picture with him, this must be the Brandy he has heard so much about and who they were all looking for. He suddenly had a fear, it wasn't the same feeling he had felt when he had found the girl and the guy, but it was a fear for Alex.

He knew he had to check the bathroom in Alex's room; he sucked in his breath, as if in a way that would prepare him for whatever he might find, he turned on the light. Surprised not find anything in there, he exhaled the air. So why would he be here, in Alex's home.

He racked his brain, trying to remember, but he was getting frustrated. He didn't remember anything other than Gina, Alex, and himself talking about what needed to be done while they were all at Gina's store. Then he remembered a conversation, one about him coming over to Alex's with him to get something of Alex's mothers so that Gina could try locating her.

This must have gone totally wrong. He was at a loss as to why he couldn't remember anything. He remembered seeing a box lying on the bed in Alex's room so as he turned and left the bathroom he grabbed the box as it had pictures and some personal items that looked like it could be his mothers.

Now he was torn, he didn't know what to do about the dead people in the house. If he called the police he stood the chance of being delayed while Alex, his mother, and Brandy could be transported anywhere in the world by this time, or even worse since he couldn't remember anything he stood the risk of being arrested for the murders of these two people who he had never met before.

He made a quick decision. He would wipe down everything he had touched starting in the kitchen where he found himself when he woke up. Grabbing a towel that lay on the kitchen counter, he began to wipe down the counter top, the bar stool; he grabbed the water bottle that was sitting there and stuck it in his pocket. Making his way around to all the rooms he wiped down everything he had touched including the light switches. Demetri was finally satisfied he had wiped everything clean and made sure he got the front door handle as he made his way outside. To his delight, his Jeep was still there, and there were no neighbors outside. As he shut the door behind him, he focused on the door lock until he heard it turn and lock.

He heard sirens in the background sounding like they were headed his way. His heart sunk. Whoever had done this to these people obviously thought they could frame him for it. He couldn't let that happen. He sprinted to the Jeep, and turned the ignition, happy to hear it fire up. He quickly thought to himself *if you wanted to frame someone for murder, you should at least disable their car so they couldn't get away from the police that were called to come collect him.*

He backed out of the driveway and headed down the opposite way to the main road. He wanted to make sure he was taking back roads as he eluded any of the police that would be arriving. Someone must have given him some kind of short term amnesia drug. It was working, because he didn't remember fuck. The only good thing was Alex and his captor must not be too far ahead of him if the cops were just now coming.

Pulling his phone out of his pocket, he dialed Gina and began to tell her what he had found. She was not a bit thrilled with what he was telling her and, quite frankly, he wasn't either. He had obviously been duped and fallen prey to this person they were all looking for.

He was far enough away from Alex's; he felt he was safe enough the police would not be suspicious of him and pull him over. He was still trying to catch his breath as he was soaking in all that had happened. Gina had filled him in on all that was talked about at her place before Alex and Demetri left to go over and look for his mother's belongings. He did tell her he had them with him. But why kill the other roommates, and in such a brutal fashion? This was just a deeper, weirder mystery that kept getting more intense as the days quickly kept moving towards the full blue moon.

When he arrived back at Gina's, she was busy crafting some spell that would help with the location of the three. He watched as she had been trying a scrying spell for almost two hours now, using her most powerful crystal, which she had him help her charge it with energy. She had a map of greater Tulsa, some hair from the brushes of Alex's mother and Brandy and a glass Alex was using to drink from before they left to go to his house. They were not turning anything up, which wasn't necessarily a good thing, as this spell was to locate a living being or object. They were doing the best they could to stay calm and hold out faith they were still alive and would be found.

There was an odd thing that kept happening with the locator spell for Alex. The crystal kept landing back onto a specific spot on the map, one that couldn't be accurate. It kept landing on the location of Gina's store, the exact spot they were standing in. The first couple of times it happened Demetri had went and searched the entire place, store, living area, and even the parking lot, but there was no Alex. This was maddening.

He was beginning to have his doubts they were dealing with just one man. The way this was playing out, even with unlimited resources, one man could not have pulled all of this off. He had to admit, the man they had encountered at the bar was a strong one, but even with the strength, he couldn't be everywhere at once. No, there had to be multiple players in this and they have had to been watching for some time, which gave them the upper hand. He didn't like that one bit. He was used to being able to handle most situations and come up with a plan, but on this one he wasn't doing too well on formulating one.

He needed to start getting his thoughts together, start centering himself, and definitely start tapping into the power he had control over in his past lives. In the past life, his soul had mastered some impressive powers and was hopeful that he could call on them again when the time came. Maybe it would take some practice which he was running out of time for or maybe once his soul came into contact with Bastiquil again, it would conjure up some emotions that would help to win this fight.

They have been on the outside looking in this entire time. They hadn't known who the players were, nor what the game was, until now. They are speculating at best, on what it is even now. It was a big task to protect the ones you love and have to protect the city in the process. If he wasn't able to control this, to keep it contained in the city the outcome could be catastrophic. He couldn't think like that now, he couldn't allow himself to. He had to focus, start building energy around himself and jump start these powers somehow. It was all in a day's work.

Chapter Forty-Nine

When Alex felt the SUV come to a halt and heard the key shut off, his stomach began to turn again. He was hoping to see Brandy and his mother unharmed and okay. He had thought of every worst case scenario and didn't like any of them.

He had thought on the ride over here about how wrong he had been about John. How blinded he was by this man who had lived with him for years and he felt like he actually never knew him at all. John betrayed him, lied to him every day for years and in the end, killed his other two roommates and appeared to have had a hand in kidnapping his mother and Brandy. He must have done something drastic to Demetri, for Demetri not to have smashed his brains into the side of a wall. He was torn by this thought because as much as he would have liked to have seen Demetri tear this piece of shit to bits, he would much rather see that his mother and Brandy were alright.

The driver's side door of the SUV opened and he assumed it was John getting out and would be coming to open the back and to let him out. He was correct, the back door suddenly opened then he heard John's voice telling him to sit up so he could lead him out of the vehicle and into the house. He did as was asked of him because he had just one mission at this time and it was to see his girls. He allowed John to lead him from the vehicle into what he thought was a house as he was being pushed down into what seemed like a living room chair as it was plush, soft, and big.

As he sat there waiting he heard some men in the background talking. He could make out John's voice, but the other man's voice, he didn't recognize. He heard it from a distance and through the bag, so he wasn't surprised by the lack of recognition. Their voices got louder; then he heard one of the men walking away in the opposite direction and one walking towards him.

"Okay Alex, I am going to take the bag off of your head and I am only going to tell you this once and only once. Are you ready to listen to me?" John said to him as he started to untie the bag that was secured around his neck.

"Yes, I'm listening."

"Okay, here are the ground rules. I am going to remove the bag from your head then I am going to take you to a room where you will wait without question for 48 hours. When those 48 hours are up, you will get to see your mother and Brandy again. Am I clear so far?" John asked.

Alex acknowledged he was clear.

"If you attempt to escape, contact anyone, or in any way try to harm anyone here, I will first slit Brandy's throat, just because I have wanted to for years, then I will slit your mother's. Am I still being clearly heard?" John asked of him a second time.

"Yes, I understand you completely," he said to John, but he was seething with hatred on the inside.

"Good, now, I am going to take you to your room, then I will remove the bag completely from your head and I will remove the ropes that are around your hands. You will be in a nice room, where you will sit out your 48 hours, be fed three times a day and at times someone will come and take you so you can wash up and shower. I know how much you enjoy your showers. They were enjoyable for me too." John said to him as he cringed inside a little. This kidnapping, murderous pervert must have been watching him for a long time. The thought was unnerving.

"I understand," was all he could muster up as he was still reeling on the inside.

"Good, now stand up and follow my lead. Don't try anything stupid." John said as he led him down some hallways, then up a series of stairs then down some more hallways. He was trying his best to keep count of the steps he was taking in the hallway, as well as how many steps he was taking on the stairs, but in the end he was so upset that he knew he just better give up because he had lost count anyway.

When they came to a stop, he heard a key being placed into the door and the door opening. It creaked a little at first, and then he was being led through the door into a room. As the door shut behind him and locked, he was led over to a bed where he was forced to sit down. As he set there, John finally removed the bag from his head and as his eyes adjusted, he could see that he was in a beautifully decorated room. It had a large bed on which he was sitting and a chair along the wall with lighting in the ceiling; no lamps as he assumed that they could be used as a weapon if one so wanted. There were some magazines, which he figured are there to keep him occupied.

John started working on the ropes that bound his hands. As John worked on removing them, he couldn't help but just stare at this man who he had many talks with over the years. The same man who just a week ago had helped him when he was sick from his dreams. I guess it is all making a little more sense now; if you plan on abducting someone, wouldn't you infiltrate their life, get to know them inside and out, then strike when the time is just right?

He had nothing but contempt for the man untying his hands. He didn't know this John if John was even his name at all. He just wanted to punch him in the face, but if he did that he risked something happening to his mother or Brandy or both. So he just sat there until the ropes were completely off.

John stood up, turned, and started walking towards the door. He couldn't help himself and burst out with, "John, when can I see my mother?"

John stopped, turned, and looked at him, smiled then turned and walked out. He heard the key in the door lock then heard the footsteps of John fading down the hallway. He was stuck here, for 48 hours John had said. Forty-eight hours until he was to be reunited with his mother and Brandy. Let's just hope that wasn't a lie to get him here. He had no other choice than to believe John, no other choice because the alternative wasn't something he could deal with.

Chapter Fifty

Demetri and Gina had been out on the streets trying to chase down any leads they could on what had happened to Alex. Demetri was using every resource he had in the city to try and find him. Luckily, it had not been found out yet he had been at Alex's house, the scene of a brutal and vicious crime. If things went according to plan, Demetri hoped it would never be found out.

There were many speculations being tossed around by the TPD. One was that he had been kidnapped along with his mother and Brandy. Another one being tossed around, is he had snapped from all of the stress of losing his mother and his best friend, and went on a killing spree and killed two of his three roommates. What they couldn't explain, was where the third roommate had disappeared too. There is a third theory in which the remaining roommate kidnapped Brandy and Ella, killed the two roommates and now has Alex.

This was yet another mystery they had to solve. The TPD were good at their job, but they didn't have all the facts of the case that Demetri and Gina had. They wished they could share the details with the TPD, but neither of them saw anything good coming from it. So they were on their own, hitting the streets, looking for clues as the ticking clock got ever closer to the approaching full moon. It had already reached its formation of the first day of a three moon cycle. The third day would be when the moon is blue, so time was quickly running out.

Demetri put some feelers out to the supernatural underworld, asking for any help they could give for information, locating or help in general, when the time came to do battle, which he hoped that day wouldn't come. But they were getting desperate, running out of time and resources.

Gina had received a call from Demetri asking her to meet him back at the store. They needed to regroup and come up with another plan of attack. This one wasn't working for them.

As Gina was impatiently waiting for him to get back, relief swept over her to see him walk in with some Starbuck's coffee and Danishes, her favorite was their pumpkin loaf. She was famished and feeling a bit drained lately. She knew she was under stress from worrying about Alex and his family, but it felt like something more.

As they set at the table debriefing each other on what they both had found so far, they concluded that they had a big pile of nothing. Gina had decided she would try and summon her grandmother through a sacred ritual and see if she could offer them any knowledge or guidance from the other side. She had not summoned her grandmother in quite some time so it would be nice to commune with her again. Too bad it wasn't under better circumstances.

Demetri was quizzing her on whether or not the same concept could be used to summon your past life, well not your past life per say, but to summon that part of your soul, the one that he saw in his past life meditative trance. He wanted to meld the memories of the souls together so that he could incorporate the powers, hidden within the memories of the past lives this soul has lived.

Gina pondered the thought for a moment and wasn't quite sure what to make of it. She wasn't sure if his body, first of all, would be able to sustain such power and, secondly, if it did, would make him one of the most, if not the most, powerful person on this planet. It was a huge risk, with even bigger consequences if they failed or succeeded.

She truly believed it was skirting around a belief that she has held out for a long time and that is, the body and mind will find its way to its own powers. Basically, your powers are revealed to you at a time when the body and mind are ready for it, not when you will them to be. Being that the mind is the center point for the conduction of the power source, what if it overloaded his brain or even worse, fried it? She wasn't sure if she wanted to take a chance or not.

He was making a good argument though; sometimes it comes down to what's better for the world. Letting a demon take over or unleashing a power source that has stopped him in the past? She thought about what she wanted to say to him before she just blurted it out.

"The last time this person, soul, being, what have you, had this power, they abused it. They vanquished Bastiquil, not because it was the right thing to do, but because he wanted all the power and glory that came with ruling the known world at the time. What makes you think that wouldn't happen again?"

"Well I am in charge of this soul, in this life, in this moment, and I think you know me well enough to know that I have a good heart and don't want to rule or destroy the world," he said to her while looking hurt at the same time.

"It isn't the current you that I question. It is unleashing the part of your soul that once had the ability to rule the world. That is a frightening thought. What if you couldn't control that side of the soul? What if we screwed up and all of the soul's memories, from eternity and beyond, melded with you? It might fry your brain, even kill you."

"Well, I think it is a good option to consider and one that we should not put on the back burner. If we are going to do it, it should be sooner rather than later so we can actually see what will happen." Demetri argued his point hoping that she would give in.

"Let's just say that I'm not ruling out that it may be our only hope for defeating Bastiquil. If he is able to cross back over into this world, this realm, but shouldn't we exhaust all efforts before we take such a big risk with your life?" She asked of him, seeing him soften just a bit.

"Well, let's agree that if we have no other options by tomorrow morning that we will proceed forward with it. I'm hoping to only tap into the one memory of the soul from Bastiquil's time. I don't want any of the other memories," he said to her knowing that it wasn't necessarily the truth. He would love to have those memories with Aldrik when they were young. He knew nothing about him back then. To know that they had shared a life together, albeit they may not have knew each other all their life, or if it was just that moment on the boat; were they lovers then or just friends? There was so much he wanted to know about Aldrik, but if he didn't survive this it would all be for naught anyway.

"Okay, as much as I don't like this idea, I will concede that I don't have a better one. So we give it until tomorrow and if we haven't come up with anything better, we will try it your way." She said to him regretting it the moment it slipped off her tongue.

Chapter Fifty-One

Victor had grown weary of all the surprises the Balashon was throwing his way. He was shocked, no, not shocked, frustrated to find out there has been a sleeper cell, of sorts, in Tulsa. Someone that had been lying in wait for the right moment to rise up just before the full moon. Come to find out, they have been here for years filtering themselves into the lives of the vessel, the vessel's mother, and best friend. You would think the least they would do for their head assassin was give him a heads up they were here. They could have been killed in the process had they gotten in his way, but maybe they didn't care; maybe it truly was about the end game.

Victor had been surprised when this Balashon sheep, John, had shown up with access to the mansion with the vessel. *What the fuck was that about?*

Victor and John had an exchange of words and, in a matter of minutes, John had the head of the Balashon on the phone telling Victor to back down and fall in line. The head of the council informed Victor he should be prepared for a great many more guests to be arriving. This was not quite what Victor had in mind for the Balashon's entry into Tulsa for the raising of the master, but Victor would never go against what the Balashon council ordered of him.

Victor was not just an assassin, he was a life-long loyal member of the Balashon and he would make the best of this. He had hoped he would be the one that finished the preparation for the master's arrival, but as he had learned before with this council, he should expect the unexpected.

But there was still salvation for him; he had still laid out the plan of all plans; one the Balashon could not have predicted. The master would love this with all of his being, with all of his glory; he will see this as a true measure of his faithful service to him.

The salvation of his legacy would not be dictated by some warriors who have been silently waiting in the wings while he has been here doing battle on the master's behalf. He would have his day, he would have his redemption in the master's eyes, and he will command an army for the master, one that would reap worldwide destruction. Man's weapons could not harm the master; he would be immortal, invincible. The witches of this day and age do not hold the power to condemn his master back to the hell in which he is clawing his way back from. What awaited now was the time, two more days until the moon is full, until it shines blue for the master's return.

It was time for the vessel to come face to face with the man who has kept him out of harm's way for the past month. He wanted to see his face, hear his voice, and look deep into his eyes. He was born and bred for this, he was born a vessel. His destiny was made three thousand years ago and it is almost upon them. All of their destinies lie in wait; all are aligned with the same end, the same beginning. Yes, he must meet the vessel for it was only right that he see the man who helped him reach his highest potential in life. Many of his family have been guarded by the Balashon all of these thousands of years, waiting for the moment when the master would return.

As he walked down the hallway towards the stairs leading to the room holding the vessel, his heart beat a few beats faster than normal. He wanted to talk to him, to be near him, but he had not wanted to reveal himself until today. Before, it was about anonymity, but today, it was about destiny.

With each step up the stairs, he felt as if he were walking towards his master. He knew that his master had not yet come forth to take root inside this vessel's body, although, he would in just a matter of days. He would take back the life that was stolen from him all of those years ago and reclaim his throne on this earth by resuming his life through the body of his great grandson. The vessel, this Alex, has not yet figured out who he is, but he comes from royalty. The vessel comes from a long blood line that flows all the way back to Bastiquil, his great grandfather.

He found himself standing outside the room where the vessel was being kept until it was time for him to be prepped for the ritual that would bring Alex and Bastiquil back together again. He placed the key inside the lock and turned it, he heard the lock snap back and he opened the door, pushing it so that it was open all the way before he walked in. He didn't want the vessel to be hiding behind the door; he wanted this to be a peaceful introduction, an exchange between a guardian and a prince. He held the vessel up in the highest regard as he was a sacred body, an ancestor to the master, a prince among men.

Walking into the room he found Alex sitting on the window's ledge, looking outside at the grounds below. Alex turned to look at him for a brief moment then turned his head to look outside again. Alex was growing weary of this isolation, of not seeing his mother or Brandy. The knowledge he was the reason his other two roommates had been killed, that other people in Tulsa were being murdered, and that an ancient evil was to return to reign down hell on earth, weighed heavily on him. None of this made sense to Alex, but his mind had grown weary and tired of the endless scenarios that kept playing over and over in his head. *Were Gina and Demetri alright? Would they end up dead like the rest if they kept looking for him?*

"Hello, my name is Victor. It is an honor to meet you."

Alex continued to stare out of the windows, not stopping to look at or acknowledge Victor had said anything to him.

"Why the troubled look young one?"

"Why? I think you know why I am troubled. If you are a part of any of this, then you know perfectly well why I am troubled, so please spare me the insincere concern and cut to the chase." Alex said to Victor, stinging him slightly as he wanted to put the vessel's mind at ease. To let him know what a great honor it is for him to have this birthright, to be a holy vessel, a walking tribute to the most powerful force to walk this earth.

"I just want you to know your mother and your friend are safe, no harm has come to them. They are being fed well, taken care of, and given the luxuries this house has to offer them. They are being treated with the utmost respect." Victor said to him in hopes of getting him to soften a little in order to have a dialog with him.

He turned to Victor and gave him a look that Victor took as gratitude, for the information of his loved ones. Alex had been worried about them. He had been promised to see them if he had agreed to come along, but that was not the case when he arrived. He was told he wouldn't be able to see them until the day of the full moon.

"Why the cloak and dagger routine; why tell me you will show me my mother and Brandy if I agreed to come, if you had no intention of doing so?"

"It isn't my intention to upset you young one. In all honesty, would you have come on your own free will had we asked? Would you have been satisfied to see them only to be removed from them and locked away for the next few days? I know this doesn't seem fair to you and maybe it isn't since you didn't choose to be born into this royal family, but life isn't fair, sometimes we have no choices, sometimes our destiny is so much greater than ourselves that we are forced to comply rather than defy." Victor explained.

"What do you mean born into this royal family?" He asked of Victor, perplexed.

"You are a prince young one, the grandson of a great power, the direct blood descendant of the great Bastiquil. You were born for this moment in time. You were chosen by the

291

stars to be born so Bastiquil could live again in this world," Victor was talking to him as he looked on in obvious bewilderment. "The great Bastiquil's reign on this earth was cut way too short thousands of years ago. Before he left this world, he had impregnated a young woman, your grandmother many times removed. You have been protected by my people, your entire bloodline has been protected by my people so this day we are living in now, could come to pass. Your life, your entire existence is because of Bastiquil."

"So you are saying I am the great great grandson of a demon?" Alex asked of him in shock and disgust.

"That is precisely what I am saying Alex, but he is no ordinary demon. He is a great and powerful one, one of the most powerful of the underworld. He ruled thousands of years ago until he was betrayed by his closest ally and was driven back to the underworld to await this day, to patiently await your birth and your rise to adulthood. You are a great creation Alex; you are blessed and lucky to be the chosen one." Victor believed all he was saying to Alex as it was the entire foundation his life had been built upon. If he didn't believe this then everything in his life would be built upon falsehood, a lie. Victor didn't think he or anyone else destined to be in this moment in time to witness this celebration of the bonding, the unification of grandfather and grandson was a mistake or a falsehood. This was pure destiny.

Alex continued to look on at Victor, to listen to the craziness coming out of his mouth, the pure and heartfelt belief in his convictions. "So you are telling me all those people who died, the one on the jogging path, and the couple at Woodward Park were all because of destiny. Of something much greater than themselves, and they should be honored to have their life cut short for the glory of Bastiquil?"

"That is exactly what I am saying to you young prince."

"Please stop calling me that, I'm no prince," Alex said to him, who seemed to ignore the request.

"From the time you were born, the stars aligned, the universe was set into motion for reunification to happen. Do you honestly think anything that has happened to you in your life has been by accident, by pure dumb luck? Nothing is as simple as that when you are dealing with destiny. Your first tattoo, do you remember how you came about knowing you wanted that particular tattoo?"

Alex just looked on at him in utter disbelief, thinking, *how does this man know all of this?*

Victor continued, "You came about it through a dream as you did the rest of your tattoos. They were all put into your mind by Bastiquil, by his pure love for you, so you would be prepared for his coming. You were already connected to him by blood, but by bearing his symbols on your body, he was better able to communicate with you, to know you inside and out. He wanted you to be prepared for this, to accept it as we all have. You have been a life mission for many of my people and you will continue to be the mission of my people when you are rejoined with your proper family."

Alex looked on at this man who was speaking so proudly, so honestly. Alex realized he was a true believer, he was a man led by conviction, which made him a dangerous man to cross. This type of man would not be stopped short of fulfilling what he believed his destiny to be, and from everything he was saying, that destiny lay with Alex and this Bastiquil. This man was a dangerous man, more dangerous than a caged lion; in fact, he thought he would have more luck with the caged lion than trying to dissuade this man from completing his mission.

"Can I ask you something?"

"Anything, young prince," Victor replied.

"Was it you at the bar, in the mask, who was protecting me in the basement and then again when Demetri was attacking me?" Alex asked looking at Victor.

"It was me and I was honored to be able to assist you. Please know you are loved here that every one of my people would gladly die for you," Victor said showing emotion for the first time since this conversation began. "There are forces out there that will stop at nothing to make sure this union between you and Bastiquil doesn't happen, but I can assure you, it will happen. You will be joined with your grandfather. You will know his joy, his power, his rage as well as his happiness. If you think the witches can help you, can stop this, you are most wrong young prince. They will fail."

"Please don't hurt them," Alex begged. "They are just trying to help me; they love me as well."

"They don't love you, young one; they don't even know you, to be honest. If they did know the real you, the reason for your birth, the blood flowing through your veins, do you think they would be so quick to help you? Please don't bother to answer me with naïve answers; the answer is no, they would not. They would try to find a way to destroy you and Bastiquil. But my people will not let that happen. We are strong; many have trained for thousands of years for this very moment. They will fail young prince if they try to stop us."

"You keep referring to your people. What are you talking about?" Alex asked of him.

"We are the Balashon, the keeper of your secrets, the people of Bastiquil. We are many and we are one. We move within society to keep the work of Bastiquil going and growing. We protect Bastiquil's family, we protect you. We are thought to be extinct; we have lived for thousands of years allowing that belief. It has made us strong in our resolve and our strength and beliefs will make us triumphant." Victor glowed as he said this.

Alex was watching him closely and somewhat admired his resolve. He still knew he was a dangerous man, but he never had in his life met someone with more dedication, more devotion to his cause.

"How were you able to fight back against Demetri?" Alex asked of him. "I felt his power, he threw me up against a wall with his mind and I was unable to move; how did you fight back?"

Victor looked at Alex and made a disgusted look. "Those wretched creatures, witches, are nothing more than a conduit for a power they will never understand. I was chosen into the Balashon because of my beliefs, my convictions. I know what true power is and knowing that gives you the power in itself, the ability to fight back against someone wielding something they don't understand. Believe me; it didn't happen all at once; that I was able to do what I did. It took years of daily practicing with a powerful witch, to be able to do that. But as you see how their power is used, typically, carelessly, you can understand their vulnerabilities and are better able to beat them at their own game. I believed this witch had no power over me, so I was able to fight back. We are taught strength in our training at the Balashon. We are taught discipline. That is one thing your friends, the witches, are lacking; a pure belief and understanding of their powers; lack of control."

As he listened to this man he began to realize, Gina and Demetri were up against more than just Bastiquil, they were up against his army too. These Balashon were led by a pure, unadulterated belief in what they are doing. They will die for him, for Bastiquil. Unless Gina and Demetri are able to come up with something quick, he didn't see any chance of getting out of this. It would most likely mean they would both be killed if they were able to find him and decided to attack this place. He shuddered on the inside, thinking of any harm coming to Gina. He had just met her, but she appeared to be a true friend, someone he would have loved to have gotten to know better.

"May I ask you another question?" Alex said looking at him again who had a slight smile on his face. Alex at that moment knew that Victor loved him, but not because he was Alex, but because of whom Victor believed Alex was. "What will happen to me when and if this Bastiquil takes over my body?"

Victor smiled at him and thought for a second, then began to speak. "Let's make no mistake about this young prince; there is no if in this equation. Bastiquil will be rejoined with your body, his body. You would not be in existence if it were not for him. As for you, you will cease to be Alex, you will become Bastiquil. You may still be in there somewhere, more like a person on a ride at an amusement park, but you will cease to have control over your body and mind. The power that will be wielded from your body will be like nothing you have seen or felt before. You think this Demetri, this male witch has power; he has nothing compared to what is coming into you. It will be a glorious day for you, for the Balashon, but most importantly, it will be a glorious day for Bastiquil."

Chapter Fifty-Two

Gina had just finished placing the five candles at the points that make up a pentagon, one large enough to hold a human spirit. She had decided that she needed guidance, and the type she needed was one that would require magical intervention since her grandmother had already passed on to the other side. She missed her so much and often times found herself talking to her out loud and sometimes she actually thought she heard her talking back. But, as she thought more about the predicament that Demetri, Alex, and herself found themselves in, she knew that her grandmother would have some sound, logical advice for her.

Taking her athame out, her ritual knife, used to direct her magical energy, she pricked her fingertip and used the blood formed on her finger to draw an eye on her forehead. This was to represent her third eye, or mind's eye. She then began to concentrate on the five candles placed in front of her and as she pictured it in her mind, the candles lit up with a flame all at once. She had mastered this ability many years ago when her grandmother was still alive.

All of the lights were out in the room except for the five burning candles she had lit. She tried to concentrate on the here and now. She listened to the sounds in the room, listened to the noises of her home, her store. She could hear the ceiling fans in the other rooms rotating around. She heard the fridge in the kitchen, heard the wind as it brushed up against the side of the building and pushed on the windows from the outside. She pictured in her head as she closed her eyes, her grandmother standing before her.

When doing this type of spell, this particular part was important, known as a standard control component. This is where you let your mind realize that random everyday noises are a part of your day to day life and the only time we typically notice them is when we are anxious, scared, or extremely nervous. Your mind likes to play tricks on you so it's important you understand this particular concept.

She acknowledged all of the sounds around her, and then began to focus on shutting them out. She needed complete concentration for what she was about to do. She spent the next ten to fifteen minutes getting her mind centered and her head clear. She was in a total clear space in her mind.

"I summon thee, the one to be, the one who lost their life. I summon thee, the one to be, the one who lost their life. I summon thee, the one to be, the one who lost their life. Power of the witches rise come to me, I call you near. Come to me and settle here. Blood of my blood, I summon thee, blood of my blood, return to me. Elizabeth Helen Petran, blood of my blood, my grandmother, I summon thee." She chanted as she was calling out to the universe, calling out to her dead grandmother to come to her. She dug deep within herself to pull on all of her power, ancient and current, to bring her grandmother across that divide.

As the flames on the candles shot up and burned three inches higher, she opened her eyes to find, in fact, an ancestor had returned. It wasn't the one that she had planned on. Her mother, Katherine, was standing within the pentagon. A blurry, see-through version of what she looked like when she had passed away. She wasn't in the same clothes and she didn't have any injuries, she was her mother, standing here smiling at Gina.

"Mom, what are you doing here? I mean, I am glad to see you, but I was calling on grandma; how did I get you mom?" She asked the ghost of her mother with a confused look on her face.

298

"I am sorry she didn't come, but we are a collective energy over here. The universe thought I might be able to help you my dear," Katherine said to her daughter, not hurt by her daughter's question, but wanting to get to the point. "I don't know how much time I will be given so please tell me how I can help you?"

"Well, I was hoping to find out if there was a way for Demetri and I as witches to fight a demon?"

"A demon; what kind of demon are you wanting to fight?" Katherine asked of her daughter.

"A powerful demon, an upper-level demon in the hierarchy of demons; its name is Bastiquil," Gina said to her mother.

At the sound of this name, her mother recoiled in disgust, and then looked at Gina in fear for her daughter's life.

"Gina, you must promise me to stay clear of this demon. You must promise me you will go far away from this demon. He has a reputation even on my side and he isn't a demon that a mortal witch, even ones as strong as you and Demetri are, can defeat. He is an eater of souls, he is manipulative, and he will toy with you while eating away at your soul Gina. Promise me you will run from this evil beast," Katherine pleaded with her daughter.

"I'm afraid I can't promise you, mother," Gina said to her. "As we speak, someone has kidnapped friends of ours and is planning on using one of them to bring back this Bastiquil from wherever he is from," Gina said.

"He is from the deepest, darkest depths of hell Gina," her mother pleaded with her. "He cannot be defeated. Your friends are lost if they have been taken to him. They are dead and you need to accept it, mourn it, and move on quickly."

"Well, that isn't going to happen until I see it with my own eyes," Gina responded. "I made a promise to one of them and I plan on keeping that promise, no matter what the cost."

"You always were such a stubborn little girl and now you are a beautiful, talented, stubborn young lady," her mother said.

299

"You say there isn't anything we can do as witches this day and age to stop him, but what about Demetri? Mother, he is the strongest witch I have ever met. He is still receiving his powers and what he is capable of doing just blows my mind each and every time. He is a good man as well. He isn't drawn to the dark, he lives and practices for goodness, for the just and the right." Gina informed her mother.

"We are well aware of what Demetri is capable of and what he has the potential to become. Some fear it is too much power for him, too much of a burden for him to bear, that he may be drawn to the darkness, whether he wants it or not," Katherine revealed to her.

"Not Demetri, I don't believe for one minute he would be drawn to the dark side. He has too much love inside of him," Gina said defending her friend.

"So this is why he shares his love with a vampire? This is why he shares a bed with a vampire?" Katherine said to Gina in a questioning tone, but it came across to Gina as an insult.

"The times are not like they were when you were part of the living, mother. Things have changed and what were once thought to be our enemies have now become our allies. What Demetri does and who he loves, is none of our business. He has shown on more than one occasion he will always do what is right, no matter what the cost." She said to her mother with conviction in her beliefs.

"What if the cost is you Gina? What if he doesn't choose you? Demetri will be shown a great test of his will and he will either choose good or he will choose evil, but both have a price that comes with them. He will have to pay a deep price." Katherine said her voice trailing off into sadness.

"What do you know mother that you are not telling me?" Gina pleaded with her mother.

"You know as much as I do. You read his cards; you know what he found when you helped guide him through his past life journey. What else can I show you that will help you with what is coming?" Katherine said to her raising her shoulder slightly in a gesture of indifference to the question, but she felt there was more behind it.

"Okay, so you know about the past life journey he took and you know what he saw. If we are able to join the memories of his soul together, meld them together so they recognize each other, if he is able to tap into the knowledge of the magic and powers each life had, will it be enough to defeat Bastiquil? Will it destroy Demetri?" She asked of her mother desperate for an answer.

Her mother looked around as if she was stalling, but as Gina watched her, she realized she was actually worried about something. "Someone is coming Gina, you must release me," her mother said to her.

"But I am not finished mother, I still have questions that I need answers to." Gina pleaded with her mother.

"Then ask them child and release me. It is coming and you need to release me, now," Katherine said anxiously looking around the room. Gina knew it wasn't the room she was looking at, but rather the veil between the realms in which the living and the dead are separated.

"Tell me mother if we are doing the right thing with Demetri, is it too much power for him to consume, too much knowledge of his past lives? Is this the only way to defeat Bastiquil?" She begged of her mother.

"All I can tell you is yes, yes, and yes. It is too much power and knowledge for one person to bear, but it is the only chance you both have of defeating Bastiquil. But it will come at a great price, not only for Demetri, but for you as well. He will never be the same again and he will have to make decisions that might lead him down a dark path where he may never find his way back again. But yes, the answer is yes. It is your only hope. No other person on this earth will have the power to defeat him. There are strong witches around that are growing stronger by the day, just like you my dear, but they are far from ready to take on such a powerful demon, the prince of hell. I just want you to know that even though he may not seem like it when the time comes that you must always try to show him the light. Show him the goodness in people, for he may lose that ability with the knowledge he is about to acquire. Now, I have already told you too much. You must protect yourself; you are at risk as well. Be safe child and blessed be." Katherine said to Gina feeling like she just laid out the heaviest burden of the world on her daughter's shoulders.

"Blessed be to you too mother, I love you," she said to her mother.

"I will always love you my child. Now you must let me go, it is close by and able to see me. Please release me, for your love of me, release me before it's too late," Katherine begged of her daughter.

"Katherine Isabel Petran Lungu, blood of my blood, I release you," she said, as tears rolled down her face, Then her mother was gone and with her the candle flames as a great wind swept through the room. She thought about what her mother had said, about Demetri and about herself. Then she couldn't help but wonder what her mother was talking about when she said it was coming for her, to release her before it was too late?

She just hoped her mother was safe and she was doing the right thing by helping him with combining the memories and power of his past soul's experiences. She believed in him and his love for her and life in general. He would always do the right thing. Time would tell if her mother was right or wrong, but for Gina, she couldn't see him wielding his power to hurt people, for evil. She just couldn't and wouldn't allow herself to ever think that about him.

Chapter Fifty-Three

Alex woke up the morning before the full moon. He was surprised to see someone had delivered him a breakfast of eggs, bacon, fresh fruit, and English muffins, with a glass of orange juice and a carafe of coffee. He forewent the food and went directly to the coffee. *It was probably not the smartest thing to do considering nobody needed to be all jacked up on caffeine and locked away in a room. Let alone in the house of a secret society that is determined to raise a demon from hell.* He laughed to himself as he thought about it and how ridiculous it sounded, but it wasn't made up and it wasn't going away. He was here with these men, held captive, along with his mother and Brandy, although he was not able to confirm that they were even here other than promises made by Victor and John.

As Alex drank the coffee, which he had to admit was amazing, he thought back to his conversation with Victor. The one whom he had thought to be his savior, but turned out he wanted him alive so he could kill him at the right moment. Kill, is not the word he had used, but he may as well have. He is trying to get a demon to possess his body which will render him basically non-existent, he will be an unwilling participant to the destruction and murder of the human race.

He had asked Victor why they had sent people to spy on him. Why they had planted his roommate John in his house? He had been informed that Dr. Grant had been in on this the entire time. Victor told him that he was much too important to take any chances with anything that could

303

possibly happen to him before the full blue moon came to pass, when his master would take control, and he would be indestructible.

As he took all of this in, he thought back again to all of those people who had died those horrific murders, his two roommates dead, and for all he knew, his mother and Brandy. Victor had assured him that the first two sacrifices were necessary for the ritual to be performed correctly that he had nothing to do with his roommates being killed. He pointed the blame towards John, calling him sloppy and self-indulgent in his inability to do his job without bringing unneeded attention to himself.

As for his mother and Brandy, Victor told him they were alive, being treated with great hospitality in this very house. He also reminded him again no harm would come to them as long as he cooperated with the Balashon. The minute he didn't, someone would have to be hurt. Victor had got a little emotional with him saying he wanted nothing more than to see Alex happy, he was the chosen one; he was beautiful and perfect in every way.

"You need not worry, Alex. You are a prince, who will become King when the moon is full. Everyone will bow at your feet." Victor had said.

"I don't want this. I didn't ask for it."

"The fact is, young prince, it no longer matters what you want or do not want. Your destiny played its hand many thousands of years ago, and now it has come time for you to play your part in this destiny."

"This too is my destiny," Victor had said. "I am here to serve you, not the person who sits here beside me, although, I would lay down my life for you, but the great being you shall become in just a few short days."

He was amazed and confused, conflicted, and bewildered. *How could all of this be happening? Were they just men that were crazed and delusional?* But he remembered the dreams, the realness, the details of them, and how he felt in them. It wasn't him in control, but rather an unwilling witness, which at this moment made total sense to him. It was what Victor

304

had told him would happen to him when Bastiquil took over his body, that he would be an unwilling witness to such great power.

He didn't want this, didn't want to hurt people, he wanted nothing to do with this. But it was too late now, unless Demetri and Gina were to show up with an army to rescue him. Tomorrow evening, when the full moon rises, they will go forward with the ritual to raise Bastiquil.

"When you saved me from the basement at The Other Side," Alex recalled asking, "what was really going on down there? It seemed so much more than just a bondage den."

"There are creatures out there, freaks of the underworld, creatures that didn't deserve his respect. They are low-level demons, who for one reason or another were able to escape through the thin veil that divided the worlds and make claim upon human victims. They are unworthy of my time and I would kill any of them on site if they interfered with him or his work." He had said to Alex, seeing the struggle in his eyes to comprehend what he saw in The Underside.

"You see, my beautiful prince, there are people who come to a bar like The Other Side, who would willingly give themselves over to disgusting creatures like vampires, werewolves, and other things. They are freely giving themselves over as sex objects to be tortured and taunted; some give themselves for food, some give themselves for both." Victor had explained further. "This has gone on for centuries, dying down for a while and then having a pop culture resurgence when it becomes the popular thing to do. Human beings have once again lost the respect of life, what it means to be alive. So these creatures of the night have a never ending altar upon which they feed and take sexual delight in torture and sometimes killing of humans."

The fact that he had ended up down there and didn't get hurt was a remarkable thing in itself, but he had Victor to thank for that. *Why would Gina and Demetri frequent a place like that? Why wouldn't they have told him about this underground world that existed? That would make sense now that he thought about it, for the glowing eyes of some of the people, no not people but rather creatures down there. It would explain the creatures that attacked him at the end right before he was once again saved by Victor and allowed to flee up the stairs to safety.*

But upstairs had not been safe for him either; he was attacked by Demetri, who had supernatural strength. *Maybe that was why they didn't tell him, because they were technically a part of that underground world. But what did that make him? He was bred to become a vessel for a demon.* According to him, that is a supernatural event in itself. He was no better than the others in that aspect, but he can say that he has never killed anyone, yet.

"But how will Bastiquil possessing my body make me any different from these other creatures? Won't I become what you say you despise about these creatures?" He had asked him honestly.

"There is a huge difference in these filth for creatures and the beautiful being you are to become," Victor had said, offended by the question. "You are to be the host to one of the greatest powers known to this and other worlds. Your body was created for this, not attacked and possessed by some bottom scum feeder. Bastiquil, my master, is the most powerful demon to come from hell itself."

He had a hard time wrapping his mind around how that was any different. He was still going to be the host to an escapee from hell. He was a demon, one who would possess him, control him, and wield his powers through him to destroy and kill. How that was any different than what Victor despised about any of the others, vampires, werewolves, and such, he wasn't sure. Maybe Victor was such a believer in his cause that he was blinded by the fact that it wasn't any different.

Alex's thoughts were interrupted by a knock on the door, then a turning of the lock. Victor came walking in carrying a bathrobe. He smiled at Alex, looked over at the tray of food that was uneaten, and looked back again at Alex with a confused and hurt look on his face.

"Why have you not eaten anything today young prince, you must keep your strength up?"

"I'm not hungry this morning, but I do thank you for the delicious coffee," he said to Victor, attempting to be somewhat civil and thankful for what he was given. He knew he wasn't going to charm Victor into letting him go, but it didn't pay to piss him off either.

Victor looked at him and then softened his emotions. "I guess you will eat when you are ready to eat. Until then, I have come to take you to your morning shower. Please remove your clothing and we will put this robe around you. While we are gone, someone will come in to refresh your bedding and clean up your room for you. We want you to remain as comfortable as possible".

He eyed Victor for a moment and at that moment he thought he saw genuine love looking back at him through Victor's eyes. He could feel the devotion that Victor displayed towards him. It took him a little off guard when he realized that. He smiled at Victor in a gratitude and turned to take his sleeping attire off. They had provided him with satin sleeping pants and a satin shirt. Usually, Alex would have slept in the nude but he wasn't ever sure what was going to be happening around here. He didn't want to be in a position where he couldn't react if needed. Removing his shirt and laying it on the bed, Alex turned slightly to see that Victor was still staring at him with that look in his eyes. Alex couldn't help but indulge the idea that it might be something he could use at some point in the near future to help further his cause of finding his mother and Brandy and getting them the hell out of here.

As Alex let the satin sleeping pants drop to the floor, he bent over to pick them up placing them on the bed with the shirt. Alex standing completely nude at this point turned back towards Victor and stood there looking at him. He wanted Victor to react to him; he wanted to test his devotion, the look of love in his eyes. Victor smiled at him, unfolded the robe and held it open in the air for him to step into. He just continued to stare at him, looking at Victor intently. After what seemed like an awkward passing of time, he finally spoke.

"Do you find me attractive?" Alex asked.

"I find you the most beautiful thing on this earth. The master has made you how he wants you to be when he inhabits this body of yours, so yes, you are most beautiful and most sexy. You are going to be a wonderful host for the master. You should be proud and honored." Victor said.

"But the master isn't here right now and we are. I'm not trying to run from you; I have no illusions that I can escape you. I know I can't overpower you, but I can do something for you. Something that will be most enjoyable for both of us," he said to Victor actually surprising himself as his cock began to respond to his taunting of Victor with sexual gratification. He was not above using sex as a tool, a means to an end.

Victor looked at him with the most curious, yet devilish eyes. For a minute, he thought that he might have just enticed him into it, but Victor walked over to him, kissed him on the lips and told him to get into a robe. He looked at him with hurt in his eyes and as Victor helped him into his robe, he spoke to him.

"Young prince, I find you the most beautiful man I have ever seen and it's not just that you are the host body for my master Bastiquil. You are amazingly stunning in your own right and my master will be so pleased with you. If you still desire me when my master arrives, or should I say if he so desires me when he arrives I will be more than happy to pleasure this body of yours in any way the master so desires."

"So if I wanted you now, even before your master takes hold of my body and soul, that doesn't matter to you?" He asked of Victor sounding hurt, trying to make it sound real.

"I know you have no love for me young prince, how could you? I have killed for you, taken your mother and best friend from you and you stand here before me with a hard cock telling me that you want to pleasure me? I am flattered, but I am not a stupid man. I know when I am being used and taken advantage of. So let's not waste any more of our time on this and let's get you down to your morning shower and shave."

As Alex allowed Victor to lead him by the arm down the hallway into the spacious and beautifully decorated bathroom, his mind was still spinning with thoughts and ideas. Victor opened up the glass door to the large marble tiled shower. The shower had to be at least fifteen feet by ten feet with shower heads all along the sides of the walls and overhead in the ceiling as well. It was made for luxury. It had a steam feature which one could use while sitting on the bench that lined the far wall.

Victor was warming up the water and came back to Alex. He stepped behind Alex and stood so close to him that Alex could feel Victor's hot breath on the back of his neck. Victor reached around him and untied the tie around his waist that held the robe together. Victor could feel that he was hard again and he smiled to himself that he was able to get the young prince hard. Victor then slid his hands up his chest to his pectoral region and pulled the robe open and off of his arms to where he was once again standing nude in the middle of the bathroom.

"You may enter the shower now young prince," Victor said softly to him still standing behind him.

Just out of curiosity, he reached behind him to feel of Victor's cock, to see if he was having any reaction on Victor. He was rewarded to find that indeed Victor's cock was responding to him. He turned around to find a handsome man standing before him, where before he had just been his captor, now a strikingly gorgeous man. As they stood almost face to face, their eyes connecting and looking intensely into the others, Alex quickly found himself feeling something other than hatred for this man. He wasn't sure why he hated him, oh, yes, the kidnapping of his mother and Brandy, but to him he had been nothing but respectful, polite, intelligent, and caring.

He wasn't blind to the fact that he knew Victor needed his body. Not in a sexual way, although, it seemed like he actually did want it that way; but that Bastiquil needed his body or he wouldn't be able to make his return to earth. There had been times since he had been here that he thought about ending his life so that this would not happen. So this evil being wouldn't be able to take over his body and use it as a weapon for destruction, murder, and mayhem. But they had cameras in his room so any attempt at hanging himself with the sheets or strangling himself would just be met with intrusion of guards who would stop him.

But what was stopping him now, in this moment with Victor? He wanted to distract Victor, to get him to emotionally connect with him as a person and not just with him as a 'vessel for his master' as Victor would say. Staring into his eyes right now he felt something, he felt emotion coming from Victor. He could see and feel that Victor felt something too; it was obvious by his hard cock and the way he was looking at him.

He decided that he had nothing to lose here. Reaching up, he started to unbutton Victor's shirt. Starting at the top button and working his way down to the last button that he had to pull out from where it was tucked into Victor's pants. When he had the shirt unbuttoned, he slid it backwards until it was lying on the bathroom floor behind Victor. Reaching down he started to unbutton Victor's pants, one button at a time and when he looked up at Victor, he found that Victor was still staring back at him with the most wanting of looks. As he bent down to the floor so he could slide Victor's pants down, he helped Victor lift his legs out of his pants. Victor hadn't been wearing any shoes or underwear so he was standing before him totally nude, with a rock hard cock and a beautiful specimen of a body.

"I am not sure what you are thinking is going to happen here young prince. I can assure you that I will never allow my sexual desires to violate you, to hurt you," Victor said, for what seemed like the first time in his life. He had something much more to live for than his sexual fetishes and fantasies; he had the master coming tomorrow night. He had trained, worked, and waited for this moment his entire life. And, yes, he will admit that the vessel was a gorgeous, beautiful man, but he could not allow his attraction to outweigh his common sense.

"You can do as little or as much as you would like, but I would really like for you to join me in the shower," he said.

He led Victor to the glass door of the enormous shower opening the door so they could both walk inside. Water hit them from all directions due to the placement of the showerheads. The warmth of the water created a relaxing moment for him. He loved warm showers, sometimes much warmer than the temperature was now. He laid his head back as the water from the overhead showerhead hit his face and neck, running down his body onto the tiled floor of the shower and disappearing into the drain below.

Victor watched him in the shower with a sense of awe, the pure joy that the young prince was experiencing from a warm shower was bringing the same joy to Victor's heart. He loved this man, this vessel, how could he not love him? He was to be the host body for his master Bastiquil, who would be here tomorrow night. What a joy it would be to have Bastiquil here, to be by his side and do his every command. But as he stood there, thinking of Bastiquil, he could not deny the human man that was standing before him now. He was so remarkable, so outstanding and different that his beauty was so pure, his body a work of art.

Victor dabbed some soap into his hands and walked over to him and begin to apply the soap to his back. He rubbed it in, lathering it up, using his strong hands not only to cleanse the prince's back, but to massage some of the knotted muscles that Victor could feel on his back and shoulders. His head leaned back as he let out a moan of pleasure as his captor stood behind him cleansing his body and massaging out some of the worries he had been feeling ever since the dreams started.

Victor stood close to his back; so close, in fact, that he would feel his manhood pressing up against him and his warm breath on his neck. Victor was rubbing down his arms with the soap using some pressure on them as well knowing that the prince loved every minute. Victor couldn't help but relish at this moment, this one time where the vessel and he had a connection, a shared space and they were both enjoying it.

As Victor's arms reached around and was lathering up his chest and stomach, his moans of pleasure intensified. When Victor found his hands rubbing the lathered soap in Alex's crotch, Alex's back arched somewhat allowing Victor to wrap his hand around his cock. He used the soap as he stroked the cock of the prince, who would be king tomorrow. As he did so, he couldn't help but think of this moment, they were sharing something so intimate. It was not offensive, but special and tomorrow just before the master would enter Alex's body, there would be a moment when Alex would hate everything about Victor.

The events that will play out tomorrow will make this beautiful man hate me to the core. As Victor was deep in thought about those events, he was brought back to reality by the intense moaning sounds coming from Alex as he shot his load all over the shower floor.

His body relaxed, falling backwards into Victor's arms as the water continued to rush over them, cleansing them of their dirt, sweat, and transgression they just shared. As he was breathing heavily against Victor's body, he was thinking about what had just happened. How he thought that he might be able to seduce this man into helping him because of something he had seen in his eyes, a longing, and a deep lust for him. But maybe, he was wrong about it, but if he were wrong, then why did Victor participate in this? Why did he allow Alex to undress him? Why did he still hold him in such a way that implied that he cared for him?

These were questions that Alex would probably never have an answer to, and he was not sure how he felt about it. A part of him thought he should feel guilty, that he indulged in self- gratification with his captor, while his mother and Brandy lay locked up somewhere in a room in this mansion, or so they tell him. But his intentions were honest in that he wanted to make this man care for him in hopes that he would in the end do what was right. Had he succeeded in his endeavor?

Victor finished rinsing off his own body as Alex did the same. When he had turned to him and tried to stroke Victor's cock, Victor stopped him gently, and whispered that a prince was too good for a lowly assassin, but if a King so desired him after tomorrow, he would be there in an instant.

He understood what he was saying and even though he didn't like it, he respected it. A devoted man; he took care of him, but had no intention of letting someone service him. Once Bastiquil was imbedded inside him, if Bastiquil wanted Victor, then Victor would be ready. Until then, Victor had turned off the water to the shower and was holding a large terry cloth towel for Alex to dry off with. Victor did the same.

As Victor finished drying off, he walked over to a rack hanging on the wall and grabbed a white terry cloth robe off of the wall and slid it on. Then he grabbed another one off the wall and walked over to him, holding it open so all that he had to do was turn around and slide into it. He did so as Victor pulled it up over his shoulders and walked around to where he was standing in front of him. He tidied up the robe before securing it with a tie around the waist. Victor had yet to tie the strap around his own and was standing there with it half open as he could see, again, what a beautiful man he was. He was stunning. But he knew he was a professional killer and even though he may have been charming, respectful, and a little bit loving in this moment, he could turn on him at any time.

Walking him back to his room, Victor made sure that he had everything he needed before he leaned over and kissed him. He accepted the kiss and felt that it was more of a thank you, but I have a job to do or we would have ravaged each other's bodies. Whether it was or not, he didn't know; Gina and Demetri had the mind reading abilities, not Alex.

As Victor turned to go, he made his way to the door and turned around to him. "I want you to know that tomorrow will be a glorious day for you, for all of the Balashon and for the world in general. I know, at times, it will not make sense to you what is being done, but I know that once the master comes he will help you make sense of it all. So please, do not sit up here on your final evening in despair,

313

try and enjoy it and know that tomorrow you will be reborn again and all will be well with the world." Victor smiled at him as he was saying what he believed to be the truth from Victor's perspective.

"Well if this is to be my last evening on this earth, will you not spend it with me, talking with me, holding me, kissing me?" He tried pleading with Victor one last time.

"Young prince, I would love nothing more than to hold you and talk with you, to help you prepare for what is to come, but I have work I need to do as well. There are great and powerful men coming in from all over the globe to witness the rebirth of the master and I must make sure that they are greeted and attended to. But I will tell you this, if I get a chance later, I will come back and check on you." Victor said smiling.

Alex smiled back as best he could, and then Victor turned and walked out the door.

Chapter Fifty-Four

Gina spent a lot of time thinking about what her mother said, and as much as she hated to admit it, there didn't seem to be any better options for fighting off a demon of Bastiquil's level. Helping Demetri to find a way to unlock the memories of the past lives his soul has lived seemed to be the only answer.

But should they wait until the demon presents itself or do they go ahead and do it so they can make a preemptive strike? What were the ramifications for Demetri? This would make him the most powerful being on the planet, at least that they know of. He would have access to hundreds of past lives, each one with a special gift or insight into a magical ability. Gina believed if anyone could control such power, it would be Demetri; but what if he didn't have to fuse his past lives, what if this demon didn't actually come.

She did know Alex was missing, along with his mother and Brandy and then there were the murders. Someone was definitely planning something, but they still didn't know who or where. Demetri had come out of his past life meditation more convinced than ever Bastiquil was coming and he was meant to stop him; that he was the only person who could stop him.

Gina had told Demetri to come over at 9:00 a.m. and she would let him know what she had found out. It was getting close to that time and she was still fighting with herself on what she should do. Her head was convinced that helping Demetri to open the memories was the right thing, but her heart was telling her another story. She didn't want him to get hurt or to lose himself in the process. But she knew Demetri well enough to know if she didn't help him he would find another way to do it.

So when Demetri arrived she would tell him they would proceed forward with the past life memory spell. They had just around 36 hours to get this completed, find Alex, and stop this demon. Things were not looking good for them.

Gina was looking through her Book of Shadows, searching for a spell she might be able to tweak a little so they could do the past life memory spell on Demetri. They didn't have the luxury of taking their time with this, they had to do it right the first time.

Demetri had to be able to control whatever powers came his way. There was a part of Gina that thought she should call Aldrik and speak to him for his guidance on this issue. But she also knew Demetri would be furious with her if she tried to get Aldrik to stop him.

Just as she had almost talked herself into calling Aldrik, she heard the door open to the store and knew it had to be Demetri because she had locked the store a bit ago. She had been closing early a lot lately and it was beginning to show in her bottom line.

She had been putting off hiring help, but the store was getting so much business, it was an inevitable reality, a reality she had been delaying way too long. Gina had many plans for the store and had started an online website a while ago. Sales from it were picking up and with everything going on in her life lately, well, she needed help.

Demetri came bouncing into the reading room where he knew Gina would be. She was most comfortable there and he knew it. He came over to her and kissed her on the cheek.

"So what is the verdict my love?" Demetri asked her coming right to the point.

"Well, hello to you too," she said to Demetri in an attempt to stall.

"Nice diversion G, but it isn't going to work. What's it going to be?" Demetri said.

"I have been sitting here worried sick over this entire thing. I have gone through every scenario I could think of and it all comes back to you Demetri," Gina said. "I will help you get your memories from your past lives."

"Thank goodness," Demetri said as he leaned in and gave her another kiss. "I had a voodoo priestess lined up in the wings to do it if you bailed out on me." Demetri was laughing at the shocked look on her face. She reached over and punched him in the arm, and then she broke out into a big smile. She had been so stressed lately she hadn't allowed herself the opportunity to just let go and laugh. It felt really good.

"I have been doing some research on the best way to go about this. I am extremely worried about the lasting affect it will have on you Demetri. You will never be the same person after this. You will have knowledge that most people only dream of having; you will have powers that no other person on earth will possess. Are you sure you are ready for this and have you thought about all the possible things that could go wrong?" Gina said, as he looked at her with a smile on his face that softened, as he realized that she was genuinely concerned for him.

"G, I love you for your concern, but can you allow yourself to think about what possible good could come from this as well? Just as much as this could go horribly wrong, it has the potential to go wonderfully right." Demetri said to her trying to give her comfort and hope.

"Always the optimist," Gina smiled at him.

She was showing Demetri the spells she had found and how she thought they should construct them. She told him all of her research thus far in past life recollection stated it is best done on a Monday which worked to their advantage

317

since it is Monday and the day before the full blue moon, due on August 20. It was going to take a lot of magic to bring this all together, to get three thousand years of memories to meld into one.

What they had not considered was this soul had shown them visions as far back as three thousand years, but a soul is infinite, it is energy that has the ability to charge and fuel many lives for many lifetimes. It is the platinum of supercomputers.

She was contemplating on telling Demetri her other thought, then decided to go ahead and share with him. "What do you think about us calling Aldrik to see what he thinks about all of this?" She said gauging Demetri for his reaction.

"Aldrik knows of the issues that face us here and he has chosen not to join us; if he had he would have been here by now. So if we move forward, we move as a duo, a united front, an army of two." He said stoically and full of hidden emotion.

She decided she would not press the issue. If they needed him, she would call him, but according to his reaction to the question, it is best to not bring it up again.

She started writing a list of items that they were going to need and gave half to Demetri. They both headed into the store and started gathering the items they had on their individual list. As they found what they needed, they brought the items to the reading room where they began to form a pile.

Using the same area she had used to summon her grandmother, but actually got her mother, she anointed the circle with a magical potion elixir in which she and Demetri would perform the spell inside of.

She brought a small portable altar inside the circle and placed two purple candles and some past life charcoal incense onto the altar. She anointed the two candles with past life oil and lit the wicks and placed a mirror in between both candles. Using the anointed candle flame, she took the past life resin, then placed it onto the charcoal and lit it.

She then instructed him to settle in front of the altar, legs placed in lotus position and start breathing in deeply and exhaling completely. With each exhalation, she wanted him to feel all stress and nervousness leave his body and with each inhalation she wanted him to feel his body becoming heavier, more relaxed.

She told him to clear his mind and let all thoughts drift away as he inhaled the incense. Let it carry your thoughts to a time long past. As his body became heavier and more at one with the earth, she told him to open his eyes and look at the mirror in front of him. She instructed him to focus on the center of his forehead, the place where his third eye is and then unfocused slightly so his third eye is his view.

"Let your focus move from everything around you to focus only on the third eye." She guided him. "You will see your face morph into other images, once that begins to happen, go with it. Ask questions, ask to see your life back from now to the time when Bastiquil had ruled the known world three thousand years ago."

To Demetri's surprise, he begins to see the flashes again, to see the images he had once seen in the past life meditation, he even saw some new ones. She was letting him go deeper and deeper into the trance, deliberately not telling him what she was planning to do when the time presented itself. She needed him fully relaxed, mind open, and fully concentrating on his past lives.

While he was focusing on his visions, his past life images, she had been focusing on her energy, building it up and letting it go, then bringing it back up and letting it go. It was almost as if she were flexing her muscles, doing crunches, but with her energy. She was preparing for the most important, most intense mental mind invasion she had ever performed. She had to get inside of his mind while he was focused on the past, and get his mind to open up doors most people would have closed off forever.

He was already susceptible to having the walls of his mind down, most people with his talents and powers already had a tendency for this, as she probably did as well. She had to go deep inside, to push past those walls and bring them crashing down. She needed to find his spark, the bright light inside of his mind that fueled everything, including his soul. She needed to bring it to the forefront in this past life journey and then perform a connection spell that would, basically, weld all of his past lives into the one he was now living.

His breathing had become shallow and labored. He was deep inside, experiencing some things for the first time as Demetri, but as a soul he was reliving the past. What he was to become after this, no one really knew. There were no recorded events of anyone trying this before. She just prayed that she didn't fry her best friend's brain or leave him stuck out in limbo. She knew the time was drawing near, she could feel it and she could tell by his demeanor and body language that he was just about primed and ready for the brain invasion.

As she flexed her energies for one last check, she came up behind him and whispered something into his ear. Upon hearing the question, he answered back "Zamaranum."

As soon as she heard this, she knew the time had come; he was in the time when he and Bastiquil ruled the world. She went up to him placing one hand on each of his temples then she sent energy bursting into his brain, traveling around inside of it as he shook a bit but maintained the connection with the past.

As she traveled deeper inside of his brain, she was bringing down virtual walls as she found them and going deeper each time she is allowed. She was searching, searching for the elusive source; one many a person searched for sometimes a lifetime and relied mostly on faith when it wasn't found. The soul was a pivotal part of the human existence and of the afterlife. If it were easy to find, then there would be no need for organized religion, mediation, or faith.

She visualized in her own mind what she was searching for and sent more energy into his brain, moving it throughout every vital piece of his brain and even into his spinal cord. Moving back up into the brain she saw a light, a small spark that generated itself to all parts of his body.

She was looking in all the wrong places. His soul was everywhere. It encompassed his entire being. Once she realized this, she sent forth a spell to bind all the memories of

320

the soul into this one soul he was living in today. She was a bit surprised when she felt energy being pushed back at her, the soul was fighting back. It wasn't designed for a total emergence of all the lives into one.

Gina thought she might need help, so she called upon the powerful witches of her past. She needed her ancestors to send forth powers from the other side and to let those powers flow through her and into the soul of this man she loved and cared about so deeply.

When it hit her, it was like a lightning bolt, it jolted her and Demetri. The binding spell was said and it seemed to be complete and intact. She let herself ease out of his mind and then she began to try to talk him back from the time in which he was in when she invaded his mind.

He gasped for air as he was propelled back to his current state of mind with such force it took his breath away. He found himself laying on his back on the floor, legs unfolded and almost in a panic attack. So much was going through his mind right now he wasn't sure what was real and what was not.

Was the melding a success or a complete failure? He kept seeing things, hearing things, sensing things. *Was this real power from the past or was this just melted brain from the surprise attack Gina made on his brain?* As the images kept coming, he began to panic. He began to crawl across the floor frantically until he reached the corner of the reading room, up against the corner wall, knees to his chest, and arms around his shins with his head cradled on his knees.

He was crying, but he wasn't sure from what. The pain he was feeling was not a physical pain as much as it was a feeling of loss, remembrance, confusion, overwhelming feelings of gain, and so much power coursing through him, but not feeling connected with it. He was crying and rocking back and forth, each time he rocked backwards his head was hitting the back of the wall.

Gina was recovering herself from what had just happened, the journey into Demetri's mind, the incredible energy she had coursing through her body. She could not believe the sensation of it; it was wonderful and dark at the same time. It was like a beautiful waterfall, when you reached out to touch it, instead of feeling the sensation of coolness, there was a feeling of being burned. And the incredible knowledge of knowing that his soul fought back, his soul was not going to let this happen, but it did! Amazing!

When she finally got her wits about her, she realized he was in trouble. She could tell he was being hit with so much knowledge and emotion, it was a too much too soon kind of ordeal. People spend a lifetime just trying to gain access to maybe five percent of the knowledge he was force fed within just a matter of minutes. He rightfully would be feeling overwhelmed and scared. She had to do something, but she wasn't sure what she could do.

Gina went over to him as he was rocking and gently placed her hand behind his head. As he was rocking, he no longer hit his head on the wall but rather the blow was softened by hitting her hand. She was talking to him, trying to reach out to him and get him to focus on her voice. She wanted to guide him back to this reality, back to her. She couldn't imagine what he was feeling, what he was seeing, but she knew she had to get him back and soon.

As he tried to navigate his way through this rush of emotions, this rush of images he felt like a man lost in a vast forest where all around him was everything and nothingness at the same time. He felt like he heard a voice, someone calling to him, but it seemed so far away. At least the thumping, pounding noise had stopped in his head.

He was aware of what they had done. Aware of the fact that it must have worked, or at least partially worked for him to be where he was now, in a memory that he knew was distant, far away and forgotten to him for hundreds of years. He knew he had to focus on the present and move forward in time. He had not time traveled back to this place, but rather he was reliving a memory, and that was knowledge that he could work with. Yes, it was real, but it was a real memory, not a real physical place in current time.

322

Demetri began to focus on home, his current home, he begin to focus on Gina, on getting back. He knew if he tried hard enough, he could do this, he could get there. The more he tried, the more the images of the forest began to give way to images of another place another time. It was a beautiful place, a serene place. There was a meadow of flowers, which led all the way up to the base of a large mountain, with snow covered peaks. It was the most wonderful view. He felt empowered just by looking at it. It was majestic and powerful. It was a memory. *Focus, Demetri, focus, and don't let these memories fool you,* he kept saying to himself.

Then the voice again, but this time it was closer, more familiar. As he listened intently, he realized it was Gina. Gina was the one calling out to him and he so wanted to find her. He was turning and turning trying to see her, but he realized she must be with his body, talking to him, trying to guide him back to his current self.

Demetri began to run; he ran towards where he thought the voice was coming from and as he ran, he came to a large river flowing just below the mountain. As he neared it, he was thinking that this river will not stop me from reaching Gina, from following her voice. As he was just about to run right into the river, an amazing thing happened. Demetri pushed off with his foot and was airborne, jumping over the river and as he did he looked down to see it was flowing intensely and purposefully. This all had a purpose. As he landed on the other side of the river, he could clearly make out Gina's voice.

Closing his eyes he focused only on her voice, breathing in, taking in the fresh mountain air and exhaling. He was listening to her voice, it was telling him to let her bring him home. To follow her voice, listen to it; use it as a beacon to come home. With his eyes closed he started seeing a prism of lights coming fast and towards him, and as it passed he felt its rush, its passing of time, but time was moving forward at great speed. It was a beautiful sight to behold, but a scary one as well. When the light stopped, he was still; his mind was still,

323

the thoughts were still, everything was still. Then he heard it, the sweetest voice, it was Gina.

"Demetri, are you back? Did you come back to me? Open your eyes," Gina said to him.

As Demetri slowly opened his eyes, the focus was blurred at first, but then the blurriness cleared and he saw his best friend, sitting next to him. Gina had done it; she had helped take him to the edge of his soul's existence and brought him back safely. Or at least he felt safe for the time being.

She reached out and hugged him tightly. Kissing his cheek she said, "I'm so glad you are back. I thought I might have lost you forever."

He smiled at her, a pitiful smile, but a smile nonetheless.

She helped him to his feet and as she did so, he held onto her as he steadied himself. He felt drained and charged all at the same time which he wasn't sure was possible. But as he thought about it, he realized a simple analogy. He compared it to how it felt when someone drank a pot of coffee and although they find they still feel tired there is an energy coursing through them keeping them awake, moving them through their purpose for the day.

Demetri had a purpose and he was going to finish it. He could feel that the time was now; he felt the power of the day, the power of the Blue Moon.

A Blue Moon is the third full moon in a four-full-moon season. Most seasons only have three. But this is a special one even outside of that fact. It is the Full Red Moon, the Grain Moon, the Green Corn Moon and the Full Sturgeon Moon. The Full Sturgeon Moon came by its name from the Native American tribes that lived along the Great Lakes. It was called this because of the sturgeon fish, which were easily caught during this particular full moon in August.

Demetri had no idea how he knew these things, but he knew the day was upon them, the day that the demon Bastiquil would try and make his way back into this world. He knew he was going to stop him, he was going to send this demon back to hell once and for all and no future generations would have to deal with this parasite again.

Demetri found his footing and was already pacing the room. He had asked Gina to begin her scrying again for Alex, Brandy, and Alex's mother. Gina looked at him with curious eyes as she had been trying this for days now with no results. The only result she had was when the crystal, actually, pointed to her store, which they both knew wasn't accurate for they had searched everywhere for Alex with no results. Then she heard him inside her head asking her to trust him.

Walking over to the table where she had the map of Tulsa set up, she grabbed the crystal tied onto a string and had three small items of each of the missing three. She held the crystal over the map and started moving it around in a circular motion. She did this for a few minutes and was getting, once again, no results.

"Demetri, this isn't working. I have tried this about a hundred times over the last few days and it gives me nothing. I don't know if they are dead or if the person who took them has them blocked somehow, but regardless, it is giving me nothing." She pleaded out of frustration.

Without saying a word, Demetri looked at Gina with a look she had never seen before, approached her and the table. Reaching out he gently placed his hand on top of hers and as he did so the crystal stopped moving midair and landed directly at an address not far from the Philbrook Museum. Gina inhaled deeply as she was struck with excitement and amazement. They found them. They must be alive.

Chapter Fifty-Five

As the dawn broke on August 20, 2013, Victor was so happy, so full of excitement, he could hardly contain himself. He had gone against his better judgment and went back to Alex's room last night and found him there, lying in bed with nothing on. Victor had felt so much love for this man, even though his death wasn't needed for the ritual to be completed, he was still an essential sacrifice. He must give over his body so that another can take over it.

He had respect for Alex as well and as he lay there sleeping, he couldn't help himself. He had removed his black pull over robe the Balashon were known for wearing, and climbed into bed with him. As he climbed in behind Alex, he ran his arm under his pillow and put the other over his shoulder and chest, pulling him close to him. In the dark, he smiled as he knew Victor had come back to him and he knew that meant he cared for him. *There might still be hope*, Alex thought.

He woke up to find Victor gone, but had left him a note on the pillow beside him. It read he hoped that it helped him have a better night's sleep by him being by his side. Today was a big day for Alex and for the world. All of their dreams were coming true today and it ended with, love Victor.

As Alex read the note again, his heart sank. He realized Victor had planned to go through with this ritual to bring back the demon and let it possess his body. Alex lay in bed and his eyes filled with tears. He couldn't help it; he didn't know what else to do.

Victor was busy in the other part of the house making sure everything was in place for the big night. There were catering trucks coming, flower trucks delivering flowers all for the big celebration of Bastiquil's arrival. It was going to be a party to remember. His master was going to come into this world in style. But tonight, Victor was giving it to him on a silver platter. The master could dine if he wishes, laugh and dance if he wishes, fuck if he wishes, or kill if he so wishes. The world was his to take and Victor would see to it that he gets it.

He wasn't surprised when some limos started showing up this early, he knew that other members of the Balashon were just as excited as he was. This was their holiday, their celebration that was three thousand years in the making. This time there would be no stopping them, this time the ancient powers that overcame his master and sent him back all those thousands of years ago, died the same day, by the hand of the grandmother of Alex. Victor couldn't count how many great grandmothers that was, but he didn't need to, blood was blood and it was Bastiquil's demonic blood that fueled her that day, the blood that flowed through the baby that she was carrying.

Time was moving at a queer pace today. Things were happening around Victor left and right and decisions were being made by the butler and the party planner that the Balashon had sent in. All Victor had to do was make sure that Alex was cared for, that the guards did their job, and that Bastiquil's entrance into this world was a smooth one. The timing had to be just right. The slow aspect of the day was his impatience for the moon to be upon them, for his master to come forth. He had waited his entire life for this moment and it was now upon them.

His thoughts came back to Alex. He respected a man who accepted his destiny with dignity and calmness. Alex had not tried to fight them over anything. Maybe this was because of his mother and Brandy, but whether that was the reason or

327

not, he was still conducting himself with the honor of a true gentleman who was embracing his fate. He had to admit that he found that he had a soft spot when it came to Alex. From the first time that he saw him he knew it was more than just protecting the vessel. Alex was a true beauty, a handsome and sexy man.

Victor had never met a person, male or female, that he had wanted to be gentle with, that he wanted to hold and protect. In his entire life, he had always had a vengeful, murderous nature towards sex, never allowing himself to feel love. He couldn't even say that he had a genuine love for his parents; they had given him over to the Balashon at a young age and his memories of them were faded and far away. He didn't begrudge them for it because his entire life is about the Balashon, but he would say that it had a huge impact on his sexual prowess. But what he felt towards Alex was new, something he had never felt before. He wanted to protect him, hold him, watch him smile, watch him sleep. He had spent much of the night last night just observing him sleep, feeling him breathe and wondering what he was dreaming about. He hoped that at least Alex's last dreams were sweet and filled with good thoughts.

Victor was so torn by his emotions and feelings right now. He couldn't trust them; they were foreign to him. He was almost mad at himself that he had allowed these feelings to creep in; but had he truly allowed it or was it one of those things that one had no control over? Maybe it was that saying 'love at first sight' coming into play. Whatever it was, he had to fight it, and he had to stay strong. This was foolish thinking about love. He loved his master. He didn't love Alex the man, it had to be that he was to be the host body of his master that made him feel the way he did. It had to be, for it to be anything other would be to betray his training and his master.

Victor noticed that some of the Balashon dignitaries had arrived. He was excited to see them. They were starting to form in the library of the mansion where they were being served cocktails. He knew that each of them were excited as well as most of them had spent much of their life being devoted followers; hell, some were even born into this. They were a hidden force at work, but far from silent. Their work was done in business, politics, agriculture, technology, warfare, and numerous other fields that have allowed them to become some of the most powerful men in the world.

The Balashon needed that; they needed the protection and anonymity that money could buy. Each member may be in the spotlight as an individual, but their wealth was amassed because of Balashon influence and served one purpose and that was to promote the agenda of the Balashon.

Victor was busy moving back and forth between the members that were arriving, the guard detail, and preparing for the upcoming sacrifice. He was almost certain that it was going to be a show stopper and that the master would forever hold him in his utmost regard.

If he could make the sun go down and make the moon come up any faster, he would. He was so ready to get on with the ritual that he could hardly contain himself. He was just full of pent up energy. But he had to control himself; he didn't have time for a break. He didn't have time to go looking for someone to pleasure him. He didn't have time for anything other than planning for his master's arrival. His mind went back to Alex; *would Alex think he was a monster?* He was sure that after tonight's sacrifice that he would, but by then it wouldn't matter what Alex thought would it, for he would no longer be in control, his master would be. When his master was here, he would make sure that Victor never had these soft thoughts again. They were destructive to his cause; they undermined him.

Victor went in the sacrificial room to look around. It was a vast room within the mansion, a ballroom made for entertaining large groups. Well, they were sure to be entertained this night. This must have been some old oil barons home; its intricate details, lavish architecture and grounds were reminiscent of someone with lots of money to burn. He had learned since he had gotten to Tulsa that it was made famous by its oil barons, but not many of those remained, if any. Just the structures of a booming time long ago, it seems that the homes are bought up by someone that either has the money for upkeep on such a lavish home or donated and turned into a museum like the Philbrook, just down the street.

Well, Tulsa was going to reclaim its former glory of the past; it was going to be a party like none other. *They would be dying to get in, or out. However, you want to look at it.* Victor laughed to himself. He wanted so badly to punish those who didn't tell him the whole story of what and who were in Tulsa. The fact that someone trusted him to come and make the sacrificial way for the master's entry back into this world, but didn't trust him enough to let him know that people were already here watching over the vessel. That information would have been valuable. It could have saved him numerous hours of watching and observing, gaining the knowledge he needed so that he could make the moves necessary to make this night happen. He knew that he would be told that it was none of his concern that they were doing their job and he needed to do his.

Well, welcome to the night of your life gentlemen. He did his job well, so well, in fact, that he was sure he would have a special place beside the master's side. He knew that the master wouldn't need a body guard as he was full of power and strength, but to be in the master's presence would be an honor.

The sacrifice room looked amazing already. He had a spot in the middle that he had already made symbols on, that he had prepped early on, in anticipation for this day, this night. He could feel the power of the day rising and building. It was a glorious day and would be an even more glorious night. Victor walked around the room, looking at every detail. He had made sure that it was filled with huge floral arrangements and had the best smelling scents. The detail that was missing was the blood spilled on the center of the floor, the dead body lying there that would allow his master to come forth and reclaim this broken world. For all their efforts to make sure that everyone knows how united they were, the human race seemed to be falling apart at the seams. You would think that a race as intelligent and technologically advanced as humans were, could have progressed further than they have, but they spend too much of their time in conflict, in turmoil.

Well, they would get turmoil alright, they would get a weapon of mass destruction, but this one cannot be controlled by any man, this one was his master. His master would lay waste to anyone that wasn't bowing down to him. He would make them beg for mercy, but there would be no mercy to have. This was to be Victor's legacy to this earth, this was his destiny and he was a proud man. He had the vessel, he had his backup insurance, and he had his sacrifice. Now all he needed was the night to come bringing with it the glorious blue full moon.

Chapter Fifty-Six

Gina beamed with excitement at getting a break on locating Alex. She decided it best if Demetri stayed back at her place while she went to check out what they were up against, besides his behavior had her concerned. He had been somewhat withdrawn, deep in thought and had moments when he looked completely bat shit crazy. She hoped that some time alone to collect his thoughts would be good for him.

As Gina had made several passes around the area where the crystal had said that Alex was, she came to the conclusion that he had to be in the huge mansion that was located here. It was a fortress and may as well have been Fort Knox for all they were concerned. It had fences all around it, guards everywhere, and the perimeter was the equivalent to a city block. There was a lot of ground to cover and was heavily guarded. She did notice that they had dogs with some of the patrols too.

This had to be the place, why else would someone be throwing a party on a Tuesday, at least she assumed it was a party. There were catering trucks located outside and it was a full moon after all. If this was a cult, they were going to make sure they did it up big time. They would go all out. She wasn't sure if this helped their situation or not. At least they knew that they would have to come up with some type of plan before trying to get inside, because of the fence, armed guards, and the dogs.

Why did there have to be dogs? Gina thought to herself. *I don't want to have to hurt dogs.* This was like a bad movie waiting to happen she thought to herself. Their only hope at getting inside this place was if Demetri could pull himself together and overcome whatever it is that this melding did to him.

As she drove back to the book store, she was going over scenario after scenario in her mind and without Demetri firing on all cylinders they didn't stand a chance in hell of pulling this off. She was hoping to walk into the store and find him, if not fully aware of his new powers, at least back to his old self. She knew when they did this they were taking a huge risk. He was convinced there wasn't another way to defeat the demon, and her mother also told her that there wasn't any other way around it. So as she got closer to the store, her anxiety was only getting more heightened.

As she pulled into the parking lot and drove back behind where she usually parks her car, she was immediately hit with a sensation she couldn't quite identify. It hit her as odd and her mind went directly to Demetri and that something was wrong. She put the car into park and ran to the door. When she opened it, she was in complete and utter shock and amazement.

What the hell is going on, was all she could think. Everything she could see from the entry of the door that wasn't fastened down to something was floating in the air.

As she slowly walked inside, her freak factor was at an all-time level red. She didn't know what was going on and she didn't know what she was going to find inside. Moving past the laundry room and into the kitchen, she was still moving slowly and with her mouth completely open. She was speechless. Making her way through the kitchen, trying to avoid hitting or knocking into anything, she kept wondering what she was going to find. *Where was Demetri? What am I going to find when I do find him?*

She wanted to yell out to him, but she knew she ran the risk of all of these things coming crashing down on her head if she did. If this was Demetri doing this, she didn't want to interrupt him abruptly by screaming out and scaring him. But she had to wonder, *who would really be scaring who?*

Making her way into the dining room, she was still in awe. No matter how heavy something was, it was still floating in the air. Her dining room table, the chairs, her grandmother's china cabinet all floating. Her only thoughts at this moment please let it be Demetri doing this and please let him have control over it. If he didn't, then she was in trouble.

The reading room was next, that was where she had left Demetri; it was the last place she had seen him before going to check out the mansion where the crystal had located Alex, Brandy, and Ella. Turning the corner, she peaked around and looked into the reading room. To her astonishment and relief, she saw Demetri in the middle of the room, still sitting in the lotus position, but he was not on the floor, he was far from the floor. He was floating at least four feet off the ground, eyes closed, deep in meditation.

Gina eased into the room, trying to stay clear of anything floating. When she couldn't avoid it, she at least made sure it wasn't anything heavy that would crush her if it came falling down. She made her way into the room, she walked past Demetri and made her way to the door leading out to the store. Opening the door a little and peeking through, she could see that all of the books, shelves, jars of herbs, everything in the store was floating. Gina couldn't help but think to herself *this wasn't going to end well at all.* She was right, this was the beginning of a bad movie.

Fearing for Demetri's safety she eased back into the reading room and was contemplating how she was going to help him without hurting or startling him or without him hurting her. She was going back and forth in her mind as to the best method, she about jumped out of her skin when she heard him speak to her.

"It's a cool meditation isn't it?" Demetri asked.

She composed herself, proud she had not screamed when he spoke to her, but still aware of the fact he had not yet opened his eyes.

"How are you doing this? How can you make all of these things float, meditate, and still speak to me at the same time?" She asked, almost scared to make him think about anything other than keeping everything from crashing down around them both.

"I wanted to clear my head of all the crazy images going around and around, all of the memories flooding back to me, so I decided to meditate for a while. At first it was difficult to silence my mind, but then I thought about all of the knowledge I had just gained, all of the wisdom. I wanted to pay respect to it, honor it, by being able to, not control it but to let it help me become a better man. It was then, the thoughts seemed to settle, seemed to become collected, then silenced," Demetri said, still floating and still with closed eyes.

"I decided to start with one object to see if I could meditate and make the object float, then I went with two, then three, and so on. It has really helped to calm me down." He said to a still astonished Gina.

"Well, I would say it worked," Gina said, hoping for the best. She had to admit she was glad to hear a little of her Demetri in his voice.

"What do you mean?" Demetri asked of her.

"Um, I mean everything in my entire home and store that isn't nailed down is floating; everything. Even you are floating," she said to him with a scared tone in her voice.

"That is really cool. I am amazed I can do that. Are you being serious that everything is floating? I wonder why I couldn't tell I was floating." Demetri said the last more to himself, than to Gina.

"I am not sure why you can't tell you are floating, but you have all of my belongings in the air, even my grandmother's china cabinet, with her china still inside it. I would appreciate it if you would just concentrate on what you are doing now instead of wondering why you didn't know you were floating," she said to him with a nervous edge.

"Oh, I'm sorry, G," he said to her as his body started to lower to the floor. As he was almost to the floor she noticed other items around her were lowering as well and at a safe, slow pace. Demetri was level with the floor and everything around her was in its original place, nothing out of sorts and nothing harmed. She walked around and poked her head into the dining room and saw everything was fine, nothing harmed.

Walking back over to Demetri he was still sitting in lotus position, eyes closed. She was beginning to worry if he ever planned on opening them again. Then just as quickly as she had that thought, he opened his eyes, letting them focus on her, and smiled at her.

"Wasn't that amazing? I can't believe how peaceful I felt, how in control." He exclaimed to a relieved Gina.

"I'm happy you were in control. I didn't know what to expect, but I sure as hell didn't expect to come home and find all of this." She said turning around making reference to everything floating.

"I'm sorry; I didn't mean to worry you. I just had all of these thoughts running through my head at lightning speed and I couldn't get them to stop, to let me catch up and make sense out of them. So the only thing I could think of was to meditate. My head then went from a splitting painful headache to a peaceful state of tranquility." He said looking at her to see if she was still upset.

"I am glad that you were able to get a handle on this. I'm not upset; I was just worried about you. I was scared going into this thing and what would you be like when we finished the spell. I don't think I would have ever forgiven myself had anything happened to you." She said tearing up.

He walked over to Gina and wrapped his arms around her. He hated to see her upset or emotional, especially when he was the cause of it. They both were stressed regarding the day and knowing that they only had hours to figure out what they were going to do about the situation. He led her over to the reading table where they both took a seat.

"Why don't you tell me what you found out when you went to look at the location that was on the map?" Demetri said.

Gina, wiping her eyes free of the tears, collected her thoughts and began to speak. "Well, the place is enormous. Not just the mansion; the grounds are expansive. It is heavily guarded, with a stone wall all the way around the place. They have dogs, too. There seems to be a lot of activity going on. I saw catering trucks there, limousines were lining up along the drive, and like I said, security seemed to be on high alert. For us to get in there, find Alex, Ella, and Brandy, well, it's going to take a miracle." She said to him in a defeated voice.

"We are not worried about all that. If you get us there, we can handle it." He said to her with a look of relaxed confidence.

"Who are you referring to?" She asked him.

"I'm not sure if I understand the question," Demetri said with a look of confusion on his face.

"You said 'If I get us there, we can handle it.' We who? Who are you referring to?" Gina asked him starting to get a little worried.

"Hmm, did I say that? I'm not sure why I would say that." Demetri said brushing it off as coincidence. "I guess I was referring to you and me."

"You think you and I can handle all of that on our own? We need some major reinforcements. Have you considered calling the police and letting them storm the place?" She asked him trying to figure out how they were going to get past the gate, across the grounds, into the house, find the three of them, and get them out safely. It didn't even sound plausible. This was crazy. But Alex was in there and he trusted her. He trusted her with his mother and Brandy. She had to do everything possible to get them all out of there. She only hoped they could rally some support from some locals and come up with a plan that didn't involve anyone getting hurt or killed.

"The police will only hinder us from doing what we need to do. By the time the police got warrants to enter, and that is a big if, because we would have to convince them Alex, Brandy, and Ella are in that house with no back up evidence other than your scrying spell. And they would want to do

337

everything their way, the legal way, and when you are dealing with the supernatural, the underworld; they don't really care about the legal way." He said to her, trying to convince her they were on their own.

"Night is quickly coming, we have no plan of action, we have no backup, we have only us, and this is fucking crazy. We are going to get shot and killed." She said in an agitated voice.

"I will let nothing happen to you. And I can feel the night coming, I can feel it like I can feel the blood pumping through my body, like the air touching my skin. I can feel so many things I had not felt before. The night has a feel to it, a longing. It wants to have its way tonight, but we can't let it. We must fight back with all we have, even if it means someone must die. But I can tell you, it won't be you that dies tonight. They will all die for what they are doing, what they are trying to bring back to this world, the unholy, the foul, wicked creature that belongs in the depths of hell. They will all go with him. They will all burn like he is burning." He said as he looked at Gina, but was he really; it felt to her like he was looking through her, at someone else, something else.

"You're scaring me a bit. Your talk of the night and killing all of those people. Why would we need to kill them all? Why couldn't we just get the three of them out of there without having to kill anyone?" Gina asked.

"It doesn't work like that. We are not going to be able to get inside there without someone getting hurt or killed and I would much rather it be them than us." Demetri said to her as if putting the debate to rest.

"What do you need me to do?" She asked of him deciding not to push him too far. She needed him now, more than ever, and she didn't want to push him to the point where he fell apart like he did earlier.

"I need you pulling out every Wiccan trick you have up your sleeve. I'm sorry to say this, but you will have to get your hands dirty with these guys. They are ruthless killers. I will do my best to make sure I am the one they are after. I need you to use every mental skill you have to find Alex and the other two as quickly as possible and get them out. I will do the rest." He said to her as if it were the only plan they had available.

"Why does it all fall on you? I can help with this; I can help you take down some of these men. I have been practicing with my energy balls and I think I have enough control over them. I can focus them on the men and knock them out for a bit." Gina said, trying to let him know he wasn't alone in fighting these men.

"That will only stun them for a bit; we need them not getting back up. We need them to never get back up. These are evil men, who deserve to die. I know you don't get that yet, but you will when you get there, when you see what they are capable of." Demetri said with disgust in his voice.

"You act as if you already know them. Do you know these men?"

"Yes, some of my past life memories have dealt with these men over the millennium and, rest assured, they are not saints that deserve to be saved. They have two agendas, one is chaos, and the other is destruction."

"Then why have we not heard about them before now? If they have lived for thousands of years, why haven't we heard of them?" Gina asked.

"They didn't want us to think they existed, they actually faked their extinction by killing some of their own to make people believe they were extinct. They sank to the shadows and as the world changed, they changed with it. They evolved and became bigger, darker, and deadlier than ever before. They amassed riches greater than you and I could imagine. They have been working all of these years, waiting for the one to be born, that would come of age and take Bastiquil's demonic stink into him. Over the years, Alex has been manipulated through his dreams to create the body Bastiquil would need. The body that he could hide in without anyone knowing it was him. Until he was ready to reveal himself to the world, that is. We both know and have known it is Alex he is going to possess and take over. We have to stop this from happening. I need you to get Alex, his mother, and

339

friend out of there before that happens. If you don't, then I'm afraid that I will have to kill Alex, if necessary, to get Bastiquil from staying in this world." Demetri said without emotion, without feeling. He seemed cold and matter of fact.

"Kill Alex? That was never part of the plan. And do these people, this cult have a name?" Gina said in shock and her voice raising a few levels.

"They are called the Balashon and they are ancient, they are old, they are ruthless and they will kill us at the first opportunity they get. They will not allow us into their home without a fight to the death. As for Alex, he was born into this world to be a body for this demon. We cannot change that any more than we can change you being a witch, me being a witch, or the sun from rising and setting. It is destiny at play here, and you have to accept that he may be a causality of war between good and evil."

"Alex is our friend, he is our ally. He didn't ask for any of this, any more than we did. I will not allow you to walk in there and kill him. He came to us for help; he came to me for help. I am not sure where your fucking head is right now, but you need to get my Demetri back in the driver's seat," Gina said getting upset.

He looked at her and reached out to grab her hand. "I can assure you, your Demetri is right here, in control. I see things clearly and just because you don't like the clarity of what I am being shown, it doesn't mean I am wrong. Do you think Alex would want to let this demon inhabit his body, to let it take control of him, basically killing him anyway? This demon will use Alex's body to go on a worldwide killing spree. If we let this happen then we are guilty as well. We have the ability to stop this from happening and if we do nothing, then we may as well have gone out and killed those people ourselves. Having the ability to make change, but doing nothing is just as bad as the evil we are fighting. People look for help. They look for good; they, also, look for light in the darkness. Sometimes that light comes in the form of two Tulsa witches, who just happened to be blessed with some pretty amazing abilities." He said trying to get her mind at ease with what was about to take place.

Her eyes filled with tears for she knew he was speaking the truth, a harsh truth she didn't want to hear, but had to. They were going to have to do whatever they needed to do to make sure this cult called Balashon didn't succeed in summoning this demon. And as much as she hated to admit it, she knew that Alex wouldn't want this either. She would make sure that Demetri did everything he could to save Alex. If they were not able to, then she would have to accept the fact that Alex's death would stop this demon from entering this world.

He reached over and wiped away the tears from her face. He was looking at her and was filled with love. Gina has always been his anchor in life, she was always there to pull him into goodness, never allowing him to get overly confident and overly cocky. He truly believed she was put in his life to keep him from becoming too out of control. She was his foundation in a rocky storm at times. But, as he looked at her, he could see her hurt, but he saw her resolve. He knew she was going to do everything in her power to help Alex, to make sure he wasn't hurt in this battle to take place.

"Can I do something for you?" Demetri asked.

Looking up at him with those beautiful eyes, she smiled at him. "What is it? What would you like to do for me?"

"I would like to just enter your mind for a moment and organize your thoughts a little. Help you to tap into your raw natural power. I know you are a strong witch, much stronger than you even know. You rule by your emotions which is admirable, but I need you to be clear, focused, and just as ruthless as those men who will try to kill you are going to be." Demetri said to her with as much love in his voice as he could muster.

"As long as you don't take away my resolve to save Alex, Ella, and Brandy, then, yes, I will allow you to focus me," she said to him sternly

"You have me all wrong. I am not going in there with the thought that I am going to kill Alex no matter what. I am going in there with the knowledge it may be a possibility I have to consider. I am going to fight for Alex, Ella, and Brandy. I am fighting for you and me as well. I am fighting for Tulsa and the world. You have no idea what this demon is capable of, what his powers are capable of. He is the most powerful entity next to the devil as far as evil goes. And if heaven isn't going to send us help, then we have to be willing to do what we can to stop this evil from destroying the earth." Demetri pleaded with her to understand where he was coming from.

"What if heaven did help us? What if God allowed us to merge your past lives into one giving you the power you have now? What if you are heaven's earthly weapon? Do you think God would want innocent people killed?" She asked him, hoping he would consider that possibility too.

"My answer to you is yes, I do think he would want an innocent person to be killed if he becomes possessed by this demon. He would be dead anyway. This demon will eat up his soul, his life force and take over every cell, every molecule of his existence. Alex will cease to exist when that demon enters him. I have seen this before, do you not remember that? I have seen what this demon will do. You have to trust me on this one." Demetri said to her with complete resolve.

"I have always trusted you, maybe to a fault. And I will continue to trust you; until you show me, I shouldn't. When that day comes, I will have to make a decision, a tough one." She said to him, finding her resolve. "Go into my mind, do what you need to do. The sun is starting to set and we need to get there before the moon is at its fullest. Most rituals like this call for the moon to be at its fullest, which is when it is most powerful."

He nodded his head in agreement with both statements; the one about the moon and the one about her having to make a decision about him if he were to ever cause her to distrust him.

"Close your eyes, allow me inside. Think about your minds eyes, the third eye, the one that gives you the ability to read others' minds, the one that allows your guttural instinct,

342

your intuition. I am turning it on fully; I am allowing you to see what needs to be seen so that you can do what needs to be done. I'm opening up your energy, allowing you to tap into it without effort. The brain has this wonderful ability of being hard wired; but with every system that has been wired, it can be rewired so that a person can rethink all things, become something new, something more." He said as she concentrated and allowed him inside.

As he did so, he showed her his true self, his true intention going into this night. He showed her he had every intention of trying to save Alex, but showed her some of the destruction this demon has the ability to wield. As he showed her, her breathing became labored and she was getting excited, agitated. He slowly withdrew himself from her mind and let her open her eyes. As she did, she gasped sucking the air back in.

Her tears were flowing down her cheeks as she became aware of the death and destruction that this demon has already wrecked on this earth once before. They cannot allow it to happen again. This demon has had three thousand years to sit in hell and give thought to this. Gina was sure he was going to want some revenge as well. He would not go as willingly this time around, not be as trusting as he was.

"Are you with me?"

"Yes, I'm here," she answered. "I'm here and I'm as ready as I'm ever going to be. I feel like you did some spring cleaning inside of my head. I feel renewed, recharged. It's a good feeling. I know that this demon has to be stopped. I am going to be fighting like hell to make sure that we send him back to the rotting depths of hell that he comes from and we will be walking out of there with Ella, Brandy and Alex. If I can promise you anything, it's that." Gina said to him, who was smiling at her.

He was glad to hear that she was ready to fight. He had not been convinced before, but he was now. She was ready for this and that was what he needed to see from her to be able to do what he needed to do.

As they were gathering items they thought they might need, he jokingly asked her where she kept her weapons. She thought for a split second about feigning as if she didn't know what he was talking about. Then she remembered all the armed guards, dogs, and the visions Demetri showed her of the demon's powers and thought it might come in handy to have something physical they could use if for some reason their powers faltered or failed them altogether.

Walking into her bedroom, she knelt down and pulled a case out from underneath her bed. As she opened it, he was extremely impressed by the different array of weapons she had amassed over the years. She had swords, hunting knives, ritual knives, throwing stars, and a plethora of other items, but he had to smile at himself when he saw the brass knuckles. He picked them up and looked at her.

"Really, aren't these illegal here?" Demetri asked her. "I'm rather surprised a Wicca, nature loving, 'don't want anyone to get hurt' kind of girl would have this massive of a collection of weapons."

"Hey, people will trade all kinds of things for herbs and such when times are hard. Don't judge." Gina said to him as she hit him in the arm playfully.

"Not judging at all; actually, I'm extremely impressed," Demetri said.

They both loaded up on various weapons large and small, putting on belts she had in the case, a belt one could slide knives and swords through. Then she pulled out two handguns, checked to see if they were loaded, which they were and put one behind her in the waist of her pants and handed the other to Demetri. She handed him some extra rounds of ammunition just in case. He was really impressed with this one. Gina was ready for this battle; he knew she would have gotten there eventually.

As they walked towards the back door of the shop where they were both parked, the anticipation was growing. They were both jacked up and ready for this. Demetri was ready to take on this demon and Gina was ready to save Alex, Ella, and Brandy. They were both dressed in black, which

344

wasn't unusual for them. Black leather was typically the clothing of choice, but it seemed fitting tonight as they headed out to do actual battle with a small army of men and a demon.

Demetri was silently hoping the man from the bar would be there, the masked one. He had some unfinished business with him as well.

Putting her hands on the door knob, Gina turned the knob and opened the door. They were both shocked to find Aldrik standing there looking at them both.

"Demetri, what the hell have you done?" Aldrik said, as he looked at them both from head to toe, shaking his head.

Chapter Fifty-Seven

Alex was starting to wonder how they were going to go about this. Were they going to come in and tie him up, put another cloth bag over his head until the demon entered his body, or would there be much more pomp and circumstance to it. The looks of this room and the bathroom he had been in was making him think the latter. Either way, he had given up hope anyone was going to save him, that Demetri and Gina were going to storm in, and that Victor would opt to help him escape. Those were foolish thoughts anyway. He barely knew Gina and Demetri, and Victor helped to kidnap him, his mom, and Brandy, so why did he think any of them would go to such great lengths as to help him?

As he laid there on the bed for what seemed like the entire day, he was getting anxious. The sun had gone down and he knew at some point tonight, they were going to do whatever it was they had planned to him. He got up off the bed and was pacing the room.

There was no escaping on his own and he had given up on the thought, actually. After Victor had spent the night holding him, he had some hope when he woke up, but after the note and then Victor not coming back today, he knew it was too late. Victor had a job to do and he had done it well. So now it was time for him to accept what fate had dealt him. Maybe it was true what Victor had told him, he was born for this moment, this transformation. His body was made to host the demon they call Bastiquil. The tattoos he dreamed about and had inked all over his body were put in his head by the demon. He had to admit, it was cunning of them, very cloak and dagger.

He was starting to get himself worked up and was just about to go start banging on the door and yelling at them to get on with it. Just get the ritual going so their demon could take over the body the demon had created. Then there was a knock on the door.

He stopped pacing and turned to face the door. As it opened, he was taken aback by Victor standing there. It wasn't the fact he was standing there, but it was more about what he was wearing. He had on a small, black leather bikini type outfit that looked more like it was supposed to resemble a loin cloth than an actual bikini, somewhat medieval style.

All over his body he had symbols and drawings that looked like tattoo ink, but Alex knew they were too crisp and fresh looking, no redness to them so they had to be henna. The symbols were all over his body, lines drawn from head to foot. His eyes were wide with amazement as he looked at Victor.

"It's time to get you prepped, young prince. You have to wait no longer." Victor said as Alex thought he saw a hint of sadness to him. But, he knew by what Victor had on and the trouble he had gone to for the henna tattoos, Victor meant to go through with this. He didn't even bother to protest.

He walked up to Victor and for a brief moment had thought about leaning in to give him a goodbye kiss. He knew how lame it sounded just thinking about it, but before he could decide whether to do it or not another two men presented themselves at the door.

"These men are here to take you to the showers, where you will be well-taken care of. They will cleanse your body with soaps and essential oils, and then they will take you to a purifying room where you will be clothed and wait until they are ready for you to join the ritual." Victor said as he was looking at him with sad eyes.

"What about seeing my mom and Brandy?"

"All in good time young prince, all in good time," Victor said trying to pacify him.

"Why are you doing this Victor? You don't have to do this." Alex pleaded.

"As hard as it may seem my friend, we all have a part to play in this. I am just playing mine." Victor said as he reached up his hand and placed it on his shoulder. He was tempted to shrug away from his touch, but he thought to himself it might be the last time he felt another human touch him with any emotion. Not too long from now, the demon would be summoned and he would cease to exist.

He tried to wrap his head around all this, but the harder he tried, the more it didn't make sense to him. He knew from meeting Gina and Demetri and, of course, the basement of The Other Side, supernatural beings and creatures do exist; they were thriving in Tulsa and the world. He was to be a vessel for a supernatural being; this was beyond the stretch of his imagination.

"Tell me one thing Victor?"

"What is that young prince?"

"Are you going to let my mother and Brandy go if I don't fight this? If I let the demon take my body without a fight, will you let them go?" Alex asked almost begging.

Victor looked at him, as he thought about what he was going to say to him he couldn't think of a way to tell him the truth without making things worse. So when he spoke, he did so with a heavy heart and a big lie.

"I know they will be present for the ritual and when it is done, they will be escorted out of the house," Victor said. Victor, uncharacteristically, was ashamed he was lying to a man he should not even care whose feelings might be hurt, or if he would be upset with him.

But he did care and he didn't want to hurt Alex any more than he had too. There would come a time tonight when he would know the truth, he would know Victor had lied to him and this weighed heavily on him. He would hate Victor with a great passion, but just as quickly as he had time to hate him, he would be gone as the master entered his body and fed upon his soul.

"Thank you, for not hurting them. They didn't know anything about this; they couldn't have known what I was or what I'm supposed to be. They are innocent in all of this, so I will not fight, I will do what I am told, so they can live and be set free." Alex said, as his eyes filled up with tears.

"Young prince, don't cry. Your life is not in vain; you will live on and do great things with my master as your guide. I know you do not feel this now, but take heart, the price you pay today, will not be for naught. You will forever reign as the prince who was transformed into a king and ruled the earth." Victor said trying to make him see the big picture of this event. He wanted him to know that this was a great and wonderful thing.

"I said I wouldn't fight this, but I never said that I liked it or that for one moment, I believed in your cause. I find it appalling and psychotic, but I am going along with it for one reason and one reason only. Let's not pretend this is something it's not; you have come here to say your last goodbyes. You came to me last night, because you wanted one more night with me, one more chance to feel something for someone greater than yourself, greater than your cause. So please, just say goodbye and let me get to this preparation so I can be done with this life, done with this pain. I cannot stand it any longer; if I am to die tonight then let's get on with it." Alex said as his tears no longer flowed and his resolve was more stoic than wavering. He had said what he wanted to say to him and he was at peace with it. Victor had his chance to make this go away, to make this not happen, but he chose hell over the living. He hoped he burned in it.

Victor leaned over and gave him a kiss on the lips, but he did not return it. Victor felt the coldness coming from him and even though it hurt, Victor completely understood it. He would have done the same thing if he had been cornered and found no way out; he would have gone out in style like Alex. But it still wounded Victor.

He for once in his life had truly felt something for someone that was genuine that was real and passionate. He wanted him sexually, without pain, without death, he wanted to feel his love, but that was never to be. Their lives crossed in this lifetime due to destiny on both parts, but it would have to be an entirely different lifetime for them to cross again.

Victor turned and walked out the door. As he did, the two men came in and took Alex by the arms, one on each side of him. They led him down the hall to the shower room where he and Victor had just shared their intimate moment the day before.

We all know we will die one day, but when one knows when that day is, when it will happen, all kinds of thoughts and emotions run through your mind and body. You go from love to hate, I should have done this, or I wish I had done that. You are angry one minute, sad the next, and then laughing at a memory from the past. It is a gamut of emotions and he could honestly say he was feeling them all.

He was stripped of all clothing when he reached the shower room. As they led him into the large shower, his mind was off elsewhere, thinking of all the things he never did and wished he had. He was oblivious to the fact these two men were rubbing his body down with soap, lathering it up all over, under his arms, between his toes and even in between his ass cheeks. It didn't faze him a bit.

He had always wanted to travel Europe, visit the tattoo shops there. He had always wanted to travel throughout Asia and study the ancient techniques of tattooing, using sharpened bamboo and a mallet. It hurt a lot worse than today's modern tattoos, but the precision and technique was what he admired most about it.

Alex had always thought one day he would quit his wild ways and really start putting his art first. He wasn't just a tattoo artist, but he loved art in all styles. He loved to paint, do charcoal drawings; he loved to sit in a park or out in nature anywhere for hours and just sketch the things he saw. People looked at him and automatically drew conclusions about him. He was tattooed from head to toe, so, therefore, he must be a delinquent, who did drugs (even though a little bit of that was true), lived on the streets, was worthless, and would never amount to anything. Most thought him a gun-toting outlaw just because he had used his body as a canvas for his art.

People would be surprised at how he was a hopeless romantic; how he had longed to love and be loved. He had so wanted to have a relationship with his father, had wanted his father to have never left. He had wanted his father to be there for all of his successes, his graduation from high school, and the day he got his first car. He hoped his dad would have been proud of the road he took as an artist and of owning his own business. Yet, another item on the list of things Alex would never know.

But the real artist here was the demon, Bastiquil. He had actually created this canvas, this walking wall of art. He had used Alex, invaded his dreams, and manipulated them into making him think these tattoos were something he had thought of and wanted. The first one had come to him when he was just sixteen years old and he was so psyched that he even could remember it after the dream. He had dreamed the design and even in the dream, he had gotten it tattooed on the back of his neck. Everyone at school, in the dream, loved it and that is why when he woke he had thought it would be a wonderful idea for him to get it.

He had no idea he was being led down a path that was hard wired to Pandora's Box. He had opened it by getting the first tattoo and from then on he was hooked. The demon had his hooks in him even at the age of sixteen; hell, for all he knew, he could have been dreaming about the demon long before that.

As he was stuck in his thoughts, the men were busy washing his hair. Once they were done, they dried the water off his body and begin to rub him down with essential oils from various flowers and herbs. The smell was something he couldn't ignore even in his deepest thoughts. It smelled so good.

Bastiquil should really like his work of art. It was clean, oiled up with the finest smells and now, dressed in a black linen robe that was split down from the shoulder to the chest, all the way down to his navel. As they dressed him they buttoned up the slit that contained three buttons, which allowed some skin to show through, even though it was buttoned up. He really didn't care what they put on him. That he had nothing on but the robe was actually fine. It was, basically, a death wardrobe anyway. Hell, they could have put him on display nude and it would not have mattered to him at this point.

It wasn't until they finished putting the robe on him that he realized they had been chanting the entire time, incense burning, and a crowd of people gathered watching them as they prepped him. The people he assumed were members of the Balashon, who were now wearing linen robes as well. *Weren't they all just one big fucking cliché? This couldn't get more stereotypical cult-like if they tried.*

As they finished up with him, the two men grabbed a hold of each of his arms, one on each side of him and led him down a series of hallways. He was taken into a room that looked to be a library. He was walked to the sofa and made to sit down on it. All around him stood men in robes, staring at him.

He wanted to kill them all. He didn't consider himself a violent man, but he would definitely make an exception. What a pathetic life they must have, to live only to serve a demon. To have lived, bred, and kept this charade up for three thousand years was almost laughable, had it not been such a deep act of devotion. One could associate this to the devotion of the people who believed in and kept up with Y2K and the Mayan end of the world theory. This Bastiquil must be a piece of work to command such loyalty. Alex figured he would find out soon enough what the big deal was.

He wondered if they were going to sit here and stare at him until the time came for the demon to take over his body. Watching them, watch him, was just pissing him off. He wanted to spit on them, lash out at them, but he did nothing but sit there, loathing each and every one of them.

Then out of the corner of his eye, he saw him. He was walking towards him; and, as he did, every eye in the room turned to look at Victor. As he approached him, Alex wished he had a knife hidden on him so he could slash his throat. This was all his doing; he had set this all up, hadn't he?

No, this was something that Victor was brought into as well, something he was pushed into. The fact he was good at what he did and was loyal, was the reason he was promoted through the ranks of the Balashon and the reason he was given this assignment. As much as he wanted to hate him, wanted to kill him, he couldn't. He just didn't have it in him to hate him anymore.

As Victor approached him, Alex looked up. Victor stood in front of him, looking down and smiled. Alex knew Victor was trying to acknowledge him, trying to say he looked nice or smelled good or something to that effect. But with all of these Balashon members standing around, he couldn't for fear of being put to death.

"We shall begin shortly, young prince. You will not have to wait much longer. You will soon meet your grandfather, our king," Victor said, this time bowing to him, and as he did, the entire room bowed as well.

"Hail Bastiquil," the room chanted as Victor turned and walked out, leaving Alex once again with his thoughts

Chapter Fifty-Eight

Aldrik had spent the last ten minutes lecturing them both on the dangers of what they had done by merging Demetri's past lives together. In essence they have created a potential killing machine, if Demetri so wanted, one maybe more powerful than the demon they were trying to stop. Aldrik was furious with them both, but more with Demetri, for not talking to him before he did this.

"What were you thinking? What possible good could come from this, outside of defeating the demon? Can you control the urges that will come from this increased power and increased knowledge?" These were the questions he laid out to both of them. This was such bad judgment on both of their parts. Aldrik was beside himself.

"Why didn't you ask for help? Did you think I would not have helped you? Have I ever not been there when you needed me? Did you not think you were strong enough to defeat this demon without having to do something this life threatening?" Aldrik asked of Demetri.

"Actually my coming to you in Kansas City was a cry for help. Why didn't you offer to come back and help me? Why do you always have to be so cryptic? If I thought I had the power to defeat him without the spell, I would have done it, but I didn't think I could. All of the visions and dreams I have had of this demon are really bad. He is really powerful and he will be out for blood. He has been vanquished now, for three thousand years and he will be pissed off." Demetri said.

"Together Demetri, we three, could have defeated him. We could have taken him and the entire Balashon army on and won. But now you are a loose cannon, a wild card. I don't know what I can expect from you. Are you going to be able to stay focused and control your new found gifts and personalities or are they going to control you? You will not get an opportunity once we are there to sit down and figure out what you can and can't do. These people are going to be trying to kill you at their first opportunity." Aldrik said.

"And you," Aldrik said turning his attention to Gina. "You thought this was a good idea?"

"Actually, I didn't, but after consulting with my mother and Demetri, I came to the conclusion, this was our best chance at defeating Bastiquil and saving the world," Gina said to Aldrik. "Listen, whether we did the right or wrong thing is still yet to be seen. I believe in Demetri more than I believe in anyone. I believe he can control this, I believe he will defeat this demon and I believe that he will remain in complete control. So since the moon will be rising any minute now, I say we can't stand here debating something that has already come to pass. We have to get out there and stop this thing. We can't have gone through everything we have, just for it all to be in vain. So are you with us or against us, either way, we are walking out of this door right now and anyone who tries to stop us will have to go through me first." She said in a matter of fact tone.

Aldrik looked at Gina and then at Demetri. Demetri just shrugged his shoulders as if to say to Aldrik, Gina was right and that they were walking out the door. Aldrik finally gave up his lecture and decided to help them. If dying for world safety isn't a good enough reason to die tonight, then he didn't know what was.

"Lead the way then," Aldrik said to Gina, stepping aside and raising an arm in invitation allowing her through.

As they walked to the car, she began filling Aldrik in on what she had seen when she had done the drive-by earlier. "We know the fence is made up of stone and wrought iron, and it will be heavily guarded by men with dogs. Even if we make it through the grounds, we will still have to get into the house, which is enormous. Then we have to find Alex, Ella, and Brandy, get them safely out, and still take care of the demon. Of course depending on if we can save Alex before the demon comes, would determine if we, actually, have to battle Bastiquil. If we save Alex first, then the demon can't appear."

"Sounds like a walk in the park," Demetri stated.

"Not," said Gina in an aggravated voice. She was happy to have Aldrik along as backup, but he had slowed them down by about thirty minutes. They had to hurry, because they were not, actually, sure when the Balashon would start the ritual.

As they got closer to the compound where Alex was being kept, they had formulated somewhat of a plan. They were going to park a block or two down on the back side of where the house was located, then move up to the fence perimeter. They would need to scale the fence, if it wasn't hard-wired with sensors that would trip if anyone came near them, or went through the laser. If it was wired, the three would have to, basically, jump the fence, which shouldn't be too difficult for Aldrik; actually it wouldn't be difficult at all. It was possible for Aldrik to get all of them over the fence.

The moon was getting higher and higher by the minute.

The biggest part of their plan was to attack as silently as they could. If they could reach the house without any guns going off, then they might stand a chance of getting into the house undetected, which would be the best possible result. Aldrik had his vampire speed on his side, so he may have to take the lead once they get over the fence.

After pulling in where they had decided to park, they unloaded their gear and proceeded to go over the plan one more time. Once completed, they headed up the street to the fence, which faced the back of the mansion.

When they arrived, they found there were guards everywhere. The fence was hardwired with a laser sensor that would let them know if anything climbed over it. Demetri imagined it would sound a large siren, letting the guards and the people in the house know they had arrived.

Aldrik was looking the fence over closely; he had concluded the fence was at least ten feet in height, which, typically, wouldn't be an issue, but he had other people to worry about. He could see with his vampire vision, there was only the laser nearest the top of the fence. With that knowledge, he grabbed Gina by the waist and bending his knees, he leaped into the air with her in tow and easily landed on the other side. Turning to go back for Demetri, both were surprised to see Demetri standing next to them on the other side of the fence.

"How did you do that?" Aldrik asked of Demetri. Gina was curious herself, but then remembered Demetri and the floating objects in the house earlier.

"It comes with the new integration, my upgrade so to speak," Demetri kidded.

Just as they were getting ready to turn and make their way to the house Aldrik picked up a sound. As he turned at lightning speed he quickly caught a guard dog, mid-air and tossed it over the side of the fence. Whether the dog survived or not Gina and Demetri did not know, but they were sure glad Aldrik was here and had heard it before it was upon them.

Running for cover to the nearest tree, the three of them tried to keep as far away from the guards and lights. This wasn't a small feat. Aldrik had the night vision, hearing, and speed to get them to the safest positions as possible. While they were working their way to the house, they stopped at another tree and as they were waiting for their next opportunity to advance further towards the house, an armed guard appeared behind Gina, barrel pointing straight at her head.

As the guard was pulling his finger to fire the gun, the gun was suddenly pulled out of the man's hands by something other than a physical hand. It was pulled by Demetri's thoughts. He was looking at the gun as it dismantled itself in mid-air, taken apart like it was child's play, even the bullets floated in the air. As the man started to talk into his walkie-talkie, one of the bullets that were floating suddenly shot at super speed and entered the man's forehead destroying his brain. He fell to the ground dead. Both Aldrik and Gina looked at Demetri with surprised looks on their faces.

"Just one of the perks," Demetri said to them, as he turned to move on towards the house. Gina and Aldrik followed, with Aldrik taking the lead.

As they approached two guards, who were talking with their backs to them, Demetri did something with his hands and immediately the two guard's necks were snapped and they too, fell to the ground dead. Gina picked up one of their guns and pulled the strap over her shoulder.

"Since we are getting closer to the house, there will be more guard detail. Shouldn't we get rid of these bodies, so no one will stumble upon them?" Aldrik asked.

Demetri turned to the tree a few feet away from them and looked upward. The next second, the two guards were flying upward from the ground and placed where they were hanging over a heavy, durable limb.

Gina couldn't help but think, even though this had not been as bad as she had thought it would be, things were getting ready to go from bad to worse.

They made their way up to the exterior of the house, noticing a large room, where lots of people were gathered. They were all thinking this must be where they are planning on completing the ritual.

Gina was told to stand watch outside the window and they would give her a signal when it was safe for her to come into the house. Demetri was going to go to one side of the house and Aldrik was going to go upwards, both trying to find a way inside so they could try and stop the ritual before it started. Gina crouched down in the shadows as much as possible, outside of a large paned glass window and every once in a while, she would peek through the lower window pane to see what was going on.

Chapter Fifty-Nine

The time had come for Alex to be brought to the sacrificial room and as Victor walked to the library, he tried really hard to take his mind off of anything other than the master's coming. He would be here within the hour, maybe less. His adrenaline was flowing and he was still feeling loss, a mourning for Alex and his feelings for him. But he could not let that enter his mind right now. He had a job to do and he was going to do it to the fullest.

As he entered, all eyes in the room were on Victor, as was Alex's. Victor nodded to the two men who had brought Alex into the library. They walked over in formation, reached out their hands to Alex, indicating that he should stand up. As he did, they both placed a hand on his arm. They proceeded to follow Victor out of the room and down the hallway.

Alex had a look of stoicism on his face, as he was marched down the hallway into a room of at least a hundred men in robes that matched his own. They were all chanting in unison, but Alex was unaware of the language or what they were saying, yet it seemed somehow familiar to him. Maybe the same chanting he had dreamed Victor was chanting when he killed those people.

Oh, Alex thought, *this is going to be another ritual sacrifice. Another poor soul would be taken so that the demon could live.* Alex was starting to boil at the thought of it. As he was brought to the front of the room and put up on a platform that was set up near the windows, there were two ornate pillars that were affixed to the ground. They bound his wrist to the pillars with a metal chain, which was cloaked with red crushed velvet material. Obviously, they didn't want the dignitaries to know it was metal holding back the vessel or that it was hurting his wrists.

As they finished with Alex, the chanting intensified for a few minutes, with ritual drums being played. The room was abuzz with activity. Then suddenly, it stopped. There was complete silence in the room. All Alex could hear was his own breathing.

A door opened on the side and as it did, Alex turned his head to see who was going to be walking through it. His heart sank to the pit of his stomach when he saw Brandy come walking through in a white tank top and loose linen white Capri style pants. They brought her to the middle of the room where the symbols from his dreams had been painted on the floor of the room. Once she was there, she was made to get on her knees, and then she was bound by metal chains around her wrist so that she could not move. As she was locked into place, she looked up and saw not far from where she was kneeling, Alex was looking at her with terror and sadness on his face.

"No, this isn't the way it was supposed to happen," Alex screamed out. "Victor, you promised me, you promised me they wouldn't get hurt." Alex was crying, as it was sinking in what was happening.

Brandy had been chosen as the third sacrifice. Victor had betrayed him. Victor had lied to him. As Alex was seething on the inside, vowing that if any part of him was still in control once the demon came, he would make sure Victor lay dead on this very floor.

Brandy was in tears as she looked up at Alex. *What were they doing to him? Why was he tied up there like he was on display?* Brandy could see he was distraught and this must be something bad; to her it appears cult-like, but she couldn't be sure of that. They had taken good care of her up until now, but she was in tears, chained to the floor, and looking at her best friend chained to some pillars on a stage-like platform.

There were men all around them, dressed in the same robes as Alex, chanting something, but the only word she could make out, was the word Bastiquil.

Brandy struggled against the chains but to no avail. She was stuck there, chained to the floor, at the mercy of these perverts who had kidnapped her. She saw the one that had, actually, taken her, standing to the side of the platform where Alex was. He was dressed like a leather wannabe Tarzan and he was covered with tattoos all over his body. *What the hell was going on?*

"Victor you son of a bitch, you promised me, you promised to let her go," Alex screamed at Victor, who continued to look forward. "I hate you, you fucking bastard, I hate you. I wish you were dead."

Brandy couldn't tell why Alex was screaming these things to the man he called Victor. *What was Alex talking about? He had promised to let her go? Oh God, what was going on here? Were they planning on killing her? Were they the people behind the recent killings? There was talk about them being ritualistic cult-like killings and this was sure the makings of one.* Brandy started to panic more as the idea of what was happening started to sink in.

As the men started to chant louder, there seemed to be a movement on the other side of the room. As the door to the room opened, an immediate hush fell over the room. A smaller man came wobbling out of the adjoining room, wearing a red linen robe, with a red linen hood. He had no shoes on. His face looked downward, so it wasn't visible to the room. On each side of the person, was a guard.

As the person took their time, making their way to the center of the room, the room was hushed, no words were being spoken. All that could be heard was Alex in the background crying and occasionally saying "no, no, no."

Brandy was crying, but she was more concerned about the man approaching her. As he was only a few feet away from her now, Alex could make out the horrified look that came to Brandy's face. It was a look of pure terror and as she looked from the person to Alex, he could see that she was mouthing a word silently, but Alex could not make out what that word was.

Victor picked up a satin square pillow about twelve inches by twelve inches, which had a ritual knife lying atop and walked to the center of the room. Alex was watching intently, seething with anger and hatred for what they were doing, what Victor was doing. As he passed by Alex, Victor looked over at him for a brief second and gave him the saddest look. Alex snarled at him, thinking it insincere. But in the moments that followed, Victor's intent was sincere, he knew what was to follow would probably go down as the hardest moment in the life of Alex Rogers.

As Victor reached the center of the room, he stepped to the side of the person in the red linen robe, slightly in front of them and held the pillow outward. The person in the linen robe reached their shaking hands out to the knife and wrapped their fingers around it. As they did, the crowd began to chant.

Upon hearing this, the man in the red robe held the knife upward and bringing it down and into the right side of Brandy's chest. Both Brandy and Alex were screaming. It took only a few seconds for Brandy to fade, to fall silent, and fall backwards onto the floor, knees still bent from where she had been made to kneel.

The man with the red robe then turned towards Alex, who was screaming obscenities at him. Reaching up, he pushed the hood backwards off his head. Alex's face became distorted in horror. He couldn't believe what he was seeing.

"Mom!" Alex yelled, but it came out more like a plea.

This had to be a dream, it had to be, but he knew it wasn't. His mother was the person in the red robe. His own mother had laid a knife into his best friend's chest and was a part of this entire ritual? How could that be? As Alex was playing scenario after scenario over in his head, a thought came to him, a thought he had not had in a long time.

Alex was a little boy when his father left him and his mother. He had just taken off without ever trying to contact them again. But Alex remembered the last thing he heard his father say to his mother, "I'm not going to watch this happen

363

to my son." He knew, the bastard knew this day was coming, and he still walked out on his son.

As his mother raised the blood covered knife to her head, Alex was brought back from his thoughts as his mother begins to carve symbols onto her forehead. As she did so, Alex began to see they were taking the shape of the symbol on the back of his neck. The crowd of men were chanting louder and faster now, making the energy of the room pick up and become frenzied. The drums were beating faster and harder now.

As quickly as they begin to chant, a hush came across the crowd as his mother once again raised the knife into the air. Looking at Alex, his mother mouthed, "I'm so sorry," to Alex. She then drove the knife into her abdomen, pulling it out; she did it again and again, until she fell to the floor on her knees, blood coming up through her mouth. She fell onto the floor with a loud thump, as her head hit the marble floor. Blood flowed around her as she lay dying.

Alex was crying as he was wrapping his head around what had just happened. His mother and Brandy had been the sacrifice and it was at his mother's own hands.

Alex's anger grew within him until he screamed, "VICTOR!"

Chapter Sixty

Gina could not hide her confusion and anger. She was sitting there watching this horror of a ritual unfold and before she could do anything, Brandy had been stabbed by what she thought was an elder of the Balashon. Her anger turned to rage when it was revealed; it was Alex's mother. Then out of nowhere, Ella turned the knife on herself. When Gina saw this, she looked at Alex who was so distraught from anger, the betrayal by his mother, and the subsequent death of both Ella and Brandy.

Gina's emotions overcame her as she laid in wait in the shadows, watching through the lower window pane. She was stricken with guilt, with fear and with anger for what Alex had just witnessed, for the betrayal his mother had just shown him. She felt her anger building, growing inside, feeding her, fueling her to act. Gina could stand it no more; she was not going to let these men get away with this.

Standing up Gina bowed her head, clearing it, thinking only of creating energy, letting her adrenaline feed it, like yeast to flour. When Gina felt fully charged she opened her eyes, looking at the massive ball of energy she was holding between her hands. As she screamed outward, the energy ball was thrown at the large window, shattering it inward towards the group of men.

They were all taken by surprise as the broken glass came flying at them. For some of the unlucky ones who had turned to look, they were met with shards of glass in the eyes.

Others into the jugular of their throat, throughout their chests, legs and arms, but most fell to the ground. Either way, Gina was glad to have inflicted pain on them even if for only a minute and she knew some of the hits would be fatal. This made her happy, which was a new feeling for Gina. It was then, Gina realized what Demetri had been telling her, these men deserved to die.

Jumping inside the window, Gina ran over to Brandy and Ella. Gina could tell Ella was dead, but she was still sensing a pulse from Brandy, a weak one, but still a pulse. Brandy's heart had not stopped yet. Men started advancing towards Gina, as Alex yelled at her to run. As she stood her ground, she made an energy ball and cast it at the man closest to her, knocking him off his feet, sending him flying backwards about ten feet.

"Come on assholes," Gina yelled at them. "Bring it on."

As Victor stepped out to where he was in Gina's line of vision, she started to make an energy ball just for him. Victor smiled at her and pointed to the ground. "I would be more concerned about what is below my feet, than what is standing to my side," Victor said to Gina as he once again stepped out of her line of sight, this time moving up on the platform where Alex was tied up. He wanted to be present when the master arrived.

Gina looked down at the floor below her and saw the symbols were lighting up on the ground. She heard a man chanting in the background but was unable to see him anywhere. To her surprise, she looked over to see the spirit of Ella standing next to her. This too was a new experience for Gina. In the past she had to summon the dead to be able to see them, but Gina still was not sure if it was her doing this or if it she was in the middle of spell being cast by the Balashon.

Ella looked scared but relieved, as if she had just been lifted from a lifelong burden of guilt. But, as they both watched, the ground where the symbols were drawn, turn from light to a swirling circle of air. Looks of horror adorned their face when they heard the nerve shattering cries and howls of what sounded like hounds. But the howls were close and they didn't sound like any hound Gina had ever heard before.

Gina looked at Ella and told her to run, but Ella just shook her head as the fear rose on her face. Gina then realized part of the sacrifice was a binding spell being chanted by the Balashon, one which bound Ella to this spot, not allowing her soul to flee. Brandy would have been in the same predicament, but they had failed to make sure she was dead before they did the final spell.

"Gina, run. Run now. They are coming," Alex screamed at Gina loudly and with a broken voice. He was tortured by all of this, broken, and betrayed.

As the ground, swirling beneath her, started to give way to what appeared to be fire, Gina jumped backwards just as the ground fully gave out and flames shot up from the hole. A large beast, resembling a hound on steroids, came crawling out of the hole. Gina was horrified, Ella was screaming and Alex was crying, not only of his mother's betrayal, but of the knowledge her soul was lost for eternity. She would be eaten and absorbed by Bastiquil. Alex finally had a grasp on how this all worked and it made his hatred for Victor soar to greater heights.

As a second hound leapt out of the ground, they were circling Gina, Brandy, and Ella. Snapping in the air at them, sniffing the ground by where Brandy lay.

"Leave her alone," Alex screamed at the hounds, who quickly turned their heads to Alex and growled at him, as their drool was hanging lower and lower from their mouth. Turning their attention back to the three women, the hounds were circling the women once again. As one of the hounds jumped at Ella grabbing her waist within its mouth, Gina tried to reach out to her to help her, but was unable to grab hold of her spiritual form.

One of the hounds stood in front of Brandy, as if waiting for her to die so it could take her soul into the pit. The chains binding Brandy were broken and her limp body was moved out of the circle, away from the preying hounds.

All eyes moved to Gina, who was looking toward the entrance of the room. Gina smiled as she saw Demetri and Aldrik standing there, both had blood on them, but she was not sure it was either of theirs. Aldrik she was sure would not be bleeding, for he had healing properties as a vampire, and at his age he healed quickly.

The hell hound then turned its attention to Gina, but just as it did, Demetri lifted Gina upwards and placed her safely beside him. Both hounds jumped back within the pit as it closed behind them.

A rumbling of the house started. It was subtle at first, but then became more intense as the men in robes resumed their chanting, louder, and louder. "Hail Bastiquil, our master has risen; hail Bastiquil, our master is raised" they chanted in unison.

Demetri looked up to the platform where he saw Alex's tear stained face and an arrogant looking Victor standing next to him.

"You!" Demetri said to Victor, as he made a run at him. Just as he was nearing the platform and Victor had braced himself for the impact of Demetri, the flooring where the hounds had just returned to hell cracked with great force, at least six feet in length. Red fiery mist rose from the crack in the ground, as everyone stopped what they were doing and all focus turned to the crack, even Demetri's and Victor's faces were turned toward the red mist.

Up through the mist rose the dark shadowy figure of a man, who was standing waist deep in the red mist. Gasp of joy filled the room from the men in robes and Victor's face was smiling from ear to ear. He was overcome with happiness and pride. As the dark figure stood there looking at Alex and then turning its head taking in the crowd, landing its gaze on Demetri.

"Finally, we meet again, my old friend," Bastiquil said to Demetri in a deep, unearthly voice, sending shivers down Gina's spine. Bastiquil made a movement with his upper chest and dark wings rose out from behind his back spanning the length of at least ten feet across. The wings were not full wings, as one would think of when we think of angel or demon wings, but rather they were sparsely there. Some spots were intact where others were like the broken window panes where the frame existed, but the glass was no longer. Either way, it was an intimidating and impressive wingspan.

Bastiquil laughed a guttural, unnatural laugh and then flapping his wings he was airborne. He made a sudden lunge at Demetri, more so to frighten him, but to let him know, he was back and he was pissed off. As Demetri ducked out of the path of Bastiquil, the dark one flew up to the ceiling and stared at Alex. "My son, the time has come for my blood to reconnect with my soul."

Bastiquil made a diving lunge at Alex. As Alex opened his mouth to scream, Bastiquil's form was spinning as it made its way towards Alex and the shape that was Bastiquil, changed just enough to fit itself into the mouth of Alex, disappearing into his body.

"No," Gina screamed. "Demetri, do something." Gina was pleading with him, but Demetri knew as well as Gina did there was nothing he could have done to stop this from happening. Father and son were rejoined as one and the ritual was complete. All this time, Gina and Demetri had spent trying to figure out what was going on, what or who was up to this, what was their end game; well, all of those questions were just answered. The father and son rejoining each other was the end game. The Balashon had three thousand years on them to plan this and even with Demetri's joining of his past lives, he had been unable to stop it from happening.

The best they could hope for would be Demetri was still able to defeat the demon even if it meant he had to kill what was once Alex to do so. Gina cried for Alex, for Ella, and for Brandy. This was not supposed to have happened; this was not how she had envisioned this would end.

As Alex fell to the ground on his knees, his head fell towards his chest as if he were unconscious. But a few seconds later his body lurched, with his back arching and bending backwards, his head fell back and he let out the loudest scream Gina had ever heard. His body was flopping around now as if seizing and Gina was terrified for him. She couldn't stand it any longer and started to run towards the platform where Alex was secured. As she made an attempt to step onto the platform, Victor stepped in her way blocking her path to Alex.

Gina made an energy ball and flung it at Victor, but he just reached out and knocked it away with his hand. Gina made one after the other and kept flinging them at him and each one he successfully knocked to one side or the other. Gina was furious and hell bent on revenge. She grabbed a knife from her waist belt and lunged at Victor. Aiming it right towards his heart, but as she was just inches from him he reached out and grabbed her hand with the knife He spun her around to where she was leaning with her back up against Victor's chest.

"Not this time witch," Victor whispered in her ear which infuriated Gina more. As she struggled to free herself, she found his grip was strong.

Demetri had been watching Alex this entire time and had finally snapped out of whatever trance he was in. Seeing Gina in Victor's snare, he made a gesture aimed at releasing Victor's grasp on Gina. Victor felt his arm being tugged at by an energy source not visible to him and he knew Demetri's powers were at play here. Victor struggled against them and continued to try and hold his grip on the girl, but the male witch had grown in power.

While all of this was taking place, a group of assassins that lay waiting in the corner of the room advanced towards Demetri and Aldrik. Without hesitation, Aldrik hurled himself through the air at a speed that left one seeing a blur behind him. As he reached the assassins, he began clawing and hitting at them. They were almost as powerful in their strength and technique as Victor, so they were a challenge for the old vampire who still held the face of a young man in his twenties.

Demetri was still attacking at Victor's hold on Gina and as Victor's arm slid up to Gina's neck he wrapped his fingers around her throat and started to squeeze it tightly, cutting off the oxygen to her lungs. Gina's face was turning a deep red from the intense grip he had on her and her lack of oxygen.

Demetri intensely focused in on Victor and as he did, one by one Victor's fingers started to be pulled away from Gina's neck as if he were doing it himself, but he wasn't. This was the work of the male witch. Victor tried to fight against it, but the witch was so strong. Gina was still struggling against Victor as she fought for air.

Then a loud roaring voice came from Alex, "Victor; stop this now." The voice was so loud and so intense everyone in the room stopped and looked over at Alex. His body was no longer shaking and his head which was looking downward, begin to lift up, revealing to them all, eyes as dark as the night sky. No white could be seen in them.

He, one leg at a time lifted himself upright until he was standing. As he looked at the metal chains which bound him to the pillars, they instantly unlocked from his wrist and fell to the ground. Alex, who was now, Bastiquil started to stretch out his muscles and arms as if he were waking from a deep sleep and working out the muscle cramps. He smiled at all who were still in the room and looked around until his gaze landed on Gina.

"Let her go Victor, she is our guest and it is so thoughtful for her to join us for this festive occasion," Bastiquil said to Victor who immediately obeyed and released Gina from his grip. Gina was gasping for air and stumbled into Demetri's arms. As Bastiquil watched this, he raised his eyelids as if a surprise had just been revealed to him and then he started to laugh. "Zamaranum my friend, I am surprised to see you here; surprised indeed." Bastiquil looked at Demetri, who looked back at Bastiquil.

Demetri was looking at him as if he didn't know what he was talking about but realized Bastiquil was too intelligent to fool. So Demetri just smiled at him and nodded.

"You have some nerve Zamaranum coming here before me after you betrayed me. I should rip your beating heart right out of your chest and have it as a midnight snack." Bastiquil said.

"Well, I must say Bastiquil, you have some nerve, thinking you can come into my world, threaten and kill my friends, and think there wouldn't be consequences," Demetri said to Bastiquil, trying to bluff a little and stall for more time to think of a plan.

"Oh, my old friend, I have had three thousand years to think about what I would do to you when our paths crossed again and I had hoped they would. I will make you suffer unthinkable pain. You will watch your entire loved ones suffer the same pain. And, if you still have a bloodline from that time, I will hunt them down and stomp their lives right into the depths of hell where they belong." Bastiquil said to Demetri, still smiling at him.

"You won't be around that long my old friend," Demetri said to him mimicking his wording so that he might get a reaction from Bastiquil. "I have evolved over the years and am ready to put you to rest once again as I did all those years ago."

At this Bastiquil gave a roar and raised his hands and at the same time Demetri and Aldrik were both lifted into the air. With a smile and a wink, Bastiquil sent both men flying through the doors in which they came. Both men landed hard on the floor, before rolling to a stop. The doors slammed shut and any attempt made by Demetri or Aldrik to open them was to no avail.

Gina stood there speechless, as she turned to look at Alex, only to no longer see any signs of him left. She couldn't sense him, feel him, or make mental contact with him, nothing. He was gone. "If you are going to kill me then please spare me the gross indulgence of spreading it out with your cryptic lies and arrogance; kill me and get it over with," Gina said to Bastiquil who looked at her impressed.

"I applaud your bravery young witch; you are full of passion and lots of power yet to be tapped into. It would be a great loss to see you not reach your full potential. I have no need of killing you and have no plans for it. I don't see you as an enemy, although, I don't think you could say the same about me." Bastiquil said to Gina, who was looking at him with uncertainty.

"Is this a riddle you expect me to figure out?" She asked of him.

"Not at all, right now I simply wish for you to sleep, so you do not get hurt in the crossfire," Bastiquil said to Gina.

"Well, that will simply not happen because..," Gina did not even get her sentence out before she started to fall to the ground only to be caught by the arms of Victor. She was fast asleep in Victor's arms.

Bastiquil walked over to Victor and leaned into his ear whispering something in great length. As Victor listened, with ever widening eyes, he nodded at his instructions, then picking Gina up into his arms he walked out of the side door and away with her.

While this was happening, Demetri and Aldrik were outside making attempts to knock the door down screaming Gina's name. As they were getting ready to make a grand attempt at smashing the door in, they were suddenly blown off their feet as the door exploded towards them, and Bastiquil walked in smiling at them both.

"So this is the best you could do Zamaranum?" Bastiquil said looking at Demetri. Of course, Demetri knew who he was referring to, but Aldrik did not. "A male witch who hasn't even learned his true purpose and strength yet and a vampire; come on Zamaranum, I expected more from you."

Aldrik made an attempt at using his vampire speed to distract Bastiquil from Demetri, but Bastiquil just matched his supernatural speed with his own, using his mind to stop Aldrik in his tracks.

"Bastiquil, it's me you want, Zamaranum, not Aldrik. You don't have to hurt him. You don't have to hurt any of them." Demetri said, as he was getting up off the floor and back onto his feet.

"Well witch that is where you are wrong. You may have Zamaranum's memories, but you have yet to show me any of his powers. I don't want to waste time with a juvenile witch, I want the most powerful one to come out and play.

We have unfinished business," Bastiquil said to Demetri as he laughed slightly to himself.

"Well, you have got me," Demetri said as he hit Bastiquil with his most powerful burst of energy that he could gather. It barely fazed him. He stumbled slightly but regained his composure quickly and sent Demetri flying through the wall behind him with the wave of his hand.

Demetri was grunting with pain as he struggled to get up, to fight back, but Bastiquil once again waved his hand and Demetri was again thrown backwards through the wall behind him, knocking him unconscious. At this rate, he wouldn't survive many more blows like this.

Aldrik was struggling as well to free himself from Bastiquil's grip he had on him, but was unable to do so. The more he struggled, the tighter the grip seemed to get.

Bastiquil turned to Aldrik and shook his head at him. "You know, I expected you to be a little more receptive to me. We are not so far removed you and I. Of course, a demon of my level doesn't have much to do with the likes of your kind, but at least there should be a level of respect. Your kind of demon is a unique one, in that you were able to turn yourself into a blood virus and spread yourself through many humans, killing them, yet allowing them to remain the walking dead. But, to fight me, you must have some nerve? I will say that about you; and make no mistake about it, I am talking to the demon inside you, the one living within your blood, if you defy me one more time, I will annihilate your entire species."

Aldrik was looking at Bastiquil with a curious look. "I am no demon; I am nothing like you."

"Well, you are both right and wrong. You are right in, you are not like me; I am much more powerful than your kind of demon. You are wrong in the aspect you are born of a demon. A blood demon runs through your veins, pumping through your body and it feeds on the blood of others. Why do you think there is such a thirst for blood? You think it is by happenstance you crave it? You must have known at your age what you are made from?" Bastiquil was looking at Aldrik with a curious look as if he were looking at a buffoon.

374

Aldrik didn't bother to speak for he knew what he was saying was most likely the truth. No one had ever put it to him like that before; no one Aldrik had known over his many years, had an answer. Even his maker didn't bother to share it with him had he even known.

"You either stand down, now or I will rip your heart right out of your chest," Bastiquil said.

Aldrik fearing he would and he would be no good to Demetri if he were dead decided to give in, for the moment. He nodded at Bastiquil letting him know he understood.

"Wise choice," Bastiquil said. "I, typically, wouldn't bother even talking to your kind, but it seems such a waste to kill something with such beauty, even if you do have such a nasty little demon running through your veins. Now, let the fun begin. I have three thousand years to make up."